Mark Greaney has a degree in international relations and political science. In his research for the Gray Man novels he has travelled to more than fifteen countries and trained alongside military and law enforcement in the use of firearms, battlefield medicine, and close-range combative tactics. He is also the author of seven *New York Times* Tom Clancy bestsellers, including three written with Clancy: *Locked On*, *Threat Vector*, and *Command Authority*.

The Gray Man series

MARK GREANEY
ON TARGET

sphere

SPHERE

First published in the United States in 2010 by Berkley,
an imprint of Penguin Random House LLC
First published in Great Britain in 2010 in ebook by Sphere
This edition published in 2021 by Sphere

1 3 5 7 9 10 8 6 4 2

A CIP catalogue record for this book
is available from the British Library.

ISBN 978-0-7515-5026-9

Papers used by Sphere are from well-managed forests
and other responsible sources.

MIX
Paper from
responsible sources
FSC® C104740

Printed and bound in Great Britain by
Clays Ltd, Elcograf S.p.A.

Sphere
An imprint of
Little, Brown Book Group
Carmelite House
50 Victoria Embankment
London EC4Y 0DZ

An Hachette UK Company
www.hachette.co.uk

www.littlebrown.co.uk

For my aunt, Dorothy Greaney.

*Thank you for a lifetime of love and support
(and sorry about all the bad words).*

ACKNOWLEDGEMENTS

Much thanks and appreciation to Karen Mayer, John and Wanda Anderson, Devin Greaney, Mireya Ledezma, Trey and Kristin Greaney, John and Carrie Echols, Nichole Roberts, David and Suzanne Leslie, Chris and Michelle Burcky, Bob Hetherington, April Adams, Dana and Nancy Adams, Jeff and Stephanie Stovall, Keith Cleghorn, and Jenny Kraft.

Thanks also to Svetlana Ganea, Gavin Smith, James and Rebecca Yeager, Jay Gibson, Alan Webb, Paul Gomez, and the rest of the cadre and support staff at Tactical Response in Camden, Tennessee. To ALL the guys and girls on getoffthex: you've taught me more than you'll ever know, and have helped me more than I'll ever admit.

I'd also like to thank my badass editor, Tom Colgan, and my kickass agent, Scott Miller. You guys are the best.

MarkGreaneyBooks.com

PROLOGUE

Dark clouds hung low above the Irish Sea, fat in the moist morning air, and tracked slowly over the assassin as he stood on the wooden foredeck of the fishing boat. A few screeching herring gulls had encircled the vessel while it was still miles offshore; now that it had entered the harbor channel, a flock one dozen strong swarmed above and around, churning the mist with their white wings.

The seabirds shrieked at the vessel, bleated warnings to the Irish coast of the arrival of a killer to its shores.

But their warnings were lost in the vapor.

The boat docked in its harbor slip just before eight a.m. The assassin climbed off the deck and onto the quay without a glance at the two crewmembers. Not a single word had been exchanged in the three hours since the forty-foot Lochin had picked its passenger up from a Lithuanian freighter in international waters. He remained on the deck, moving fore and aft, vigilantly scanning the roiling sea around him, his black hooded raincoat protecting him from the salty spray and the occasional shower, as well as the curious eyes of the father and son who operated the boat. The crew remained in the wheelhouse during the journey, following strict instructions. They had been told to pick up a passenger and then keep away from him, to return with him to Howth Harbor, just north of Dublin. After delivering this odd catch of the day, they were to enjoy their payment and hold their bloody tongues.

The assassin walked through the seaside village to the tiny train

1

depot and bought a ticket to Connolly Station in central Dublin. With half an hour to kill, he stepped down the station steps and into the basement pub. The Bloody Scream served a full Irish breakfast for the fishermen in the harbor; the long narrow room was more than half-full of men wolfing down plates of eggs and sausage and baked beans, washing it all down with pints of ink-dark foamy Guinness Stout. The assassin knew how to assimilate in unfamiliar surroundings; he grunted and gestured to hide his foreign accent, and ordered the same as those around him. He dug into his plate and drained his beer before leaving the Bloody Scream to catch his train.

A half hour later he trudged through Dublin. He wore his brown beard thick and a blue watch cap down over his ears and forehead, a scarf tight around his neck, and a dark blue peacoat into which his gloved hands dug deep to hide from the frigid air. Hanging over a shoulder, a small canvas bag swung with his foot-steps. He headed south away from the train station, then turned right at the quay of the River Liffey and followed it as chilled rain began to fall.

The assassin walked on.

He looked forward to getting this errand behind him. He had not been comfortable at sea, nor was he comfortable now in the morning crowd growing around him as he neared O'Connell Street.

But there was a man here in Dublin who, it had been decided by someone with money and influence, should cease to exist.

And Court Gentry had come to see to that.

1

At a pharmacy he bought a pack of acetaminophen tablets and a bottled water. He'd been injured a few months back, a bullet through the thigh and a knife blade into his gut. The pain had lessened by the week. The body had incredible power to heal, so much greater than that of the mind. Court had grown dependent on the pills and injections: Vicodin and OxyContin, Demerol and Dilaudid. A surgeon in Nice had kept him supplied since the operation to clean and close his abdominal wound, and Gentry had popped pills each day since. But he'd purposely left them behind when he boarded the freighter; he'd gone over a week now without his meds, and this self-imposed detox was making him miserable.

The acetaminophen was no substitute for a heavy narcotic, but his mind found comfort in the ritual of swallowing the tablets nonetheless.

Three hours after leaving the boat, he checked in to a Chinese-run budget hotel in a narrow alley off Parnell Street, a half mile north of the river. His room was dark and dank and smelled of mold and frying grease; the restaurant two floors below him blew the stench through the vents. A near-horizontal rain beat steadily on the dirty window but failed to clean it; the oily grime covered the inside of the glass.

Gentry lay on his back on the sagging mattress and stared at the ceiling, his thoughts unfocused. He'd been on a boat for over a week; it felt odd not swaying back and forth, rising slowly up and down.

It took hours to drift asleep, the cold rain unceasing on the pane next to his head.

In the mid-afternoon he sat at the Chinese restaurant in the tiny hotel, ate noodles and pork, and used a store-bought mobile phone to log on to the Internet. He accessed a bulletin board on a Web site that sold adventure tours of the Ural Mountains, entered a password to log on to a forum for employees; with a further code he gained entry to a thread with one other viewer.

Court typed on his phone with his thumb while he drank tepid orange juice.

I'm here.

A few seconds later the tiny window in the phone refreshed. Someone had replied on the forum.

In Bangkok, I trust? This was the code that confirmed the identity of the other party. Gentry's identity was established with his reply.

No. Singipore. Only by the misspelling was the identity check complete.

Nice journey, my friend? came the next reply. Court read it, bit into a fried wonton as greasy as the window in his upstairs room.

He tried not to roll his eyes.

It had *not* been a nice journey, and Gregor Ivanovic Sidorenko was *not* Court Gentry's friend. Court had no friends. And it was unlikely Sidorenko, or Sid to all those in the West who knew of him, had any himself. He was Russian mob, an overboss in Saint Petersburg. He ran an organization that controlled illegal gambling and drugs and hookers and hit men and ... out of desperation on the part of the American assassin, he now ran Court Gentry, the Gray Man.

While ostensibly in the same line of work, Gregor Sidorenko was no Donald Fitzroy. Sir Donald had been Court's handler for years, ever since the CIA had chased Gentry out of the US with a burn notice and a shoot-on-sight directive. Fitzroy had taken him in, had offered him good jobs against bad men, had paid him fairly for his work, and had even once hired him to protect his own family. But then Fitzroy had been pushed into a corner, had turned on Court, and though he'd apologized profusely and even offered up his life to his American employee in recompense, Gentry knew he could never trust him again.

He would never trust anyone again.

Sid was scum, but he was a known quantity. Court knew he couldn't trust the forked-tongued Russian fuck as far as he could throw him, but Sid could supply access to some of the most lucrative contracts in the industry. And Sid agreed to Gentry's caveat that he would only accept those hits he deemed righteous, or at least those that tipped slightly to the good side of the "morally neutral" category.

Which had led Court here to Ireland.

This trip to Dublin was Court's first op for Sid. He'd read the dossier of the target, agreed to the job, argued online about the low wages offered for the contract, and then reluctantly accepted.

He needed to stay operational. The downtime and the wounds and the drugs were softening him, and he was a man who absolutely could *not* afford to soften.

Court had memorized the relevant portions of the target's dossier. Standard operating procedure before a wet operation. Name: Dougal Slattery. Age: fifty-four years. Nationality: Irish. Height: big. Weight: fat. He'd been a boxer as a young man but couldn't break out of the thick midlist of local pugilistic talent. Then he found work as a tough guy, a bouncer in Dublin nightclubs. He branched out, did some rough stuff for a local syndicate, slapping around lazy Polish hookers and knocking Turkish drug dealers' heads together for not making quota. He graduated to some low-level killings: gang versus gang stuff, nothing fancy till he was sent on an errand to the Continent. In Amsterdam he'd made the big time, killing his boss's rival in a hail of bullets after using his gnarled fists to bash in the faces of two of his bodyguards.

From there he'd climbed to the second tier of the killer-for-hire trade. Wet jobs in Ankara, in Sardinia, in Calcutta, in Tajikistan. He did not run solo, Court had noticed in his file; he wasn't the brains behind his operations, but his curriculum vitae included some respectable kills. Not respectable in the moral sense; no, he'd reportedly killed a police detective, an honest businessman, a journalist or two. But Court appreciated that the operations themselves had been, if not spectacular, at least competently executed.

But his last hit on file was six years ago. Court couldn't help but notice that Sid's dossier on Slattery went wafer thin after that. A few speculative inferences aside, all that was known about his life since then was that he played the drum in a traditional Irish band that performed five nights a week in the touristy Temple Bar section of Dublin.

Hardly work that got your name scribbled onto a termination order.

Gentry found this to be one of his more morally neutral operations. The man was a killer, but so was Court. Court rationalized the difference; he vetted *his* targets, made sure their deeds warranted extrajudicial killing. Dougal Slattery clearly did not. According to Sid, the Irishman was now on retainer for an Italian-run international criminal organization. His next victim might well be a recalcitrant prostitute or the owner of a restaurant that failed to pay protection money to the Mafia.

Killing Dougal Slattery wouldn't much improve the evil ways of the world, Court decided, but it certainly wouldn't hurt.

Well, it wouldn't hurt anyone who was *not* named Dougal Slattery.

Hello? You still there? Sid's previous post was three minutes old. Court had drifted off-mission for a moment. He forced himself to concentrate on his phone's tiny screen.

I'm here. No problems.

How long will you need?

Unknown. Will assess situation tonight. Act at first prudent opportunity.

I understand, my friend. Don't take too long. I have more work after.

There was always more "work," Court knew. But most "work" involved contracts Gentry would never accept. Court would be the judge if there was "more work after." He didn't argue the point with Sidorenko, though. Instead he just replied, *Okay.*

I look forward to good news. Do svidaniya, friend.

Court just logged off. He shut down the phone and stuck it in the side pocket of his peacoat. He finished his meal, paid, and left the hotel.

In the late afternoon he walked the neighborhoods around Grafton Street. He'd spent an hour looking at the dress and mannerisms of the locals, trying to assimilate. It would not be hard for the trained professional; Dublin was an international city full of Poles, Russians, Turks, Chinese, South Americans ... even a few Irish here and there. There was no one look or walk or attitude to parrot; still, Court stepped into a used-clothing shop on Dawson Lane and stepped out with a bag. In the bathroom of a department store he changed into worn blue jeans, a hooded sweatshirt, and a black denim jacket. Black athletic shoes and his dark blue watch cap finished off the ensemble.

By nightfall he was a local, moving with the masses. He ran a security sweep, backtracked, stepped on and off a few trains on the DART—Dublin's mass transit—all to make sure he was not being followed. There were more people in this world who wanted Court Gentry dead than would ever give a rat's ass about Dougal Slattery, and Court kept this in mind, just to keep his operation in perspective. His secondary objective was to kill the Irishman; the primary objective, as always, was to keep his own ass alive for another day. His PERSEC, or personal security, needed to remain at the forefront of his thoughts.

Satisfied he had not grown a tail, he headed to the Temple Bar neighborhood on the southern bank of the River Liffey.

At ten o'clock he sat at the bar at the Oliver St. John Gogarty.

Although it was a Wednesday evening, the touristy pub was packed full. Americans, Continental Europeans, Asians. The only Irish in the bar were likely the barmaids, the bartenders, and the band.

Court hadn't spent much time in raucous juke joints in the past few months. He'd laid low in the south of France, lived in the tiny attic room of a tiny cottage in a tiny hillside village and rarely ventured out past the little corner market for canned foods and bottled water. Even his few visits into Nice to see his doctor were tame. It was the winter season; the nightclubs and the kitschy shops on the Promenade des Anglais, always bursting at the seams during the tourist season, were nearly empty or boarded up. That was the way Court liked it. The Oliver St. John Gogarty was anathema to his standard tradecraft; already the female bartender had asked him his name, and two Englishwomen next to him had tried to engage him in small talk. He'd ignored their overtures, sipped his Guinness, scanned the room, wished he had four milligrams of Dilaudid to relax him, and then angrily told himself to unfuck himself and get his head back on this job.

There are two types of people in the world. Only two. Sheep and wolves. Court was a wolf, and he knew it. The past few months had weakened him somewhat, but a wolf was always a wolf, and it had never been more evident to him than it was here at the bar, surrounded as he was by a hundred sheep. No one in the crowd scanned for threats like he did. No one in the crowd had pinpointed the exits and the fit men in the room and the type of glass in the front window. No one in the crowd had taken note of the paucity of law enforcement on the street or the lighting scheme of the back alley. No one in the crowd knew where to sit so no mirror's reflection cast his image about the room.

No one in the crowd had a plan to run for his life if necessary.

And no one in the crowd had a plan to kill everyone else in the crowd if it came down to it.

Yes, he was in a crowd full of sheep, but there was, in fact, one more wolf in the room. According to Sid's dossier, the drummer onstage was a hard man as well. There were five in the traditional, or "trad" band, and though Gentry was no expert on such matters, from the reaction of the patrons, he supposed they must have been very good. The big man with the white hair sitting on a bench to the side of the stage played a bodhrán, a traditional handheld Irish drum. He took his work seriously, kept his head down and leaned forward as if to pick up on the subtleties of the music. He looked to Court more like a middle-aged musician and less like a middle-aged hit man. Maybe it had been a while since he'd worked his "day job." Next to him, a young thin man played a tin whistle into his microphone, the guitarists strummed and sang in harmony, and the crowd of sheep went wild. Court couldn't make out many of the words of the song, but it had something to do with a beautiful young woman and a bad potato harvest and a husband dead from drink.

Court finished his stout and headed out the door.

2

Dougal Slattery said good-bye to his bandmates at eleven thirty, covered his thick white hair with a Donegal wool walking cap, and left the Oliver St. John Gogarty with his drum in its leather case hanging over his shoulder. It was a cold but clear evening, like a thousand other nights he'd played in the bar, and also like most other nights, he fancied a pint before heading back to his flat. There were three dozen pubs within a few minutes' walk, but his flat was a mile away on the other side of Pearse Station. He'd do what he usually did: head to his local watering hole for a nightcap.

Slattery walked with a limp, a bad knee. Actually, a bad knee and a worse knee, but limping on both legs was out of the question, so he leaned into the better of the two weakening joints, his thick body lumbering on through the cold night.

It took the big Irishman nearly thirty minutes to make it to the Padraic Pearse, named after the Irish Catholic leader executed by the British in the 1916 Easter uprising. It was a staunch Catholic pub; photos and relics of the Rebellion decorated the windows of the small establishment.

Dougal limped in, placed his coat and his bodhrán in a corner booth, and headed to the bar for the pint of Guinness already being poured from the tap.

Court Gentry found a darkened doorway and sat down on the stoop. He'd done more walking today than he'd done in months, and he was surprised to feel the ache in the muscles of his thighs and his calves and thought he sensed a faint sting where the bullet had torn into his right leg the previous December. He wished he had a Vicodin, but he knew he couldn't be doped up and operational at the same time, so he just sat there and stared at the front door of the pub across the street. Tonight was reconnaissance only; he'd follow his target home and then assess where and when to act afterwards.

The Padraic Pearse it was called. A tiny saloon by the looks of it from the outside. Probably Slattery's regular haunt, seeing how he'd made a beeline here past countless other opportunities to sit and drink. There were more bars per capita here in Dublin than in any city in the world. The Irish loved their pubs, and Court was not surprised to find himself spending a portion of his evening watching the front door of a tavern, waiting for his target to down a couple of brews.

Gentry rose stiffly to his feet. He wanted to move his muscles, he was cold as well as sore, and he needed a toilet or a back alley. He knew the most reasonable place for a young local such as himself to be caught taking a piss would be the narrow passage alongside the Padraic, so he crossed the empty street and headed into the dark. Once there, he sniffed his way to a wall beside some rubbish tins, undid his belt, and then quickly retightened it. A noise farther down the alley had caught his attention: two men exiting a back door, a shaft of light fifty feet down from him, and the sound of other men talking from inside the building. The men went to a back wall and pissed, then returned inside a minute later with no idea a stranger stood nearby in the dark.

It was clearly a back door to the Padraic Pearse that they'd passed through. So the pub was much larger than Court had originally thought. He did his business against the brick wall and then walked to the back door. On the other side he heard the cracking of a pool cue against a cue ball and gruff men's voices, audible but unintelligible. Looking ahead, Gentry saw the back alley gave access to a side street, and he wondered if Slattery had already left the bar via this route. Perhaps he'd even made the tail on him, but

Court had seen no hint of that at any point in the half-hour walk from the Temple Bar.

Shit. Gentry knew he either needed to knock off the surveillance tonight and try again tomorrow, or head into the pub and take a look to see if his man was still there. The danger of being compromised in a tavern this large would be minimal; it sounded as if there were dozens inside, and the Gray Man knew how to melt into his surroundings indoors as well as outdoors. He headed back to the front door, tucked his neck deep into his denim jacket to make himself an inch shorter, and then pushed open the front door of the Padraic Pearse.

Gentry entered the pub and immediately knew he'd made a grave mistake. It was incredibly small. The pool area he'd heard from the back was shut off with an access door against the back wall of the tavern with a large sign that read MEMBERS ONLY. The room Court had entered contained just a small bar, three tables, and a few snugs along the wall. He strolled to the bar and took a stool, did not turn his head left or right, just pulled out his wallet and stared straight ahead at the bottles behind the bar. He felt the eyes of the dozen or so patrons, but he did not yet know if Slattery was in the room with him.

There was a hard edge to the pub and its clientele. Court sensed it immediately. Malevolence filled the air.

This was no place for strangers.

Finally he glanced up into the mirror behind the bar. Every man in the pub, Dougal Slattery and the two young mates seated with him included, stared at him through the glass.

Tough crowd, Gentry thought.

A sign taped to the mirror caught his eye: NO SINGING ALLOWED.

Tough joint.

Shit.

The bartender eyed him for a long moment over his newspaper, finally laid it down, and raised his red eyebrows slightly.

"Pint of Guinness," Court said.

*

Slattery sipped his beer, listened to the two young blokes in his snug complain about a bad call in the rugby match the previous evening between Clontarf and Thomond. Dougal was a Wanderers supporter himself, couldn't give two shits about how bleedin' Clontarf had been bleedin' robbed by the bleedin' referee, but he enjoyed the company of the two young regulars nonetheless. He looked up when he heard the door open; it was late for anyone to come in for a pint, but certainly not unheard of. He cocked his head to the side. His eyes tracked the stranger as he headed to the bar.

Dougal quickly tuned out his tablemates.

Inside Dougal Slattery's large frame alarm bells clanged as loud as those in the belfry of the Christ Church Cathedral a mile to the west. A stranger in the Padraic Pearse was a queer enough sight, but this bloke had been in the crowd at the Oliver earlier in the evening. Moreover, he was young and fit, and just one shade too nonchalant for Slattery's taste.

He wasn't local. He dressed the part, true, but Slattery saw through it somehow. As the man sat himself on a barstool, the Irishman looked hard for evidence of a weapon in his clothing, either the printing of a handgun or that particular hitch a man with a sidearm must make to accommodate the iron on his hip as he sits. Dougal saw nothing, but the stranger's right side was shielded from him.

He heard the man order. "Pint of Guinness"—nothing foreign or odd there. He even sounded a bit Irish, but his voice was low and soft.

Was he police? Interpol? Dougal knew that cops in a half dozen countries would like to put him in shackles and drag him off his blessed island. No. This man did not appear to be a cop; he seemed somehow too relaxed for that line of work.

He also knew how to order a Guinness, and that was something. Uninitiated foreigners tended to reach for the glass as soon as it's placed on the bar, a cardinal mistake. The stout requires a two-part pour; the bartender allows the foam to settle for a couple of minutes, at which time the beer sits teasingly close to the patron, inviting him to show his ignorance by pulling the glass to himself.

But this stranger knew his manners.

Slattery caught a glance from the man through the mirror, just a quick, impassive, fleeting look. The other regulars in the bar were all staring at the stranger, as well. He looked them over before returning his attention to the bartender. George wasn't any happier to see a stranger at his bar than was Slattery, but he served the pint and took the money and went back to his newspaper.

Dougal leaned forward to the men at his table. He spoke to them softly. There was an affectation of levity, but the words were said with no smile at all.

"Listen, laddies. How would you fancy a little action tonight before your ma's tuck yas into your beds?"

Court had been made, and he knew it. He sat at the bar, stared into his beer, his body feigning relaxation but his mind tense, going over the protocol for dealing with a dozen men in a room not much larger than the interior of a school bus. There would be blades in this crowd, Gentry had no doubt. Brass knuckles, too, more than likely. Maybe even a sawed-off double-barreled shotgun behind the bar. Court wore a pistol in a holster in his waistband, but it wasn't much of a defensive weapon. A Russian Makarov. With the silencer in his coat pocket, he could make it an effective assassin's tool, but the .380-caliber bullet was too impotent to count on as an effective man stopper, the eight-round magazine capacity seemed woefully inadequate for the mass of beef around him in the room, and the magazine release mechanism was poorly placed and inefficient. Yes, Court knew, he could poke bloody holes in a few of these Micks if it came down to it, but if they moved on him in force and with motivation, he'd be good and well fucked.

He took a chug of his Guinness. Never had a pint looked so large. He thought he'd never drain down to the bottom of his glass so he could head out and get back to the dark street. Behind him he heard Slattery whisper something to the men with him. Court did not look up into the mirror. Slattery had seen him earlier at the Oliver St. John Gogarty; that was clear enough. Now he'd be letting his friends in on the situation. With good luck, Slattery would bug out, set up some sort of confrontation in the street. Send his men outside to hide in the dark and leave with them. With bad luck, it would go down here and now. Dougal would stand and proclaim to the room that the man who pitched the stranger through the front window would earn himself a year's supply of Guinness.

Son of a bitch, Court thought. Recuperating in France, he'd really wanted to get operational again, but this was much too fucking much.

Court began to stand. His pint was half-full, but he thought if he could leave this pub under his own power at any time, it would be right now, before Slattery got his plan together. But before Gentry could slide all the way off his stool, the bartender lowered his newspaper.

"Don't fancy yer pint, eh?"

The redheaded, barrel-chested sixty-year-old must have sensed the bad juju in the room between Slattery and the stranger.

Court didn't want to say too much. Instead he shifted on his stool, like he was just rearranging himself, and lifted his glass. Tipped it to the bartender and took another gulp. "It's just grand," he said. He thought he sounded Irish but wasn't sure.

To his left the two men in the booth with his target stood and left through the front door. Two more at a table behind him stood; Court tracked them through the mirror as they approached. They sat on either side of him menacingly.

The man on the left spoke first. His breath was hot with Irish whiskey and tobacco.

"Woar ye from?"

Court looked straight ahead. He dropped the attempt at an Irish accent. "Workin' a Maersk freighter. We docked this afternoon. Leave out in the morning."

"Woar are ye from?" The other man repeated his mate's question.

15

"I told you."

"You born on the freighter? 'Where you from' means where you come from?"

"Lads. Leave the man to enjoy his pint in peace." It was Dougal Slattery speaking. He had stood, strolled over to the bar with his limp, and made eye contact through the mirror. "Always good to see a new face here. Travelers included. Don't pay the lads any attention, friend."

Court wondered why it was that everyone was calling him "friend" today.

3

Five minutes later Gentry left the Padraic Pearse. Slattery had gone first, just after rescuing the stranger from the two locals, who had returned to their table without another word. The bartender had not looked up from his paper through it all.

Court walked east on Pearse Street, moving deftly in the shadows a hundred yards behind the limping man with the drum on his shoulder.

Everything had changed now; the entire operation had been accelerated by Court's decision to walk through the front door of the pub. He could not just do a soft recon as he'd originally planned. No, his target was spooked, and his target would run or build up his defenses. It did not take a brilliant tradecraft mind to thwart an imminent attack from one man. Run away or circle the wagons and pass out the guns. It was page one from the *How to Avoid Assassination* manual, and Gentry had no doubt Dougal had read it.

If the Gray Man was going to complete his contract, he knew he'd have to do it tonight. Slattery turned right into the open front gates of a drab block of flats and did not look back as he began climbing up a slanting car park towards a door. Court moved on through the darkness, closer to his prey, a prey that would be expecting him, yes, but hopefully not quite so soon.

A thick young man in a black rugby shirt stepped into the street from his hiding place behind a large waste bin twenty-five

17

feet in front of Court. Gentry slowed, stopped, faced the man, his hands down at his sides. It was one of the young men who'd been with Slattery in the Padraic Pearse. The Irishman exposed a long length of chain from behind his leg, began swaying it slowly like a pendulum.

"What the fek ya' doin' followin me mate?" His brogue was almost incomprehensible, but it hardly mattered. Court was not listening. Instead, all his attention was focused on softer noises, tuned to hear the footsteps that would be approaching from behind any second. This rugby boy's buddy was out there somewhere, and he'd make his move from the rear, Court had no doubt. He might go for a headlock or, more likely, swing a chain or a piece of metal at his target's exposed back. Normally, as an elite contract killer, Court dealt with more determined foes with better training and equipment. But in cover working in dockyards or hanging in seedy bars in scummy parts of shitty towns, he'd seen beatings and batterings by thickheaded ruffians often enough to memorize the standard operating procedure.

It didn't matter where you were, really. There was something of a universal language to an ass-kicking.

The man in the black rugby shirt shouted something else, this time fully indecipherable, and then there it was: soft footsteps, getting louder and quicker behind him as they closed in. Court made himself look straight ahead at black-shirt rugby boy and pretended to have no idea he was about to be jumped from behind, until the last possible moment.

The steps were on him now, and Court moved like lightning, executing his first force-on-force encounter in months. In one motion he sank low and spun and moved to the side, saw a bald young man in an orange rugby shirt move in a blur and swing a length of bent rebar at the empty space where Gentry's back had been three-quarters of a second before. The weight of the iron and the swing itself as well as the Irishman's own momentum carried him through the space, and he kept moving forward long after his mind had registered that his target had avoided his strike.

Court stood quickly as the man passed by him, used his left hand to guide the flying man past him, shot a clenched fist through the black night like a firing piston, connected perfectly with the area just under the man's right ear, cracking the jaw and snapping the head to the side and rendering the man unconscious even as his out-of-control energy propelled him onwards.

The rebar clanged in the street and the Irishman followed, fell chest-first and rolled, all arms and legs flapping, to a stop at the foot of his mate.

He did not move. Blood on his face from the road rash acquired when his skin met the asphalt glistened in the cobalt streetlamps.

Black rugby shirt swung his chain wildly now, his eyes dropping to check on his friend and then darting back up, with equal measures of fury and terror, to the bearded man in front of him. Court walked towards the man, arms low, eyes and shoulders relaxed.

A man in his element.

The chain whipped forward.

The Gray Man stepped into the path of the chain, caught it deftly with his left hand, and yanked hard, knocking the young man in the rugby shirt off balance, bringing him closer with a jolt.

A right-hand spear to the throat knocked the Irishman to his back. He rolled in the street, gagged and wheezed, choking on his bruised and swelling airway as he stared at the bearded man who now squatted above him. When he spoke, the American sounded calm, in complete control, as if *he* were the one who had planned this ambush in the dark.

"Slattery's flat number, please. I will only ask you once."

Four minutes later the tip of a handgun's silencer pushed open the unlatched door of flat sixty-six of the Queen's Court Condominiums. Behind the silencer was a Russian Baikal Makarov automatic pistol. Behind the Mak was the Gray Man. All senses were alert, more so because the door had been left open invitingly, and that was odd, considering the fact that the man who lived there was surely aware that someone was coming for him.

As Gentry entered the well-lit living room behind the door, he did not have long to wonder about the location of his target. Slattery sat at a simple wooden table in the middle of the small room, facing the door, a bottle of Irish whiskey and three shot glasses in front of him. Court noticed that the man had changed shirts. He now wore a blue on black rugby jersey, open loose at the collar and straining tight around his thick midsection. Perhaps his favorite team?

Slattery looked up at him for a long time. He took one of the shot glasses and turned it upside down. He had been expecting two guests, no doubt the two left lying in the street. Dougal recovered, lifted a second glass slowly. "Care for a drink, lad?" He was nervous, clearly; his low voice cracked.

Court scanned the room quickly. His weapon remained pointed at his target's forehead as he did so. He spoke softly but with calm conviction. "Hands where I can see them."

Slattery complied. "Did ya kill 'em?"

"The rugby boys? No, they'll be okay." He added, "Eventually."

Slattery nodded. Shrugged. "Like a knife through butter, was it?"

"Not much trouble, no."

"They'd have been no match if they *weren't* pissed. Have a seat first, will ya? I have some grand whiskey here."

Court continued searching the room for threats, all senses alert. His target seemed oddly resigned to what was going on, but that could have been some sort of deception.

"No."

The big man shrugged again. "Then maybe you'll let *me* have a drink first." He didn't wait. He poured Old Bushmills into a shot glass, tossed it back into his open throat, placed the glass back in front of him, and refilled it.

Court moved to the window. He flipped the overhead off on the way. Shrouded in darkness now, he looked down into the street.

Slattery said, "There's no one coming. Just the two you met already. Even if they *can* still walk, they won't be walkin' this way, I promise ya that."

20

Court checked the bedroom, the bathroom, the kitchen. They were alone. The Irishman just sat at the table, facing the doorway. He shot another whiskey. Refilled the glass again.

Waiting patiently.

When Gentry stepped back in front of him, Slattery put his hand around the bottle, tipped it towards his guest. He said, "Sure ya won't have a wee drop? I always found it helpful back when I was on the job." Court shook his head. Focused fully on his target, his Makarov rose. Dougal Slattery spoke quickly. "Look, pal. I know ya gotta do it. No argument from me. I was on the job once, and I know the score. There's just one thing. A little favor. I got a kid. Not a kid, he's 'bout thirty now, I guess. He's in Galway."

"Do I look like I give a shit?"

"He's got the Down syndrome. Good boy, but he can't look after himself. No ma—she was an aul whore in Belfast, OD'd twenty some-odd years back. I've got him in private care. I'm all the boy has."

"I could not possibly care less."

"I'm just sayin'. I send money, enough to keep him out of state care."

Court pulled the Mak's hammer back with his thumb.

Dougal kept talking, faster. "Without the money he'll go to state care. It's a fecking mess, believe me. Me boy is my punishment for me life. You can have me fecking life, mate, but don't make *him* pay for it."

It occurred to Court that he should have just put a bullet through the man's head when he walked through the door.

"Everyone leaves someone behind. I can't help you."

"No, you can't help *me*. But you can help *him*. I'm askin' for twenty-four hours. One bleeding day, and I'll knock over a bank or a currency exchange or something. There's an armored car that makes stops up and down Dawson Street in the afternoons. A lot of options for a quick job. If I just had time for a score, I could get some money to the home so he'll be set. If I had any idea you were coming for me, I'd have done it already, but this is a bit of a surprise. I've been off the job for a long time. I thought I was out of it. Look. I won't run. I'll send the home in Galway one hundred percent by wire tomorrow afternoon and then I'll come back here and you can drop me dead. I swear on me ma's grave. You'll get your payday for me scalp, I'll get me boy the money he needs so he can be looked after when I'm gone. I'm sitting here now showing you respect. Showing you that I'm not a runner. I'm not a fighter. Not anymore. I'm sittin' here handing myself over to you, hopin' you'll do the right thing and give me one bleedin' day to sort out some decent future for me lad." The man was near tears. Desperate. Court had no doubt the story was true.

Still, he steeled himself. He raised the weapon to eye level. "Sorry, dude. That's not going to happen."

Slattery's eyes began to water before he tossed down another shot. He did not refill the glass afterwards this time. "I figured you for a man with a soul. My mistake. So it's off to state care for me lad." He smiled a little. "All's not lost, though. There is some wee consolation. I know someday Sid will send some bloke after you."

Court lowered the pistol slightly.

"Sid?"

"You're Sid's new lad, yeah? I'm Sid's old lad, so you see your future before your eyes, don'tcha? He's sent you on this wee errand to make room for yourself in his organization. This is your audition to replace me, ya know." When Court did not speak for several seconds, Slattery's watery eyes widened. "He didn't tell you, did he? What a bastard he is! You thought he was passing on a contract from someone else that wants me dead? No, pal, this is Sid's doin', all of it."

Gentry lowered the pistol farther. "Why?"

Slattery poured another shot glass and tossed the contents down his gullet. "Five years back, Sid came to see me. I'd been doing some . . . some stuff for another Russian. Sid tells me he likes my work, wants me to come work for him. I say, 'What's the catch?' Everyone knows Sidorenko gets the juicy contracts. He tells me the only thing I have to do is rub out the guy holding the job I wanted. Create the vacancy myself, ya see? Seems this bloke, an Israeli, had outworn his welcome. Dunno why. Sid tells me once I sort out his Jew, I'll be top stallion in his stable."

"So you killed him."

"Bloody well right, I did. 'At's the business we're in, ain't it? And now I'm too old, too broken and beaten to execute the big contracts anymore. I'm not making the cash I once was, so he's sending ya to shut me off, so ya can take over. He figures if there's a one percent chance I'll talk, call a newspaper or Interpol and tell on him, then he might as well off me just in case."

Court was stunned. Sid had lied about the very existence of a contract on the target. It was only in the personal interests of his handler that he should kill this man. He recovered a bit and reminded himself of some of the dirtier parts of Sid's dossier on Slattery. "He told me you'd done some ugly hits in your past." The Makarov rose again with new resolve.

Slattery cocked his head, genuinely surprised. "Ugly hits? Ugly hits? What the feck is a pretty hit?"

Court took a moment. "You've killed innocents, I mean."

"Bollocks. You gonna sit there and judge me, based on what Sid has told you? A feckin' joke you are. Go on then, be done with it. Put a bullet up me nose and feel good about yourself! Ugly hits? Innocents? Aren't you the most pretentious fuck for a hit man that's ever soiled this godforsaken planet!"

Dougal Slattery's nostrils flared as he stared down the suppressor at the end of the barrel of the little Makarov. The alcohol showed in his eyes, but not a shred of fear.

After a long pause, Court lowered the gun to his side. He pulled out the wooden chair and sat slowly down at the table across from the Irishman.

"I guess I'll take that drink now."

Slattery did not take his eyes off the American as he poured for them both.

4

Ten minutes later Court had reholstered his weapon. He'd decided not to kill the man in front of him. He'd told him as much. The Irishman did not smile or breathe a sigh of relief, but he did strike out a hand, and they shook. They sat mostly in silence in the dim light from the streetlamps outside the tiny room. Court was careful to leave his hands on the small wooden table to keep Slattery relaxed.

After a while Dougal said, "Sid's not gonna be happy with you."

"We had an agreement. I told him I would only execute contracts I approved of. If he gave me bad intel, I reserve the right to pull out. Fuck him."

Slattery lifted a Bushmills into the air.

"I'll drink to that. Fuck Sid!"

"He'll just send someone else after you, you know."

"Aye. Suppose he will. Maybe I should just go ahead and have you do me in, just to get it out of the way."

Court said, "I don't take requests."

The thick Irishman laughed heartily. "That's a good one, mate. Maybe my two lads will be out of the hospital by the time the next hitter shows. Hopefully Sid feckin' Sidorenko will send someone they *can* handle."

Court chuckled. "I doubt that."

Dougal Slattery poured another shot of Old Bushmills for himself and then, seemingly as an afterthought, pulled Gentry's shot glass to his side of the table and began to fill it.

Court tried to stop him. "No. I'm good."

Slattery kept pouring. "It's the third, me boy. The third wee shot will make a man of ye, I swear it!"

Court shrugged, shook his head, reached across the table for the drink, hoped the hard liquor would substitute for the pain meds his body craved. He said, "You might want to think about leaving town until—"

The table rose into the air to meet Court's face. The shot glass slammed into his mouth before he could grab it, the wooden table's edge hit him squarely on the chin. Gentry's head snapped back, and he flew backwards off his chair.

The big Irishman had flipped the table up on him. Slattery lunged over it, took hold of Court before his back hit the floor, and Dougal's meaty hands wrapped around the American's muscled neck.

Court tried to shout but could not make a sound. He felt two thumbs digging into his throat, pressing his Adam's apple to the point of crushing. Though dazed by the blow from the table, he had the instincts to turn his head sharply to loosen his opponent's grip. He swept an arm up to try to knock away the hands entirely, but the big man's thick arms barely budged.

"Stop!" Gentry gurgled. He had every intention of leaving Dougal Slattery alive. Either Dougal Slattery did not believe that, or he felt, for some reason, Sidorenko would only convince this killer to return someday, and the Irishman wanted to preclude that event here and now while he saw an opportunity.

On his back, with the big Irishman on top of him and his hands choking the life from him, Court saw only one option. He scooted around on the cheap linoleum flooring, used the heels of his shoes to rotate himself and his attacker around to where Court's legs were bent against the door to the little flat. From here, still using his hands to try to push away the iron grip on his throat, he walked his feet up the door. Six inches, two feet, three feet. This raised his lower torso off the ground and caused Dougal's dead weight to roll forward onto Court's face and shoulders. Quickly, with all his strength, Gentry pushed off the door with the balls of his feet, executed a sloppy headstand, then a backwards roll. His head popped free of Slattery's grip when he spun back over the top of him. Court landed on his knees on the overturned table, leapt back to get away from any wild punches from the prostrate former boxer.

In one second both men were on their feet. Court looked at his attacker; the Irishman's fat face was beet red and slick with sweat, his eyes wild from fury. He shouted something; it was Gaelic, perhaps, as Court could not understand.

Gentry wanted to tell the man it was a mistake, that he just wanted to leave, but there was no use. Slattery took a step forward and threw a right jab that half connected with Court's left cheekbone. It stung and stunned him, and instantly his right eye filled with water and his vision blurred.

Court had vastly underestimated the flabby man's brute strength and blinding speed. It was a mistake that he could easily find himself paying for with his life.

Court backed away into a corner, created just enough space from the big man to reach for his Makarov, but he found his holster empty. He was certain it had fallen loose when he did the headstand, and was somewhere on the floor under the overturned table or the broken chair.

Slattery noticed Court's empty holster. A wild-crazed smile broadened across his cherry-red face. "You're feckin' dead, laddie!" The Irishman fired another jab. This one Gentry leaned away from and avoided all but a brush against his chin.

A left hook came next, thrown from Dougal's body, his torso and legs shifting along with the punch to get full force behind it. Gentry blocked it, but it still knocked him down. The fist failed to impact him, but just the power Court absorbed in his forearm sent him tumbling in the tiny living room. He ended up against the wall on his knees.

He stood quickly, just in time to recognize and then duck below a jab. Gentry then quickly retaliated with a finger spear into Dougal's solar plexus, followed with an instep kick to the big Irishman's crotch.

Slattery was unfazed. "Jesus sufferin' fuck, ya fight like a Molly!"

Then Court remembered Slattery's weakness; he'd followed the limping man for half an hour through the night and had watched him struggle to put weight on his left knee. Court kicked viciously to the inside of the knee, and it buckled outwards. Dougal screamed and stumbled but did not fall.

Instead he kept coming, though the American's attack caused him to telegraph his next move.

Court dropped low and to his right, ducked the right fist as it whipped the air just above his left ear. The American moved in on his attacker with all his speed, leapt off the ground, and got his right arm on top of the Irishman's right shoulder. From here, in a blur of perfectly practiced execution, Gentry reached high with his right arm, rolling his own shoulder forward to turn his fingers in. His hand came behind Slattery's neck and back around in front of his face from his left side, then it hooked back around under his chin. Court's hand grabbed the right collar of Dougal's rugby shirt, pulled it back across his throat, yanked it all the way around his neck in the back, and handed it off to Court's left hand.

"Fight like a bloody man, you feckin'—"

Dougal's words were replaced by a choking gurgle. Gentry cinched the collar tight like a twisted garrote, using the man's own shirt to strangle him. He wrapped his right arm around Slattery's neck as if he were hugging him passionately, wrapped both his legs around the man's back, and held on for dear life as his left hand pulled and pulled and pulled on the rugby shirt digging into the boxer's fat throat.

In the panic of loosing his airway, Slattery moved across the flat, wobbling on his bad knee, crashed the American assassin's back into the glass window, slammed him into a wall hard enough to crack the Sheetrock and knock cheap imitation lithographs of

27

mustachioed bare-knuckled boxers onto the floor, and then spun him sideways into the heavy wooden door.

Just then, above the crashing and the panting and the shouting, a pounding came from the other side of the door. A woman screamed frantically, asking Mr. Slattery if he was all right. Asked if she should go for help. Dougal could not speak. He tried to reach for the door latch with his left hand, but the strength was leaving him with the depletion of oxygen in his lungs. Just as he got a finger on the latch, Court reached back with his right hand, flicked the dead bolt to lock it, and then used his legs to push off from the door.

Both men went crashing to the floor in the middle of the flat.

Slattery still could not breathe, but he had plenty of fight left in him, and he managed to use his legs for leverage as he flipped on top of Court. But Court did not, *would* not, let go. He forced the momentum of the roll to continue and again found himself above his target.

For thirty seconds they grunted and kicked at one another among the shambles of the broken furniture and furnishings of the little flat. Gentry got both legs over one of Slattery's arms, but the other fist hammered down on Court's back and the top of his head with frantic repetition.

The big Irishman tried head-butting Gentry, as well, but their heads were pressed against one another already; there was no room for him to get his skull back so that he could slam it forward.

And then the fight slowed. And then the fight ceased.

Court kept the pressure up on his victim's throat, but he leaned back a bit to check Slattery's face. His eyes had bugged out, his face had turned impossibly red and was covered with sweat that smelled like whiskey and vinegar and body odor. Court was over him, could see his own blood dripping off his lips from where the shot glass cut them. The red splotches speckled the Irishman's forehead and stained red the sweat rivulets running into his eyes.

The bulging eyes blinked weakly.

Court let the rugby jersey loosen a bit. Quickly Dougal sucked air, gagged, and wheezed.

Court's face was inches from him. Gentry spoke through gasps from the exertion of the brutal fight. "The kid. Your boy ... with the Down's? He's real?"

Slattery's tongue was swollen, his throat was nearly closed. He coughed bloody sputum. "I swear it."

Court nodded. He wiped sweat from his own brow. Still he spoke through gasps from his near hyperventilated state. "Okay ... okay. Don't worry. I'll see to him. He'll be okay."

The bugging eyes of the Irishman turned to him. Blinked tears mixed with blood that streamed down both sides of his face. Mucus sprayed from his nose as he sobbed. He nodded. Spoke through a clenched throat. "That's just grand, lad. I take it back. You've got a soul. You're a good man."

"Yeah." Court brought his fingertips to the Irishman's forehead. "That's me." He smoothed the man's sopping-wet gray hair back gently.

He nodded again.

"I'm a goddamned saint."

In a swift single motion, Court Gentry scooped the Makarov from its resting place on the floor beside him, punched the suppressor into Dougal Slattery's fleshy neck, and fired a single round up through his chin, through his tongue, through the roof of his mouth, through his sinus cavity, and into his brain. The .380-caliber hollow point projectile danced inside the skull of the fifty-four-year-old Irishman before coming to rest behind the left ear. Slattery's protruding eyes turned glassy and remained wide-open in death.

Court rolled off of Slattery's chest and lowered himself onto his back on the floor next to the dead man. He was exhausted, drained, sapped of all energy and emotion. His face hurt where he had been punched, his stomach and leg hurt where he'd been stabbed and shot last winter.

Together he and Slattery lay amid the shattered shambles of the little flat and stared vacantly together at the low ceiling.

29

5

The landing launch cleared the fog bank a half mile from shore. Behind it, lost in the mist, the Lithuanian freighter that had been Court's transportation both to and from the Emerald Isle had already turned to the north, brought its engines to full power, and begun steaming for its home port. Court stood at the front of the small launch, squinting towards the docks of the Gdansk shipyard in front of him. He was the boat's only passenger.

He continued speaking into his satellite phone.

"Paulus, I want to be very clear. Except your commission, every last cent goes to this patient. I don't care how you do it. Just do it."

"That is no problem. We can set up a small trust. Regular automatic withdrawals for the institution. I checked into it as you asked. It is the best establishment in Ireland for people with such conditions."

"Good."

He paused. Court could sense discomfort in the call. "Sir. You understand I will need to contact Sir Donald."

"Go ahead. But since you'll be talking to him anyhow, tell him this. This money isn't his. It isn't mine. It belongs to the kid. He touches it . . . and I'm going to—"

"Herr Lewis. Please do not threaten Sir Donald. He is my employer. By duty I will be obliged to relay whatever you say—"

"I'm counting on it. I want you to tell him word for word. He touches the account, looks into it in any way, and I will show up at his door."

"Herr Lewis, please—"

"You have the message, Paulus."

"I know he will fulfill your wishes. And I will handle the account as agreed. My standard commission will apply to the funds."

"*Danke.*"

"*Bitte schön.* Sir Donald is very fond of you, Herr Lewis. I am not sure why you two parted ways, but I hope maybe someday the two of you could sit down and—"

"Good-bye, Paulus."

A frustrated pause. A polite good-bye. "*Auf wiedersehen,* Herr Lewis."

Gentry stowed his sat phone in his canvas bag. Then he focused all his attention on a new threat ahead.

Court had noticed it three hundred yards out: a large black car on the docks. At two hundred yards he could just make out men leaning against the vehicle, all wearing dark gray. At one hundred fifty yards he counted four of them, could tell they were big. At fifty yards he had them pegged as Slavic, wearing suits, and their car was a limousine of some make.

These would be Sid's boys, here to pick him up and take him for a ride, and this made Court furious. He'd planned on getting off here in Gdansk, losing himself for a few days on the Polish coast, and then contacting Sid via the Ural Mountain Tours Web site when he was good and ready. Sir Donald, his ex-handler, never made him work face-to-face, but these goons, sent by his soon-to-be ex-handler, had no doubt come here on a babysitting mission to make sure Gentry came along peacefully to kneel before the throne of his liege.

"Fuck this shit," Court said it aloud at twenty-five yards. The men were up off the hood of the limo; cigarettes were thrown on the ground and crushed out. Court could see the glint of thin gold chains around their necks. Russian mob boys. Who else? The men stepped up to the edge of the dock, coming to the water's edge to prevent him from running away when the ferry landed.

As if.

Court looked up and down the landing to see if there was any place to run to.

Nope. Shit.

Gentry stepped off the swaying launch and up onto the floating wharf. He stood in front of the four goons. No words were exchanged. The only communication between them was through the looks of five men filled with testosterone, all of them on the job, none of them here particularly willingly. Court's old CIA Special Activities Division team leader, a foul-mouthed ex-SEAL named Zack Hightower, referred to it as "eye fucking," a crude but accurate description of men simultaneously sizing up one another and projecting their own power and prowess through their cold stares.

Slowly Court opened his peacoat to reveal the butt of the .380 Makarov on his hip. One of the younger Russians stepped forward and yanked the gun free of its holster, sneering at Gentry during his backwards draw stroke as if he had discovered the weapon himself. He then patted Court down front to back, pulled a knife from the foreigner's pocket, and slipped it into his own. He looked through the canvas bag on Gentry's shoulder, yanked out the satellite phone and pocketed it, but he did not find anything else of interest. Satisfied he'd disarmed the Gray Man, the Russian stepped back, and with an impatient gesture, he beckoned the American forward to the car.

Court unslung his bag from his shoulder, then tossed it underhanded to one of the men to carry. The bag hit the thick man on the chest, and he let it fall to the ground in front of him; his "eye fuck" stare neither wavered nor diminished.

Court could not help it. He cracked a smile, stepped forward, and scooped it up with a chuckle, then walked to the black limo and opened the back door of the car and climbed in.

An hour later he was airborne. A Hawker 400 light corporate aircraft had been waiting for his entourage at Lech Walesa International Airport. No passports or customs inspections were performed that Court could see; certainly no one asked him any questions or solicited from him any documentation. The Hawker shot upwards through the wet clouds and into a clear mid-morning Polish sky. With him in the seven-seated cabin were the four men who'd picked him up at the dock. They showed him where the food and the booze were stored on the plane, and in broken English they said the flight would only be two hours. They did not tell him where they were headed, but they did not need to.

Court knew. He was being taken to the boss, and the boss lived in Saint Petersburg, Russia.

Gentry leaned back and relaxed, sipped bottled water, and listened to Sidorenko's henchmen chat. Court's Russian comprehension had been fair at its peak, a dozen years earlier, but it was extremely rusty at the moment. By concentrating on the chitchat of the men around him with his eyes closed for over an hour, he felt like he was retuning his brain to the nearly impenetrable language.

He was reasonably sure that Sid and his men would have no idea that he spoke a word of Russian, and he thought he might be able to use their ignorance to his advantage in the hours to come.

The Hawker dipped a wing and descended, landing just after noon. Court's assumption that he'd be heading to Saint Petersburg to meet with his employer was confirmed when, upon their descent, he spied the Gulf of Finland out the port side window. He recognized the airport, as well. Rzhevka was to the east of Saint Pete, less convenient to the city center than the main international airport, but Court had been to this airfield more than once.

In the old days, ten or more years before, Gentry had worked as a CIA singleton operator living undercover and alone overseas. Theoretically his missions could be anywhere on the planet, in either friendly or enemy territory, but in practice he operated more or less steadily in the former USSR. Russia, Ukraine, Lithuania, Georgia, Tajikistan—the CIA had reasons to send operatives from their Autonomous Asset Program into the badlands of the East, tailing and chasing and sometimes even killing traders of weapons or nuclear secrets. For a time it seemed the only things worth selling from behind the former Iron Curtain were the surviving relics of doomsday left behind by the former evil empire, and for a time it seemed the only thing Court Gentry and other Double A-P men were ever asked to do was to head over there, follow a target, report on his activity, and/or bug his house and/or buy off his friends and/or plant evidence to incriminate him of a crime.

And/or kill him.

But those were the nineties. The good ol' days.

Pre–9/11.

He'd been to Saint Petersburg just once since, in January 2003. By then he was a member of Task Force Golf Sierra, the Goon Squad, a CIA Special Activities-Division/Special Operations Group paramilitary black ops team that hunted terrorists and their associates around the globe. Court and the Goon Squad flew into this very airport on an agency jet. Part of the team stayed in a safe house out in the countryside while Court and Zack Hightower billeted in a ramshackle tenement a couple of blocks away from the posh hotels on Nevsky Prospect. And then, on their third week in town, the Goon Squad boarded Zodiac rubber raiding craft and hit a freighter leaving the Port of Saint Petersburg. On board was supposed to be nuclear material heading to Saddam Hussein and Iraq. Instead it was conventional weaponry, stuff that went *bang* and not *boom*, as Zack Hightower had reported to Langley from his satellite phone at the time. They were ordered to leave the guns behind, to hop off the boat, and to get out of Russia. Perplexing, but it made sense later, sort of, when that very lot of goods was "discovered" in Basra, Iraq, and paraded in front of the media, Russian packaging and all. The ship had been tracked all the way to Iraq and the cargo monitored by satellite. The Marines who found it had been told where to find it, and the embarrassment for Russia nudged them a bit in their support of the US mission there. Not much, really, but a little.

It was politics, and politics wasn't the Goon Squad's stated mission. Court didn't like it, but as his boss, Zack, had said at the time, he wasn't paid to like it, he was paid to do it.

From Sidorenko's airplane Court was shepherded across a

hundred meters of frozen tarmac to a black stretch limousine. His minders led him to the front passenger seat. One man said, "You get in front. The back is for VIPs." He smiled, enough metal around his neck and in his teeth to pick up local AM stations. "You are just a *P*." He laughed aloud, then translated his joke to his colleagues, and they laughed, too.

Court shrugged and climbed into the front seat. The minders, hardly VIPs themselves, got into the plush back. An absurd security violation: Court sat up front with only a late-middle-aged driver, but Sidorenko's security men did not appear to be the smartest henchmen around.

As they drove west towards Saint Pete, Court did his best to retain information about the trip, in case he needed to find his own way back to the airport. He planned on making this a very short journey. Thirty seconds to tell Sid he didn't appreciate being dragged up here, a violation of his and Sid's agreement, another thirty seconds to tell him he didn't appreciate being deceived about the hit he'd just performed, and a final ten or so seconds to tell his Russian handler that he quit, and if Sidorenko's gold-chained, skinhead mouth breathers tried to stop him from leaving, then there would soon be more vacancies to fill in Sidorenko's organization.

But, in the end, it did not work out quite the way Gentry had envisioned.

6

After an hour on the road, Court was taken to a massive home on the northern outskirts of Saint Petersburg. He had never been in this suburb and admitted to himself that he could not even find this place on a map. The streets were wide and tree-lined, the properties were large and landscaped, the homes were old and stately.

The limousine turned up a drive, and Gentry immediately focused on the home ahead. It was breathtaking from a distance. Architecturally speaking, it was magnificent.

But as they got closer it appeared to Court as if Sid's crew of dumb-ass henchmen also moonlighted as his landscapers and housekeepers, tasks for which they were even less suited than security. There were tents erected on the grounds, like a small military encampment, with smoking fires and young men standing around, apparently doing little or nothing. Several four-wheel-drive vehicles, mud-covered and poorly maintained, were parked on the shredded lawn on both sides of the driveway.

The facade of the mansion was covered in flaking paint, and the gravel roundabout parking space was covered with bottles, cigarette butts, and other trash. Gentry climbed out of the limo and was led through a kitchen that looked like something from a frat house whose house mother had run away after a nervous breakdown: dishes upon dishes in the sink, plastic carry-out trays covering every flat space, and vodka bottles rimming the floors like some sort of shabby chic glass trim work.

Court was no neatnik, but he could not help but wonder about the prospects for wildlife in this kitchen during the summer, and he felt thankful for the frigid air that made its way through the thin kitchen window to keep bug life from flourishing, and the three or four fat cats he'd noticed strolling around both the interior and the exterior of the mansion to keep furry vermin at bay.

Next it was two flights up on a wide, circular staircase. Men sat on the steps, played handheld video games, chatted on mobile phones, read newspapers, and smoked, each man with a submachine gun on his lap or a shoulder holster stowing an automatic pistol under his arm. Some wore typical Russian mobster suits, but most of them were in camouflage or army green, though not in any sort of coherent uniforms—more like the attire of survivalists or hunters.

And they were all skinheads. Most stared up at Gentry with malevolence. He presumed it was his long hair and scruffy beard that served as indicators that he was not from the same club as they were. He even wondered if they thought he was a member of whatever particular ethnic group they blamed for all the problems in their shitty lives.

Fuck 'em, thought Court. He knew he could kick any five of their assess without breaking a shine on his forehead.

The only problem with his macho self-assuredness, he recognized, was that he'd seen at least ten times that number of men so far on the property.

Sidorenko's security setup clearly placed a much higher premium on quantity than quality.

Finally Gentry passed through a massive gilded double doorway and into an outer office. A male secretary sat behind a desk. He was well-dressed and instantly appeared to Court to be incalculably more competent at his job than were the fifty or so other jokers lounging around this regal shit hole.

"May I take your coat, sir?" the man inquired in English as he stood behind his desk and stepped around to greet Court.

"I won't be staying."

37

The secretary seemed momentarily nonplussed, but he recovered nicely. "As you wish, sir. Please, right through those doors," he motioned with a gracious smile, but then he spoke to the four guards. "Stay close to him." It was in Russian, but Gentry understood.

It was another set of gilded doors, and on the other side it was dark, a large hall, the only light coming from a fireplace to the right of a massive desk at the far end of the wooden-floored room. There was no other furniture in the room, and it was as cold as a meat locker, even with a crackling fireplace. The room echoed like a cathedral as Gentry moved through the dark towards the man behind the desk.

"Wonderful to meet you finally, Mr. Gray." Gentry recognized the voice of Gregor Ivanovic Sidorenko. It was high-pitched and nasal, and it matched his face somehow. The man was small of frame, with tiny eyes and narrow features; his eyeglasses seemed as fragile as the rest of him.

But he was younger than Gentry had imagined him to be. Maybe mid-forties, though he did not seem to be healthy. His thin face made him appear underfed, and his sunken cheeks were sallow even in the dim of the room.

Sid reached out a hand to Court. Court ignored it. He knew everything since Gdansk—the men, the plane, the limos, the guns, the attitude—was all orchestrated to demonstrate Sid's authority and control over Gentry. Small men with big power sometimes exert this power disproportionately to compensate for what they consider to be their shortcomings. Nothing Gentry had not seen before, but he knew that he had to fight fire with fire, to exert his own dominance on the situation.

"We had an agreement. We were not to meet face-to-face. You violated this agreement. I am not like the others that you control. You can't impress me with a third-rate crew of gold chains and poorly lubricated firearms. I only came along willingly to tell you this, and to tell you that I quit."

The young minders around Court could not understand his

38

English, but from the foreigner's angry and aggressive tone they moved closer to him and looked to their master for guidance. He stayed them with a raised hand, then wiggled his fingertips at them, as if brushing them back into the corners of the room. They complied. Court could hear their retreating footsteps behind him.

Sidorenko did not take his eyes off of Court. Instead he slowly backed up behind the desk and sat down. He sipped purple tea from a gold-leaf glass. Court thought the man to be intimidated, but the next words out of the Russian mob boss's mouth came forth calmly and with no discernible tremor.

"Have you ever seen a man boiled alive in a tub of acid?"

"Is that a rhetorical question?"

"A colleague of mine." Sid held out a hand as if to allay his guest's fears. "I did not do it. It was shortly after the auctioning off of state-owned enterprise; ninety-three, I think it was. I was with a team of accountants and lawyers working for a mobster in Moscow. He was no oligarch, no great genius either. But he loved money above all, and he strong-armed his way into several department store chains and then scared off or killed off the co-owners. Anyway, he decided one of his employees had been siphoning funds from his legitimate holdings, and he brought us all to a meeting at his dacha in Odessa. There, waiting for us, were some very hard men: Spetsnaz paramilitaries moonlighting as henchmen for this cretin. We—there were nine of us—were all taken to a barn, stripped naked, and shackled to railroad ties. We were beaten and sprayed with cold water for two days. It was October. The oldest man, an attorney, died that first night. During the second night our employer entered the barn and told us that if one of us confessed, he would, by doing so, save the lives of the others. No one spoke. The beatings continued for another twelve hours."

Court looked around the room while Sidorenko spoke.

"On day three another man was dead. I can't remember his face, a regulatory affairs expert, if I'm not mistaken. Our employer returned again and made the same offer as before. Again, no one confessed. I was certain he would kill everyone, but fortunately for the rest of us, the oligarch had a deep-seated mistrust of Jews. He noticed, lying there in the muck and blood, that one of us was circumcised. Natan Bulichova. He took him for a Jew, decided he was the deceitful one, and had a wooden water trough brought in from outside. It was filled with a solvent used for stripping lead-based paint, powerful stuff, and Natan was thrown on the ground next to the trough. For nearly an hour our Spetsnaz tormentors used shovels to splash the acid on poor Natan as he writhed on the straw. He turned red, and then the skin began to bubble and pop off him, leaving him covered in the most brutal sores. The rest of us were forced to watch. Finally, because the men with the shovels grew tired of the work, they grabbed hooks used to lift bales of hay, and they pierced them into Natan's arms and legs. They threw him right into the acid bath. The rest of us, Natan's friends and colleagues, willed him to hurry up and die, for both his benefit and ours. He screamed a scream I will never forget, until finally his melted face went under the liquid and did not emerge. It was a horrifying experience."

Court recognized that Sid enjoyed telling the story. He did not know what to say, so he said, "Sounds like stealing from this man was not a good idea."

Sid shrugged, reached for his tea as he replied matter-of-factly, "Oh, Natan was perfectly innocent. I am the one who embezzled the money. Used it ultimately to go into business for myself. Our employer let the rest of us leave. He himself was killed in ninety-four, shot in the back while getting fitted for a suit in Moscow."

Court sighed. "Is there a point to this story? Because if there is, I don't get it. Or am I just supposed to be frightened by it? Because I am not."

7

"The point is, I want you to understand who I am. I can be your friend. I *want* to be your friend. But if you come into my home and speak to me as you have just spoken to me, if you show me no respect, I can be your enemy. Do not let my pleasant regard for you allow you to think you can disrespect me in my home. I am a man who has evolved into where I am. I did not begin like this. To be a success in Russia, you need equal measures of two things: brains and brutality. This mobster I spoke of, he was a brute. Killing a man like that was effective, but then to go out by yourself to buy a suit and get shot ... surely he did not have the brains to understand the consequences of his brutality. Other men, accountants like me, for example, they have become involved in crime because they have the brains for success, but in this vicious environment of competition and institutional corruption and the bloodthirsty hunt for money at all costs ... the accountant criminals were swept from the chessboard even faster than the brutal fools.

"I realized there was no one who had both the brains and the stomach. Someone with the brains for business and the stomach for violence could survive and thrive in the new Russia like no one else. I had the brains ... this I knew. But the stomach? That took a while to develop."

"So, do you throw your employees in acid?"

"No, my employees are treated well by me. They are National Socialists, if you had not yet guessed. They beat immigrants for fun. They think you are from the Caucasus from your complexion and hair ... so they are no fans of yours. No, I do not threaten them; I let these young men live as they wish, give them free run of my home, and I pay them extremely well."

"In gold chains?"

Sid laughed, genuinely amused. "Ha. No, not in gold chains. In euros. Used to be in dollars but, well, time marches on. You can come here, angry as you are, and you can tell me you do not want to work with me any longer. But, Mr. Gray, I promise you, I am the best that there is for what you need."

On the wall to Gentry's left and Sid's right was a huge painting in a massive gilded frame. In the smoky light of the room, the square face and penetrating eyes of Joseph Stalin stared back at Court.

"Cute picture," Court said as he sat down in an uncomfortable wooden high-backed chair in front of Sid's desk.

Sidorenko regarded the portrait as if he had only just noticed it. "Yes. I respect the authority that it conveys."

"You don't strike me as one of the old guard."

"What do you mean by that?"

"A commie. I thought all of you billionaire mobsters were capitalist pigs like the rest of the civilized world."

Sidorenko laughed with his mouth open and a high gurgle in the back of his throat. "Oh yes, I am a pig, but not an ideological one." He stared at the portrait as he said, "He was a terrible man, yes, but Uncle Joe said perhaps the most brilliant words ever spoken. He said, 'Death solves all problems'—"

Court finished the quote. "'No man, no problem.'"

Sidorenko smiled appreciatively. "Of course you would know this. It is your own personal mission statement, is it not?"

"It is not."

Sid shrugged. "An operational credo, then?" He did not wait for Court to answer. "Stalin, the Romanovs, the Great Patriotic War, the current skinhead Russian nationalist phenomenon. I have, you see, an affinity for terrible, terrible things. I am a fan of the power of cruelty. A man who has the ability to inflict death

42

and misery on his fellow man is more powerful than the rich, the famous, the good."

"*Your* operational credo?"

"Not really. A pastime, nothing more. Most of my business interests are rather benign: prostitutes, money laundering, stolen cars, credit cards, drugs ... moneymakers, yes, but money is not my true passion. There is, you see, nothing to me so fulfilling as to be a player in the industry in which you ply your trade. I am speaking of the industry of death. I am Russian. Our history is gloom and destruction. There are many sufferers and only a few dealers in suffering. I chose to be one of these. Awful, but preferable to the alternative, yes?"

Court said nothing. He was accustomed to working for, with, around, and against total nut jobs. This Russian freak was just par for the course on which he played.

Sid continued, "You are my instrument. You are my tool."

"If I choose to be."

Sidorenko smiled. "Yes. If you choose. Which is why I brought you here today."

"I thought you brought me here to intimidate me."

"Are you intimidated?"

"Not in the least."

Sid smiled. "Ah, well, good thing I have another reason. I have a job." He took another long sip of his purple tea and leaned forward on his desk as if to get down to business. "If you could kill anyone in the world right now, who would it be?"

"Greg Sidorenko."

Sid laughed. Court did not. Sid's levity chilled and morphed into a slight smile. "The best assassin on the planet wants to kill me. I should be frightened. But I'm not, because once I tell you who your new target is, you will thank me, and you and I will be the best of friends."

Court stood and turned on his heel. Quickly the four men by the door behind him pushed off the wall and moved closer. Court said to Sid, "I'm leaving. These guys try to stop me, and they *will* get hurt. I get the impression that you might get off on watching that, but you'll have to find yourself a new crew of hoodlums."

"President Bakri Abboud," Sid shouted the name, the name echoed in the long hall, and the Gray Man stopped dead in his tracks. He did not turn around immediately.

Court said, "I don't mind difficult, but I insist on the possible. He is an impossible target." He began walking again.

"Normally, yes, it would be so. But I have a way in, I have his schedule, I have access to him, and I have a way out."

Court chuckled derisively. "Then do it yourself."

"I did not say it would be easy. But *you* . . . *you* can do it. Just listen to my plan. You may still walk away, of course, if you do not like it. But I am sure you will be satisfied."

Court turned and took a few steps back to the desk. "The president of Sudan knows he is a wanted man. There is a warrant for his arrest by the International Criminal Court in The Hague for the genocide in Darfur. A hunted man who is surrounded by bodyguards, controls a national police force, an intelligence agency, an army, an air force, a navy . . . who rules an entire fucking nation? One man cannot get to him."

Sid sipped his tea again slowly. "Nine days from now a Russian transport plane will depart Belarus with military equipment for President Abboud's army. The aircraft's destination is Khartoum, the capital. It is a secret flight. No manifest, no customs, no problems. Four days after that is April 10, Abboud's birthday, which he always spends in his hometown of Suakin, an ancient port city with no military garrison and no major government installations. He will travel there with his close protection detail, two dozen or so men, but that is all. His farm will be well-guarded, to be sure, but he will go to the local mosque three times a day while he is there. In the morning, at dawn, the president will perform the muezzin's call to prayer himself from the minaret of the mosque. Suakin is also surrounded by ancient ruined towers and buildings from the time of the Romans. A competent man equipped with a sniper rifle could find many good places to position himself, yes?"

"I don't know," said Court, an affectation of annoyance in his voice, but he *was* listening.

"Mr. Gray, I can put two million dollars into your bank account tomorrow. I can put you on that transport plane into the Sudan in nine days, and I can arrange for you to slip out of the airport facility without being detected. I have a man who can drive you to Suakin. One week after this, presuming you accomplish your mission, I can similarly arrange for you to get back into the airport with no trouble from the locals, and fly back to Russia on a Russian jet. Once home, you will find two million more dollars in your account."

"Four million. Plus whatever cut you are keeping for yourself. You must have been commissioned by a party extremely interested in the termination of President Abboud."

"Indeed I have."

"Who?" Court sat back in the uncomfortable chair.

Sidorenko cocked his head but did not seem too surprised. "It was my understanding that you don't normally care who the payer is, only whether or not the target is worthy of the punishment you are being paid to dole out."

"I am not in a very trusting mood after the last contract."

Now Sid *did* show genuine surprise. "Slattery? He was exactly who I said he was."

"But the payer was not who you claimed him to be," responded Court flatly.

The Russian weighed the comment carefully, his beady eyes nearly turning in on themselves as he thought. His pupils flickered in the light from the burning logs in the fireplace. At first Gentry thought Sid was going to argue, to feign confusion, to deny. But instead, the Russian just raised his hands in sheepish surrender, shrugged, and said, "Yes, true. I deceived you. I am sorry. But in response to your question, no less than the Russian government wants Abboud dead. They are putting up the money. They are commissioning the contract. Through intermediaries, of course."

"You're lying again. Russia and China are practically the only two countries who *do* have good relations with Abboud. Why would Russia—"

"Because Russia's relationship with the Sudan is not as good as China's relationship with the Sudan. Three years ago China was given expanded mineral rights in the Darfuri desert, specifically a large sector called Tract 12A. At the time Moscow did not care; it was just desert scrub land on the Chadian border."

"But China found something," said Court.

"Not just 'something.' The most powerful 'something' of all."

"Oil."

"Yes. A tremendous amount. The Chinese are running all over Tract 12A as we speak. Bringing in equipment and experts. Drilling will begin very soon. And Abboud has allowed this. But if Abboud were out of the way, powerful members of the Sudanese Parliamentary Council, people within Abboud's own party, have made it clear to Moscow that the new leadership will throw the Chinese out on their ears and give Tract 12A to the Russians with an arrangement beneficial to both countries."

"If the Sudanese already have an agreement with the Chinese, how can the new president just ignore this?"

Sidorenko looked momentarily disappointed in his assassin. He answered as if the man's question was dangerously naive. "This is Africa."

Court nodded. "And what will this new man do about the genocide in Darfur?"

"One cannot say for sure; you must know that. But it is logical that without President Abboud, the situation will improve. Abboud has a personality cult under him, his minions do his bidding, and he has no similar successor. Also, Darfur has become important for something other than eradicating a broken and hopeless people. His successor may end the genocide in order to get the UN to look elsewhere for a place to waste Western money." Sid smiled. "And then my countrymen will come."

Gentry said nothing, just looked off to his left, into the crackling fireplace under the portrait of Joseph Stalin.

Sid pushed. "So your act will take a very powerful and very bad man off this earth. Further, it is possible that it will go a long way to ending the genocide that has been perpetrated there for the past decade or so."

"So you say," muttered Court, still looking into the fire. He knew Sid didn't give a damn about genocide or an evil man walking the earth; it was just his attempt to create excitement for the operation in the mind of his killer, a man Sid no doubt thought to be a Goody Two-shoes.

The Russian behind the desk smiled. "It would be nice if you trusted me, but our relationship is new. Trust will come with time, I feel certain. In the meantime, feel free to look into this matter yourself, do your own research. I'll have my men take you to a nice hotel. You can spend the evening looking through material I have prepared for you, learning the players, the affiliations, studying the maps. You can come back here tomorrow morning and give me your answer. I am confident you will make the right decision, so after that, we can immediately begin preparing the operation to fit your requirements."

Court nodded slowly. He asked, "Your men . . . Am I to assume they are under orders to remain at my side?"

Gregor Sidorenko smiled, but his eyes were serious. "You may assume that, yes. Saint Petersburg is not a safe place for the uninitiated. They will watch over you." Then he said, with eyebrows raised and a bit of a mischievous smile on his sunken face, "You will have much to do tonight, but I can provide you with companionship. You've been working hard; there is no shame in a little . . . shall we say, recreation, before beginning your next operation."

"A hooker, you mean?"

"A companion."

Court's shoulders slumped. This was just one more thing to deal with. "Sid, don't send a hooker to my door."

"As you wish, Mr. Gray. I only thought it would improve your disposition." He said something in Russian to the guards and laughed along with them when he finished. Gentry did not pick up a word of it. With a wave of his hand, Sid moved on. "Until tomorrow, then."

8

Gentry dined alone at a Russian restaurant with no other patrons. He sat in the back, and his minders sat towards the front and turned potential customers away while the waiters sat by themselves and smoked morosely but did not complain. After his meal he was taken to the Nevsky Palace on Nevsky Prospect. The limousine pulled into a loading dock, and five of Sid's men ushered the American through an employee entrance. A staff elevator shot the entourage to the twelfth floor, and they continued down a long, bright hall to a corner room. Court was led inside a junior suite and was told his minders would be outside the door and in the next room all night. They would wake him at seven for breakfast and then drive him back to Sid to give him his answer.

A young man with a shaved head closed the door on his way out.

For a junior suite it was opulent, hideously so, and it had clearly been modified by Sidorenko's men. A large seating area led to a narrow balcony. The telephone was conspicuously absent. A hallway off the living room connected to a large bedroom—again, with no telephone—which was connected to a large, modern bathroom. Court found a massive stock of toiletries on the vanity, enough for a soccer team to prepare for a night on the town. On the bed he found a single change of clothes: a silk tracksuit, multicolored—black with a thick trim of purple and a gold V shape under the velour collar. Obnoxious anywhere in the world except for the countries formerly behind the Iron Curtain.

Back in the sitting room he saw a thick stack of papers, books, and booklets, open and bookmarked and at his service. Presumably Sid had these put here so he could check out everything the Russian mobster had said about the Sudan, the Russians, the Chinese, and Tract 12A in the Darfuri desert.

Court ignored his homework and instead stepped out on the balcony and watched the heavy traffic clogging the road below. He spent a minute scanning the buildings around, squinting down into the streetlights' glare. He then returned to the bathroom. He scooped up a can of shaving cream and a washcloth and slipped both inside the pockets of his jacket before stepping back onto the balcony. Deftly, he went over the railing with one leg and then the next. He shimmied down the ornamental drainpipe running along the wall next to the balcony, descended to the floor just below him, swung twice for momentum, and then kicked his legs forward. Immediately upon landing on the eleventh-floor balcony he could tell the corresponding room was occupied. Lights were on and clothes were strewn about, but no one seemed to be inside at present. Perhaps, he thought, they were out to dinner. The balcony door was locked. Quickly he shook the can of shaving cream and then pressed the button to discharge the white foam on the sliding glass door, concentrating it just next to the door handle. By the time the can was empty, the shaving cream had created a thick covering over the glass the size of a dinner plate. He wrapped his right hand in the washcloth and quickly punched through the thick cream, creating a fist-size hole with an audible crack but without the loud shattering sound of broken glass, as the foam both muffled the impact and muted the clanging of glass on the tile floor. He let the washcloth fall from his hand inside the room and then he reached in and unlatched the door.

He entered the room, checked the clothing in the suitcases and on the floor, and was disappointed to find nothing that fit. Disappointed, but not surprised. Nothing in his life was too easy; rarely did he pull off any scheme without a single hitch. He left through the door of the room and took the hallway to a stairwell.

He descended four flights and then walked along another hallway, entered another stairwell, and then exited into the lobby. From here he found employee-only access that led him to a laundry room. No one paid any attention to him as he entered.

Thirty minutes after slinging a leg over the balcony on the twelfth floor, Gentry was dressed in fresh clothing and entering a tiny guesthouse a quarter mile from the Nevsky Palace. Court remembered the place from his last trip here. This was the non-descript hotel he'd stayed in back in 2003 with Zack Hightower, team leader of the Goon Squad, while they waited to take down the cargo ship full of Saddam's guns. Then, as now, it was pretty much a dump, but it was quiet and secluded and at the end of a narrow cul-de-sac that gave a good view of all who came and went.

He paid an elderly lady in euros for one night. She asked for a passport, but he shrugged his shoulders and fanned two more twenty euro notes. She shrugged herself, and took the money. He asked for the second-floor room that faced the street, and she took him up one narrow flight of stairs, past the community toilet, and down a shoulder-wide second-floor hallway that creaked with each step. She opened the door with the key and then turned and shuffled back to the staircase without a glance.

Court much preferred spending the night here, as opposed to being held captive in his suite at the Nevsky Palace, surrounded by skinhead goons. He just wanted to crash, lie in bed, and think about his options as far as making a run for it or working with Sidorenko to get into the Sudan, maybe even return to his suite in time to thumb through some of the documentation left there to help him make up his mind.

Court entered his darkened room and flipped the light switch. Nothing happened. Shit hole. He breathed a slight sigh of frustration and felt his way forward, using the dim illumination from the streetlights outside the vinyl curtains. He stepped around the tiny twin bed and drew open the curtains and turned around to survey his room.

Five men faced him in the low light. Still as statues, they were positioned against the walls, but all were within a couple of steps of the Gray Man.

Court's fight-or-flight response kicked on in a single heartbeat, and he attacked. He ducked low and charged the man on his far right, slammed into him as the big man's arms came down hard on the back of Court's head. They crashed into the wall together. Gentry raised his left leg to deliver a groin kick to whoever would surely be attacking from behind. He connected with inner thigh, not a debilitating blow, and while he brought his right palm up hard for an open-hand uppercut on the man embracing him, he felt an airborne body hit him hard from the right. Court's palm connected with the first man's face just as he spun away, crashed onto the bed on his back, and felt two more men grab his legs and pin them.

With his one free arm he delivered a vicious punch to the solar plexus of a man moving towards him. He felt a Kevlar vest under his dark clothing and knew he'd done no damage.

As he struggled and fought, he recognized plainly that the men attacking him were competent. No, they were damn good. They were fast, strong, and well-trained. More important, they worked together and didn't shout or scream or freak out as they fought him. He managed a solid elbow to the side of a smaller man's head, sending him hard against the headboard of the bed and then off the side onto the wooden floor. But the others filled in the gap left by their wounded comrade in an instant, their body weight pinning his appendages to the bed as he wrestled desperately to get free.

Looking to his left, he saw one of the men had retrieved something from somewhere in the darkness and approached now with careful confidence. Court saw the sharp glint of thin metal, a stubby piece of clear plastic. Even in the negligible light he recognized the outline of the syringe. The needle approached, and whatever noxious goo it had been filled with was on its way to his bloodstream unless he could stop the man trying to punch it against his skin.

Instantly Gentry decided these were CIA Special Activities Division Paramilitary Operations officers, an entire field team, and he knew he was in deep shit. There was a termination order on him. He'd ducked them for years, but they had found him now.

Bound to happen sooner or later.

Court relaxed his left arm for an instant, gave the man holding it down a moment's respite from the struggle. The ruse worked, and Gentry shot his arm down, under the man's grip and to his side. From here it was free, and he jetted out a fierce jab to the needle man's face. The needle man's head snapped back, and he dropped the syringe as he folded back on his legs and grabbed his nose, but the operator pinning his left leg down reached out and grabbed the instrument off the floor, buried its business end into Court's thigh, and pressed the plunger as Gentry tried and failed to kick free.

"Son of a bitch!" Court shouted, not knowing what he'd been injected with but recognizing that, no matter what he did now, he had just lost the battle.

He stopped moving immediately. There was no point. He was as good as dead.

A sixth man entered the room—slowly, but with an unmistakable swagger in his step. Court tried to focus on him, but already he could feel a drug taking hold of his central nervous system. Whatever they'd given him was powerful; he'd worked with poisons and incapacitating anesthetics enough to know that he'd been dosed with a hard and potent sedative. His muscles relaxed; he felt as if his body were melting into the mattress.

The new man in the room leaned over him as the others climbed off. Two of the original five were down; the other three calmly tended to their associates' injuries, while the new visitor to the dark room just looked down on Court with curiosity. Gentry tried to focus on the man, to fight against the growing fuzz from the drugs in his blood. For a moment he thought the face looked familiar, but a wave of dizziness wiggled the image out of his mind.

The man above him spoke. "Hiya, Court."

Through the haze Gentry knew the voice somehow. The man grabbed Court's cheeks and pinched them until his mouth opened. Saliva oozed out past his protruding tongue and down his chin.

"Twenty seconds and he's out," said the man above him to the men standing around. Then he turned his attention back to Gentry. "Predictable. I knew you'd sneak out of the hotel and come here. Haven't you picked up any new travel tips in the past eight years?" He smiled. "Unlucky for you I just happened to remember this shit hole."

He turned back to his colleagues. "Sierra Six never was the luckiest dude around. We used to say that if it were raining pussy, Court Gentry would get hit with a dick."

Sierra Six?

As Court felt himself falling into blackness, his numb mouth moved, and he whispered a single word before the lights went out completely. "Zack?"

9

"You remember me, don't you, Gentry?"

Gentry hadn't even remembered that his name was Gentry. His eyes were well open when he became aware, and he wondered if he'd been conscious for a while or if he'd just now come to. He was not dead, of that he was certain, though the rest was unclear. He then felt the cold, looked down at his bare chest and underwear, found himself sitting on a chair. Four walls surrounded him, and his wrists were bound behind his back. He saw four men standing around him, over him, and felt their malevolence, but their faces were difficult to focus on, drugs coursing through him still. In his training at the CIA's secret Autonomous Asset Development Program in Harvey Point, North Carolina, he had been injected with, had ingested, or had been aspirated with somewhere in the neighborhood of twenty-five mood-altering substances to test and improve his dexterity, agility, and cognitive ability while under the influence. He'd once even successfully climbed a three-story rope ladder and picked a lock while completely numbed by Versed, though he had no recollection of performing the drill twenty minutes later. He'd learned much about opiates and other anesthetics in his training, but now all he could say for sure was that he was seriously fucked up.

In a flash he realized that he had not taken any heavy pills in nearly three weeks and had seemingly kicked the painkiller addiction he'd been suffering from for months in the south of France. Now he wondered if having these drugs forced into his bloodstream would just undo all the work he'd done to get past his problem.

Of course, he reckoned, if one of these men did what he was supposed to do and put a bullet into his brain, then the problem would be remedied in short order.

Death solves all problems.

Three of the four men backed out through a small door in the room, leaving just the one who'd spoken. "Hang on a sec," the standing man said. "We took you off the drip a few minutes ago. You'll come down in a flash. Let me know when I'm coming through loud and clear, okay, bro?"

Court knew the voice before he knew the face. He fought the drugs, shook his head to clear the cobwebs. Blinked hard. Then he knew. His eyes furrowed. His head cocked. "Didn't I kill you once?"

"Negative, Court. Why would you kill me? We had a little misunderstanding way back when, but nothing major."

"Hightower. Zack Hightower," Court said the man's name as if the man didn't know it himself. Court's words did not come out past his tongue as clearly as he'd intended.

"Are you hurt?" asked the standing man.

"Na . . . negative."

"Let me fix that. Now pay attention, bro. I've been waiting four years for this moment. I'd sure hate for you to miss it." He snapped his fingers in front of Gentry's face. "You with me still? Outstanding. Now . . . *this* is for Paul Lynch." Hightower punched Gentry in the jaw.

Court fell off the chair and onto the floor with a brilliant starburst in his eyes.

"Fuck!" said Court.

"Fuck!" said Zack. Court looked up and saw the other man holding his fist, in obvious pain. Court licked his lower lip and spat blood. Zack pulled him by the hair back up into the chair. Gentry's movements were sluggish from the drugs, but the punch had gone a long way towards focusing his senses.

"And *this*, Court, is for Dino Redus." Hightower hit Court again in the face. Gentry dropped back onto the floor, felt his left eye swell instantly, heard Hightower cuss again in pain.

After a moment Court said, "Redus tried to kill me! You all did!"

"Shut your dick trap, Gentry! We're not done here yet!"

Court rolled up to his knees, fought with his balance for a moment, then climbed back up to the chair without Zack's help. His left eye had all but shut, tears running and blurring his vision further. "He, Lynch, Morgan, you, *you* guys came at *me*! What the fuck was I supposed to do? Just let you murder me?"

"Would have been helpful," said Hightower. "Keith Morgan's wife sure would have appreciated it." Hightower smashed his left hand into Court's head. Not as hard this time, but again he shook his hand to cool it after the impact.

Court wobbled but kept his seat this time. He spat a mouthful of blood on the floor and said, "Too bad you've got more piece of shit dead friends than you do hands."

"They were your friends, too, Court! Before you killed them!" Hightower balled his left fist again, reached back for another punch.

"Come on!" shouted Court. "I know about the sanction! It's shoot on sight! You keep swinging at me like that, and we'll be here all fucking night! Pull out your gun and do your goddamned job!"

Zack held his fist high over Gentry's face. Then slowly the fist lowered. His jaw tightened. He nodded slowly. He reached behind his back and drew a snub-nosed nickel-plated revolver from his waistband.

Zack swung it around and pressed it to Court Gentry's forehead in a single motion.

Court blinked, his cheeks twitched, but then he looked up at Zack, up the tiny barrel of the gun. His voice was soft. "Might as well just tell me why. What's it going to hurt now?"

Zack ignored the question, just held the gun against Gentry's head steadily for five, ten, twenty seconds. Then he said, "Just so you know. Whatever happens after this, Six ... for the rest of your life. Everything from now on ... is a gift from me." With a cruel look in his eyes he lowered the gun, slipped it back into the small of his back.

Court blinked away a bead of sweat that had trickled into his right eye.

Zack put his hands on his hips, still looking down at his prisoner. Through heavy breaths brought on by the physical activity of the beating and the intensity of the moment, he asked, "Did ya miss me, Court?"

Court blinked again. Said, tentatively, "Like a hole in the head."

Zack smiled wryly. "Easily arranged."

Without another word, Hightower left the room, giving Court the opportunity to calm his nerves a bit and take stock of his surroundings. Immediately he decided from the thick white paint and bare furnishings of the small space that he was on a boat. Near the engine room, he surmised, from the humming in the walls. He could not feel the motion of water, but he knew that his equilibrium was toast at the moment, so that didn't mean much.

Hightower returned with a clear plastic bag full of ice and a small utility knife. He stepped behind Court's chair and, with a well-practiced single motion, cut away the flexi-cuffs binding Court's wrists. Zack then grabbed another chair from the hallway, dragged it across the floor with a painful screech, and sat facing Gentry, dropping the bag of ice into his prisoner's lap. Court immediately brought it to his eye and lip to deaden the growing pain there.

Gentry looked the man over with his right eye. It had been four years since they last worked together in the CIA's Golf Sierra unit, unofficially known, to those few who knew of it at all, as the Goon Squad. Hightower had been Sierra One, the team leader. Gentry was -Sierra Six, the youngest, most junior man on the team, but always the first through the door. Hightower was now forty-five or so, but his eyes were still as bright and blue as a baby boy's. He was razor lean and square-jawed. His hair was cut in a classic military high and tight; flecks of silver now blinked in the sandy blond. He was six one and two hundred pounds, not an ounce of it excess fat. He moved with confidence, walked with his broad chest leading the way. Court knew Zack was Texas born and bred, had joined the navy after college baseball, spent a decade on the storied SEAL Team Six before joining the CIA's Special Activities Division as a Paramilitary Operations officer. Zack was smart and tough and sure of himself, exceptionally charming with the ladies, and popular with the guys.

In short, a typical SEAL.

"How ya been?" Hightower asked as he looked down to his own injury, a hand swollen at the knuckles. Court thought briefly about leaping off the chair and spearing the bigger man's windpipe, but he knew the drugs in his system would slow his reflexes still. Zack didn't seem worried about Court attacking, and Court figured Zack would know better than he did what was still pumping through his bloodstream.

"Some days better than others, I guess."

"Scuttlebutt is you're doing all right. You've run three to five ops a year for the past four years. All over the map. Making some pretty good bank is the word on the street. Langley thinks you smoked both of the Abubaker brothers, one in Syria and the next a few weeks later in Madrid. French intelligence says someone fitting your general description blew up half of French-speaking Europe last December. The Ukrainians are even running around saying you did that shit in Kiev. You didn't, did you?"

"Don't believe everything you hear. How'd you guys find me?"

Zack shrugged. "Echelon picked up some cell phone traffic from Sidorenko's hoodlums. They have a code name for you, I guess, but some dipshit referred to you as *'seryj muzhchina'* on an open line."

"Gray Man," Court translated with a frustrated sigh. "Brilliant."

"Fucking geniuses, these Ivans," said Zack sarcastically. "They said you'd be coming to see the boss today. NSA sent word to Langley; Langley passed it on to me."

Court nodded. "It's shoot on sight, Zack. You drugged me just to bring me here to slap me around first?"

"Nah, the SOS is officially on hold, at least while you and I have a little discussion. The ass-kicking? That's personal."

"You call that an ass-kicking?"

"Who says I'm done?"

Court's brown eyebrows drew together. "Back in Virginia. I shot you, point-blank. Forty-four caliber. I saw you go backwards out a window. Two stories down."

Zack grinned. Like a hyena, he smiled but did not look happy. "Don't remind me. My vest caught the round, but I landed pretty fucking hard on an air-conditioning unit. Broke my pelvis in two places. Collarbone and a couple of ribs for good measure." Zack winced as if he were remembering the event, until something popped into his memory. He added, "Never knew you to carry a Derringer."

"Never had cause to mention it. Good thing I didn't."

Zack shrugged. "Depends on your point of view. To tell you the truth, I'd have loved to have known about it."

"So why were you guys there? What did I do?"

Zack shrugged, like the answer was obvious. "Termination order from on high. You know how it is."

"No. Actually, I don't. What the hell did I do wrong, Zack?" Court's voice was plaintive.

Hightower shrugged again. "Dunno. I'm just a worker bee. I got the term order on you, and I went to work that day, just like any other."

"Bullshit. They gave you a reason."

"Kid, when have I ever needed a reason to follow an order? I'm not like you, all navel-gazing and introspective. I do my shitty day job with a smile on my face."

Court was certain his former team leader was lying; no one at CIA would order an SAD field team leader to delete his own man without so much as an explanation, but he decided to let it go. "The men, the guys with you who jumped me tonight, they're your new Goon Squad?"

"More or less. Not Golf Sierra but Whiskey Sierra, so I'm still Sierra One. Bureaucratically we're set up different than the old gang. Mission and rules of engagement are more restrictive these days. But basically it's the same idea. My new crew consists of a couple of ex-SEALS, an ex-Delta, two SF guys who crossed over to CIA black ops way back when. Pretty good bunch, but certainly not Court Gentry caliber. You'll always be my best door kicker." He smiled. "You fucked Todd up pretty good: busted nose and a dislocated jaw."

"Sorry," replied Court, but he didn't mean it.

"Shit happens." Zack shrugged. Clearly he didn't mean it either.

"So why am I here?"

Zack Hightower reached out for the ice bag, took it from Gentry's face, and wrapped it over his swollen fist. "Abboud. President Bakri Ali Abboud."

10

"What about him?"

"You're goin' in to whack him on an op for Sid."

Court saw no point in playing dumb. If the CIA knew this much, they probably knew more details about Sid's op at this point than Gentry did himself. "I haven't agreed to anything."

"Yeah, well, you will. We want you to."

"What makes you think I give a shit what you want?"

"Just listen to my spiel, kid. It's that or the term order, so why not?"

Court pulled the ice pack back, repositioned it lower, leaving his black eye uncovered but soothing the growing pain in his lip. From behind it he said, "I'm listening."

Hightower leaned forward. "Here's the sit rep, kid." Gentry was thirty-six years old, but Hightower had called him kid since the first day they met, eight years earlier. "We want you to take Sidorenko's job, use the Ruskies to get into the Sudan. They have a solid op to get you in, better than anything we can orchestrate without using agency transportation and logistical assets, which we're not allowed to do."

"And then?"

"Then you make like you're going to pop Abboud, but at the last second, we want you to snatch him."

"Kidnap him?"

"Affirmative."

"And then?"

"Then you pass him off to me and my boys. We'll be on site, outta sight but close by. You hand him over to us and exfiltrate over water with my team."

"Why does the USA want Abboud? Washington wants to clean up the Darfur thing as much as anybody, and Abboud is almost single-handedly responsible."

"Yeah, he is, but POTUS and his people want Abboud sent to the International Criminal Court; he wants to hand over Abboud on a silver platter to them. There's been an ICC arrest warrant on him for three years."

"I know. But whacking him will do it quicker and cleaner, with no CIA comebacks. You guys could have just let me do the hit for the Russians."

Zack chuckled. "I know, Court. Your prescription for any disease is a double dose of lead to the head. But it's a new day in D.C., bro. The president and his crew at the White House are all into making nice with Europe, bolstering international institutions and all that shit. They want to take credit."

Court couldn't believe what he was hearing. "You've got to be kidding me. The White House actually wants to save Abboud's life so that he can be turned over to the Euros?"

Zack shrugged. "There's more to it than that. Tit for tat, quid pro quo, and a bunch of other phrases I don't get paid enough to understand but ... basically ... yeah."

Court shook his head, "Not like the old days, huh?"

"Yeah, right? Five years ago we would just whack whomever we needed to whack. To hell with the ICC. Listen, I'm with you; this seems like a lot of work just to hand the guy off to the fucking UN or whoever the fuck, but someone at Langley has convinced someone at the White House, who has convinced POTUS, that we have a surefire way to get hold of Abboud and deliver him to the ICC with no comebacks on us if it doesn't go to plan."

"And that way is me," Court said.

"Exactly. Every intelligence agency worth its salt knows the

CIA wants the Gray Man dead. So that makes you the epitome of plausible deniability. If this deal breaks bad, it won't smell like a CIA op."

"This was the CIA's idea?"

"One hundred percent. SAD has been lying too low for our taste. CIA and military drones are buzzing around at thirty thousand feet, taking out bad guys left and right with their Hellfires, but Paramilitary Operations teams like Whiskey Sierra are just sitting around. The White House has restricted everything we do. Even our training regimen has suffered. We aren't killing terrorists, we aren't running in friendly countries, we aren't wiping our asses unless we use extra soft TP. SAD needs this op to go ahead, to show POTUS that SAD's Special Operations Group can still be viable in a kinder, gentler CIA. You are our proxy boy; you'll take the risks, you'll hand Abboud over to us, we'll hand him over to the Justice Department, and they'll hand him over to an appreciative International Criminal Court. POTUS and his risk-averse flunkies will give SAD more to do if they see how we can make his Euro fag buddies all warm and fuzzy by giving them Abboud tied in a bow. There isn't a UAV out there that can kidnap someone. At least, not yet."

"What about Sidorenko?"

"We pull it off, and Sid will just think you got whacked by us and we snatched Abboud in the same op. You don't want to work for that caviar-sucking psychopath any longer, trust me. Even in comparison with the rest of the Russian mob, Greg Sidorenko and his Nazi henchmen are fucking loony tunes."

Court cocked his head to the side. "If you guys are going to be in theater for the handover, how are you going to ensure there are no comebacks to the CIA?"

Zack waved his hand. "Details. We'll lie low, spend most of our time in international waters, shoot in for the op. You'll do the heavy lifting, and we'll support you. CIA Sudan Station has an informant in Suakin who knows Abboud's schedule for his trip there. This guy is involved in contingency planning for any emergencies; he knows the op orders for the president's body-guards and their tactics."

"How does that help me?"

Zack smiled. "The security detail has a protocol for an attack when the president is making his morning walk to the mosque. If there is a threat while they're in the square in front of the mosque, they take Abboud into the local bank and lock themselves in the vault until help arrives."

"And I am guessing you have a way to make them think there is some sort of a threat?"

"Sudan Station does. They have a force of one hundred Sudanese Liberation Army rebels who can hit Suakin at six thirty-five a.m. on Sunday, ten April. Exactly when Abboud and his entourage hit the square. The president and some of his close protection detail will enter the bank, which of course will be empty."

"But it won't be empty."

Zack smiled and nodded aggressively, "You got it. You'll be in there, ready to disable the guard force and snatch Abboud, get him out of town while the SLA blows some shit up and jumps around for a few minutes, distracting the locals and the rest of Abboud's team. Then you meet up with me for the handoff." It was clear Hightower was excited by the operation; his hands and his body had not stopped moving since he'd begun his explanation.

Court sat there silently for a moment, then asked, "Is this where I start clapping?"

"This *is* a good plan, Six. Operation Nocturne Sapphire, we're calling it."

"A thrill just went up my leg," said Court sarcastically, still unfazed by Zack's vigor.

"But the best part is the deal I've been authorized to offer you."

Gentry looked at his former team leader a long time before speaking. "The CIA has wanted me on a slab for four years. What kind of deal could you offer that would interest me?"

"No slab, for starters. We call off the dogs. Not just CIA, but Interpol, too."

"Interpol doesn't scare me."

"I know they don't. You don't scare easy. Never did. But I know what *does* scare the Gray Man."

"What scares me, Zack?"

"*We* scare you. Wouldn't you like to be free of us? Free of the shoot-on-sight sanction? I know what your life is like, bro. People talk about the Gray Man like you're some sort of flashy-assed James Bond, jet-setting around the world, partying at the best clubs, and drinking martinis with the beautiful people on the Côte d'Azur. But I know what it's really like: living on the run, bouncing from one shit splat town to the next, no one loves you, no one likes you, no one fucking *knows* you. Always looking into the shadows for crazy mother-fuckers like me hunting you down. Eating beans out of a can in a stairwell in a roach-infested flophouse while the real tuxedo crowd is around the corner dining on lobster tail at the Four Seasons."

Truer words had never been spoken, but Court was not about to give Zack the satisfaction of admitting he was right.

"I like beans."

"No, you don't. You don't like any of it, except the job. The job is you. The rest is just your fucked-up temporary predicament. I know the score, Sierra Six. Being the Gray Man sucks."

"So let me guess. You're here to take me away from all that?"

"Damn right. I can keep you on the job, but you won't be hunted anymore, at least by us."

"On the job? Working for who?"

"The CIA, of course." Zack reached across and held Court's face by the chin, turned it from side to side. "I thought we just covered that. What, did I hit you too hard?" He took the ice pack from Gentry and returned it to his hand.

Court said, "I do this gig in Sudan for you, but after that, you're offering full-time work? Just like the last four years didn't happen? Everything goes back to the way it was in the old days?"

"Negative. I'm offering *contract* work. Keeps Langley's hands clean, and it pays a damn sight better than a real government salary." He smiled. "We want you back." Then he shrugged his shoulders. "Well, let me rephrase that. I'm not talking about a desk and a reserved parking space at Langley. That doesn't happen to guys like you. CIA won't acknowledge working with the Gray Man. But from time to time we run into situations where I hear people say, 'Sure wish Sierra Six was still here, instead of out in bumble fuck, doin' private hits for pimps and drug dealers.' I swear, we miss you sometimes."

He paused before saying, "You always were the best. We want you alive, Court. Doing the dirty jobs under a false flag."

"How do I know you aren't just going to kill me when the Sudan op is done?"

"Because we *need* you. We aren't asking you to go raise daffodils in Iowa in the Witness Protection Program here. We want you to keep doing what you're doing, living out here in the cold, and we'll keep up the front that we're still after your ass. Look, this shit is in your blood, and the agency can still use you, despite your fuckup in '06. Washington won't let the SAD get its hands dirty these days. But if we play this right, we can let *you* get the dirty hands, and we can support you. It's fucking perfect, man. Like coke off a whore's ass. Know what I'm saying?"

Court shook his head slowly. "Not really, no."

"Look, you act all cynical, but I *know* you. You are a patriot, kiddo. You piss red, white, and blue. The White House has a need, I have a need, you have a need. We can all help each other." He grinned. "Everybody wins."

The discussion steered to the potential operation for several minutes. Zack had an answer ready for every question Gentry posed. When there were no other operational details left to go over, Court grabbed the ice pack back from Hightower and pressed it to the swollen flesh on his face. Zack looked at it longingly a moment but did not reach for it. Behind the ice pack Court said, "I need to hear this deal from somebody above you."

"Like who?" asked Hightower with no appearance of surprise.

"I'd settle for Mathew Hanley. I figure our old supervisor is probably running SAD now, if not higher up than that."

"Matt's out of SAD. Riding a desk in South America last I heard. Paraguay, maybe?"

Court did not hide his puzzlement. "He used to be the wunderkind of black ops. What happened?"

"*You* happened, fucko. Having one of his door kickers go nuts and shoot up his own squad didn't help his ascendancy to the top."

"So I get blamed for that, too?"

"History is written by the victors. You may have survived, sorta, but the CIA is still around to write the official version of what you did and why."

Court thought a moment. Finally he just repeated himself: "I need to hear this deal from someone above you."

Hightower nodded. "That's cool. Sit tight, and I'll be back."

Court was given his clothing back. He dressed, and then he waited.

11

Over an hour later two of Zack's men returned to the room where Court was being held. He'd spent the time massaging ice into his face. He wondered how he was going to explain the obvious bruising to his Russian colleagues/captors. Two of Zack's men, one big and black and the other older and white, led him down a narrow and low hallway, past water and steam pipes, up a narrow flight of stairs, and into a room on the upper deck. Zack's men didn't like Court, that much was plain by their *eat shit* looks and the way they bumped him with their muscular bodies to get him to turn into the new room. Gentry recognized that taking down one of their team with a cracking shot to the face wasn't going to endear him to these hardy boys.

But he didn't care. He wasn't looking to make friends, even if they were all going to work together on the mission to come. These guys would be pros, just like him, and the op would take precedence.

They didn't need to like each other to do their jobs.

Once Court was seated in the new room, he noticed a blue monitor on a desk in front of him. Zack entered a moment later, stowing a sat phone in a pouch on his hip as he did so.

"Okay. You are going to talk to somebody. He's read in on this op, and he knows who you are, but for all intents and purposes, you are not a NOC, not a CIA employee, not a former CIA employee, not an American citizen. You are a foreign national agent and will be treated as such. Your code name will be your old Goon Squad call sign, Sierra Six."

Court nodded.

"And the code name for President Abboud will be Oryx."

"What's an oryx?"

"I had to ask, myself. It's some kind of an African antelope or something."

Court shrugged. This type of code word protocol had been his life for many years. When he was in the Goon Squad he'd been Sierra Six, though he'd used literally dozens of cover names for his assignments. And before working for Zack, back when he was in the Autonomous Asset Program, his code name had been Violator. The code words were supposedly randomly selected by computer, but Violator seemed uncannily accurate. The CIA had pulled Gentry out of a south Florida penitentiary, where he was serving a life sentence for the triple second-degree murder of three Colombian drug runners, and presented him with a job offer he could not refuse.

He had never believed for a second that it was a computer who dubbed him Violator.

The screen in front of him flickered to life.

The image of a man in a gray suit and a Brooks Brothers tie in a full Windsor. He was over sixty, thin glasses low on his nose. The face and countenance of a soldier. After a short moment Gentry recognized the man.

Court was surprised. Shocked, even.

"Sierra Six. Do you recognize me?" His voice was clipped and curt. There was no smile nor emotion of any kind.

Gentry answered immediately. "Yes, sir." He turned to look at Zack. Hightower smiled and raised his eyebrows, obviously proud of the juice he possessed to command a video link with this other man.

The man was Denny Carmichael, currently the director of US National Clandestine Service, and recently the head of the Special Activities Division. He was a legend at the agency, a Far East specialist and a longtime station chief in Hong Kong.

Denny Carmichael was, in short, the top guy in CIA operations. Court knew this mission was big, but this kind of dirty work usually went on without the fingerprints of the top brass of the US intelligence community.

"I understand Sierra One has laid out our proposal to you regarding the extraordinary rendition of Oryx. I am prepared to reaffirm the details of Nocturne Sapphire."

"Yes, sir," repeated Court. It was all he could think to say. He'd never spoken to anyone this high in the food chain. He found himself almost starstruck. It felt odd, doubly so since Carmichael would certainly have been a signatory to the shoot-on-sight directive against him that had been in place since 2006.

Carmichael laid out the general plan that Zack had discussed, though he spoke in more euphemistic terms. Court would "detain Abboud with force," not "snatch him" as Hightower had instructed. He would "neutralize all threats from Abboud's close protection detail," as opposed to Zack's suggestion that he "pop a hollow point or two into each bodyguard's snot box."

This dissimilarity in the vernacular was a common distinction between labor and management in this industry. Court was accustomed to hearing more from Zack's ilk and less from men like Carmichael, but he knew the results would not differ depending on the political correctness of the vocabulary used. The operation would be the same, no matter how pleasantly or corrosively it was explained.

Men would die.

While Carmichael spoke, Hightower leaned against the wall of the ship, occasionally making an open and closed hand gesture to mock the verbosity of the man on the screen. But otherwise Sierra One minded his manners.

When Carmichael finished his explanation of the operation, he moved on to the part of the deal most important to the Gray Man. "You do this for us, Sierra Six, and our operation to eliminate you will simply go away. That means any existing sanctions or directives against you within the agency will be dropped. Existing

70

warrants via Interpol will be rescinded. Existing communiqués from Central Intelligence liaisons to foreign intelligence agencies regarding you will cease. The CIA request for Echelon intel and other data mining regarding you from NSA will be allowed to expire. Other loose ends will be cleared up. FBI, Joint Special Operations Command, Immigration and Customs Enforcement, the Commerce Department ... you will no longer be a person of interest to any United States federal department or agency."

Court didn't know JSOC had been involved in the hunt for him. JSOC meant Delta Force, the Unit, and the Unit meant some tough hombres. The Commerce Department, on the other hand, didn't quite fill him with the same sense of dread.

Gentry said, "I understand."

"Fine. So do we have an agreement?"

"Will you tell me what this is all about?"

Carmichael looked a little annoyed. Presumably he did not feel comfortable offering deals to outlaws. But he nodded and said, "President Abboud is wanted by the International Criminal—"

"Excuse me, sir. I meant ... Can you tell me what the shoot on sight is all about? Why you went after me in the first place."

There was a long pause. Denny Carmichael looked off camera to someone on his side, perhaps for guidance. Finally he replied with a grave tone, "Son. If you truly do not know what you did, it is probably better for everyone's sake that I do not tell you."

"I don't understand."

"Let's move forward. Forget the SOS. *We're* prepared to forget the SOS. Do we have a deal regarding President Abboud?"

Court looked at Zack. Zack looked back. Finally, Gentry said, "Yes, sir. I will do my best to uphold my end of the bargain. I will rely on you and Sierra One to uphold yours."

Carmichael nodded but did not smile. "Very well. We will not speak again, Six. Sierra One will be the team leader and on-site commander for Operation Nocturne Sapphire, the rendition of President Bakri Ali Abboud from the Sudan to the International Criminal Court in the Netherlands. Arrangements will be made

71

for further operations, presuming all goes well in Africa, at the appropriate time, via the Special Activities Division Special Operations Group case officer assigned to you."

"Understood. Thank you."

A curt nod from the man on the screen, and the screen went blank.

Immediately Zack said, "I thought that dude would *never* shut up."

Court stood, looked at his watch.

"So, we good, Six?" asked Zack.

A pause of resignation on the part of Court Gentry. He was going to do this, but it would not be easy. He said, "You'd better get me back to the hotel. Can't let Sid's goons catch me away."

Zack smiled. "Roger that. A couple of my boys will take you back and tuck you in. Don't mind them if they aren't too chummy at first. They're a little grumpy about all this. They somehow got the impression that you were the dickhead who'd killed several men in your unit and then ran off to seek fame and fortune in the private sector."

"Where did they get an idea like that, Zack?"

Sierra One put his hands up in surrender. "I might bear some responsibility for their distrust of you. Also, you put Todd out of action for this op." Then he smiled, slapped his hand on Court's back, a little too forcefully. "Hey, it's good to be working with you again. Last thing. Let's talk about gear."

"What about it?"

"I'll have all the specific equipment for Nocturne Sapphire in the Sudan. I'll meet you there to hand it over the night before the operation. But as far as personal gear, let me know what you need, and I'll see what I can do to have it ready by next week."

"A sat phone that I can reach you on. Something that works well in North Africa. A Hughes Thuraya should be good. And a good supply of batteries. That ought to do."

Hightower looked at Gentry. "You gonna bash a sat phone over the bad guys' heads? I was talking about guns, Six."

"I'll get all the guns I need from Sid. He's got better shit than you guys."

"Oh, that hurts. But hey, you'll save the taxpayers a few bucks, so I guess I'm cool with that."

12

Court made it back to his suite at the Nevsky Palace at four forty-five a.m. He and Hightower had discussed operational details for another hour, then he was led out of the belly of the yacht and over the side, onto a dinghy with two of Zack's men. No words were spoken between the three as they negotiated the frigid black waters of the Bay of Finland, making landfall at nearly four in the morning. A car was waiting on the dock, and Court was ushered into it, driven back to the hotel, and delivered to a room. Hightower had thought of everything, even renting a suite directly above Gentry's. From here the SAD men went to the balcony, dropped a rope over the side, and gave Court a small pad of contact information for the team.

"Hey, man," said the black operator. He'd been introduced as Spencer, and the other guy, a younger man with an accent Court recognized as Croatian, as Milo. "People talk. Rumors and shit. Normally I don't listen ... but ... Were you the guy in Kiev? Just a yes or no."

Gentry took the pad, stuck it in his back pocket, and uttered his only phrase in the past hour of the transport. "Fuck you." He ignored the rope and kicked his legs over the side of the railing. He swung down to his balcony below unaided and dropped silently.

Spencer leaned over the railing and called down, "Fuck you, too, Six. We'll see you in two weeks down in the stink."

*

74

Gentry showered, stared into the foggy bathroom mirror at his bruised face, and looked at the clock on the vanity. Five a.m. In two hours he'd have some explaining to do about how he managed to get a shiner and a fat lip while reading papers alone on a bed in a junior suite. Naked, Court turned to leave the room, but he stopped, turned back, and opened the medicine cabinet on a hunch. He peered in, and simultaneously his heart raced and his shoulders slumped. Sid's men had stocked the cabinet with over a dozen prescription meds: decongestants, antibiotics, medicines for temporary relief from erectile dysfunction. All these could not possibly be less relevant to his present circumstance. But he saw the painkillers almost immediately. Dilaudid, four milligram tablets. His heart raced in anticipation of the respite of relaxation one tab would give him. But his shoulders slumped in resignation that he was not in any real pain, he knew he wanted but did not need the strong opiate, and he knew his three weeks of self-imposed detox would be coming to an end in about five seconds.

Court popped two tablets, swallowed them with water from the tap, and then in a moment of anger and shame, he poured the rest down the drain of the flowing vanity basin.

Next he dressed in the butt-ugly purple tracksuit Sid's men had left for him, and he lay on the bed. His mind would be useless to him soon enough; he had to think before the medicine took its full effect.

He thought about President Abboud. If Nocturne Sapphire was successful, the murderous despot would live. This bothered Gentry mightily. It was *too* simple perhaps, but Sid's quote from Stalin had a plain truth to it that did resonate with Court, even if he would never admit common ground with Uncle Joe. "Death solves all problems. No man, no problem." No, that wasn't Court's exact thinking; few problems were solved with political assassination. But certainly many short-term goals were achieved. And most assuredly, killing a bad actor ended the bad actor's commission of the bad act.

Killing Abboud would *kill Abboud*. Other than that, Court Gentry did not give a damn.

The Dilaudid kicked in suddenly. An inaudible whoosh of contentment waved through his brain, like an egg cracked on his forehead and trickling down around his skull. For a moment he just lay there, staring at the canopy above the bed and taking pleasure in the quilted patterns in the fabric. *Damn*, he said to himself, simultaneously happy for the drug-induced relief on his heavy mind and mad for succumbing to the temptation of the tablets.

He fought the next wave of relaxation and went back to thinking about his predicament.

No, he didn't like the thought of kidnapping the most hated man on the planet. Sid's op would certainly have been more satisfying to him than Hightower's, but Hightower's op offered a more satisfying reward. Having the shoot-on-sight directive rescinded by the SAD would not solve all of Court's problems, but it would be better than having four million dollars in the bank. The money was no good if he was not around to spend it, and with the CIA on his tail for the past four years, he'd been unable to slow down from the around-the-globe flight from his pursuers.

Yes, he'd love to get back in the good graces of the CIA. Whatever he had done that had earned him the SOS sanction, perhaps he could make amends for it by handing Abboud over to Zack and his Whiskey Sierra team on a silver platter.

There was a knock at the door. Court looked to the clock on the side table and saw that it was seven a.m.

Shit. He did not know if he'd slept at all, or if the drugs and the worry had consumed him for two full hours.

Court heard the door in the sitting room open. Seconds later three men entered his room. They were from the same stock of hoodlums who'd dropped him off last night. Their suits were wrinkled; perhaps they'd slept in them in the hall or in the room next door. Or maybe they'd stayed up all night partying. He stood slowly, rubbing his eyes, and felt the meds in his blood slowing his movements and affecting his balance. He caught the men eyeing his black and gold and purple tracksuit appreciatively. Then their eyes rose to his face. Even through his beard he was sure they could see his fat purple lip, and his black eye was totally exposed to them.

"What happened to you?" asked the first man in Russian. Court understood, began to respond, but then caught himself just before the first word left his mouth. Fuck. The Dilaudid was heavy in his brain; he could not operate effectively.

He shrugged his shoulders, perhaps too dramatically, and waited for the man to realize his mistake and ask again in English. When he did, Court said, "I fell out of bed. These silk sheets are slippery."

13

Court was taken back in front of Gregor Sidorenko just after breakfast. This time the Russian mob boss was outside in his courtyard, a cold gray morning and a light but steady spittle of hard needles of sleet from the sky did not deter him from taking his morning tea in his robe in his bare gardens. He sat at a small metal bistro table under a red canopy, gold pajama bottoms and fluffy slippers intertwined due to his crossed legs. Two young men armed with machine pistols stood amid the bushes already defoliated by the long Saint Petersburg winter. The men watched Court closely, but Court knew that at the distance they kept from him, if they felt the need to shoot him with their little fully automatic peashooters, they would no doubt perforate their principal just as quickly as their target.

The American winced in the face of such lousy security protocol. To him, witnessing such amateurish tactics by men with guns was like fingernails on a chalkboard.

Gentry approached Sid with two of his minders. He'd been with the men an hour since the hotel and had not said a word to them since leaving his suite. With a curt nod to his employer he said, "Let's do it."

"What happened to your face?"

"Nothing. Did you hear what I just said?"

Sid hesitated, nodded, clapped his hands, and gave two thumbs-up, which somehow lost something in the translation from

English to Russian. "Excellent. This will make my government extremely happy."

Court continued, "Understand this. This is *my* op. You follow my instructions to the letter, or I walk away."

Sid sat up straighter, nodded swiftly.

"I leave here alone. I need time to prepare and research, and I don't need your Nazi freaks watching over me. In a few days I will contact you with an address. Your boys can come and get me." Court pulled out a handwritten sheet and handed it across the bistro table to Sid, who took it willingly. "They will have this equipment with them. They will take me out into the country, a place of your choosing, and I'll test-fire the rifle, check the rest of the gear. From that moment on I am operational. I will follow your instructions as far as getting into the Sudan. When I leave the airport in Khartoum, I will meet up with your agent. Together he and I will go to the coast. I will remain out of contact, in the black, until the operation is complete. I will notify you via sat phone, my own sat phone, that the job is done, and then we can talk about extraction."

Sid was almost giddy with excitement. "Brilliant. I will do *exactly* as you say."

For the next week Gentry test-fired and zeroed weapons, exercised rigorously on the hills and in the forests to the east of Saint Petersburg, did his best to build up his stamina by running, climbing tall trees, and carrying a rucksack filled with stones. He made daily visits to a tanning salon in Pushkin, an affluent suburb south of Saint Petersburg proper. He pored over maps and books and printouts regarding the players in the Sudanese region, from the smallest, most poorly equipped rebel group to the structure, tactics, and training of the NSS, the dreaded Sudanese National Security Service. He studied the history, the laws, the infrastructure, the roads, the ports, the location and disposition of the airports and the military garrisons.

He paid special attention to the Red Sea coast of the country, because this was where he would act, first as an assassin in the employ of the Russian mob and then as an extraordinary rendition operative in the employ of the Central Intelligence Agency.

This might get complicated, he told himself with cynical understatement.

He met again with Zack Hightower after the rest of Whiskey Sierra had left to join up with a CIA-owned yacht, named the *Hannah*, customized for their needs and already in Eritrea, about to sail for Port Sudan, thirty miles north of Suakin. Zack and Court spent an entire day together going over codes, maps, equipment, and operational plans. No aspect of this mission was too small for discussion or too trivial to troubleshoot. Hightower explained how the SLA, the Sudanese Liberation Army—an anti-Arab, anti-Abboud rebel force—would create a diversion the morning of the kidnapping of President Abboud that should distract the majority of his guard and force the president himself into the bank. CIA Sudan Station had an agent who was a former member of Abboud's close protection detail, and he had indicated the standard operating procedure for an attack while walking to the mosque in Suakin was to get inside the bank and defend the inner sanctum until helicopter troops could come from Port Sudan. It was considered a low--probability location for an attack on the president. The SLA was nonexistent in the area, and Abboud had visited the town dozens of times without incident.

Court would be waiting in the bank to snatch the president and then take him out of the city, while Whiskey Sierra stayed on the outskirts of the town, doing their utmost to refrain from direct action if at all possible. They would then all be picked up by an inflatable Zodiac boat and ferried to the *Hannah*, at which time they would pull anchor and head north. Then Hightower would put Abboud in a mini-sub attached to the bottom of the yacht, and from there Sierra One and Oryx would link up with a CIA fishing trawler in international waters. This way, if the *Hannah* was boarded by Sudanese coastal patrol boats, there would be no evidence of this group's involvement in the kidnapping.

The *Hannah* would then just motor up the Red Sea coast and eventually dock in Alexandria. By that time, Abboud would be imprisoned at the ICC facility in The Hague, Netherlands.

It was a bold, audacious plan. Court could see no specific part that seemed impossible or poorly thought out. That said, there were a tremendous number of things that could go wrong. Human error or failings might derail the op at any time. As could intelligence failures. So could the "shit happens" phenomenon, Murphy's Law.

But more than anything, this smelled like an operation that, though it might well come off just as planned, was thought up by a department desperate to remain viable under an administration for whom covert, paramilitary-style operations had been all but ruled out.

On Court's third night on his own, he called a number given to him by Sidorenko's henchmen. Sid's secretary answered, and Court told him he'd suffered a slight injury while training for the mission. He would require, Court declared, a small bottle of mild painkillers to get him through his recovery. Court went to a dark hallway in Vitebsk Metro Station, where he met one of Sid's young skinhead goons. A paper bag was exchanged without a word.

Court downed two of the Darvocet while still on the platform waiting for his metro ride back to his hotel on Zagorodny Prospect. He had convinced himself, sort of, that he was in pain. The stomach wound he'd received four months earlier did seem somewhat aggravated by his abdominal exercises—the knot of scar tissue pulled at the muscles and caused them to stiffen in protest—but truly it was not pain he would have batted an eyelash at had he not developed his penchant for narcotics.

Court knew this, and he wondered if—despite all the big, bad men in this world who wanted him dead—in fact, that friendly old doctor in Nice who'd hooked him up with the morphine would end up being the man who would ultimately bring him down.

81

14

The Russian transport, an Ilyushin Il-76, was massive, with a tip-to-tail length of more than 150 feet, and a similar width from wingtip to wingtip. Court stood in front of the plane before dawn and inspected it through the faint illumination of frigid moonshine. Next to him stood Gregor Sidorenko. He'd flown with Gentry from Saint Petersburg to Grodno, Belarus, in the Hawker and landed at the main airport there just thirty minutes earlier. There was, unequivocally, no operational reason for Sid to be there; it was anathema to every relevant procedure and tactic that Court had learned in his sixteen years as an operative. But his Russian handler had wanted to go along for this part of the ride. Even though it was below freezing out here on the tarmac, Sid looked ridiculous bundled as he was in wool and cotton and leather and fur, his thin nose and his pointed chin jutting out from the mound of fabric and dead animal that blanketed him.

Court was perplexed by his handler's bizarre excitement over the operation. It was night-and-day different than the cool distance kept by his former employer, the English ex-spymaster Sir Donald Fitzroy. Sir Donald would no more fly along to stand around at the departure point of one of Court's wet operations than he would execute the op himself. But Sid was a fan—a freak, in Court's eyes—of this sort of thing.

Sid's Russian accent broke the still. "Everything is prepared. Takeoff at ten a.m."

"I know."

"Seven hours fifteen minutes to Khartoum."

Court just nodded.

"They say your pilot is very good."

Court said nothing.

"Takeoff will be to the south. That's Poland back there behind us, so he will probably fly south until he reaches the border with—"

"Sid. I really don't care which way we fly."

The Russian was quiet for a moment. Then he said, "I do not know how you can be so calm. Everything that must be running through your mind. Everything that you must do in the next days. The danger, the intrigue, the physical peril. And you just stand there bored, like you are waiting for a train to take you in to your office."

Court's eyes remained on the aircraft ahead. Sid did not know the half of it, of course. Sid's op was relatively—and relatively was the key word—easy, compared to what he really had to do. Shooting a man at five hundred yards and then hiding out in the hills for a week or so until he could just walk through airport gates and board a flight out of the country seemed so much simpler than pretending to prepare for an assassination but instead executing a split-second kidnapping and a perilous rendezvous in enemy territory to transfer a prisoner.

Court so wished he could just shoot that murderous fucker Bakri Abboud in the head and be done with it.

"How can you possibly remain so relaxed?" Sid asked Court.

The Gray Man turned to the Russian mafioso, the first time he'd made eye contact with his handler all morning.

"This is what I do."

Gregor Sidorenko's narrow mouth formed a surprisingly toothy smile. Even in the predawn light it glowed. "Fantastic."

The aircraft was a behemoth, and it exhibited function over form. Called the Candid by NATO forces, the Ilyushin Il-76 had huge, high wings that sagged slightly when at rest. The plane looked big and fat and slumbering there in the dark. Court wanted to walk over and kick it awake, but he knew soon the Russian crew would handle that, and the aircraft would effectively transport him and whatever war goods it carried to Khartoum. It was not a military flight in the strict sense. The plane and the crew were property of Rosoboronexport, the Russian state-owned military export entity. Rosoboronexport flew cargo aircraft all over the globe, to the Sudan, to Venezuela, to Libya, to India, transporting exported Russian arms to some sixty countries in all, fanning and fueling the flames in trouble spots all over the earth.

With only idle curiosity, Gentry asked Sid, "What is the cargo?"

"Other than you? Crates of heavy Kord machine guns, ammunition, and support equipment."

"And they are allowed in by the UN? What about the sanctions?"

Sid snorted in the cold morning air. "The sanctions are obtuse. Russia is allowed to sell military equipment to the Sudan, as long as the equipment is not to be used in the Darfur region of the country."

"If Russia is shipping machine guns to Sudan, they can be damn sure they are being used in Darfur. That's where the war is."

"Exactly, my friend," Sid smiled, not picking up on Court's derision of the arrangement. "Moscow takes President Abboud's word for it. That seems to satisfy the UN."

"Unbelievable," said Court, almost to himself.

Sidorenko patted him on the back. "Yes. Very good, isn't it?" The Russian turned and headed back to the warmth of the terminal.

Court lay on his back across four of the Ilyushin's red plastic seats. Next to him in the tight floor space between his resting place along the wall of the fuselage and the huge crates of cargo in the center of the aircraft was positioned a single MultiCam backpack. Gentry was a master at packing light. Inside the fifty-pound ruck was a disassembled Blaser R 93, a German sniper rifle, caliber .300 Winchester Magnum, and twenty rounds of ammunition. Also binoculars, two fragmentation grenades, two smoke grenades, and a small supply of dried food, water, and oral rehydration salts. A medical blow-out kit for major trauma was included, but for cuts and bruises he'd packed nothing. On his belt and in his cargo pants he wore a Glock nine-millimeter pistol, a combat knife, a multi-tool, and a flashlight.

He was covered in a long white thobe, a robe customary in the Sudan.

The flight crew had left him alone. Their higher-ups at Rosoboronexport had ordered them to ferry a man to Khartoum, but that was *all* they knew.

Gentry had told the crew chief in Russian before takeoff that he was not to be disturbed except for emergencies, so when a member of the five-man cabin crew appeared above him and shouted over the shrill engines, he knew it was time to either be mad or be worried. The man summoned him to the cockpit, and Gentry followed him up the narrow channel alongside the gray wooden cargo crates, which hung from rollers attached to rails on the ceiling that ran down the length of the craft. There were no windows in the cabin; instead, quilted padding and netting and fastened equipment hung from the walls of the fuselage. It reminded the American of another cargo plane he'd been in, four months earlier, over northern Iraq. That flight did not end well for Gentry; his thigh throbbed where the bullet had torn through the muscle, but it ended even less well for the five other men who'd been with him in the cargo hold.

The cockpit of the Ilyushin was expansive; four men fit themselves in the upper-level crew area, and the navigator sat below in the nose among a sea of dials and buttons and computer monitors. The pilot, a redheaded Russian in his forties named Genady, who wore aviator glasses too large for his face and appeared, to Gentry, to be unhealthily thin, beckoned him forward. A young and heavy-set flight engineer passed the American a radio headset so he and the pilot could communicate comfortably with each other.

"What is it?" Court asked in Russian.

"Sudanese air traffic control has contacted us. There is a problem."

"Tell me."

"We have been diverted. We are no longer going to Khartoum."

"Where are we going?"

"Al Fashir."

"Why?"

"I don't know, but I think perhaps the Sudanese Army must need the guns there in a hurry."

Court pulled a laminated map off the flight engineer's table. The man looked up at him but did not protest. "Where the hell is Al Fashir?" asked Gentry as he unfolded the map.

The Russian pilot turned and looked back over his shoulder and answered the question with one word, delivered in a grave tone. "Darfur." He put his gloved finger on the far edge, completely across the country from where Court's operation was planned.

Court looked up from the map. "Fuck."

"It is a problem for you, *da*?"

"My job is not in Darfur."

Genady said, "Nothing I can do. I have to divert; I don't have clearance to land in Khartoum."

"Shit!" said Gentry now. He tossed the headset back on the console and turned to leave the cockpit, yanking the map out with him.

Five minutes later he was on his Hughes Thuraya satellite phone, talking with Sidorenko. He'd spent the time waiting for the connection to be established looking over the map. "This is not acceptable! How am I supposed to get out of the airport at Al Fashir, cross a hundred miles of bandit-covered desert, plus another three hundred miles of Sudanese territory? I've got the fucking Nile River now between myself and my objective."

"Yes, Gray, I understand. It is a problem. You must let me think."

"I don't have time for you to think! I need you to get this flight back on track!"

"But that is not possible. My influence is with Moscow, not Khartoum. You will have to land where the Sudanese instruct you to land."

"If you can't fix this, then this operation is dead, you got that?" In fact, Court was concerned about Zack's op, Nocturne Sapphire, and not Sid's contract, but he did not mention this.

"I will do my best." Sid hung up, and Court continued pacing the narrow alley between the wall of the fuselage and the crates of guns.

This snafu was of the "shit happens" variety. It was no one's fault, but Court knew from much experience that no blame need be assigned to an operation for it to fail completely and miserably.

To Sidorenko's credit, he called back much quicker than Gentry had anticipated.

"Mr. Gray, we have a solution. You must fly out again with the plane after it off-loads in Al Fashir. Return to the air base in Belarus. There will be another flight to Khartoum in three days' time. It will be helicopter repair equipment, goods that are not likely to be diverted to Al Fashir. Everything will be fine." Sid seemed satisfied with the new arrangements.

"Three days from now?"

"Correct."

"One day before Abboud goes to Suakin? That's not enough time to get there and prepare." It would have been, thought Court, if Sidordenko's operation was the actual plan he intended on carrying out. It was not enough time, in Gentry's estimation, to adequately recon the area to increase the chances for success in Zack's operation. Again, he could not very well explain this to the man on the far end of the satellite connection.

Sid shouted back across the line, his stress getting the best of him. "I can't help it! I had no way to foresee this. The Russian government did not foresee this. Just stay with the flight crew and come back. We will try again in three days."

Court hung up the phone and continued pacing the narrow corridor of the aircraft next to the weapons. "Son of a bitch."

He next used his phone to call Zack. Hightower took the call on the first ring. He was clearly surprised to hear from Gentry. "You're about twenty-four hours ahead of schedule, Six."

"I'm about to fall behind schedule." Court told Sierra One what was going on. When he was finished he asked, "You know anything about this airport? Any way I can get out of here and over to Suakin?"

"You might as well be on the dark side of the moon. It's a war zone all around Al Fashir. The Red Cross, private NGO relief agencies, and African Union troops working for UNAMID, the United Nations Mission in Darfur, are about the only foreigners in the area. You might be able to buy a ride to the east from some local ballsy enough to brave the Janjaweed militia and the government of Sudan troops patrolling the badlands, but I wouldn't recommend it. Stick with Sid's change to the op orders, retrograde out of the Sudan with the aircrew, and reinsert in three days. It's the best we can do at this point. We'll just have to rush things when you get there. I'll let Carmichael know what's up."

"Roger that, Six out."

"Wait one," Zack said, "Just a piece of advice. Don't know what your turnaround time is in Al Fashir, but stay the hell inside the airport grounds. If you get popped by the authorities over there, they'll take you to the Ghost House."

"That sounds charming," Court said over the whine of the Ilyushin's engines changing pitch. They had just begun a turn to the south and a slight descent.

"It's anything *but* charming. It's the name the locals give to the government's secret prisons across the country, but the one in Al Fashir is extra special. You go in the Al Fashir Ghost House, you don't come out, and you don't die quick. It is legendarily miserable."

"Understood. I'll avoid the local tour, then. Six out."

15

Ellen Walsh's low spirits rose instantly when she saw a ray of the late afternoon sun glint off metal in the distant sky. It was an airplane, big and lumbering, turning onto its final approach, a thousand meters above the brown highland plain of north Darfur. An aircraft landing here at Al Fashir airport meant a potential way out of this miserable place.

Ellen had been stuck here since arriving on a UN transport plane ferrying in aid workers. There had been a problem with Walsh's documents; her UNAMID travel authorization was missing the requisite stamp that would have allowed her entry into the UN camp for internally displaced people in Zam Zam. This oversight meant she was not allowed to leave the airport, unless it was on a plane out of Al Fashir.

So for three days she'd waited for a flight that would take her back to her office. UN aircraft had arrived, but they remained parked on the hot tarmac awaiting a resupply of UN jet fuel from a UN tanker. Chinese state-owned oil company planes had come and gone, but they'd returned to Beijing and not Khartoum, and they'd made it clear she could not go with them. Sudanese military flights had arrived and departed, as well, but they weren't providing taxi service for some white woman.

But this new aircraft, this mysterious arrival floating in the hazy mirage to the north and lining up on the runway, could be her ticket out of here. It wasn't military, it wasn't painted in UN white, and it did not have the same shape as the Chinese planes she'd seen. Ellen knew aircraft, and normally she could ID a cargo plane in a second, but this craft in the distance was now banking across the late afternoon sun and was therefore impossible for her to identify. But she did not care. Whatever type of plane it was, whoever was flying it, and wherever it was headed next, she determined to do everything in her power to see that she was on it when it left.

Ellen was neither vain nor any sort of slave to fashion, but even before the lumbering aircraft touched down at the far end of the runway, she hurried back into the terminal to the restroom. She passed a pair of local Darfuri tribeswomen on their way out, dressed head to toe in colorful orange drapings, ushering three small children on ahead of them. The ladies' head wrappings were high and wide and, Ellen Walsh now realized, served as an effective foil for all the dust in the air. As she stepped up to the mirror for a look at herself, she nearly recoiled in horror. Her auburn hair looked ashen from the gray dust floating about, the faint creases around her eyes on her thirty-five-year-old face were exaggerated by the dust and grime and salt from the sweat that had dried there.

Quickly she untied the white T-shirt from the outside of her backpack and drenched it in the dingy water flowing from the tap. She wiped her face with the makeshift washcloth. She had used the same shirt for the same task so many times in the past seventy-two hours that it was streaked and dulled from the filth scratched off her skin. She turned away from the tap, dipped her head forward towards the begrimed floor of the bathroom, and used her fingers to comb through her hair as she leaned over, pulling a dust cloud out of her shoulder-length locks. She rose, blew the bangs out of her eyes, and replaced her hair band.

One more look in the mirror didn't fill her with relief, but it was an improvement. She retied the wet T-shirt to her backpack and hoisted it over a shoulder, then left the bathroom to return to the tarmac.

She heard the huge engines long before she saw the aircraft. It taxied to a parking spot on the other side of the ramp from the four UN planes, some four hundred meters from the door Ellen stepped through. In the dusty afternoon distance she could not identify the four-engine plane, but she did see there were no airline markings or country designation. Still, from its shape she could tell it was a cargo ship. She was momentarily caught up in the bevy of traffic as she began walking towards it. Several customs men and airport ground crewmen passed her on foot, as did two dozen soldiers hanging off the sides of a pickup and two dilapidated flatbed trucks. She thought about letting all the activity approaching the new arrival die down before making her approach, but she decided to keep going. She had no idea how long this flight would be on the ground. Days were doubtful; everyone who'd landed heretofore had gotten out of Al Fashir as soon as possible if they had the fuel to do so. Hours would be likely if they were going to be offloading cargo. Minutes only if they were just here to take on fuel.

She was not going to miss her chance.

As Ellen walked towards the aircraft at the distant end of the ramp, it was partially obscured in the haze of a heat mirage pouring up from the cracked tarmac, the late afternoon air dimming just slightly but not yet cooling. The air above the plane's hulking form quivered as vapors poured from the idling engines.

After a moment, the pilot shut his engines down. The whine of the four big turbojets was replaced by the voices of the soldiers in the distance and the ceaseless sound of insects in the sandy scrub brush that ran along either side of the taxiway.

The entourage of local army and airport workers was between her and the plane, moving purposefully across the hot taxiway, and they commanded her attention for the majority of her walk. She hesitated more than once, weighing the pros and cons of waiting for them to do their business and leave the aircraft versus pushing right on through the gaggle of black men, some uniformed, some in business suits, and some in flowing white tobes, to speak immediately to the flight crew. Neither option looked particularly promising, but she quickly arrived at the conclusion that the latter choice seemed preferable to sitting back and waiting for a plane that might well just take off again into the sky without her.

So she decided to walk right up the lowering rear hatch and take her chances. This decision caused her to look past the men fifty yards in front of her and turn her focus fully to the aircraft another twenty meters beyond them, and only then did her certain gait slow a bit. After a few yards she slowed even more.

And then she stopped dead in her tracks on the blistering tarmac.

With her eyes steady on the plane, she unslung her backpack and put it at her feet, unzipped it quickly, let a couple of sweat-stained blouses fall to the pavement as she pulled out a small black three-ring binder. She knelt on her backpack as she quickly leafed through it; her knees would have blistered had she placed them directly on the ground. Three quick glances back up to the cargo plane, and a few licks of her bone-dry fingertips helped her find the page she was looking for.

Another look down at the page. Another look up at the plane in front of her.

Yes. She muttered an exclamation that was not completely drowned out by the locusts and crickets around her. "Oh my God."

It was an Ilyushin Il-76, and from the look of its sagging disposition on its ten-wheel undercarriage, it was full of cargo. The Il-76 was an extremely common Russian-built transport aircraft, in service with aid agencies and transport services and militaries throughout the hemisphere. But unless Ellen's eyes were deceiving her, this was an Il-76MF, an upgraded version with a longer fuselage.

Slowly she looked away from the plane as she collected her belongings off the tarmac. Slower still she turned and began walking back to the terminal.

Her excitement grew and grew as she sauntered nonchalantly in the afternoon heat, retracing her steps of moments ago. This excitement was tempered by the knowledge that she would not be able to make a phone call inside the building, as there wasn't a single public phone, and she'd been told the administrative line had been down for the past seventy-two hours. The airport administrators were lying, she had no doubt, but the effect was the same. She could not call her office.

The excitement, tempered as it was, helped her think quickly as her mind raced to formulate a hasty plan. The scale of the opportunity before her could not be exaggerated, and she determined to control her emotions and focus on the opportunity at hand.

Certainly in her professional career, and almost certainly in her entire life, Ellen Walsh, special investigator for the International Criminal Court, had never felt so determined.

Nor so alone.

16

This white woman is going to be a problem.

Court had changed into an extra jumpsuit to match the rest of the flight crew, climbed down the rear ramp of the aircraft with the others, was slapped hard in the face by the heat and the stink of dry earth, and immediately squinted into the low afternoon sunlight, scanning the area to get his bearings. To his left he saw an old white UN aircraft off in the sand, its tail broken off from the fuselage and evidence of a fire on board from the soot-covered windows and the partially melted and completely smoke-stained engines. To his right a row of UN helicopters sat in the haze generated by the heat pouring off the engines of his own plane, the propellers of the choppers dipping low as if melting. Behind them were several airplanes parked wingtip to wingtip. They looked like they could be small UN transport craft. A tiny, new-looking terminal was up ahead several hundred yards. To the right of it was a fence line out in the sand that ran alongside a road, with several more junked and wrecked aircraft deposited nearby.

Bugs were everywhere: flies, mosquitoes, locusts that he could not see but could easily hear out in the thickets alongside the dusty taxiway.

And then he noticed her in the mid distance; it was hard to miss a white female alone on a sunny airport tarmac in western Sudan. From fifty yards away he watched her take note of his plane and drop to her bag, pull out a book, and thumb through it. He watched her pause to read the page, then stand slowly with her hands on her hips. Then she began retreating, slowly but unmistakably, to the terminal, well aware, Gentry had a strong suspicion, that the aircraft behind her was not supposed to be there.

Yep, this white woman was definitely going to be a problem.

Court remained in the background of the conversation and listened to the pilot Gennady speak English with the Sudanese military officials at the foot of the ramp. The trucks coming to off-load the guns were behind schedule; it would be another hour before they reached the airport. Fuel for the Ilyushin was available and would be provided immediately, and an airport official would show the men the way to the washrooms and the restaurant. They had parked alone at the far end of the taxiway. This was to keep the few civilians and foreign aid workers milling about the terminal from getting near enough to the unmarked cargo plane to see something they shouldn't. Still, Gennady and his flight crew were invited by the Sudanese to enjoy the comforts of the terminal while they waited for the plane to be unloaded and refueled.

After the Sudanese had wandered off, Gentry asked Gennady to keep his men on the aircraft. From a security perspective, Court saw no benefit in the Russian men wandering among civilians. But the pilot was in charge, not the stowaway, and he told his men they would be wheels up in three hours and would need to be back to the aircraft in two, but until then they could do as they pleased.

Twenty minutes later Court and the Ilyushin's flight crew stepped out of the oppressive late afternoon heat and into a stairwell at a side entrance to the terminal's concourse. Court almost stayed behind himself, but he wanted to keep his eyes on the Russians to make sure they behaved themselves. He did not have any gear with him at all. His gun remained back on the plane in his pack. He had no idea what security measures he might find here and did not want to run the risk of getting frisked by some local version of the TSA. Only his wallet full of euros, rubles, and Sudanese pounds bulged the lines of his olive-drab flight suit. The stairs led up one level into a nearly empty concourse, smaller than a typical American supermarket. A few locals milled about, and GOS soldiers sat on the floor or strolled around with their assault rifles hanging upside down off their backs. The flight crew, with their secret foreigner hidden in with them, found the bathrooms and used them, then found the tiny restaurant and sat down. A waiter who proclaimed himself Egyptian, as if these Russians cared, energetically greeted the men and passed around menus. None of the Russians spoke Arabic. Court, on the other hand, had spent more than enough time in the Arab-speaking world to order a meal, but he held his tongue. He was not about to differentiate himself from the rest of the flight crew by becoming their translator.

Gennady ordered for the table. He'd been here in Al Fashir many times before, which, Gentry realized, should not have come as a surprise. Flagrant disregard for international sanctions by the government of an African despot was de rigueur, as was the Russians' eagerness to benefit from it, as was the United Nations' shock and outrage each and every single time that they became aware of it.

While they waited for their food, Court's eyes continued scanning the environment. They were still adjusting to the low light inside the terminal compared to that on the tarmac. He looked back over his shoulder down the hallway and cringed inwardly.

Shit. Here comes the white woman.

This he didn't need.

"Excuse me. Do any of you gentlemen speak English?" Ellen smiled broadly, directing her question towards the pilot as she knelt next to him at the head of the table. She could tell he was in command by his countenance and bearing; he sat erect at the table full of men in sweat-soaked jumpsuits.

There were five men in the flight crew; all wore matching green uniforms, no names or emblems or markings of any kind. None of the men were particularly military looking in their hairstyles or fitness levels, but Ellen knew better than to draw too many conclusions too quickly. These could be military pilots working for Rosoboronexport or former Russian military. Either way, it didn't matter.

"Yes, I speak a little bit." The redheaded pilot smiled at her, then slowly and suggestively, he looked her up and down. Ellen realized his actions were for the amusement of his colleagues; she knew she was not much of a sight to behold at this moment. Immediately she determined the man to be a pig, but she also told herself she could use this distraction of his to her advantage. Some of the other men leaned in closer to her, as well.

"Great," she said with a wide, friendly smile designed to put the men at ease, although they surely didn't seem on guard. "Ellen Walsh, United Nations." It was a lie, but it was delivered without a batted eyelash. "I sure am glad to see you boys. I've been stuck here at Al Fashir for three days. I'm looking for transport out of here, Khartoum, Port Sudan … at this point I'd go just about anywhere just to get out of this terminal. I'd be happy to pay you cash for the trouble, and I'm sure my office could work it out with your employer."

The lecherous pilot clearly didn't understand every word. His head cocked a couple of times. She knew she was speaking a little fast; the pace of her words seemed to follow along with her elevated heart rate.

"Perhaps we can make an arrangement. Join us for dinner first, please, and we will discuss this."

"Delighted." Ellen sat, smiled, but she could tell this guy wasn't going to let her fly on his plane. He was stringing her along for personal reasons.

She knew now that a flight out on this mysterious aircraft was too much to hope for, but she would string this bastard right along as well, to see if she could glean information from him or even just get a closer glimpse at the Ilyushin or its cargo.

Two could play the game he was playing. She leaned in close to him.

"Chto vy delaete?" came a voice from the end of the table. Ellen looked to the speaker, saw that somehow she had miscounted the Russians before. There were six men at the table, not five, and this sixth man was asking a question of the pilot. He, like the majority of these guys, wore a thick beard and scruffy hair; his was longer than the others. He seemed more athletic than the rest, and darker complected. When the pilot did not answer him, he repeated himself.

"Chto vy delaete?"

"What do you mean, what am I doing?" replied Gennady in Russian. "I am asking this lovely woman to have dinner with us."

"You must not allow her on the aircraft," Court said flatly, straining his Russian abilities to do so.

Gennady looked at him and replied, "You do not tell me who I can and cannot allow on my plane. I don't know who you are, but I know who *I* am. *I* am the pilot. *I* am in charge."

Court looked away. His eyes drifted back out over the concourse. Turning away from what was beginning to look more and more like a fucking mess in the making.

The Canadian woman introduced herself as Ellen. She shook each man's hand with a smile. Court did not make eye contact when he shook her hand limply and grunted out the name "Viktor."

"So, where are you guys from?"

"We are Russian," said Gennady.

"Russian. Wow. Neat."

Court turned to study the woman's face carefully now, like an art student studying the brushstrokes of an oil painting on a museum wall.

"What brings you gentlemen to Darfur?"

Play cool, Gennady. Court said it to himself in Russian.

"What is your job with UN?" the Russian pilot asked warily, responding to a question with a question and not exactly "playing cool" in Court's eyes.

The woman smiled at the Russian, asked him to repeat himself, though Court sensed she understood him well. Gentry was trained to look for clues in the limbic system, the part of the brain that controls subconscious actions. Court knew how to discern the movements and expressions and postures that were indicators of deception. This woman glanced away quickly to the right when asked what she did, and to Court this was a signal that she was going to attempt to deceive with the next words out of her mouth. That she delayed by asking him to repeat himself was only more indication that a deceptive or untrue answer was being prepared and would soon be on the way.

Finally she replied, "Oh, I'm just an administrative officer for relief supplies." She shrugged her shoulders, "Logistics and such. Nothing very interesting." Her right arm reached across her body and rubbed her left arm.

Bullshit, thought Court. Gennady, on the other hand, seemed eased by her air of nonchalance.

"Yes. Well, we bring oil equipment into Darfur," the pilot said as the Egyptian waiter brought steaming cups of tea to the table.

Court wasn't satisfied with Gennady's answer; he'd much prefer he'd said it was none of her business. But at least he didn't say he was schlepping in tons of belt-fed machine guns and ammo.

The woman seemed perplexed, and Gentry's built-in trouble meter flickered higher up the dial.

"I see," she said, but her body language indicated that she did not. A micro-expression on her face revealed excitement, not confusion. "I would have thought the Chinese would use their own equipment."

"The Chinese? Why are you speaking of the Chinese? We Russians are experts in oil. Much oil in Siberia," Gennady said with a smile that he likely thought was sexy.

Court's research of the Sudan and the oil situation during the last two weeks afforded him with knowledge that, obviously, this Ellen Walsh woman would also have. The Chinese had control over all the oil exploration sites in the Darfur region. It was clear that Gennady did not know this.

"Oh." She feigned surprise, but Court picked up clues that she recognized that the Russian pilot was lying to her about the cargo. She let it go and began spooning dingy gray sugar into her tea even as the waiter placed it in front of her.

Was her hand trembling?

"Why are you in Al Fashir?" Gennady asked.

She hesitated, again reaching a hand across her body to rub her other arm, both covering herself and comforting herself with the action. Obvious tells of anxiety and deception to a trained body language expert such as the Gray Man.

"I came out to survey the Zam Zam IDP camp. Unfortunately, my staff didn't have all my documents and permissions in order, so they won't let me out of the airport. I'm really desperate for a ride out of here." She looked at the pilot again, and he back at her. He raised his eyebrows suggestively but did not offer her a seat on his aircraft.

Gennady said nothing.

"Have you been to Darfur before?"

"Yes," the pilot answered cockily. "Many times."

The woman nodded, still smiling. "It's horrible out here. Four hundred fifty thousand murdered in the past eight years, and no end in sight. Millions more in the camps, either here or over the border in Chad."

"Da," said Gennady. "War is very bad."

Court wanted to reach across the table and slap the insincerity off his face.

After a few seconds Ellen said, "That plane of yours is awesome. It's an Ilyushin, isn't it? Looks like some we have in our inventory." Quickly she added, "I ship a lot of cargo in my job, though I've never actually been in a cargo plane."

"It *is* an Ilyushin. An excellent Russian aircraft," said Gennady, and Walsh nodded along with him, seeming to fawn all over his words.

"Here is some pilot trivia for you," Ellen said with an excited smile. "Did you know Amelia Earhart landed here at Al Fashir on her attempt to circle the globe?"

Gennady cocked his head a little. "Who?"

"Amelia Earhart. The female pilot? The *famous* female pilot who disappeared flying around the world in 1937."

Gennady just looked at her.

"Surely you have heard—"

"I have never heard of this woman, but I am not surprised she disappeared. Women do not make good pilots," he said, as if this were the most basic fact of aeronautics. A dismissive wave of his hand and a loud slurp of tea followed his comment. Court caught the woman dropping her veil of admiration for the Russian man and revealing her true feelings of disgust.

But the veil rose again almost instantly.

"Well, I've heard great things about Russian aircraft. And the Ilyushin. Our UN planes do the job, but they are a bit boring. Do you think I could possibly get a closer look at your beautiful plane? Don't worry, I won't try to fly it. I'd probably just disappear."

Her smile was wide, friendly, and, Court recognized, a total sham.

Gennady just smiled back at her a long time without answering. He gave his shoulders a shrug, but it was a shrug that indicated anything was possible.

Some of the other Russians asked her questions in broken English. If she was married—no. Where she was from— Vancouver. How long she'd been in the Sudan—a month. Court saw no deception in any of the answers she gave. But he did notice her looking at him, perhaps picking up on his scrutiny of her, and this caused Gentry to look away again.

They are all buying it except the darker one. He *is suspicious.* He *knows I am full of shit.*

Ellen tried to give a big smile to the man at the end of the table, but he turned away, bored. Unlike the rest of the crew, he did not leer at her. No, other than his earlier comment to Gennady, he had not been a part of the conversation, but it was clear to her he was listening. Either he understood her perfectly or he was struggling to do so.

But more important than the quiet man at the end of the table was the big airplane at the end of the taxiway. She just *had* to get a closer look at it, take a picture or two, somehow get some more intelligence on this flight into the heart of north Darfur. She wondered if even now the GOS army was taking the cargo off the plane.

"Will you have to unload your airplane yourself, or do you have someone from the oil company to do it?"

"The Sudanese will do it," said Gennady, and immediately followed with, "It will be an hour more, at least. My men will go back and help them, but I can stay with you and enjoy another tea." He smiled, she smiled, and the quiet man at the end of the table looked to his pilot. He spoke to him in Russian; Ellen did not understand a word.

"I don't trust her. Too many questions," Court said it in Russian and was totally unconcerned that the woman would recognize his distrust from his tone.

Gennady looked away from the woman and towards Gentry. His reply in Russian, as well. "I don't need to trust her. I am not going to marry her. I'm going to fuck her. She'd look okay with a bath and some makeup."

Court sighed. "We leave in two hours."

"I don't mean now, although that is plenty of time. I mean on my next trip to Khartoum. I am setting the table right now. When I next go to Khartoum, I will eat my meal."

Ellen followed the conversation around the table with her eyes. Obviously she did not understand.

Court sighed again. He thought about dropping Sidorenko's name. This would likely terrify Gennady into complying with his unauthorized passenger. But he did not. "Let's just get our food and return to the plane."

"That is a good idea. You and the boys leave me and Miss Canada alone." Gennady laughed heartily, as did the other men.

Court just looked away, angry but controlling his anger.

"Why do I get the feeling you are talking about me?" Ellen Walsh asked with a smile.

Court stood without a word and began heading back to the aircraft. He wouldn't wait for his food. He'd just eat the dry rations in his bag.

17

Gentry stopped again in the restroom. He washed his face slowly to calm himself. He decided to pop some hydrocodone when he got back to his backpack; it would help him relax on the flight back to Belarus, and it couldn't hurt anything; he wouldn't be operational again for a few days.

But first he had to watch out for this Canadian woman. Personally, he was all for someone taking note of what the Russians were doing here, calling a newspaper, an international organization, blowing the lid off of the sanctions violations. But just not right now. Court would need this shady arrangement to continue at least until his operation was complete. A Westerner making trouble for the Rosoboronexport flights, thereby throwing a wrench into his means of insertion into the Sudan, absolutely could not be tolerated.

He'd just turned the spigot off and dried his hands on his coveralls when the navigator entered behind him. He nodded to the American and said, "Gennady is taking the girl to show her the plane." Court could tell the navigator was not crazy about the idea, but the Russian just shrugged good-naturedly about it. "Vlady and I have a bet. I think he's going to do her in the cockpit, Vlady says Gennady's going to get his face slapped. You want in on the bet, friend?"

Unlike the navigator, Gentry had no intention of taking the pilot's obscene breach of operational security in stride. He stormed past the thick man and out into the concourse. He saw the woman and Gennady walking towards the stairwell to the side exit, she with her backpack on her shoulder, he with his plate of food in his hand.

"For God's sake," Court said softly. He thought about grabbing Gennady by his mop of red hair, dragging him into a corner, and telling him he was going to call the Saint Petersburg mob, who had set up his mission in the first place. One call from Court, and Sid would have Gennady's family thrown into a van in half an hour flat. Gennady would do what he was told if only Gentry dropped Sidorenko's name.

Then Court saw the airport security officials, standing around bored behind a high counter.

Yes, this was the best option. He could impress upon the Sudanese that this UN do-gooder was hassling the secret flight of Russian armaments.

It would make trouble for the woman, no question about it, but only until he and the Russians got into the air. If she and her curiosity could just be held in check until wheels up, Court could be on his way and get this wasted day behind him.

Court's operational security would remain in place, the woman from the UN would learn nothing that would impede this flight or his next flight in three days' time, and the Russian aircrew would not learn anything they did not need to know about Gentry and his employers.

"English?" Court asked the bored young airport security policeman. The African shook his head, as did the man next to him.

"*Français?*" Again, a shake of both heads.

"Okay," said Court in English, before reluctantly switching to Arabic. "*Asalaam Alaykum.*"

"*Wa Alaykum as-Salaam,*" came the polite but officious-sounding reply from both men.

Court continued in Arabic. "I must speak to your superior."

"What is the problem?"

"I am with Russian plane. There is small security problem."

The policeman nodded, spoke softly into a handheld radio. Court could not understand the rapid Sudanese Arabic. The cop looked back up at Gentry. "Wait one moment."

In under a minute two small-framed bearded men in black coats and ties appeared. One was probably not yet thirty, the other a decade or so older. Their suits were uniform; Gentry noticed the imprint of handguns on their hips, and he immediately suspected these men were from the National Security Service, the Sudanese secret police.

Oops. Thought Court. *Not these assholes.* He'd not intended to make that much fuss over the woman.

Both NSS men spoke English, and Court took the senior officer aside. He was small and wiry, and he wore thick glasses with frames too wide for his oval face. There was nothing menacing or threatening about him, but the fact was he and his subordinate held authority over all around. Security guards, airport officials, local police, even the Government of Sudan officers and enlisted men here knew to stay out of the way of the NSS.

Court said, "The woman. The white woman. Who is she?"

The man shrugged and waved his hand dismissively. "She is Canadian. We were told to not let her out of the airport grounds but not to arrest her. She is just UNAMID relief worker; all her papers are in order, except she did not have the stamp in her documents to allow her entry into Zam Zam camp."

"I think she wants to make trouble for us."

"She is not important; she is just a *kawaga* stuck here at the airport, waiting to go back to Khartoum."

"A *kawaga*?"

"A white person. Sorry."

"She is asking questions about the aircraft and the cargo."

That got the NSS man's attention. He seemed to put together the fact that the Rosoboronexport flight was not supposed to be in Darfur, and a Westerner was here, putting that very fact together herself. Court felt bad about turning the woman in to operatives of the National Security Service. They were tier-one assholes, Court knew. He'd hoped to just arouse the interest of airport security. But now, like it or not, the NSS was involved. If they acted on his information, she'd no doubt be detained for hours. Who knew, Court thought to himself, she might even get tossed out of the country if they were worried enough about her interest in the Russians.

No more passing out blankets and bottled water for her.

Still, he needed to get on with his mission; his mission was paramount, and he was not above using these NSS goons to help him shoo this annoying little bug out of his face.

The NSS man looked out the dirty window towards the runway. The daylight was fading fast, and the Il-76 was out of view, several hundred meters back off to the left. "Our orders were to keep any NGO flights away while you were on the ground. No one said anything about the people who were already here." The man seemed worried about his own skin. This didn't bother Court; it would certainly be a great motivator for him.

Court said, "I suggest you just take her into your office until we leave. She has not seen the cargo, she knows nothing. She has no idea we're from Rosoboronexport." Court wasn't going to mention that she'd initially approached the Ilyushin and had all but begged to be allowed on board, as that might just invite more trouble for her than he needed her to face. No, a little concern on the part of this man was all that was required to defuse the situation and put the matter to bed. Gentry was beginning to feel confident that everything would work out just fine.

The man nodded somewhat appreciatively. "Okay. Yes, okay. We will have a talk with her."

Ten minutes later the two NSS men escorted an extremely anxious looking but obedient Ellen Walsh into a small office off the main concourse of the terminal. Following them into the room were the Russian pilot and Court Gentry. Court had wanted to just board the aircraft with the crew and get the hell out of here, but Gennady had insisted on coming along for the woman's interview with the

NSS, and there was no way Gentry was going to let him do that by himself. Gennady was mad at the Sudanese for interrupting his seduction of the attractive woman, but he apparently thought that if he could help her in the questioning, to stand up to these third-world goons, then he'd have her swooning into his bed on his next flight into Khartoum.

But Court could tell the Russian was furious with him. They gave each other *eat shit* stares while they stood on either side of Walsh. Gennady obviously put together that the American had turned Ellen in to security. The Russian probably thought, Court guessed, that this was nothing more than a cock block borne out of the American's jealousy at the Canadian woman's interest in the Russian.

What a completely fucked-up day, thought Court as he stood there, exchanging threatening looks with Gennady. This better not get any worse.

The older NSS man, the one with the goofy glasses, spent a couple of minutes looking through Walsh's belongings. Court thought it was just for show, but when he pulled out the black notebook Gentry had seen her thumbing through earlier on the tarmac, he began to worry. He hoped there wasn't anything in there that would invite more trouble for the woman. The man leafed through the pages and stopped on a hand-drawn sketch and description of the Ilyushin aircraft. He looked up at the girl. "Why are you asking questions about this cargo flight? What is your interest in this aircraft?"

"I like airplanes. Is that a crime in your country?"

The man stared at her a long time. In a nation where few women are even allowed to work outside the home, a back-talking white lady was a double anomaly, and he was clearly not sure how to handle her.

Ellen found herself no longer afraid. She'd accomplished much in the past hour, and though she did not have picture proof that the Russians were violating sanctions, the actions of the NSS right now gave her all the proof she needed to be certain she was on the right track.

She'd done well to get this far, and she knew it. Under cover as a UN employee she'd thoroughly charmed the pilot into taking her on board, had made it to within twenty-five yards of the rear ramp of the aircraft when the jeep of soldiers came and picked them up. The Russian insisted on going along with her; he wanted to pretend to be her knight in shining armor, although it was obvious he just wanted to use this as a way to get into her pants.

When they arrived back at the terminal, she saw the two NSS officers who'd interrogated her days before standing with the suspicious dark-complected Russian crewmember named Viktor. Clearly he'd reported her to these guys to keep her away from the flight.

Bastard. She knew what he was trying to hide, and he was not going to get away with it.

Gennady broke in. "Look, she ships goods for the United Nations. The United Nations has Il-76s in their fleet. She has to know how big they are and how far they travel and how much they can carry. She has done nothing wrong by asking for a tour of my aircraft." He reached across the table and took the sheet of paper from the open notebook, held it up to illustrate his point.

The secret policeman regarded the Russian pilot's comments for a moment, then said, "Perhaps you are correct." He looked back to Walsh. "Who did you say you worked for in Khartoum?"

Ellen sighed, rolled her eyes. Rubbed her left upper arm with her right hand. "I've told you a dozen times, and just like my ID says, I work for UNAMID in the Transportation and Logistics Division. I came here to interview camp workers about their needs and—"

"What is the name of your director?" the secret policeman asked. He picked up a booklet that he'd brought into the interview room with him.

"Charles Stevens." Walsh smiled briefly. "A fellow Canadian."

The man looked into the book for several seconds, nodded sourly, and then put it down.

Court had just begun to relax again when he glanced over at Gennady on the other side of the woman under interrogation. The pilot had noticed something on the page with the drawing and info about the Il-76, and he peered at it intently. Confusion grew on his face now, and to Court that could only mean trouble.

Gennady spoke softly. "Ellen. The aircraft represented here is an MF variant."

She shrugged her shoulders. Too quickly and nonchalantly for Court's taste. It seemed an artificial reaction.

"It is?"

"Yes. The UN does not fly the Il-76MF." The Russian was looking up at her now, but her eyes remained to the front, towards the NSS officers.

"They don't?"

"No . . . *they* don't."

Shit, thought Court. Gennady was suspicious now. Hell, *Court* was suspicious now himself. Why would a UN do-gooder have a hand-drawn diagram of the Russian plane? He really hoped she could talk her way out of this predicament because there wasn't a damn thing he could do to help her.

"Who *are* you, and who do you work for?" Gennady asked, louder now, reaching out and turning the woman around by the shoulders to face him.

18

The Russian pilot spun her around. He'd figured her out, and she knew she could not play dumb with him like she could with the NSS.

It was time for a counterpunch.

When she was a kid her father had a saying, and she had turned it into her mantra. "Go big or go home." All her life she'd pushed herself to the limits of her abilities, did not accept second best or half measures. And now, clearly she'd found evidence of illegal weapons transfers between Russia and Sudan, *exactly* what she knew had been going on, and exactly what she wanted to prevent by moving to Holland and joining the International Criminal Court.

This was not a time to be demure, to be compliant, to run and hide. She would use the weight of her position, the power of her organization, the strength of the international community to get herself away from here, away from these thugs, and back to her office, so she could reveal what she'd discovered. Back in Khartoum, she had stared down Sudanese government officials a half dozen rungs higher up the ladder than these two little black-suited buffoons, and she was not going to let these men intimidate her. And the Russian pilot was an arrogant bastard who needed to see that women were not placed in front of him just to bow to his will.

Go big or go home?

Ellen wasn't going home until this dark secret, the secret that many had suspected, had been revealed to the world.

She was about to go big.

Say something, lady, Court said to himself. She just stood there, staring at the tall Russian. Court needed to get this over with, to get this woman tossed into the little cell here at the airport until he and his waste-of-time flight could get wheels up and out of here.

Say something! Anything, Court silently implored the woman, but when she *did* break the silence, he immediately regretted her opening her mouth.

"Very well, gentlemen. My name is Ellen Walsh. I am not an employee of UNAMID. I am, in fact, an inspector with the International Criminal Court, here in the Sudan to investigate sanctions violations concerning weapons sales from abroad."

Oh, shit, woman, you just got yourself killed, Court thought, near disbelief at what he was hearing. How could she be so stupid?

The NSS men's eyes grew impossibly wide, and Gennady looked away from Walsh and towards Gentry, an expression on his face like he'd just been poleaxed.

Walsh continued. "We've known about this flight for a long time. I was sent here to see it for myself. I can assure you my entire agency, both in Khartoum and in the Netherlands, is well aware that I am here. If I am not immediately allowed to communicate with my staff, there will be—"

Gennady shouted at her, "You lie! We were not supposed to come to Al Fashir. We were only diverted at the last moment. No one sent you here to spy on us!"

The secret policemen recovered from their surprise and stormed around the table, heading straight for Ellen Walsh.

"ICC!" Gennady began shouting outside the room to the rest of the flight crew, who were standing out in the terminal. Court couldn't stop him from doing so. The two NSS men immediately confronted her, spun her around, and put her arms behind her back. These guys did not possess more than two speeds—off and on—and she had just flipped their switch. No doubt they were concerned about their own careers, their own lives even, allowing this woman to wander the airport while the Rosoboronexport flight was parked on the tarmac.

"You fucking Canadian whore!" shouted Gennady, turning back to the woman.

The big Russian slapped her face with his powerful hand. Court started to move forward with the objective of breaking Gennady's jaw and pushing the NSS officers back, but he stayed himself. He was in two forms of cover at the same time, and neither of these alter egos would have any incentive to stop the secret police from detaining this woman. He could not show the Sudanese that he was anything more than a Russian cargo aircraft crewman, and he could not show the Russians that he was anything more than some dispassionate agent they were bringing into the country.

So he just stood there, watching, as the NSS men handcuffed her, and she kicked out at Gennady as he stood in front of her shouting in Russian. Soon four armed GOS soldiers stormed in, alerted no doubt by the shouting and wrestling in the interrogation room. Gentry's Russian cohort scooted back out the door, and a couple of the other Russians peered in, with gawking stares of fascination and even amusement.

The older secret policeman grabbed her by her chin and turned her face towards his. "There is a place we take unwanted guests. I promise you that within minutes of arriving at the Ghost House, you will regret your espionage against the Republic of Sudan."

"Espionage? I am not a spy! I have every right as a member of the international community to—"

"Don't say another word, lady!" Court shouted aloud, no attempt now to hide his American accent and stay in cover. This fool was making her own situation direr by the second. "Just shut up and do what you're told. You don't know anything. Get out of here and do what you have to do, but don't let on that you know any—"

"You speak English?" She looked at Gentry, confusion replacing her fury.

Court tried to reason with the woman in short bursts so the others would not understand. He switched to French. He hoped like hell that, as a Canadian, she understood it and hoped, also like hell, that the Sudanese did not. "You are not ICC! Do not say you are ICC, or they will kill you! Tell them you were lying. Tell them you are nobody. UN, that's all." One of the NSS men looked up at him in surprise but was too busy trying to pull the strong woman over to a chair to stop what he was doing.

Ellen began crying, screaming at the same time, "I don't speak French, asshole! Do you speak English or not? Help me!"

After she was led to the chair, her small hands still cuffed behind her back, some of the soldiers cleared out, and one of the NSS men left the room to use the phone. The Russians had all returned to the concourse, sensing that the show was over.

Court remained in the room with the girl, pacing back and forth. He stepped in front of her and leaned close. Her lip bled where Gennady had slapped her, and her rust-colored blouse was torn at the shoulder from the soldiers' rough treatment.

He spoke to her softly, quickly, so the NSS would not pick up all of it. "Listen carefully. Don't fight with them, but be firm. Demand to speak to someone from UNAMID. Don't say anything else. You are *not* in the ICC. You *saw* nothing. You *know* nothing." Gentry looked down at the floor. Not up at her eyes. "You'll be okay." He turned away and headed back out the door slowly. "You'll be fine."

"Who are you?" she called out to him.

He slowed but did not turn back and look at her. "Nobody."

Gentry and the rest of the Ilyushin's crew walked together across the darkened tarmac towards the huge aircraft.

Court was mad and worried, and he felt like shit about the Canadian woman. His shoulders sagged as he walked in the rear of the group, his head slumped down. He tried to tell himself that her outburst condemned her, and that was *her* fault, not his, and he could not do anything about it.

114

He'd told her she'd be fine, but from pretty much everything he could see and guess about the situation, he was certain she would be killed. It would be just too easy to make her disappear right here and now, and too damaging to let her walk away to reveal what she knew. Court also knew that if he could come to this conclusion, it made absolutely no sense for the NSS or the GOS to come to any *other* conclusion.

Miss Ellen Walsh was dead.

"Your fault, Gentry." He said it aloud, softly, as he walked through the night with the flight crew.

They were still a couple hundred yards from the aircraft. Court began to slow. He looked up and saw the others were ahead of him by several yards now. He slowed some more. Then his slumped shoulders raised and stiffened. He looked up from his sulk and said, "Gennady. Don't leave me."

The pilot turned, continued walking backwards. "What? Leave you where?"

"Just wait for me. I have to—"

"We are going now. Fifteen minutes for preflight, and then we are in the air. I don't know what you are talking about, but I'm not waiting for you. Come on."

Court stood firm in the dark; insects chirped and buzzed and trilled and clicked in the scrub around him. He looked back over his shoulder towards the dark terminal. A black four-door sedan pulled up to the employee access door.

"Dammit!" he shouted into the night.

"Let's go!" barked Gennady, angrier this time.

Court looked ahead at the aircraft still two hundred yards ahead. He thought about his fifty pounds of gear. He wished he had some of it with him now.

Gennady asked, "What is the matter with—"

Court interrupted him. He pointed a threatening finger in his face. "Don't leave me! I'll be right back. Do *not* take off until I get back!" He knew if he invoked the name of Gregor Sidorenko this pilot would do exactly as he said, but he was not about to violate operational security to *that* level just yet. Instead he just threw out a "Please!" He did not wait for a response. Instead, he turned on his heel and began running back to the terminal. "Dammit!"

19

The Gray Man had sprinted one hundred yards through the warm night, with no real plan other than to find the woman and to figure out some way he might help her. He wasn't going to pick a fight with an airport full of secret police and soldiers, so he didn't have any real idea where he was going with this impetuous charge, but he'd been around long enough to put some confidence in his powers of improvisation. Ahead he saw the bright shaft of artificial light from the opening of the terminal's employee access door. The two NSS men appeared in the beam, and behind them, two armed GOS army sergeants pushed Ellen Walsh forward and into the back of the four-door sedan. The soldiers climbed in on either side of her, and the NSS men got in the front. The vehicle pulled away, in the opposite direction of Gentry's run, just as he arrived at the terminal's side entrance. He knew they were heading to the exit of the airport, taking the woman away.

And he knew where they were going.

The NSS detention facility in Al Fashir.

The Ghost House.

"Dammit!" he shouted again as he stopped running. Two airport guards eyed him from the doorway, vaguely curious perhaps, but they did not come outside.

Gentry looked around for a vehicle but found nothing. Instead, he turned around and began walking back towards the aircraft. As soon as he left the dim lights coming from the terminal and disappeared from the guards' sight, he began running again. This time he turned around the side of the building and shot between several shipping containers that had been lined up to serve as mobile offices for some NGO that had apparently long since pulled up stakes. Passing these, his feet left the warm tarmac and sank into thatch-covered sand and hard dirt. A small hill rose towards the end of the airport property, another fifty yards away. There was a metal fence here. Court had noticed that it ran alongside a reasonably well-trafficked road, back when there was still enough light to see this far into the distance. Now he did not see any headlights, but neither did he see any guards out here in the desolate darkness. He ran past the wreckage of a hulking, high-winged, twin prop aircraft that had obviously crashed and then been towed here to await the eventual burial in the sand that would occur over years of swirling winds.

Court skidded to a halt at the base of the fence. It stood ten feet high and was topped with thick coils of razor wire. He untied his boots but left them on his feet, then climbed the fence quickly and adroitly. At the top he held on with one hand just below the razor wire, pulled off one boot and then the other. He struggled to put his hands into the boots, again one at a time, the skin between his toes burned as they pinched in the chain links, supporting all the weight of his body that he could not hold up with one hand. He pushed into the razor wire with his boot-covered hands, doing his best to cover as wide an area as possible. He pressed the dangerous barbs tight against the top of the metal fence with the thick rubber soles. Then, while keeping the boots stationary, his feet continued up the fence until they were near the top, positioning his body like a swimmer on the block waiting for the starting gun. From here he shifted all his body weight to his arms, kicked his legs up until he was in a sloppy handstand position on the top of the fence, and then let his legs continue forward. He completed the flip and went airborne, his boots flung off his hands as he left the razor wire, and he landed in a rolling heap in the dirt on the outside of the airport grounds.

He was not hurt, maybe a small bruise or two on his arm and back, and he found his first boot immediately in the dark. It took a few seconds for him to realize that the other was still stuck in the razor wire, and he had to climb back up and tear it free. Another thirty seconds to retie his laces, and he headed down the small hillock towards the road.

Court had not studied a map of Al Fashir, wasn't certain he'd even heard of the place before that afternoon. But he had sat in the cockpit and paid attention to the terrain and the surrounding area as the Il-76 flew its base leg alongside the airport. From this he knew that the road the NSS vehicle was taking headed off to the north for a mile or so before meeting up with the highway that ran east and west. At this intersection they would make a right turn, and it would take them several more minutes to get to Al Fashir town. Court knew that if he could commandeer some sort of vehicle, he could get in front of them and intercept them before getting to the Ghost House. A light ahead of him on the road at first filled him with optimism. Within seconds he saw the single headlight of what he assumed to be a motorcycle approaching. This was ideal. Court would like nothing better than getting on a bike. He could skirt through traffic at his own speed and find Ellen Walsh and her captors.

He ducked back into the dark to await its arrival.

Of course he had no clue where to find the Ghost House, but he knew that virtually everyone in this town would know the location of the secret police's clandestine prison. He doubted anyone would walk with him up to the front door and knock, but he did not expect too much trouble getting directions from a local on a street corner if Court whipped out a small wad of Sudanese pounds.

Court hurried to the side of the road now. His plan was border-line brutal, certainly cruel, but he did not doubt its effectiveness. He would wait for the driver of the motorcycle to get within a few yards of him, and then he would step into the road and knock the man and his vehicle over. He prepared himself for this action, but noticed the bike was moving slower than it should have been with so much open road. He then presumed it to be only a motor scooter, which would still be an effective vehicle to make his way through narrow streets and thick third-world traffic, even if it wasn't going to move very fast, even with an open throttle.

But then, after an eternity, the vehicle appeared behind its single headlight, and Gentry cussed aloud. It was a tiny motorized rickshaw, a scooter with a covered three-seat bench behind the driver, a feeble two-stroke engine, and a wide tricycle-type rear axle.

Gentry was pissed. This was probably the slowest vehicle in existence with the exception of a donkey cart. Still, he recognized it would be a hell of a lot better than jogging, so he stepped into the dark road. He did not try to topple the little vehicle; instead, he just flagged it down.

The rickshaw pulled over. A black man in a turban sat behind the handlebars. "Taxi?" he asked, no shock or surprise at the sight of a bearded white man in a military-style jumpsuit. Apparently Court wasn't the first foreigner to wander stupidly around the darkened suburbs of Al Fashir. He climbed in hurriedly, and the driver twisted the throttle forward on his handlebars, sending the machine slowly again on its way with a whine like a lawn mower in thick, wet grass.

Court told the driver to take him into Al Fashir's souk, or marketplace. Every town has a market, he assumed, and apparently this backwater was no different, as the driver did not press him further. Instead, as the fortyish Darfuri tribesman set off for town, he turned back to his fare and offered to sell him a drink from a tiny cooler he kept in the backseat. Court checked it out, saw a half dozen bottles of tepid water, the bottle caps' safety seals broken. Gentry admitted to himself that he *was* thirsty, but he wasn't about to chug old plastic bottles refilled with local tap water. Also on the floor he found a small repair kit for the rickshaw in a burlap bag. There was nothing of interest to him in the kit, save for a single red road flare and a small, rusty screwdriver.

Court pocketed the flare and the tool as the first vestiges of an idea began forming in his mind.

They headed east for no more than three minutes before they

hit the bustle of the city. Nearly a fourth of the vehicles on the road were powered by donkeys instead of engines, and suddenly the two-stroke job under the seat of the rickshaw did not seem quite so impotent in comparison. Another third of the vehicles on the road were NGOs of some sort: UN, UNICEF, CARE, the Red Cross. Additionally there were some UNAMID military vehicles on the road and GOS army men on motorcycles. The last 10 percent of traffic were locals in cars and trucks. They were very much a minority on their own streets.

He pressed the driver to hurry more than once, but even with the slow speed he imagined himself still to be well in front of the NSS sedan, which had gone far in a different direction to meet up with the highway. He knew, however, it would only take one traffic jam or missed turn to make this a close race.

They pulled up to the marketplace and stopped. "Here is the souk. Twenty pounds."

Court said, "I want you to take me to the Ghost House." He was hardly surprised that the man jerked his head around to look back at his passenger. No one *wanted* to go to the secret police interrogation facility. Court had already yanked a fat wad of cash from his wallet. He held it up for the man to see.

But, whatever the value of the currency in his hand, it was not enough. "I don't know this place. Here is the souk. You want a drink? Many soda stands still open. Tea stands. It very nice."

"I don't want a fucking soda. I want the NSS headquarters. Just get me near there. Show me where it is. I will walk the rest of the way." Court now lifted another lump of wrinkled notes out of his wallet. From the light of a storefront powered by a roaring and smoking gas generator, Gentry looked into the wide eyes of his driver. He nodded slowly at the money, then up at the insane American.

"I take you two blocks from there. I take you to soccer stadium."

"The soccer stadium is two blocks from the Ghost House?"

"Yes," said the man with a nod. Court could see the nervous tension; he felt sure the man was telling the truth.

121

"Good. More money if you go faster!" The man turned back to face the road ahead, leaned forward into his handlebars, and seemed to twist out another horsepower or two from the impotent machine.

Just then Gentry heard a noise high in the sky above him. He knew what it was instantly; he really did not even have to look. But he did look and saw the silhouette of an Ilyushin Il-76MF climbing into the starry heavens.

"Motherfucking Russians," he muttered, but he couldn't say he blamed them.

Court felt incredibly alone, but there was no time to think of that now. He needed a plan.

In seconds they were stuck in the evening traffic again. Stationary in the middle of the street. Court's driver's honking was lost in the melody of louder car horns. A donkey cart on the right of the rickshaw pushed forward a few feet, and Court caught a glimpse of the unpaved promenade running alongside the road. There, under the light of a bare bulb hanging out a second-floor window, a man sat on an overturned metal bucket resting on the ground. Beside him was a container the size of a beer keg, with a rubber hose snaking out of the top of it and looping down the side. In front of the contraption stood a handwritten sign in wood, the writing in both Arabic and English: Gas. The man picked at his dinner of rice with his fingers.

Immediately Gentry leaned into the front of the rickshaw, reached past the driver, and pulled the keys from the ignition. "I'll be right back," Court said, but this did not stop the man from shouting at him when Gentry left him behind in the center of the busy street as he ran to the gas man.

Court pulled out his wallet hurriedly, yanked another fold of Sudanese pounds free, and handed them to the man. The elderly gasoline vendor took them and stood, nodded quickly, but then looked the hurried Westerner over curiously. Court didn't get it for a second, so he said, "Gas!" pointing at the keg. Behind him cars and motorbikes began honking, and those on horse and mule carts began yelling at the stationary rickshaw blocking traffic. Court shouted "Gas!" one more time, then realized the vendor was looking to see just what the hell he was supposed to siphon the gas into. Court had no container, and he drove no vehicle. Court pulled another note from his wallet and pointed to the metal bucket the man had been using as a stool. Court picked it up himself, flipped it over. It would hold two gallons or so. The man looked at him like he was crazy, but he nevertheless began sucking on the hose to draw the gas out into the tin bucket.

It took a minute and a half to siphon the fuel and complete the transaction, and by the time Gentry returned to his tiny taxi scooter, he was certain he was the most hated man in all of Al Fashir. Horns honked in chorus behind him. He handed the keys back to the driver, who continued to berate him while he restarted the little putt-putting motor of the vehicle. Court crammed the metal bucket on the floor between his feet. Then he grabbed a fistful of money out of his wallet and, reaching up, waved it next to the complaining Darfuri tribesman. The man shut up and reached for it, but Gentry pulled it back to him, patted the man on the back instead as if to say, "Soon, my friend."

The driver pressed on. As he did so, Court opened the cooler of bottled water next to him on the bench. Even in poor lighting from the buildings as they passed them and the headlights of the other cars on the street, he could see black sediment in the liquid. Drinking it would have probably given him dysentery, but he was not going to drink it. Instead he doused himself with it, completely covering his face, his arms, and his clothing. He pulled out a second bottle and did it again, drenching himself in water.

The driver looked back over his shoulder at this odd fare, but Court motioned for him to keep his eyes pointed forward.

Court opened a third bottle and then a fourth, pouring water all over his clothing and hair and face.

The Darfuri man soon pulled over next to a large but aged soccer stadium. He pointed at the busy intersection ahead and then gestured with his hands that it was just to the left. He turned fully around in his seat with his hand out for his money now, and Court reached deep into his wallet. The American pulled out a wad of bills of a different color than the Sudanese man expected, but the Darfuri knew euros when he saw them. He nodded slowly, then became more serious when he saw how much he was being handed. Four hundred euros was enough to buy a brand-new rickshaw, the driver realized, and he could not help himself from swallowing hard.

It took a few seconds more for the turbaned driver to realize that that was exactly what the *kawaga* was asking him to do. After the driver took the money, the waterlogged white man with the tin bucket of gasoline stepped out of the back, unzipped his jump-suit, stripped to his soaking wet shorts and T-shirt, and handed the jumpsuit over to the driver. It did not take the Sudanese man long to realize he was being asked—no, forced—to change clothes with the white man. He climbed out of his vehicle grudgingly but quickly and took off his clothes right there on the side of the street. Passersby stopped and stared. The *kawaga* pulled the long tunic and the brown pants on, pocketed the screwdriver and the flare, cinched the pants tight with a leather belt, and reached up and took the turban off the Darfuri's head and used it to wrap his own face and head in a white mask. Without a word or a nod, the white man removed the cap from the gas tank of the covered scooter and tossed it in the road. Then he hurriedly climbed behind the handlebars and positioned the bucket tightly between his knees. He opened one more bottle of water and doused his new clothing with it, and then he jammed the throttle forward, and the rusty red machine leapt forward and back out into traffic.

The Darfuri driver stood in the dirt under a streetlamp next to the soccer stadium, no shirt on his back, scratching his head as a crowd converged on him with unbridled curiousity.

Court hoped he was not too late. Once Ellen Walsh was taken through the front gates of the Ghost House, it would be suicide to even attempt trying to get to her, and it would do nothing to help her chances. He just had to do something before the NSS car made it in.

Just up ahead at the last intersection he saw another traffic jam of crap cars, beasts of burden pulling wood and rusted carts, and NGO vehicles. He jacked the handlebars to the left and bumped up on a little curb, drove straight through men walking home from work or out for dinner or an evening stroll. White-turbaned men leapt to the side as if for dear life, though the rickshaw was probably not big or powerful enough to do much more than cause bruises or a few broken bones to a pedestrian.

He tried to picture the scene ahead because he had no real idea what he was going to find around the corner. But he'd seen his share, more than his share, of secret police HQs in third-world, ex-colonial outposts. There would be a squat building with a fortified wall around it, a front gate with a guard shack and some sort of movable barrier. Often there would be a sandbagged machine gun emplacement or two, or even an armored personnel carrier at the front.

This damn Canadian investigator better appreciate this, he thought to himself. Then he remembered that if not for him, she would be nowhere near the predicament from which he was now trying to extract her.

He was at the left turn now, leaving more screaming and shouting and horn honking behind him. He pulled too hard for the turn, and the little two-stroke machine rocked high, its left rear wheel off the ground for a few seconds before banging back to the dusty pavement, causing the cab of the vehicle to bottom out with an ear-piercing scrape. Gasoline sloshed on his pants leg, but he'd managed to save eighty percent of the contents of the bucket by lifting his opposite knee to compensate for the tilting in his seat.

And then there it was, right ahead of him and on the right. The wall was lower than he had expected, and the building was taller and a bit more ornate than he had envisioned. There was an access gate with a guardhouse on the near side of the road, and some sort of tin-shack bunker on the far side.

And there was the NSS car, about to make a right turn at the intersection ahead, just beyond the entrance to the Ghost House.

Shit, thought Court. Not going to make it.

But he floored the little rickshaw and leaned forward, hoped against hope something would slow down the sedan's advance on the entrance.

A donkey pulling a cart overladen with plastic watering cans entered the intersection in front of the NSS sedan, causing it to slow and honk. It was twenty-five yards tops to the entry drive of the Ghost House, and Court knew this was his chance, he *would* get to the sedan in time, though his odds for success at any part of his plan after that were still pretty lousy. He grabbed the bucket of gas by its rickety handle, held the rickshaw straight by its throttle, and barreled in on the stationary car. Just as the donkey cart began rolling out of the way and the sedan started to drift forward again, Gentry let go of the handlebar, spun out of his seat, and leapt out of the rickshaw. Though he stumbled forward and splashed another twenty-five percent of the gasoline from the bucket, he remained on his feet, running into screeching and honking traffic.

The rickshaw slammed into the front passenger-side door of the NSS car at twenty miles an hour, jolting and denting the car with a crunching crash and knocking it into the wooden cart in front of it.

20

Horns honked at Gentry, at the accident itself, in annoyance of the delay this would surely cause. Animals brayed at the loud noise of the crash and the ensuing protesting blarings.

The NSS car had stopped in the middle of the intersection, its headlights reflecting off of steam pouring forth from its grill. The rickshaw had bounced away and rolled on its side in the street. Gas flowed from its open tank.

Court arrived at the passenger-side door just as the dazed NSS commander kicked it open. Gentry grabbed the small bespectacled man by his necktie and pulled him free of the wreckage and then let him go, using both hands now to douse the bucket of gasoline over the man's head.

The two soldiers were piling out of the back of the car, and the driver was slowly exiting his side, when Court pulled the road flare from his pants pocket, pulled the lid off the top, and struck the wick on the head. With an explosion of fire and sparks, he held the flare far away from his body with his left hand. With his right he grabbed the NSS commander by his collar and pulled him tight in a headlock.

The soldiers from the back of the car leveled their guns and screamed at him.

The NSS subordinate moved around the car, his pistol high in his hands, and screamed at him.

Three uniformed guards from the Ghost House approaching the wreck lifted their rifles to their shoulders and screamed at him.

Court stood in the middle of the intersection, holding the commander tight by the neck. He spoke softly into his ear in English.

"Reach for your gun, and I burn you."

The man said nothing, but his hands pushed out wide from his body, away from the holster on his hip under his suit coat.

Court whipped the sparkling flare close to the man and then jerked it away quickly. "If they shoot me, I drop this. If I drop this, you die. Understand?"

The man clearly understood. He raised his arms high and began shouting into the chaos around him. Court understood the Sudanese Arabic. "Lower your guns! Put them down! Put them down! Do not shoot!"

No one lowered their guns, but no one fired them either. Court continued to yank the small NSS man to the left and to the right, tried to keep himself a moving target in the hopes that some sniper on the Ghost House roof or some overzealous sentry or passing cop might think twice instead of feeling confident enough to pop a shot off in his direction. While he did this, careful to keep the buzzing and burning road flare near enough to the secret police commander to be dangerous but not so close as to start an inferno, he chanced a look in the back of the black sedan. Ellen Walsh had not moved. She stared at him, her wide stunned eyes obvious under the car's interior light.

"You okay?" He asked. He moved around quickly to the other side of the car, still trying to preclude any hot shots from feeling lucky. "You okay?" he asked from the left of the vehicle now. She nodded blankly, and he worried she may have been in shock. "Pay attention! Get in the driver's seat! Hurry! Now! Get it together!" He moved forward and back a few feet. Ducked down, nearly pulling the secret policeman to the pavement. The blaring horns of the cars and trucks and bleating animals of the carts crowding the intersection continued unabated. Court knew the road flare would not last another minute. In sixty seconds he'd have to either be gone from the scene or be prepared to torch the scene.

He strongly preferred the former.

Ellen finally scooted out of the backseat. She seemed confused more than terrified. He yelled at her mercilessly, a profanity-laced tirade designed to focus her and bring her back into the here and now, to convince her that all the danger around her was real, and her own actions were the only thing that would save her from it.

"That's right," his tone softened as she sat behind the wheel. "You're doing good. See if the engine will start." The deputy NSS man from the airport backed away from the car slowly, moving to Court's left. Gentry worried the man was thinking about taking a shot, planning first to get away from the fireball that was sure to follow. His boss would die, no doubt, but for all Gentry knew, this clown was next in line for a promotion and saw an opportunity to create the vacancy he needed to make that happen.

Behind this man nearly a dozen African Union peacekeepers arrived, jumping out of the back of an APC. They began waving their rifles around at the scene demonstratively but warily, not sure what the hell was going on but damn sure they weren't going to let anyone in the crowd target them without blowing the entire fucking crowd apart in a fusillade of bullets.

Perfect. There were now easily twenty-five guns pointing at Gentry, and he had no doubt that the vast majority of people pointing these guns didn't really give a damn if this shitty little hostage of his burned alive.

Time to go!

Ellen got the car started, and Court pulled his NSS captive up the north–south portion of the intersection a few feet, told Ellen to drive alongside him. She backed the sedan away from the donkey cart, and the rear bumper scooted the demolished rickshaw a few feet before she put it in drive. Court let go of the secret policeman's neck but continued to wave the flare over him as he reached across the man's body and pulled the pistol from his hostage's hip holster. He racked the slide one-handed by hooking the rear sights on his belt and slamming the gun down and forward. Court now pointed this gun at the other NSS man, who seemed to have thought better of his plan to open fire. Gentry imagined this insane intersection full of weapons would only need the pop of a single gunshot to send every last goddamn rifle opening up full auto on the scene. Maybe the other NSS man figured the peacekeepers behind him would obliterate every breathing creature in front of them if he fired a round from his pistol at the white man.

As Ellen drove forward and alongside the Gray Man, he instructed her to continue slowly. He walked backwards, alongside the open left rear door, leaving the NSS commander in the intersection near the broken rickshaw and the smashed donkey cart and the other vehicles stuck in traffic behind the wreckage on three sides. Court pointed the pistol with his right hand, held the last of the burning road flare with his left, but then quickly flung the flare overhanded past the secret policeman and toward the rickshaw. In a swift single motion, while the sputtering flame arced nearer to the scooter with its leaking gas tank, Court Gentry dropped to a low squat, fired two rounds from the pistol, one into the chest of each of the National Security Service operatives. Then he spun low and dove into the backseat of the sedan. "Go! Go! Go! Go!" he screamed.

The rickshaw and the dusty street intersection burst into flames. The whoosh of the ignition of the fuel was audible through the open car door.

Ellen Walsh's foot stomped down on the gas pedal.

The sedan shot forward towards the north.

No one fired a shot at it before it turned to the left forty meters on, disappearing down a side street into the dark, a fireball rising into the sky behind it.

"Where are we going?"

The crewman from the Russian military transport plane, who was obviously no Russian himself, sat in the backseat of the car as Ellen plowed through narrow, congested streets, past gray tin ramshackle buildings and mud-colored single-story walls running on both sides, seemingly in all directions, seemingly for miles. Through intersection after intersection she drove, sometimes getting the four-door up to forty kilometers or so, but often slowing down to a near crawl as she used the front grill to nudge her way through the evening congestion or to push groups of cows or sheep out of the way.

"Where do you want me to go?" she yelled it this time; the man behind her didn't seem to be paying attention.

Finally he answered, his voice softer than back in the intersection. "Just keep going. You're doing great."

Yeah, she allowed herself to realize. I *am* doing great. She'd never in her life experienced shock, and she retained the presence of mind now to wonder if that was this strange sense of calm she was beginning to feel.

"You didn't kill anyone back there, did you?" Ellen asked. Her voice was shaky, confused, she did her best to swallow the flood of emotions that threatened to pour forth at any second.

"Of course not. Just a couple of warning shots. I had to slow them down so we could get clear."

She believed him. He certainly did not sound or act like a man who had just killed another human.

"Where are we going?"

"No place specific. Just keep heading this way."

"Who are you?"

"Not now," was all he would say.

"You aren't Russian," she said, looking at him through the rearview.

"Figured that out? You *are* a special investigator," he replied, sarcastic in a vague way so that Ellen could not discern if he was trying to be playful or cruel.

"American?" She knew that he was from his accent.

But he just repeated, "Not now."

They continued north for a half hour; they spoke little. The American muttered something about needing to change out the vehicle they were in, but he just told her to keep going, as if he could not bring himself to pull over in this town even for a few minutes to find another mode of transportation. He stayed in the backseat. At first she thought he remained back there to keep

131

an eye out the rear window for anyone following, but later she ventured a few glances in her rearview and saw him sitting back there in the dark, just looking out the side windows, as if he were lost as to where to go. He'd seemed resolute enough back with the flare and the pistol and the shouted commands and the little man in the headlock. But now she worried that he had somehow worn himself out, either physically or emotionally, and now she would have to make the decisions.

She said, "I need to get to a phone. Call some people who can help."

"Negative," he replied flatly. "Just keep driving." His voice was unexpectedly strong now.

"We're going to be in the desert soon."

"Not desert. The Sahel."

She looked up in the rearview. "The what?"

"It's scrubland. Between the savannah to the south and the desert to the north. Sparsely populated, hot as a desert, but not the same. The desert starts another hundred miles north of here."

"Okay, whatever the geography is, do we really need to go out there?"

"Yes."

"There won't be phones out there."

"No," he agreed. "There won't. We just need to get off the X for now. We'll find our way back to a safe place later. The National Security Service will be looking hard for us. They'll be listening in on phone lines; they'll have choppers in the air; they'll have the streets and markets and alleys and hotels in Al Fashir covered with informants. We need to just get out into the clear. Hunker down tonight, and then make our way to one of the UN-run IDP camps in the morning."

"I don't have the credentials to get into the UN camps," she protested.

"You didn't have the credentials to arrest a crew of Russian gunrunners either, and you tried that."

She shook her head. "What the hell was I thinking?"

132

"Not a clue, lady," the man said. "I just have to ask. Did you have a plan, other than to threaten them with international indictment and then ask to please use the telephone so that you could turn them in?"

"That was about it," Ellen admitted, shaking her head again at her actions. "I'm a lawyer by training. I've only been with the ICC for a few months. I had the UN documents forged myself; I got tired of sitting in my office and not doing anything. I just wanted to come out here and see Darfur for myself. Nobody from my office knows where I am, what I'm doing."

"Well, you've got guts. I'll give you that." The man's words trailed off at the end, and she got the idea that he did not want to talk anymore.

21

They headed north for another ten minutes. Her attempts to engage the quiet man in conversation were either deftly deflected or outright ignored. On the open road, outside of the city, they picked up speed. The man finally directed her to pull over and to run the car down a gentle draw by the side of the road. She asked about wild animals, and he admitted he had no idea, but he promised she'd be safe. It wasn't that she trusted him—she still didn't know exactly which side this man was on—but she knew she didn't have any other options at the moment. She would do what he said.

The low draw led them to a gully that ran towards a rocky, dry streambed. During the rainy season, in another couple of months, it would be suicide to hide in this ditch. The rills cutting into the scrubland all around would send hundreds of thousands of gallons of runoff down here just minutes after a concentrated rain shower. But right now it seemed safe enough. Thatched brush rose several feet high on either side of the dusty gully. The tops of some of the bushes had interwoven, creating a tight canopy above. It was only six feet high or so, but Court directed her to push the car into the brush and turn off the engine.

The hot metal clicked and clanged when she did so.

"Check the glove box. Any water?" He asked. She opened it and found only a plastic bag of lemon candies. Court climbed out, dug through the bushes, and checked the trunk but found nothing there either.

"We'll be okay tonight. We'll get some water in the morning."

"What do we do now?" She looked back towards the man; he was invisible in the dark now. She heard him reposition himself, lift his legs up onto the little backseat.

"Try to get some sleep."

"What do I call you?"

"I'm the only other person here. If you are talking, I will pretty much assume you are talking to me."

"Touché," she said, though she did not like smart-asses. She did her best to make herself comfortable in the front seat. She swung her body around so that her back was to the passenger door. It had been smashed on the outside by the rickshaw, but the inner frame was intact. She did this to try to get face-to-face with the man in the back who was prone with his back on the driver's side.

"I'm Ellen, if you had forgotten."

"Yep."

A long pause. "You're not going to talk to me?"

"We both need to rest. We're not going to drive out of here tomorrow. Too dangerous. We'll go up to the road on foot and try to flag down a friendly vehicle."

"How do we know if it's friendly before we flag it down?"

She heard more than saw him shrug his shoulders. "No idea, to tell you the truth," he said, and again, she could tell he was trying to end the conversation.

"Are you really a crewman for Rosoboronexport?"

No answer.

"Some sort of mercenary?"

No answer.

"A spy?"

"Go to sleep, Ellen."

She let out a frustrated sigh. "Just give me a name. Make it up if you want to, but give me *something* I can call you."

"Call me Six," he said after several seconds.

"Dear Lord," she replied. "Does that mean there are five more out there just like you?"

"Go to sleep, Ellen," he said again, and this time she endeavored to leave him alone.

One minute later she realized she could not sleep. After what had happened in the past hour, who could sleep? Plus it was miserable in the smelly car.

"Six, can we open some windows?"

"Negative."

"Negative? Why don't you just say 'no'?"

"No."

She sat up in the seat, leaned a little closer to the man in the dark. "No, we can't open the windows?"

"We can't open the windows."

"Why not? It's so hot in here. There's no way I can sleep in this heat."

Six responded matter-of-factly, "Scorpions, camel spiders, pythons, poison—"

"Okay, okay! We'll keep the windows up."

Six said nothing.

"Why did you come back for me?"

"Dunno."

"Yes, you do. You can talk to me." Then she said, "*Please* talk to me. I'm scared, my heart is still racing, there is no way I can sleep like this. I just need to talk a few minutes. You don't have to tell me anything top secret or whatever, but please help me out here."

The man remained silent. She could barely see his silhouette in the darkness, and his silhouette did not move a muscle. Of the expression on his face, even whether or not his eyes were closed, Ellen had not a clue.

She was so certain the man had turned to a statue she was startled when he finally did respond.

"I came back for you because it's my fault you are here."

"Your fault? How? Why?"

"I came here to do a job. An important job. A good job, actually, one you would approve of."

He said nothing else. He seemed to have chosen those few words he did say extremely carefully, laboring over every phrase. She encouraged him, "And?"

"And then you got in the way. I tried to get you out of the way the easiest way I could think of. It didn't work."

"Or it worked too well."

"Yeah, I guess that's it. Didn't know you were ICC. I thought you were just some annoying busybody."

She was grateful for the conversation, for feeling like she'd pried open a corner of the tough shell of this mysterious American to get a tiny glimpse of what was inside. She said, "That's actually not a bad description for my job with the ICC."

Ellen saw the silhouette change, movement in the whiskers of the beard on the side of his face, and she imagined him smiling. It was difficult to do.

"Anyway, I just wanted you on ice till we took off. Then the NSS got involved. They were going to kill you."

"You think so?"

"I know so."

"How do you know?"

"I know men like that. They'd be worried about their own necks more than anything. They'd realize how bad they'd messed up letting you get that close, and they'd do the one thing they knew how to do to make it better."

With the stranger's calm proclamation that she had narrowly avoided death, the weight of everything that had happened in the past three hours seemed to crush in on her all at once. Ellen put her head in her hands, felt her fingers tingle and shake. Her entire body went slack, tired, achy. She looked back up to the man in the dark.

"I . . . I just . . . " Ellen Walsh hesitated, but then she hurriedly spun around in the front seat, fought madly for the door handle of the sedan, wrapped her fingers around it and pulled it open while frantically pushing at the wrecked door with her other hand. She launched her upper torso out into the dark, thick brush, spewing vomit along the way as she did so. After several seconds the wave of nausea subsided, and she hacked and coughed and spat out into the flora of the streambed. A second wave of sickness attacked her, and she succumbed, vomiting again until she retched loudly into the night, her body continuing its convulsions though it had nothing left to expel. She spat again to clear her mouth, began crying openly, her head still hanging out of the car.

And behind her the stranger had not moved.

"I ... I'm so sorry," was all she could say. Her embarrassment only made her feel foolish.

"Don't worry," came a surprisingly soft voice from behind her.

She wiped her mouth on the sleeve of her blouse.

Six said, "It happens to me all the time."

It took her a full minute to get her body back inside the vehicle, to get the door closed, herself twisted into a reclining position on the front seat. Her tears and sobs had begun to subside. She wiped her face several more times, cognizant of the gaze of the quiet man in the dark, though she had no way of knowing for sure if his eyes were even open.

Finally, when she had recovered completely except for a few wet sniffs, she asked, "You think we're going to get out of this okay?"

"Yeah, you'll be safe and sound by this time tomorrow."

He sounded certain, and this helped her greatly. But she asked, "What about you?"

He shrugged. "I take it day by day."

She let that go, did not know what it meant but sensed not to press. While she wiped her eyes she asked, "Are you married?"

"Yeah."

Slowly she lowered her arm from her face, looked towards the silhouette in the backseat. "No, you're not. You just lied to me."

"Why do you say that?"

"I don't know, but you are not married."

He nodded; this she saw clearly. "You're right. Impressive."

She sat up straighter, leaned a little closer. Her eyes brightened as if she were playing a game. "Kids?"

"No comment." He had loosened up a little; he was using humor, but he was still very much on guard.

"I can't tell for sure, but I don't think so."

He said nothing.

"Mom, dad?"

"Dad." He answered back quickly, too quickly for her not to believe him.

"Where are you from?"

"Michigan, Detroit."

"Really? Me, too! Originally, I mean, before my family immigrated to Canada. Where did you go to school?"

A long pause. An admission. "Okay, I'm not from Michigan."

Ellen laughed, surprised herself by the loud noise she made in the tight, hot car, "Sucker! Neither am I."

She saw him smile again as he shrugged. "You are pretty good."

With a long sniff and a wider smile she said, "You have no idea."

22

An early April morning on the Sahel begins hot and sunny, gets hotter and sunnier by the hour, with the screech of birds and insects prevalent and energetic in the dry season. In the sweltering sedan, under the thick brown and green brush of the gully, Gentry flicked a centipede from the tip of his nose, tried to fall back asleep, but could not.

He rubbed his eyes, wiped away dried sweat that had formed on his eyelashes and on his forehead during the night. He cracked his window. Instantly fresh air entered the interior, and he inhaled deeply. He'd actually managed a couple hours' sleep, not consecutively, but his body was tuned by half a lifetime of catnapping to get maximum benefit from minimum rest.

In the low light of the morning under the canopy of brush enveloping the car, he tried to plot out his day. He did not have his sat phone, so he couldn't report to Sierra One what had happened. Not that he would have been looking forward to that call. The landing in Darfur was a snafu that was really no one's fault and could have been worked around with relative ease. But everything that had happened since? All the threats to the operation since touchdown in Al Fashir? Court knew good and well that it was all on him. A string of fuckups on his part had put him here, now, and had put the CIA's Operation Nocturne Sapphire, of which he was a crucial part, in mortal jeopardy.

So now what, Gentry? He looked over at the woman. He had

not been this close to a female in a long time, with the exception of a venerable nurse or two in France and a veterinary assistant whose amateur needlework had unquestionably saved his life and the lives of those he went on to save the previous December.

This was different. She slept a few feet from him, calm and quiet now, and as near as he could tell from his limited experience with women, content. He'd heard her toss and turn for hours last night. A few times she'd called out in fright, waking Court in the process, but he had done nothing to help her.

He had no idea what to do. He'd had no training in providing comfort.

She was pretty. His age, with short, reddish-brown hair that lay strewn all over her face as she slept. He respected her being here, in a war zone, even if he did not hold attorneys or international organizations in particularly high regard. The ICC specifically seemed, to a man like Court, to be nothing but a banquet hall full of overeducated and underexperienced bitchers and whiners who had no real enforcement arm or mandate to do what they promised to do. To a man like Court, a one-man judge, jury, and executioner, the ICC seemed incredibly irrelevant out here in the real world.

But he couldn't help but respect the woman. The way she had puffed her little chest out and declared herself an ICC investigator like that was fucking stupid, but it *was* undeniably ballsy. The girl was tough, even if she didn't have the sense to restrain herself from talking too much.

He'd lied to her about killing the two NSS men, but he felt he did that for her own good. He could tell by her questioning him about it that she would not have been able to handle that piece of information at that moment, and he needed her to drive and to keep her wits about her. He *had* to kill them, he knew, because even with the turban wrapped around his face and the change of clothes, they would easily have been able to identify him as the crewman of the Ilyushin who spoke English and French and yelled at the woman. It was lucky for him Ellen Walsh hadn't seen his

141

shooting of them, and he saw no reason to burden her with this knowledge.

She began to stir a bit, licked her lips and rubbed her nose. For an instant he wanted to reach out and brush the hair away from her face. It was a powerful feeling. It reminded him of the feeling he got when he looked across the room at his bottle of pain tablets back in his room in Nice. He knew he shouldn't reach out, but damn if he didn't want to.

Unlike those days in Nice, and some of the days since Nice, he did not reach out for Ellen Walsh.

He'd talked too much last night. He remembered this suddenly, and it pissed him off. The conversation went on for an hour, easily. She'd managed to get more info about him, more true info about him, that is, than anyone else he'd been in contact with in a very long time. Ninety percent of the conversation was about her, her family, friends, experiences with the ICC in Holland, but the 10 percent of the time he was talking, or at least the 5 percent of the time that he was both talking *and* telling the truth, he'd said too much. He hadn't given out one shred of operational intelligence, of this he was sure. But he'd admitted to having parents who divorced when he was young, and a brother who had died a few years back, and why he'd told her this he had no idea. He imagined she made one hell of a good investigator, drawing the truth out of those she interviewed, instilling in them a confidence that the two of them were just chatting while she was, in fact, sucking in each and every word, evaluating them, tossing out those that didn't fit, and building with those remaining words an impression, a picture of the people she was talking to, an understanding of who they were.

And what they were trying to hide.

He had this uncomfortable and unshakable sense that this woman sleeping three feet from him in the hot car, separated only by the backrests of the front seats, had somehow peered deep inside of him and knew his history, his past, his demons that he'd even managed to hide from himself.

It was a sickening feeling, a feeling of exposure, of vulnerability.

142

And yet, at the same time, it gave him an affinity for this woman, made him feel close to her somehow, gave him a sensation to which he was wholly unaccustomed.

Court looked at her a long time. He watched her chest move up and down with the slow breaths of slumber.

Then he turned away from her suddenly and sat up straight in the backseat.

Unfuck yourself, Court! Unfuck yourself this instant! He screamed it at himself internally. *You are shit deep in Indian country. Get your damn head in the game!* Instantly he disliked this woman; she was a threat to him now, a weakness that could kill him.

He could flip a switch in his brain like that. It kept him alone, no question, but it also kept him alive.

Court climbed out of the car, no attempt to do it quietly so that Ellen would not wake. Her beauty rest was not his goddamned problem. He crawled out of the brush hiding the sedan, stood in the gully, then he ripped off the local tunic that he'd taken from the rickshaw driver the evening before, revealing his brown undershirt.

He pulled the gun he'd taken from the NSS commander the evening before, looked it over carefully in the morning light. It was a Bul Cherokee. He found it somewhat ironic that an Arabic-speaking secret policemen should be carrying an Israeli pistol, maybe more ironic that the gun had been used to kill him. It wasn't in Court's top-ten pistol choices, but it sure as shit had done the job on the two NSS goons last night.

He scrambled out of the gully, looked out to the road a quarter mile distant, past dry scrubland, windblown and sand-strewn. He saw no cars on the road. It ran flat and straight to the west, but to the east, back towards Al Fashir, the highway turned into a winding track and disappeared down a gentle slope.

The landscape wasn't barren in the strictest sense. This wasn't a Sahara-like desert of sand dunes; there were sporadic tufts of trees, acacia and baobab, and on-again, off-again grasses and shrubs as far as the eye could see atop the brown earthen crust, a surface that looked as hard as stone and somehow even less inviting.

He heard her climb out of the car below and behind him. It took her a minute to get her bearings and find him there on the crest of the gulley. Wordlessly she appeared next to him, closer than he would have liked, and followed his gaze out on the vast expanse to the east.

"Don't suppose you spy a Waffle House that I'm missing out there in the distance."

Court shook his head.

"Did you get some rest?"

"A little."

"I had some hellacious dreams. But I feel okay. Thanks for talking to me last night."

Court said nothing.

"I got the impression you don't do a lot of that. That you were chatting to help me relax."

Still nothing.

"Anyway ... I appreciate it."

Court just kept looking out at the vast expanse of land in front of him, willing her to take a couple of steps back.

He was scanning the road, searching for vehicles in the hazy distance.

"Did someone get up on the wrong side of the stolen car this morning?"

He realized he was being an ass, was turning his anger at his openness last night into poor manners today. He felt even more childish now than when he woke up. He softened, turned towards her, but did not make eye contact. "I'm fine. Just thinking about today."

"Where are we, exactly? Do we even know?"

"We're about twenty-five klicks from the outskirts of Al Fashir. That's really all I can tell you."

"Where are we going?"

Court looked past Ellen's shoulder and saw it in the distance.

A hazy, smoky apparition on the false horizon a few miles to the west. It rose from the desert track, what passed for a road out here in the Darfuri landscape, and from the size of the dust cloud he knew it was some sort of a convoy of large trucks. It took a while to be sure, but after a time he recognized the white paint on the vehicles. They were not government of Sudan; they were not private cargo transports. No, they belonged to some sort of nongovernmental relief organization.

He pointed to the dust rising in the distance. "We're going where they are going."

Ellen and Court moved quickly together down towards the road. The Canadian woman began running her fingers through her hair, trying to fix herself up a bit. Gentry looked at her with confusion.

"It never hurts to make a good first impression." She said it with a smile, continuing to do what she could to knock dust off her clothes now. "I'd ask you if you had a mirror, but I imagine I'd have better luck finding that Waffle House."

Court was fascinated by the odd behavior of womanhood.

"Listen," Ellen said to him. He could tell before she spoke again that she was a little uncomfortable. "Would it be okay if you stood back, maybe behind one of those little trees or something, while I get them to stop for us? I don't want to scare off what might be our one chance."

Court didn't mind at all. He was a scruffy-looking white man, out here, with a big pistol poorly tucked into his pants. He assumed the convoy would have a contingent of UNAMID soldiers, African Union troops loaned to the United Nations, and he had no doubt they would stop the convoy for a pretty white woman by the side of the road. Court would be perceived as a threat, and from what he'd learned about the UNAMID's reticence to fight *anybody* around here, he didn't want to run the risk of scaring them off. "Yeah, that's not a bad idea. Don't fuck it up, though. Lie down in the road in front of those trucks if you have to, but make sure they stop. And don't tell them you're with the ICC and were involved in the fracas with the secret police. These NGOs aren't looking to get involved in that kind of trouble. Tell them—"

"How 'bout I tell them I'm a reporter and you're my photographer? We got lost in Al Fashir looking for our hotel and then got robbed, taken out here, and dumped alongside the road."

Court was ready to nix her idea for one of his own, but he stopped himself, thought about it, and realized her story was actually pretty good.

Doing his best to mask how impressed he was, he said, "That might work. Let's go with that."

Gentry moved off the road, down a small draw and into some scrub brush. Ellen Walsh walked up the road fifty meters to create some more distance.

Ten minutes later, sixty-one-year-old Mario Bianchi followed the Canadian woman along the sandy dirt road, back down the row of trucks towards her colleague, an American photographer, or so she had just informed him. Fat flies half the size of one euro coins dive-bombed his face. He pulled off his safari hat and shooed them away, but it was a losing battle he soon gave up. It was going to be a hot one today, already at nine a.m. it was nearing thirty-seven degrees. He'd wanted to get his convoy up to Dirra by noon; they'd been running late, even before this surprising event he'd just stumbled onto.

Mario had thought he'd seen everything on the road from Al Fashir to Dirra. Hell, he'd made this 125-kilometer trip well over a hundred times in the past eight years working for, and then running, the Rome-based aid agency Speranza Internazionale. Bianchi shuttled personnel and supplies from all over Europe to the SI-run camps just this side of Dirra, and he had become well accustomed to the heat, the smell, the bugs, the animals, and the dangers of this route.

He'd encountered drunken rebels, highway robbers, government of Sudan military patrols, African Union "peacekeepers," and, of course, the dreaded Janjaweed militia.

But in all his trips along this poor excuse for a road, he'd never run into any English-speaking white Westerners on foot.

What madness.

Mario Bianchi enjoyed an impeccable reputation in the relief agency industry. He'd cultivated this in his forty-year career working all over the African continent. The Italian was known as the man who could get the job done, deftly negotiating not only minefields in the literal sense but also the minefields of street-level diplomacy. No matter who he was working for or where, his convoys got through, his aid camps got built, his clinics got supplied, and his staff got paid. He did this all without discernible trouble from the local heavies. It seemed nothing less than a miracle, considering where he had been and what he had done, but somehow the marauding ADFI. rebels of Laurent Kabila passed him by, the RUF maniacs in Sierra Leone did not harass his efforts to evacuate civilians from their territory, even the teenage Liberian gang, the West Side Boys, who essentially slaughtered most anyone they saw just for shits and grins, pretty much let him do his thing in areas where they held control.

He won award after award all over the First World. Hardly a season of any year went by that did not see Mario Bianchi in a tuxedo walking across a floor-lit stage to civilized but energetic applause by the elite, themselves in tuxedos and evening gowns. His successes had piled up over the years before Darfur, and the atrocities of Darfur called to Signor Mario Bianchi the way a flame calls to a moth.

Here in Darfur his reputation had reached near mythical proportions. Somehow, when the UN wouldn't dare run convoys without escorts, when private relief concerns were hunkered down in Khartoum, too bloodied and battered by the indiscriminate slaughter of Darfur to actually *go* to Darfur to work, Speranza Internazionale convoys continued in the region; their IDP camps and clinics and warehouses and water stations remained in operation. Of course, there were sporadic raids by the Janjaweed and even the local rebels, but they were a small fraction of what any other group had experienced in the region when they dared open up shop in the Land of the Fur.

It was thought Bianchi's successes were a result of his powerful personality, that he had somehow been able to cajole the devils of Africa for decades to permit his organization's coexistence.

But that was not it at all. Bianchi was, behind the false veneer of do-gooder naïveté, in truth, a deeply cynical man. A half century in Africa would do that to anyone, but the manifestation of his cynicism was a cold, brutal, realpolitik that, most would agree, had no place in the world of relief organizations.

The truth of Mario Bianchi's success stemmed from one simple, common act.

Mario paid bribes.

Big bribes.

To everyone.

The West Side Boys in Liberia did not hassle his local operation because he paid them tens of thousands of dollars to let him work. Surely if the well-intentioned Americans and Europeans who donated money to his organization knew that a major portion of their tax-deductible donations was immediately converted into baksheesh that fourteen-year-old Liberian gunmen used to buy ganja, bullets, and porno tapes, the spigot of privately donated aid would be shut off instantly. If these same donors had a clue that after the Congolese death squads took payments for access from Speranza Internazionale, they immediately demanded payment from all NGOs working in their area of influence, and when the principled among them refused to contribute, they were targeted and butchered, thereby leaving SI as virtually the only relief agency in eastern Congo, well, they could be forgiven for feeling somewhat sullied by their well-intentioned funding of butchery.

And here in Darfur, it continued. American film stars created advertisements at the SI camps, money poured in, and the money went, in no small part, to the Janjaweed killers who roamed north Darfur and raped and killed and burned, did so on the backs of the best camels from Chad, with the best AK-47s from Egypt, communicated with the best satellite phones from Japan, all paid for with American and European money.

Bianchi justified it easily. He was here, and he was working. He did what he had to do, and who the hell were you to judge him from your armchair while he was swatting flies out of his nose in forty-degree Celsius heat on a dirt road in the center of hell?

And now his cynicism applied to his present situation. Two American journalists alone, out here in the Sahel? If he were honest with himself, he would admit that he now wished he'd ordered his drivers to continue on, to leave the white woman by the side of the road. Freelance reporters operating without GOS minders in Darfur were serious troublemakers, as far as Bianchi's operation was concerned. He had to work *with* the leaders of the Sudan—rat bastards one and all—not against them. Even picking up this woman, taking her to Dirra, was dangerous to his organization. If the GOS somehow found out what he had done, he'd little doubt there would be repercussions from Khartoum that could hurt the flow of aid to his camps. Sure, he could bribe his way out of it, but the economic downturn in the First World had affected donations, and there was only so much in bribes that he could dole out in this economy.

Bianchi saw the white man ahead.

"Where is his camera? You said he was a photographer."

"He is. Like I said, robbers stole our car last night. Everything was in it. We've been out here for hours waiting for the right people to come along."

"You are twenty-five kilometers outside Al Fashir," he told her.

"Hey, don't look at me, I wasn't driving."

Mario did not doubt the woman. Highway bandits worked the road between Al Fashir and Dirra. In the rainy season, when the roads were slow and breakdowns were common, SI tried to travel with an UNAMID armed escort whenever possible, since it was impossible to bribe *every* Darfuri farmer or herder with an AK. But this time of year they could, more or less, race on by most any small group of men bent on doing them harm.

149

Except for the Janjaweed, whom he paid well so that they would leave his convoys alone.

The Italian was just a few steps from the American man now, the lone white talking to some of SI's African drivers and freight loaders who'd left their vehicles to smoke by the side of the road. The American did not have any equipment with him, not even a pack on his back. He wore a sweat-stained brown T-shirt and some sort of local black pants. His T-shirt rode up on his back when he turned.

The man was bearded and tan, and grime from the Sahel covered the parts of his face that the beard did not. He spoke in French to the locals. French was not uncommon here, as it was a common language in Chad, and Chad was just one hundred miles to the west.

The American was facing the opposite direction. When he reached to shake the hand of another of his employees, a young Darfuri loader, Mario saw the butt of a pistol on his right hip.

The Italian relief coordinator's mouth dropped wide. He could not believe this man dared to carry a gun. An American cowboy! And he expected to just jump on one of the Speranza Internazionale trucks and get a ride out of here to safety? He would bring nothing but danger with that instrument of evil tucked so cavalierly in his drawstring pants.

Without a word to the American, Mario Bianchi angrily walked up behind him and reached out to disarm him.

And that, as it turned out, proved to be an *extremely* bad idea.

23

Putting one's hand on the personal weapon of a man with Gentry's training and disposition might not have been quite as dangerous as sticking one's arm in a rusty bear trap, but it was damn close. As soon as Court felt the pressure, long before Mario's fingers had fully wrapped around the grip, and way before he'd begun to tug the gun out of his pants, the American assassin spun towards the threat, used the momentum in his turning torso to sweep his right arm back up with incredible power and speed, knocked the arm of the threat up and away from his gun. His turn continued, and with his left hand shooting across his body, he reached in front of the threat's face, swept his left leg out behind his threat's legs, and slammed his left hand back hard under the threat's chin. This sent the man reeling backwards, over the leg behind him, falling onto his back and into the cloud of dust kicked up by Gentry's flurry of movement.

Gentry drew his gun like a phantom's blur, pointed it at the threat on the ground, and then scanned the area for more attackers.

Ellen stood ten feet away, her face white with horror.

Five minutes later all was neither forgiven nor forgotten, but the sixty-year-old Italian *had* been hauled back to his feet, brushed off, and his hat had been returned to his head. He needed a minute to compose himself, so he sat on the running board of one of the

151

trucks, drinking a cold orange soda and smoking a cigarette. Ellen Walsh sat with him and spewed apologies, more like a diplomat than the lawyer she was, or the journalist she claimed to be. Court stood off the side of the road by himself, a pariah to all, for what he saw as simply having the temerity to carry a fucking pistol in the middle of a fucking war.

"No guns! No guns!" One of the African aid drivers, a middle-aged man with silver hair, stood ten yards away from the American and waved his hand in a no-no gesture over and over as he chastised.

"You aren't getting my gun," Court said, definitively.

"No guns. No guns!" Court listened to what was, apparently, the only two English words this man knew, over and over and over, and watched him wag his finger back and forth.

"Say that one more time, dickhead," Court snapped. The man did just that—twice more, actually—before he stopped and stepped to the side to allow his boss and the white woman access. From their gait and fixed expressions, Court could see that Ellen and Signor Bianchi were still mad.

Court looked to Ellen. "You don't put your hand on someone else's weapon," he said.

"You mentioned that already, Six," she responded angrily. "Look. *I'm* riding to Dirra with them. They will still take you along, as a personal favor to me, if and *only if* you give Signor Bianchi the pistol."

"What's he going to do with it?"

Mario Bianchi spoke for himself. He was still rubbing the back of his neck. He wondered aloud if there was a physical therapist or a chiropractor at his Dirra clinic doing volunteer work today. Then said, "I will throw the gun out in the desert. What were *you* going to do with a gun?"

Court rolled his eyes. "I might have come up with something."

"We don't need guns in our convoy. We aren't looking for trouble."

Court eyed the older Italian for a long time. Finally he said,

"That's the funny thing about trouble. Sometimes *it* comes looking for *you*."

Bianchi's stare was every bit as intense as Gentry's; it conveyed the same measure of loathing for the man in front of him. "You do not get in one of my trucks with that gun."

This was a dangerous waste of time, and Court knew it. No other car had passed in the ten minutes they had been in the road with the Speranza Internazionale convoy. If he wanted to get out of here before either brigands, the GOS Army, or the secret police happened by, he was going to have to play along. With an exasperated sigh he drew his weapon. Bianchi reached out for it, but Gentry turned away from him, back towards a shallow dry streambed on the south side of the road. He dropped the magazine from the pistol and thumbed the bullets out onto the ground, kicked them down the indentation. Some fell into the cracks of the dry earth, some remained visible. Then he ejected the round from the chamber and disassembled the weapon, pulling off the slide, popping out the slide spring, the barrel. He threw these items as far as he could in the distance.

Ellen stepped up to him. Her voice was softer; she wanted to put the matter behind them. "Now then. Was that so hard?"

Court looked out at the vast landscape and scratched a fresh sand flea bite on his left wrist.

"I'll let you know in a couple of hours."

Ten minutes later Court was in the center seat of the third truck of four in the convoy. He could see little out the windshield ahead save for the dust of the two vehicles in front of them. Ellen was with Mario in the lead vehicle. The Italian had segregated the two, probably, thought Court, so that the geezer could hit on the dust-covered but still attractive Canadian. In the cab with Gentry was Rasid, the white-haired driver, and Bishara, a young loader for SI. Bishara spoke surprisingly good English, even if his geography wasn't quite as practiced. He asked Court if he was from the same town as David Beckham. Court said no, ignored him mostly, and kept his eyes peeled out the windows. He knew they weren't free of the NSS just yet. It would be another couple of hours to Dirra, Mario had told them. They should arrive just about midday. Once there, he would get Ellen to safety in the Speranza Internazionale camp for internally displaced people. She would have access to communications there and could arrange some way out of here either via air with a helicopter or overland with an escort of UNAMID troops. Court, on the other hand, planned to hire a car and driver to take him right back to Al Fashir. In the city he would find someone who could sell him a black market mobile phone, and he would call Sid, put as much blame for his missing the Ilyushin flight on the Russian flight crew, the pilot's canoodling with the girl from the ICC, and he would get Sid to find him some other way out of Al Fashir. If he could do all this in a day and a half, he would still just be able to make it to Suakin in time for the operation there.

He'd be cutting it close as it was, and he just hoped there were no more snags along the way.

Court sipped a bottle of tepid water that Bishara had passed him. He'd checked it carefully before opening it to make sure it was not a refilled container. The two SI Darfuris were listening to awful music on a poorly tuned transistor radio that hung right behind Gentry's head on the latch to the sliding access port to the cargo hold of the truck. The radio coms between the trucks were all but drowned out by the wailing away of some woman. Bishara sang alone for a moment until the older Rasid laughed and joined in.

The men continued singing into the next song, then the next. Court wished, momentarily, that he still had his gun on his hip and was still waiting in the heat by the side of the road for a ride.

Bishara only stopped his singing to question Court about various American hip-hop artists, a subject on which the Gray Man was not terribly well versed. He continued ignoring the kid, who finally went back to his music.

From time to time the convoy radio would crackle to life with the Italian-accented English of Signor Mario Bianchi up in the lead vehicle, usually reporting one thing or another to those in the convoy behind him. A large outcropping of bundled roots from the remains of a dead baobab had broken free from the hard pack alongside the road and needed to be negotiated, a dry wadi that crossed the highway required downshifting to safely cross, a hobbled camel had decided to stop in front of them, so there would be a short delay.

Court would have felt a lot better if this convoy had an armed escort. "Why don't you have UNAMID soldiers with you out here?" he asked Bishara.

The young man just shrugged while he moved to the lousy music. Then he said, "Darfur is as big as Texas in your America, and there are only ten thousand UNAMID soldiers. Most of them are at the camps. Not enough left for every little convoy." He smiled again. "It's no problem. The Janjas don't attack SI. Everybody knows that."

Court looked down at the young man, surprised. "And why is that?"

"Mr. Mario is a friend to the Janjas."

Court just looked out the window at the dust. "Perfect."

Court had not noticed that Bianchi had not transmitted in some time. He could barely hear anyway with the music and the sing-along in the stuffy cab. But when the Italian's singsong voice finally did come back on the radio, Court immediately sat up straight. Something in the man's tone was different. His cadence and sudden protocol caught the American's attention, and he reached out and turned the dial up quickly.

"SI IDP camp Dirra, this is SI Convoy, Truck One, over."

Court hushed the singing in the cab with him, reached back, and fumbled with the transistor radio to turn it down.

"Go ahead Truck One, over." A female voice. Australian.

"Margie," Bianchi's disembodied voice sounded official and serious. Court had studied voice stress patterns for over a decade. He knew this radio transmission meant trouble even before the

Italian spoke. "Our convoy has picked up a woman who claims to be an investigator for the International Criminal Court. She is with a colleague. Can you contact their office and Khartoum and confirm her credentials? If she is who she says she is, we need to have them send a helicopter—"

"Dammit!" Court shouted. The two local tribesmen in the cab with him just stared.

Court realized these transmissions would surely be picked up by the NSS, who, though certainly no tier-one intelligence organization, could sure as shit figure out that the people the SI convoy had just picked up were the same two killing government agents and blowing up shit in front of the Ghost House the night before.

Fucking lawyer bitch, thought Gentry, but he caught himself. She had no reason to trust him over Signor Bianchi. She must have felt safe up there with the head of this aid organization and just confided in him about the danger. It was understandable, even if it did just create a potential disaster.

Gentry's mind began working full throttle. What were the chances the NSS had picked up that transmission? What were the chances that they would put two and two together? What were the chances they could mobilize assets in the area and either intercept the convoy or be waiting for it outside the IDP camp at Dirra? What were the chances, failing that, that they would be allowed to march right past the UNAMID guards at the camp and grab the girl?

Court looked out into the haze and dust. He thought to himself in a near frantic mental scream, *Think! Think, Gentry! What are they going to do?* He struggled to channel the thought process of the leadership in Sudanese intelligence. They could not just let Ellen waltz into the camp at Dirra. She would reveal all about their sanctions violation. They would not wait for UNAMID peacekeepers to link up with the aid convoy. Then they would be outgunned, even if the gunners themselves were not particularly energetic about using their weapons.

No, Court thought, if *he* were running the NSS, *he* would hit

156

them as soon as possible, out here in the open. Kill everyone in the little convoy so as not to put the focus on the ICC woman as the target of the attack.

He thought about all these possibilities for less than a minute. Processing them in his fertile brain, a brain conditioned to danger, to battle, to intrigue, to deceit, and to threat.

The NSS might be able to get a platoon of GOS soldiers in the area mustered in time to cut off the convoy. But that did not seem likely. They were only a few hours from their destination.

No, the NSS had communications with and control of another fighting force who would be right in the area and ready to do their bidding.

Oh God, he thought. Not *those* assholes.

As much as he hated to admit it, Gentry could only see one likely conclusion. He nodded to himself. The muscles in his jaw flexed with resolve. He looked to Bishara.

"Give me a map."

Bishara fumbled through some papers on the floorboard. While he did so, he laughed. "Why you need a map? There's only one road. You can't get lost out here, man." Still, he pulled out the folded map, and Gentry took it from him quickly and began studying it.

It was nearly featureless, but there were some fatal funnels in the landscape, shallow crevices and narrow valleys that they would have to negotiate on the way to Dirra. Any one of these places would be a good place to be hit.

"Listen to me, kid. We're going to be attacked. Out here, on the road."

Bishara's bright brown eyes widened. "Attacked? Who gonna attack us?"

Court looked past the young Darfuri, out the passenger window, and into the near infinite landscape. The terrain rose to the south, fat acacia as big as boxcars amid dry hillocks protruding in the distance.

Court's voice was strong, but the nerves showed in its tone. "The Janjaweed."

The young black man cocked his head. Waved a hand in the cabin as if swatting a fly. "Nah, man."

Gentry turned to the driver. "Your gun. I need your gun."

Bishara answered for the older man, who spoke no English. "We don't have no gun, man."

"C'mon! I know you guys *must* keep something stashed in case the Janjas come. I'm not with the UN, I won't tell. We're going to get hit, and I need your AK, to watch for them."

"No gun, man. And no Janjas gonna come. We are SI."

"Doesn't matter today," said Court. He thought about his options. He could get on the radio, call up front to Bianchi and have the convoy stop. Then he could tell him of the danger he just caused, have him stay off the radio, and return to Al Fashir.

No, too many variables. What if Bianchi didn't comply? What if the NSS or the GOS army was racing from Al Fashir along this very road to catch up with them, in which case slowing to chat or turning back would only put the convoy in more danger.

No, the best thing they could do was to press on, try to get to the relative safety of the IDP camp near Dirra before the raiders appeared on a hilltop.

It was something to hope for, but it certainly didn't mean the Gray Man was going to just sit there with his fingers crossed.

He now tried to channel the mind of the commander of a gang of armed horsemen out here in the desert. What would his plan be?

Shit. He had no idea. Gentry possessed some training in small unit tactics. But not on fucking horseback. This was new territory for him. He tried to think back to the John Wayne movies he and his brother and his father enjoyed when he was younger, just to see if any tactics came to mind.

Nope, not really. The Duke wouldn't have been caught dead out here in Indian country without a lever-action Winchester, so those old westerns had no relevance to his current predicament.

Court stopped trying to figure out the best tactics that an attacking force would use. This was not Indians versus the cavalry. This was the Janjaweed versus an NGO. The horsemen wouldn't be looking for high ground, for sound military terrain. Shit, they would be attacking a defenseless convoy. They could swoop down any place and any time.

From what he knew of the Janjaweed, they usually did not attack UN convoys, or any convoys, for that matter. No, the Janjaweed militia raided villages, burned huts, raped and slaughtered. Then they looted.

Looted! Yes. They would want to keep the trucks intact so that they could steal whatever was inside.

Court could picture the impending action now. They would likely just stop the trucks, get everyone out, and begin the butchery.

Back at Harvey Point, the CIA instructors tried to teach Court everything, but nobody ever taught him how to prevent a mass execution while unarmed.

His head spun back to the cargo hatch behind him. "What's in the back?" Court asked Bishara, who was clearly alarmed by the American's insistence that they were heading into some sort of an ambush.

"Nothing, man. No guns. Why you say the Janjas—"

"What are we hauling?" Court asked again, more insistent this time.

"Just stuff for the camp. Beds, radios, lamps, desks, shit like that for staff office and living quarters. And tools to build a new water tower. Why you say the Janjas—"

"Let's take a look." Court spun around in the seat and slid the small access hatch from the cab to the massive cargo compartment. There was just enough room to squeeze through, climb over luggage and bags of millet and some sort of a metal rack to make it to the top of the pile of stowed cargo. "Pass me a flashlight," Court shouted at the young man poking his head through from the cab.

"Pass you what?" asked Bishara.

"A torch. Pass me a torch. Fucking British English," he said under his breath.

A minute later Bishara and Court were on their hands and knees on top of the gear. It was like a tight crawl space above a ceiling.

159

Easily one hundred fifteen degrees and pitch-black without the light. They bounced around wildly with every bump in the road. The driver must have wondered what the hell was going on, but he continued driving along in the convoy like nothing was amiss.

"Why you think Janjas are coming?" The young Darfuri finally managed to pose his question.

Court dug through boxes and bags while he spoke, throwing items over his shoulders left and right while Bishara held the light for him. Gentry explained, "The NSS is looking for the white woman. They want to kill her. Bianchi's radio broadcast told them where we were. I figure the NSS doesn't have a strike force out here on the road, so they'll probably radio the Janjaweed to come get us. If they do, maybe they will just kill me and the Canadian woman, but I wouldn't bet against them killing everybody, just to cover up the fact they are working with the NSS."

Bishara nodded, understanding the ramifications of the words of this high-strung American. "What can I do?"

"You and I are going to have to work as a team here. We work together, and we can get ourselves and some of these others out of this. You understand?"

The kid nodded.

"The driver, Rasid. Do you trust him?"

Bishara shrugged. "I am from Zaghawa tribe, he is a Masalit. But he is a good man. I will tell him to do what you say." Then Bishara asked, "What we gonna do?"

"First, we're gonna pray I'm wrong."

Young Bishara shook his head. "The Darfuri pray all the time. But the Janjas still come and kill us."

Court continued digging furiously through the cargo below him. Already he had pulled a cigarette lighter and a mechanical alarm clock from the scrum of cardboard boxes. He clutched a roll of heavy plastic trash bags in his hand and held it up in Bishara's flashlight's beam. Then he dug down deeper, past stacks of sacks of flour and small drums of cooking oil. He heaved a woven basket of clothes out of his way and reached up to the SI loader, took the light himself, shined it down on a heavy wooden crate on the floor of the cargo compartment. He pried the lid off to find an array of welding equipment, an acetylene and oxygen rig, a welder's helmet, iron joints, a torch.

Court looked up at Bishara at the top of the cargo. He said, "If they come, then we fight."

"American, I know the Janjaweed; they destroyed my village, they raped my two sisters, killed one, let the other live, but she crazy now after what they did. They killed my father, too. Only my mother and I left, and she at the camp at Dirra. If the Janjaweed come, nothing we can do. They have guns, camels, horses. If they come, we are all gonna die."

Court shook his head. "We can do this. These Janjaweed are killers, but they are cowards. They don't come to fight; they come to slaughter. We make it tough for them, bloody some noses, kill a couple of them even, and they will break and run. They aren't looking for a battle, believe me. These guys kill women and children for fun. We can do this."

"It doesn't matter if they're not real soldiers, they have guns! We don't have *anything* to stop them with."

"Yes, we do."

"What do we have?"

"We have me."

The kid's eyes grew wide. "You crazy, man," he said, a little smile growing on his face.

Smiling at a time like this meant Bishara was a bit crazy himself. Court could tell immediately that he'd be able to work with this kid.

"What's in the other trucks?"

"Uhhhh, the first truck has food, mostly. Stuff for the workers, not flour for the IDP. Also parts to repair the well—"

"Forget it. What's in the truck in front of us?"

"That's got the canvas rolls in it, plus water, the generators, six small generators for the camp. Also there is like a pump thing for the well."

The oversized tactical portion of Gentry's brain spun almost too quickly for the rest of his mind to keep up. "No good. Okay, the truck in the back?"

"Uhhh," Bishara thought for a minute. "Tools, hand tools, wood and nails and lumber to build a new latrine. Oh, and gas for the generators."

Court shined the light up on the young Fur tribesman. "Gas?"

"Yeah."

The Gray Man's head cocked. "How much gas we talking about?"

24

Bianchi was surprised to see the men blocking the road ahead. At least a dozen in strength, some sat high on large dapple-gray horses, others even higher on massive tan or chocolate camels. Their rifles hung low off their chests or by their sides, turbans of different colors piled high on their heads, covering their faces as well as their hair. Most wore sunglasses, some wore mismatched camouflage battle dress. A couple had military style boots, but most just wore sandals. There were long trench coats on a few of the men, while others were nearly bare-chested save for their tactical vests full of rifle magazines.

These were the Janjaweed. The term comes from the Arabic words for *evil* and *horse*. They were the *evil horsemen*. Black Arab tribesmen, originally culled from the best Arab horsemen of the Sudan: cattle ranchers or camel ranchers. Now, any Arab villager with a horse or a camel or, occasionally, with a pickup truck, could become a member of the government-sponsored militias who had been wreaking havoc against the non-Muslim population of western Sudan for the past eight years, killing hundreds of thousands, displacing millions, and raping and maiming and terrorizing untold numbers.

If there was evil in the world, and who could say there was not, then the Janjaweed were evil.

But Mario Bianchi was unafraid. He knew these men.

This particular franchise of evil was on his payroll.

The Italian was annoyed at facing yet another delay but absolutely not concerned. He'd made arrangements with the commanders of these men, arrangements that allowed him to travel this desert track unmolested. Occasionally he would be stopped by some band or another of the Arab tribesmen. They were not impolite; they just ordered him out of the cab of his truck while the African men working for him were wrestled more violently from the vehicles. But Mario Bianchi knew he merely had to speak with the commander leading the party, deferentially drop some names, even offer up his satellite phone if the Janjaweed underling was unaware of the arrangement in place and wanted to check with his superiors directly for confirmation.

And that was always the end of it.

Bianchi ordered his driver to stop. He looked to the Canadian woman, whose eyes were wide and fixed on the men in the dust ahead. "No problem. I know the leader of these gentlemen. There is nothing to worry about." He brushed his hand across her cheek and smiled.

"Hey, Bishara?" Court yelled out from back in the truck bed. He held a wooden and iron hand tool; he'd been nailing a frame of pine four-by-four posts together with the hammer end of the device. The opposite side of the instrument was a sharp hatchet, and there was the hook of a crowbar on the side. "Why are we stopping?"

"Men in the road!" Bishara yelled back. Court could barely hear him. He had burrowed like a mole into the gear and luggage, and his hearing and mobility were affected by the sacks and suitcases and pallets of water bottles and large rolls of tarpaulin above him. Sweat from his hairline had run into his ears and eyes. Even taking a deep breath was a challenge in the dark, claustrophobic confines in the back of the truck. Bishara had been back with him helping for a while, but two men kicking and pushing and digging through the cargo proved to be more hindrance than help. After burying one another with their own movements one time too many, Gentry sent the young man back up front to the cab with instructions for the driver. Court had then tried to use the flashlight and the hammer at the same time while he worked, but he finally gave up. Slinging a hammer in pitch-blackness had caused him to bang his thumb and forearm four times in five minutes, but not having to screw with the light at the same time sped up his work rate, even though it was hell on his extremities.

After a long delay, Bishara responded. "It's the Janjaweed!"

"Shit," Gentry said to himself. He stopped hammering, grabbed his flashlight, and began crawling back to the top of the cargo. One more thing he had to do. He only understood the theory of this project, had never built anything like this before. Doing it on the fly, in low light, had been a nightmare. There were many things that could go wrong, so many, in fact, that the only way he knew how to combat the majority of them was by erring so far on the opposite end of the spectrum that his project really only had one major danger at this point. He wasn't worried about whether it would work or not; rather, he was worried that it might just work too damn well.

Court was afraid of his project's very real, and very literal, potential for overkill.

Acetylene and oxygen, the two components necessary for a welding torch, are extraordinarily combustible when placed in the correct mixture and contained in a confined space. Court had stood the two large tanks up, filled six forty-gallon contractor bags with this mixture, tied the bags tightly like balloons, and then placed them on top of the cargo, taking up the vast majority of the empty space above the truck's load. He used the alarm clock, the cigarette lighter, and a healthy supply of strapping tape to fashion a timed detonator for the bags. He'd tested it twice, before filling the bags, of course, and found the moving hammer of the clock could activate the striker of the lighter and create a flame of burning butane.

He wanted to make a large bang, with much noise and flash, but not a great deal of shrapnel, lest he kill himself, Ellen Walsh, and the rest of the Speranza Internazionale convoy. No, he wanted only a diversion, an oversized flash-bang grenade. To achieve this effect he'd placed the bags at the top of the load, hoping the roof of the truck would blast off but all the cargo inside would not be propelled out at hundreds of miles an hour. He also did not want the truck's massive gas tank to ignite, which would create a bomb that could easily kill everyone. He really had no idea if his truck-sized concussion device would have the desired effect—there were dozens of variables at play—but he'd also had no other options that he could see.

Court had also created a second stage to his diversion, presuming that the few seconds of confusion by the enemy would not be enough for him to take any sort of advantage. He struggled and fought and pulled and pushed the iron acetylene tank to the top of the cargo load, positioned it in the back by the sliding door, with its nozzle facing the bags of combustible chemicals and its blunt bottom towards the door. He pointed it slightly downwards, and then built an extremely crude wooden cage around it, essentially rails above and below that it could travel on, like a missile on a launching pad.

Last, after the truck stopped, he opened the tank's nozzle slightly and began backing out of the cargo hold, moving the bags in front of him as he did so. At the cab end of the cargo space, he set the alarm clock, triple-checked the lighter to make sure the hammer of the timepiece would make contact with the lighter's flint wheel, and then left it there next to one of his oxy-bombs.

He backed out of the hatch to the cab, covered in sweat and exhausted beyond belief, just as the driver backed his vehicle up several meters and then turned off the engine.

A turbaned man on a horse rode by the driver's-side window, barked an order to the driver, who opened the door. Immediately the Janjaweed horseman struck Rasid several times with a heavy, braided whip before heading back to the last truck to hassle that driver as well.

Gentry followed Rasid and led Bishara out of the cab, worried as much now by his own contraption as by the armed enemy force around him.

*

Bianchi climbed out of the lead vehicle as the Janjaweed slowly enveloped the convoy. Half had dismounted and pulled their horses by their leads as they waved rifles around with their other hands. The other half, the senior men of the raiding party perhaps, remained on their mounts as they rode down both sides of the four vehicles on the hot road.

Bianchi identified the commander by his stature and by the heavy necklace of amulets hanging on his chest over his rifle magazines. These brown, square, clay charms were common among the Janjas, but the man on the largest camel, who wore the newest looking chocolate-chip patterned camouflage uniform and sported the longest beard, also wore the necklace with the most amulets. The charms were blessed by a holy man and were purported to ward off bullets.

This man was in charge, and Bianchi addressed him politely. *"Asalaam alaykum."* He put his hand to his breast in a sign of peace.

"Wa a salekum asam," responded the man with a slight nod. His head was ten feet in the air as he sat astride the huge camel. *He* made no sign of peace.

Bianchi continued in Arabic. "Brother, why do you stop us? Commander Ibrahim is a friend. He allows us to pass to Dirra."

The man on the camel just looked down at him. Then his eyes rose to the other people from the trucks, who were being led over to the side of the road. Bianchi turned to make sure everyone was accounted for and behaving themselves. His four drivers, his four loaders, the Canadian woman, who still wore a terrified expression on her face, and the American man. He was sweat-soaked, his hair matted to his forehead, his face low to the ground in supplication. Bianchi regarded him for a long time. So brave he was with a gun in his hand and facing an old man. Now, with these true warriors around him, he looked like he just wanted to disappear.

Right before turning back to the Janjaweed commander, Mario Bianchi caught the American sneaking a quick glance at his watch. Bizarre at a time like this, the Italian thought, as he once again began deferentially explaining his working relationship with the Janjaweed to the obviously poorly informed man on the camel.

"This is not going to be good," Court muttered under his breath. He wasn't talking about the marauders on horseback; he was talking about the project he'd been working on for thirty-five minutes. His life and the lives of everyone in the convoy were in peril, and not just from the hotheads with the smelly horses and flea-bitten camels. Bishara stepped up to Court on the road and put his hand on his back.

"Is it going to work?" he asked softly.

Court turned back to him. "I don't know if it's going to work. But it sure as hell is going to explode." Court put a tone on it and a look in his eyes that endeavored to convey the danger they were all in.

It was obvious to the Gray Man that young Bishara understood completely.

"Good luck, man."

Court nodded. "You, too, kid."

He wanted to talk to Ellen, to warn her about what was to come, but at that moment she was farther up the road, being led along with the rest of the SI personnel, all of them into one single group. When he did get close enough to her he could not speak. The common languages that he could have used, English or rudimentary Arabic, were likely understood by someone in the Janjaweed raiding party. So he did what he could to get next to her. She was close to Bianchi, who was standing below the leader of the Janjas. Court scooted behind the Italian. It wasn't hard with the Janjas shuffling everyone into this tight knot by the side of the road. They were fifty feet or so from truck three, Court's quickly fabricated diversionary device. He did his best to lead the SI staff a few feet farther away, but the Janjas just kept herding them back. Everyone was in a tight circle; he could literally smell the apprehension in this constricted gaggle of humanity standing together in the dirt. All eyes were on the Janjaweed commander high up on his camel, and another man on horseback with a rocket-propelled grenade launcher strapped to his saddle. Both used their angry beasts to compress the convoy personnel. Ellen shouldered up to Court, the man she knew as Six.

"Are they here because I told Bianchi who I was?" she asked breathlessly. She was on the verge of tears, as if she already knew the answer.

"I told you not to do that," Court said flatly. He had something else bothering him at the moment and had no energy to focus on the Canadian woman's feelings or fears at present.

"I . . . I thought it would get UNAMID forces out here."

"Uh-huh," Gentry said, looking down to his watch again. Nervously he glanced at the Janjaweed. They were standing around or sitting high in their saddles, as if waiting for something.

Court was waiting for something, too. But he did not know what would come first. Or which of the two events would prove to be the most calamitous.

Shit.

For the first time he tuned into what Mario Bianchi was saying to the Arab commander. The old Italian hadn't shut up since he'd gotten out of his truck. He'd been speaking Arabic, but now the one-sided conversation was in French.

"As I say, you can use my phone to contact Commander Ibrahim. He will tell you that I am a friend."

"You're friends with these fucks?" Court asked in English.

Bianchi looked around at the American, who was now right behind him on the side of the road. He nodded and said, "I have an arrangement with the Janjaweed in this area."

"Yeah? How's that working out for you?"

Bianchi ignored the American and turned back to the commander. "So, would you like my phone?"

The Janjaweed commander, impossibly high up on his huge mount, said, "No. I have a phone."

Bianchi nodded. "Can you please contact Commander Ibra—"

"Commander Ibrahim contacted *me*."

169

Bianchi's head cocked. "He did? So he told you we could pass, *si*?"

The commander on the camel simply shook his head, one time, very slowly.

Bianchi's next words were softer, uncharacteristically unsure. "What did he tell you?"

"He told me to do this." The commander barked a brief order in Arabic. Quickly a horseman shrouded with a purple turban on a large sorrel gelding moved around and behind the herded scrum of convoy personnel. Court lost sight of him for a moment behind some stationary horsemen, but when the purple-turbaned man reappeared there was a noosed rope in his hand. Deftly he tossed it out underhanded. It dropped heavily over the neck of Mario Bianchi, who was just now turning to the sound of galloping hooves behind him. The horseman looped the other end of the rope around the horn of his saddle, and he cruelly kicked his heels into the sides of his steed. The animal bolted forward, away from the road and towards the rocky desert to the north.

With a shout of surprise, Mario Bianchi was launched forward by the taut rope, yanked to the ground by his neck, and dragged forward. He crashed awkwardly into three or four of his staff, sending men spinning out of the way or knocked like tenpins in a bowling alley. Ellen Walsh screamed as the Italian was dragged off. The horse hooves and the slamming of his thick body against unyielding hard earth crust and jagged stones and dry roots as hard as hickory sticks made violent sounds that only diminished as the man was pulled ten, then twenty, then fifty, then one hundred yards away, to where finally all that could be seen of him in the distance was a dust cloud that hung in the still air.

25

Court looked down at his watch. He began quickly pushing the crowd around him farther off the road, first with nudges and then with shoves.

The Janjaweed commander then shouted something to his dismounted men. It was Sudanese Arabic, but close enough to the Gulf Arabic that Gentry understood.

"Beat them all to death."

Rifles were raised and turned upside down. The weapons' butts were then used to viciously slam into the crowd from all directions. A half dozen men hammered into the bodies of nine men and one woman; they went about their cruel business amid shouts and screams and begging pleas from the victims. At the same time those Janjas on horses and camels began shoving the group tighter and tighter together, using the thick animals' massive bodies to literally crush the pathetic group of defenseless civilians.

Court took a glancing rifle butt in the right shoulder while he was looking in the other direction. It propelled him sideways and knocked him into the haunches of the camel upon which the commander sat. The Janjaweed leader looked down at him with his coal black eyes showing through the folds of his turban. Court winced in pain but again looked down to his watch.

Then he turned to Ellen. She tripped backwards over a felled man and then rolled onto her stomach at Court's feet. She started to get back up as if to run, but there was nowhere to run to. They were completely encircled by the Arab thugs.

And only Court Gentry knew that the safest place in the world for her right now was right where she was, facedown in the dirt.

He dove onto her, used his body to slam her down and his arms to cover her ears.

Here we go, he thought to himself as he tightened his body.

From the third truck, the vehicle in which Court and Bishara had ridden, there came a muted pop, like a car backfiring through its muffler. It was audible, even above the shouts and the cracking of rifle stocks on thin arms and legs, but it wasn't one-tenth the volume Court had expected it to be.

Huh? He lifted his head, looked back, had no idea what he'd done wrong. Underperformance had been the absolute *least* of his worries.

The beatings stopped momentarily as the Janjaweed looked to the vehicle. Even the Speranza Internazionale staff, lying prostrate or fetal on the ground all around Gentry and Walsh, looked around in confusion.

Smoke billowed out of cab windows and through the slits of the sliding lift door at the back of the cargo space. But the roof did not blow off, there was no cacophonic concussion blast, and certainly no shrapnel.

Orders were barked in Arabic, and a pair of men on horses dismounted, passed their reins off to others standing around, and ran over to the truck. Court knew these men had planned on looting cargo. They needed to see why the cargo in one of the trucks was now smoldering.

The Janjaweed leader shouted another command to the rest of his men, and again Court understood.

"Shoot them all."

The men moved, formed in a single ragged line facing their prostrate victims.

Kalashnikovs were raised, and safety levers were clicked down to the fully automatic setting.

Court stood quickly. One man against dozen, he reached behind his back and under his shirt to grab something hidden there.

And then it happened. For whatever reason, stage one of Gentry's diversion had been all but a dud.

But stage two?

Stage two was a goddamned masterpiece.

As the men neared the rear of the vehicle there was another loud bang, then the demonic high-pitched scream of a missile launch. The acetylene tank rocketed out of the back, a jet of fire behind it. Almost faster than the eye could pick up its image it smashed in a downward angle through the windshield of truck four and buried itself into the cargo space of the rear vehicle.

The big four-ton truck shuddered on its chassis.

Court spun back towards Walsh, tackled her to the ground once again.

The truck exploded in a flash of fire, eardrums were assaulted with a deafening thunder, brains were slammed around inside skulls with a concussion like a brickbat to the temple. Court felt the flame envelop his body and then dissipate in an instant. The quick burn sucked the oxygen from the air and starved his lungs. He gasped and grunted, inhaled nothing until new air moved in and he could catch a fresh breath.

He fought the pain in his chest and the daze in his head, looked up to see that the concussive battering had rendered one Janja dead instantly, while three more were knocked off their horses and stunned. One more fighter, one of the men who had just moved between vehicles three and four, simply ceased to exist. Only his frightened horse running off into the distance gave any proof that he was ever there. Two more Arabs were burned and wounded by projectiles fired out of the exploding vehicle.

Six seconds after the blast, flaming scraps of debris were still falling and scattering all around them. Horses and camels alike were spooked; they danced and sprinted and wobbled on shaky legs.

Every single one of the SI crew were dazed at least and

173

concussed at worst, but they'd all been on the ground and therefore were somewhat less affected by the blast. Gentry and Walsh made out the best of everyone because he'd covered both his ears with his upper arms and hers with his hands. Still, he staggered while rising to his knees. He glanced at truck four, looked past men staggering around like drunkards. Its cab was bent and blackened and twisted but intact, its wheels and chassis and gas tanks and flatbed were still in place, but the sides and roof of the cargo container were simply gone, the gas bladders contained there were up in smoke, the other goods that had been housed in the cargo space now all over the road and burning, or even still floating through the air. Court turned now, still a bit unsteady, took a full, awkward step towards the commander, who had somehow managed to remain in the saddle on his monstrous camel. The camel and one other horse were the only animals not to scatter after the detonation. The Janjaweed leader lifted his wire-stocked Kalashnikov up towards Gentry. The white man was the only person from the convoy on his feet now, but the commander himself was slow and disoriented. He just got his muzzle up when Court knocked it to the side with his open left hand. In his right hand Gentry retrieved the instrument he'd kept hidden under his shirt in the small of his back.

It was the hammer-hatchet combo, wielded to the sharp side, and Gentry windmilled it down from over his head with all the strength in his shoulder and back, sank the hatchet's blade squarely into the kneecap of the camel-mounted Janjaweed commander.

There was no scream from the man, but his knee lurched up, and he grabbed at it in agony. The hatchet remained embedded in the bone of the kneecap and deep into the femur, and the handle pulled free from Court's grip. The man slid off the saddle on the opposite side of his attacker, fell the six feet or so backwards, slamming his neck and back into the dusty earth, his rifle tumbling back with him.

Court turned away from the now riderless camel and spun towards Ellen Walsh, who was scrambling away from the men and the trucks on her hands and knees. From behind him he heard full automatic fire from a Kalashnikov. Even though he'd covered his ears before the blast of the truck, the gunfire sounded tinny and distant. His eyes next went to the rear vehicle. Fires burned all around it from the massive detonation. He knew the gas tanks could go up at any time, they all were well within the blast radius, and every living thing could be killed if they were this close when it detonated and the chassis and drive train turned to a thousand supersonic slugs of hot metal.

Another burst of AK fire behind him encouraged Gentry to find himself his own weapon. The Janja commander's AK would be lying on the other side of the camel. Court began turning around to go after it, but then something huge slammed into his back, as if he had been hit by a bus at speed. He crumpled forward with an incredible weight on him from behind. Gentry fell to the ground face-first with a grunt, his arms askew. Instantly he knew he was pinned down on the hard earth by something massive and unyielding.

Looking back over his shoulder he saw the gargantuan camel lying on top of him, covering him from his waist down. The hairy beast's head had flopped around in its death throes and ended up facing Court: vacant eyes with oddly long lashes, flared teeth, and a droopy wet tongue hanging out. The animal had been felled with an assault rifle, and after only a second or two of scratching into the dirt with his fingers and hands did Gentry realize there was no way he would be able to get out from under nearly fifteen hundred pounds of dead weight by himself.

He reached behind his back, tried to get hold of anything fastened to the saddle of the camel that could help him unpin his legs or, failing that, at least something that would help him fight from where he lay.

But there was nothing within his awkward reach.

And the fight continued around him. Five feet from his face an SI driver clambered to his knees, blood trickling down his ears from the concussion of Gentry's overcooked car bomb. Behind him other men, both Speranza Internazionale and Janjaweed, were all moving in different directions and at different speeds, each man at a unique point in the timeline of recovery from the brutal shock wave. A Janja, also dazed by the explosion, tried and failed to climb back up on his camel. The beast was having none of it, backing up and away from the Arab, who finally gave up. Instead he yanked the rocket-propelled grenade launcher free of the scabbard on the camel's side. He spun around. Court watched but was helpless to do anything as the man then raised the weapon. He seemed uncertain of a target for a long time. Gentry knew he was surely close enough to his intended victims, the men in the dirt on the side of the road, that he would no doubt blow himself up in trying to destroy them. But the man was out of it, disoriented. He pointed the RPG and pulled the trigger, seeming to forget that the tube on his shoulder possessed an external hammer that must be cocked for the weapon to fire. He looked the launcher over. Court watched him, legs pinned down by the fifteen-hundred-pound carcass, and soon enough the Janja seemed to figure out his mistake. He charged the weapon and resighted it on the crowd of staggering men.

A burst of rifle fire from the other side of the camel forced Court's head down into his neck like a turtle escaping to the shelter of his shell. The Janjaweed with the rocket launcher stumbled backwards, fired his weapon into the air, the back blast into the dust and sand of the Saheli track enveloped the man as he fell dead.

The gray smoke from the rocket-propelled grenade shot upwards into the blue sky but angled off harmlessly towards the south.

Court looked back over his shoulder again, just as young Bishara vaulted the dead camel, ducked down on Court's side to cover himself, a smoking AK-47 in his hands.

A huge white grin on his face greeted Court.

"Man, you blew up that truck, American!" He rose and fired a short burst over the camel's brown stomach at a target Gentry could not see, pinned as he was facedown in the dirt. The return fire was sporadic, but Gentry saw dust kick up between his position and the trucks in the road. Rasid, the SI driver from Court's truck, pulled the AK from the camel of the dead RPG man and returned fire with no real skill for doing so. He held the AK out in front of him, shut his eyes as he pulled the trigger, and the gun leapt all around as 7.62-millimeter bullets snapped through the air just above Gentry's head. Bishara ducked down from this new threat, turned, and screamed at the older man. Court hoped he was telling him to watch where he pointed his fucking gun.

"You gonna fight, American?" Bishara asked Court, still smiling. He seemed to be enjoying this chance to kill the Janjaweed murderers who had destroyed much of his homeland under orders from President Abboud.

"I'm stuck," replied Court, still trying to pull himself free. He did not feel pain in his legs, only intense pressure, and he prayed he wouldn't find anything broken when he finally did get extricated from under the camel.

Bishara fired another burst over the dead animal. Its long, fat body provided excellent cover, but Court knew the Janjaweed horsemen on the other side could flank his and Bishara's position at any moment.

The young Zaghawa tribesman slung the AK around his neck, took Gentry by both arms, and, while still crouched low behind the camel, pulled with all his might. Court did not budge. One of the other SI men crawled over and shared duty with Bishara, each taking an arm, and this time Court felt his body becoming unwedged. Gentry tried to dig his knees into the dirt to help pry him out from the punishing weight of the massive animal carcass above him. More AK bursts from the Janjaweed by truck one sent both Sudanese men to the dirt next to Gentry, but they scrambled back up after a moment for another heave of the sweaty white man pinned under the camel. Their third try was successful; Court felt his legs and then his feet break free. They tingled and ached, but he could move them. Nothing was obviously broken, so he kept his head down low and clambered to his knees.

Gentry looked up to see the driver who had pulled him free keeping his own head low to the ground, but Bishara was in a half crouch, pulling his Kalashnikov back up to the firing position, his eyes fixed on a threat on the other side of the camel and a determined look on his face.

A burst of automatic fire from behind Court and, just like that, young Bishara spun around, cried out in surprise, and crumpled to the dirt, dead in an instant.

But in the next instant Court yanked the bloody, dirt-covered AK off of the hard packed dirt road and spun around on his knees. He peered over the camel, and saw six Janjaweed fleeing on horseback. They were crossing behind truck one in the distance, leaving his sight line. He managed to fire one aimed round, striking the low back of the last horseman. The Janja man tumbled out of his saddle and into the sand.

26

Men moaned and cried out. Vehicles and debris smoked and burned. The smell of cordite, diesel fuel, and charred paper, rubber, and plastic filled the hot air. Court looked for Ellen Walsh among the heaps of humanity lying in lumps around him. Some of the piles were moving, injured; others were still, dead. He finally saw her through the billowing smoke and hanging dust. She was on her feet, fifty yards away, heading towards the distant body of Mario Bianchi at the foot of a fat-trunked baobab tree. She appeared unhurt. Next he looked down at Bishara. His dead body lay in a ball, like a pile of dirty shop rags ready for the washing machine, blood rivulets running in the dry earth around him. He'd been dead under a minute, and already flies swarmed his neck wound, buzzed around him, crazed by the boon of fresh wet blood, a bonanza for them to suck to their filthy hearts' content.

Another SI man was dead, facedown, a few yards away. The remaining six had survived, though a couple of them bled from the ears thanks to Court's truck bomb. They'd have some degree of hearing issues for the rest of their lives, he guessed, but at least they had lives. A couple more had bloody arms or legs, either shrapnel thanks to Gentry or bullet or rifle-butt injuries thanks to the Janjaweed. Horses and the one camel still alive milled about. They'd scattered no more than fifty yards from the trucks; these animals were well accustomed to gunfire and explosions, to mayhem that would make uninitiated creatures run in panic until they dropped from exhaustion or dehydration. Fires still burned all over the road, and truck four was totally engulfed in flames now. Its tank would explode in moments.

What a fucking mess.

Court grabbed the closest man. "Move the first two trucks. Get everyone and all the animals up the road. The gas tank is going to blow in the last truck. It will probably set truck three off as well."

A minute later Court arrived behind Ellen Walsh. She knelt by the body of the Italian relief worker, lying alone in the dirt a hundred meters from the road. His clothes were torn, his face shredded by hard earth and harder stone. The thick rope was still wrapped around his neck.

Walsh cried in shallow sobs.

"You hurt?" Gentry asked. He was not going to be gentle with this woman. If she had followed his instructions, none of this would have happened.

"I'm fine," she said, just noticing the American. "But Mario is dead."

"Fuck him," Court said, looking down at the unnaturally contorted body. "He brought this shit down on himself."

Ellen said nothing, just looked up at him with a mixture of shock and disdain.

After a few seconds standing there, there was an incredibly loud boom. The gas tank of truck four ignited and exploded in a roar. Gentry felt the heat even at one hundred yards. The flame scorched the air; churning black smoke rose into the blue sky like a hot air balloon taking flight. Ellen just watched it alongside Court. After a moment of silence truck three went up in a ball of fire as well, an equally impressive sight.

Ellen gasped. "Where are they going?" The surviving SI men had climbed into the two remaining trucks, ostensibly to pull them forward out of the blast radius. The first vehicle kept on moving up the road, a cloud of dust behind it as it accelerated into the distance. "Where are they going?" she cried out again.

"Most likely to Dirra," Court said. Truck two idled in the

road. All the remaining men were inside. They looked like they were waiting for Ellen and Court, but Gentry imagined a heated argument ensuing right now inside that cab about whether or not to leave the *kawagas* behind to die in the sun. Court was neither surprised nor horrified by the thought of being left behind by the vehicle. He just began walking back to the road. "Calm down; everything is okay," he said to her, but he was nowhere as certain as his strong voice portrayed.

"Dammit," Court knelt down beside Bishara a minute later. The gas explosion had singed his body and burned off most of his clothing. One more unnecessary assault on the young man who had helped him so much. Court hoped that the flies that had been feasting on Bishara's mortal neck wound had been incinerated in the blast.

"What?" asked Ellen.

"He was one hell of a kid."

"You knew him for an hour," she said. She wasn't arguing with him; she truly just didn't understand this sudden emotion for one man out of all who had just died, especially considering the way he had regarded Bianchi minutes before. She counted eight bodies lying in the dirt, not including the one Six knelt beside.

"He saved us both. He was the most dialed-in son of a bitch I've had the honor of working with in a long time."

The one remaining truck lurched into gear and made a wide U-turn off the road, passing the white people in the dust. Ellen began running towards it, waving her arms frantically. It passed her by and raced back to the west.

"No!" she screamed.

Court surmised now that any argument inside the cab had not been whether or not to leave them; they were probably all in favor of that. It was whether they should head east to Dirra or west to Al Fashir. They had obviously decided on the latter.

"What are we going to do?" Ellen cried out to Gentry. He walked up the road a few meters, dropped to his knees, began picking over the body of the dead Janjaweed commander. He pulled a small bladder of water on a chain and looped it over his back. He dug a full mag for a Kalashnikov out of a black canvas chest rig. He lifted up an ornate knife in a scabbard, drew it to inspect the blade, and then pushed it back into its scabbard and dropped it back on the dead man.

"What are we going to do?" she asked again, sobbing this time, as she watched him use his boot to flip the dead SI driver onto his back. He knelt down and pulled sunglasses out of the breast pocket of the man's bloody shirt. He slipped them over his eyes and looked at the animals milling about.

"Can you ride a horse?"

"I . . . I guess so. But how far?"

He glanced at his watch. There was a GPS on it, but it wasn't working at the moment. *Perfect*. He guessed. "Twenty-five to thirty miles." Now he pulled a second AK out of the dirt. He folded the wire stock underneath the rifle, significantly shortening its length. "Thirty miles is doable," he declared. He hung the gun off his shoulder and down his back, the muzzle facing down. He poked another Janja fighter with his boot, looking for something useful to scavenge. The man groaned. He was injured but alive. "Unless we run into more of these fuckers."

She just stood there while he worked. "If the radio in one of these trucks is still intact, we can call for help."

"Yeah." Court looked up at her. "That worked so well the last time, why the fuck not do it again?" He softened, but only a little. "How do you think these Janjas knew we were in this convoy? The NSS was listening in. This wasn't random. They *sent* the Janjaweed out here to kill us. Ordered them to butcher everyone so that it wouldn't look like a government-sanctioned assassination. Trust me, we're better off not broadcasting. With a little luck they'll think we're dead. When those trucks get to civilization, you can be damn sure the SI employees won't admit to knowingly leaving us out here alive. We're dead to the world, and we can use that to our advantage."

Now Gentry kneeled over another wounded Janjaweed horseman. The Arab was flat on his back, breathing shallowly in soft wheezes. Court pulled a water flask from around his neck, a long knife from his belt. He inspected the weapon. This blade passed muster, and he took the belt and the scabbard and the knife and strapped it all to his own body.

"What about them?" Ellen asked as Court returned to his feet.

"What about who?"

"Those two men. They are injured."

"What about them?"

"Can we help them?"

"Are you a doctor?"

"No, but—"

"Me either. Pick one of the horses. We need to get moving."

She looked at the bearded American for several seconds. "But these men. What if no one comes by before nightfall? There are wild animals out here. These are human beings, Six. You can't just leave them behind to die."

"Watch me. Get on a horse. I'd like to take the camel, he won't need water like a horse will, but if we encounter another Janjaweed gang out in the desert, we're gonna want the speed of horses to get away from them." He pulled two turbans from the heads of two of the dead horsemen and tucked them into the belt he'd just scavenged.

Ellen shouted angrily, "We take these two men with us, or I don't go, Six. That is absolutely final!"

Gentry ignored her, kept speaking, more to himself than to the woman. "Camels are actually very fast, but if you don't know how to handle one, and I don't, it's easy to lose—"

"Listen to me! They need a hospital!"

Court stopped talking and looked over the wounded men. "More like a morgue."

"They are alive! And I am not going anywhere without them!"

Now his eyes turned to the shouting woman. He sighed. "Seriously?"

"Seriously. We *can't* just leave two living men out here in the desert." One of the wounded groaned softly.

Court's jaw fixed, jutted forward a bit as he stared at the Canadian lawyer. He nodded, lifted the rifle hanging from his neck, causing the woman to flinch in fear. With no hesitation at all, he turned and shot the two wounded men, once each in the chest. Their torsos jerked violently with the impacts, dark blood rooster-tailed a foot into the air above them, and both men stilled instantly.

After the report from the second round died off in the desert, Gentry let his rifle hang by its sling in front of him. "Problem solved. Let's go."

Ellen Walsh's face whitened with horror, then seconds later it reddened with rage. She charged the American. He walked away from her, heading for one of the horses, but she grabbed him by the back of his T-shirt, literally spinning him around. He did not make eye contact with her; instead, he continued marching forward alongside the burning truck.

"You bastard! You are no better than them!" she berated as she ran alongside, trying to get in front of him.

"They're dead; I'm alive. I'd say I *am* doin' a lot better." He said it mirthlessly, continuing forward. But she finally made it in front of him, put her hand on his chest. Her small sunburned fingers clenched his sweat-drenched brown T-shirt. With his free left hand Gentry snatched her hand, spun it backwards into a wristlock, and pushed her back, away from him. He angrily raised the butt of the AK towards her with his free hand as if he were going to slam it into her face.

Ellen was unafraid; her rage had pushed her past concern for her own personal well-being. "Ah, you beat women, too, do you? You fucking animal! Executing wounded men! Picking over dead bodies like a vulture! Blowing up—"

"How the fuck were we going to haul them across thirty miles of desert? They would have bled out anyway, and we would have died trying."

"We could have carried them on the horses!"

"And moved at half speed! You want to be out here at nightfall?"

"Don't make excuses! Just admit it, you *wanted* to kill them!"

He lowered the gun and let go of her hand. "I'll admit this. I don't give a fuck about those two guys, about the bodies lying around here. Other than Bishara, I could not care less."

She looked over the bodies, back up to him. "What? What *are* you?"

"I'm whatever you want me to be. The son of a bitch who shoots the wounded, or the guy who's pulled your ass out of the fire more times in the past eighteen hours than I'd like to remember," he said, climbing into the saddle of a large gray Arabian mare. "I can get you out of this alive, but you have to let me do my job."

"Your job is to shoot injured men?"

"Not if I can help it, but we needed to go, and wasting those two shitheads was a means to that end. I could have waited thirty minutes for them to die on their own, but I didn't want to wait. I could have left them behind, knowing that if the Janjas came back and one of them had enough strength to point which direction we took off in, it could get us killed, but I didn't want to do that either. Do you even know what these fuckers do? They rape and slaughter defenseless women, they burn children alive in fire pits in front of their parents for shits and grins. Four hundred thousand dead. Is that just a fucking number to you? You can cry for the Janjaweed if that makes you feel self-righteous, but I won't bat an eye after shooting the killers of women and children."

She stared at him a long time. Tears streamed down a face still wild with fury and hatred. Clean lines in the caked dust on her cheeks. She said, "Okay, they are killers of women and children; I understand that. But what does this make you?"

Court slid the AK into a strap on the rear of the saddle, then tightened his grip on the big mare's reins. He looked down at Ellen Walsh and kicked the animal's haunches. The horse was already galloping towards the east when he answered her.

"I am a killer of men."

185

27

Thirty minutes later Ellen Walsh and Court Gentry were a mile north of the desert track to Dirra, heading east through a narrow canyon that ran parallel to the distant road. Walsh's chestnut mare had nearly bucked her twice; it was accustomed to a heavier hand controlling the bridle. Gentry deftly led his horse, and he led the way without speaking.

He felt the fury of the woman behind him, sensed the hating eyes burrowing into his back like the scorching heat of the sun's rays. Off and on she would speak, continuing to berate him. "You are a war criminal now. You realize that, don't you? And the fact that you executed two wounded prisoners right in front of an ICC investigator leads me to wonder what you do when no one is around to hold you accountable for your crimes."

Court looked deep into the afternoon haze, searching for any stationary or slowly moving dust clouds ahead, telltale signs of approaching horses. He did see dust clouds here and there, but they moved quickly across the landscape, indicating they were caused by the wind and not hooves or feet or tires.

"I came to the Sudan to help bring a wanted man to justice. But you know what? I ran into someone else, someone who maybe isn't as dangerous, scale-wise, as President Abboud, but someone with just as little regard for human life. That's you, Six. I'm going to make sure you are brought to justice for what happened today."

He turned his horse a little towards the north now. The path he was on led back closer to what passed for a road out here, and he wanted to stay out of sight of any passing traffic. "Do you ever take a break?" Court mumbled it to himself. The way forward, out of the canyon and back into the scrubland of the Sahel, looked clear, for now. He spoke louder. "You know what killed them? *You* killed them. You not doing what I told you to do. Out here, if you want to live, you do what I say. If I'm on trial in Winnipeg or wherever the fuck, I will listen to you, but out here, in enemy territory? You listen to me."

Apparently his remark caught her off guard, so accustomed she had become to his ignoring her.

It took her a while to respond, and even then, her words seemed ineffectual. "I am not a trial lawyer. And I'm from Vancouver."

Court did not reply, just looked ahead, scanning for threats.

"How can you do it? How can you kill like that?"

"Training."

"Military training?"

He did not answer.

"I need to know who you are," she said. He could hear the wheels turning in her head. *He* was now the subject of her investigation.

"No, you don't."

"Do you really work for the Russians?"

"I did once, but that didn't work out."

"Because of me?"

"Yep."

"But . . . you are American. Are you CIA?"

"Negative."

"Then what?"

"I'm currently unemployed."

"Right." She didn't believe him. "So all this isn't business? It's just pleasure?"

"More fun than a barrel of Janjaweed," said Court as he swigged from the canteen he took from one of the men he killed.

187

"I'm serious, Six. I have every intention of writing a report on what happened back there."

"Knock yourself out."

"You don't believe me?"

"I don't care."

"You aren't afraid of the ICC?"

He laughed cruelly. "Terrified, but I'll get over it."

"You are a dangerous man who must be stopped."

He did not slow his mount, but he pulled the reins to the left so that he could make eye contact with the woman. "But I'm not so dangerous that you won't accept my help. And I'm not so dangerous that you aren't afraid to be alone with me in the desert while I'm carrying two firearms, and I'm not so dangerous that you aren't afraid to tell me that you are going to do all you can to have me thrown in prison. What does that tell you, Walsh? It *should* tell you that you see me as more savior than demon."

She thought about it a moment. "The justice I want to administer to you is not the same as what you administered to those people back there. I respect the rule of law."

"Well, you didn't respect it enough to get all those bastards to stop bashing heads and sit down at a little makeshift courtroom in the dirt to be judged properly. Respect the rule of law all you want, but out here, the rule of law is not going to save your ass like this rusty AK and a fistful of dirty bullets will."

"I'm not a fool, I—"

"That's exactly what you are! All of you international law people are fools. Naive, foolish sheep who think the way to get the government of Sudan to put down their weapons and stop a genocide is to draft indictments in the Netherlands and send do-gooding lawyers down here to wander the desert and write fucking reports. You can feel good all you want, but you won't change a goddamned thing."

She had locked onto something he said. "And what you're here to do, it will change things?"

Court wanted to keep his mouth shut, but he couldn't. "You're damn right, it will."

"So you smuggle in weapons with the Russians and shoot the wounded. Is that all part of your plan to make the world a better place?"

"No, it's not. All this is just a distraction."

"Then what is your mission?"

"I'm not going to tell you."

"Why not?"

"Because you are just another obstacle in my way."

"Maybe we can work together."

"Surely I don't look *that* stupid, do I?" Court said. "Until we get to Dirra, we are on the same side. After that, you go your way, I'll go mine, and we'll just leave it at that." There was a finality in his comment that Walsh recognized, and she left him alone.

They covered three hours more of hard ground with no words between them.

Just after five in the afternoon, Gentry looked back over his shoulder to check on the woman. She was sunburned and exhausted but still upright on her mount. He pulled his horse to a stop, slid off the side, and untied a bladder from the saddle. He gave the gray Arabian warm water, which the animal drank eagerly. After thirty seconds he repeated the process with Ellen's horse. As he did this, Ellen looked around, as if she'd been sleeping upright and was only now recognizing her surroundings.

After a moment Court looked up to her, noticed an odd look on her face.

"What the hell is that?" she asked, her voice more curiosity than worry.

Gentry followed her gaze into the distance, back the way they had come.

"A haboob," Gentry replied gravely. "A dust storm."

Ellen stared in awe at the sight. It was as if a huge mountain had risen out of the flat ground they had just crossed. And the mountain grew and moved towards them.

"That looks bad."

"It's not good." Court replied.

"Is it going to catch us?"

Court hurriedly retied the three-fourths-empty bladder on the back of his horse's saddle. Then he lifted a foot back into the stirrup and climbed back up. "Get off your horse. Get on with me. Hurry!"

"No," she said. But then asked, "Why?"

"We'll get separated if we're on two horses, and we *cannot* afford to get separated out here. Climb on with me, now!"

Ellen hesitated but soon slid off her chestnut mare, grabbed the water bladder off its back, and went to Court. He pulled her up behind him, and she held her arms tight around his waist. He handed back one of the brown turbans he had taken from a dead Janjaweed horseman. "Cover your face," he said. "Even your eyes."

"What about you? How will you see?"

Court threw a similar wrap over his own face. "I won't see. I'll try to keep us going in the right direction. But the most important thing is we stay on the horse. There is nowhere out here to hunker down and wait this out. We just have to barrel right on through it."

Ideally Gentry would have dismounted and waited out the storm, but commonsense action was a luxury he could ill afford. He'd seen haboobs in Iraq that lasted three days, knew every minute they were out here in the badlands was another minute the NSS had to send more men out to hunt them. The last thing he wanted was to have his horse blindly stumble down a gulley or wander smack into a camp of Janjaweed fighters, but attempting to continue on, to run these risks, seemed preferable to just hanging out in the open with little water and no protection.

A cooler breeze hit them a minute later, and the sand and dust were on them shortly after that. Suddenly it went from daylight to night; the sun's rays were blotted out above them in an instant, and then they were surrounded, enveloped. A sense of claustrophobia overtook Ellen, but all she could do was tuck her face tighter into the turban and then press her face into the sweaty T-shirt of the man in front of her. The man who had kept her alive but who considered himself the arbiter of the life of others.

Court held his watch up to his eyes, under the head wrap like a little tent. He could barely see, and hot grit dusted his corneas in seconds. The GPS function on the watch still seemed to be screwed up, but at least the compass worked. He headed east-northeast. Dirra was in this direction, but he had no idea how fast they were going in the haboob, so his main worry was passing right by the town in the dust or even in night. Surely there would be lights from the village, even if electrical power was virtually nonexistent, but there were low hills and sagging dry streambeds and wall-like rock formations that could easily obscure any distant light source, even if the dust storm did die down.

Court could feel dehydration affecting his performance. He felt dizzy, tired, even a little drunk. He needed to take in some more liquid quickly. Though he could not see an inch in front of his face, he pulled the canteen off the horse's saddle, opened it, and held it to his mouth. The grit and dirt and sand in the air and on his mouth immediately mixed with the hot, rank water, creating a mouthful of soupy mud. He gulped it down nonetheless, understanding how important hydration was for him right now, even if he didn't enjoy sucking down this hot sludge.

He reached back and put it in Ellen's hand. It took her a minute to realize what it was and what he was asking her to do. She took a swig herself, then immediately began hacking.

"It's full of dirt."

"Your face is full of dirt. Drink it. You need it."

"I'm okay," she said and tried to give it back to him.

"Drink. You have to stay hydrated out here in these temperatures."

"But it's full of dirt."

"You'll shit it out," Court said coldly.

"That's disgusting. I don't *want* to shit it out."

"Do you want to die of heatstroke? Drink the fucking water!" he shouted at her.

Reluctantly, angrily, she gulped down several more swallows. The grit and the mud made her cough several more times, but the liquid stayed down. When the bladder was empty, she dropped it in the dirt and the horse kept moving.

The haboob lasted until well past nightfall, and Court somehow managed to keep the animal moving in the correct direction. When the dust cloud moved on, he and Ellen dismounted and continued on foot, while Gentry led the big horse by its reins. The animal had proven incredibly reliable, and he wanted to give it a break by relieving it of the weight of two riders for an hour or two.

Their bodies were completely covered in grime. They could have been black Africans or Asians or space aliens under the coating of brown, and no one would know. Court realized this unintended consequence just might work in their favor as long as no one came too close. He was wrong, though. Their white skin may not have shown through, but their Western appearance was impossible to mask.

They had stayed away from the one desert track between Al Fashir and Dirra, had covered nothing but wide-open and desolate ground for hours, but as they neared their objective, they began passing through tiny villages and across dirt roads, and the traffic around them picked up. Donkey carts and small pickup trucks passed them, Darfuri villagers stared at them unabashedly, two filthy *kawagas* leading a Janjaweed horse, the man with two Kalashnikovs strapped to him and the woman wearing a turban like a man. Hardly an everyday occurrence out here in this wild land.

Court worried about the locals. He knew there existed a phenomenon in places like this, referred to as the bush telegraph, where somehow, inexplicably, news travels from community to community as certainly and as swiftly as a satellite phone. Gentry knew that at any moment he could meet up with Janjaweed or NSS or GOS soldiers and find himself outnumbered in a gun battle out here in the dark. Or he could find himself overrun by UNAMID soldiers from the African Union, who would arrest him and put an end to his operation.

But there was nothing for him to do but continue on; he had to get the woman to safety. He did his best to avoid settlements, gave the dung-fueled cooking fires a wide berth, waited for vehicles to pass instead of crossing in front of their headlights.

Ellen was dead tired. The heat and the stress and the long day and the lack of food and water all added up to put her in a temporary trance, which she occasionally snapped out of to try to engage Court in conversation. Just like the evening before, Gentry found himself talking to her more than he would anyone else. Even though she was 100 percent against him now, an adversary after he wasted those two worthless pieces of shit back with the convoy, he still kept talking to her, and it pissed him off. But it did not piss him off enough to stop.

The air finally cooled around eleven, and Ellen seemed to be reinvigorated by this. Court gave her the remainder of the water and, like a thirsty brown plant in the corner, the hydration seemed to cause her to spring back to life before his eyes.

"How much farther?"

"Not long. Another half hour or so."

"Can we get back on the horse?"

"Negative. We need her rested in case we get into trouble and have to escape."

"Okay," she said. "That makes sense." They walked shoulder to shoulder through low grass and beneath acacia trees so large they blocked out the stars. She looked over at him a few times. He could tell she was thinking about something. He ignored her, hoping her thought would pass, but it did not.

"Six, I think a lot of very bad people started out as good people, don't you?"

"I don't know."

"Be careful you don't become that which you hate."

"I have no idea what you are talking about."

"Yes, you do. I believe you. I believe that *you* believe you are here for the right reasons. Maybe in your head you are. But this place needs people who are saving lives, not taking lives."

Court stopped her from stumbling over an anthill in the dark. He led her around it by the arm, and then immediately let go. "Saving a life and taking a life are not opposites. Sometimes they are two sides of the same coin. I may take lives from time to time, but I wouldn't do it unless I felt I was saving some, too."

"Sounds like you're trying to justify it to yourself."

"I *have* to justify it to myself. But I don't have to justify anything to you. People like you will never understand. Waste of time to try to convince you."

"You will be indicted for war crimes for what happened today."

There was a tone to her voice that Gentry picked up on. She seemed to be disappointed in him for what happened but conflicted in her feelings.

"I believe you mentioned that."

"We will catch you."

"Right. You've been trying to catch Abboud for three years, and you have his goddamned address."

That sank in a moment. "We are trying. The ICC will get Abboud, sooner or later."

"Not if the ICC is sending Canadian women into Darfur alone. You people are going to need a lot of help to bring him down."

He could tell this comment made her curious. "Are you going to help us? Is that your plan?"

Court had said too much, and he knew it. "If I was here for Abboud, do you think I'd be in Darfur? No, I'd be in Khartoum, *where Abboud is*." He hoped he'd sold that to her.

She shrugged. "Abboud isn't my job, anyway," Ellen said. "I am working on illegal weapons proliferation. Armament imports are the symptom. Abboud is the disease."

"You think he's single-handedly responsible for the genocide here?"

She thought it over. "Responsible? Not entirely. But he can stop it. I believe that. He has the power."

"Somebody should just shoot him in the head; that would stop it." For the first time today, Court was interested in the conversation. He wanted to see how she'd respond to the comment.

"Your gun is the answer to every question, isn't it?"

"Not *my* gun. Like I said, I'm not in Khartoum."

"Fine, not *your* gun, but you really think killing him will fix things?"

"Don't you?"

"No, I don't. His followers could continue the war for years, decades even. If he died, all the gains the NGOs had made, just by being allowed in here, would probably be lost. Whoever takes over won't want the prying eyes of the west in Darfur, especially if the campaign of brutality continues."

"So Abboud is a good guy?" He was baiting her to get more intel on the political landscape.

"Of course not! He is as evil as the day is long. I'm just saying his death could bring about some unintended consequences."

Court knew about an intended consequence the Russians had in mind. They wanted Abboud out of the way so the Chinese would lose access to Tract 12A.

But at what cost to the region?

He pressed her a bit, trying to pull a bit more info from her. She knew more about the Sudan than he did, and he respected her knowledge, even if he assumed her conclusions to be naive at best and stupid at worst. "What about other actors in the region? The Russians, the Chinese, the US, the African Union."

"What about them?"

"Do you think any of them have an interest in what happens here?"

She turned to him, though they were still walking, regarding his question with a thoughtful sigh. The Arabian behind them snorted. "The Chinese have mineral rights in north Darfur. So far they haven't found much, but if they *did* find something, then all bets are off as to how that would change the political landscape."

"What do you mean?"

"The Chinese have a fragile alliance with Abboud. The Russians have a fragile alliance with—"

Court tried to finish the sentence, "The vice president, who would succeed Abboud if he were taken out of the picture."

"No. The vice president is as weak willed as they come. I was going to say the Russians have a fragile alliance with the government in Chad. If Abboud were killed, some people think a power struggle would ensue, and the civil war would spread to the entire nation. Chad would use that opportunity to invade Darfur with Russian help. It would start a firestorm, with two nuclear superpowers involved in the outcome. Personally, I don't believe that, as long as no major oil deposits are found in Darfur. This big conspiracy just sounds too big for Russia to fool with unless it turns out there is something really significant out here under the dirt."

She sounded like she knew what she was talking about, which gave Court the sinking feeling Gregor Sidorenko had lied to him. The Russians wanted Abboud dead not because his death would give them Tract 12A but because his death would cause chaos, into which Chad could invade and *take* Tract 12A for the Russians via a shooting war.

Son of a bitch.

Court had a thought. "But you guys want to arrest Abboud? Wouldn't that have the same effect as killing him? He'd be out of power and could not stop a civil war."

"The thinking at the ICC is that if we could give Abboud a reason to use his influence and power to our benefit, then his followers would not fall into the trap of being used as pawns by the Chinese and the Russians."

Interesting, thought Court, but he saw no possible way Abboud would have a reason to comply with the ICC.

They crested a gentle rise, palm trees at the apex. On the other side they saw the massive IDP camp splayed out in the valley below them over several square miles. It was flat and dark in the night, thousands of single-room tents. There were lights around the perimeter, and a few UNAMID vehicles in view. Camel-dung fires burned like a hundred fireflies in the distance, tiny pinpricks of amber across the wide valley floor.

"It's incredible," said Ellen, her hands on her hips.

"You see the gate?" asked Court, pointing towards an entrance in the fencing, protected on either side by white armored personnel carriers.

"Yeah." She looked up at him. "You're not coming with me, are you?"

Court mounted the Janjaweed horse.

"Nope."

"Because of what I said about having you prosecuted? Look, you are safer in there than you are out here. You won't be taken into custody here in Dirra, I promise you. We follow the law. You haven't even been indicted yet."

"I'm not going in there because I have a job to do out here. And I'm going to do it."

"So you just ride off into the sunset?"

"It's half-past midnight."

Walsh shook her head, batted buzzing insects away from her eyes. "I bet you think you are a cowboy. But you're not. You're an outlaw. You are—"

"I need three days, Ellen. Three days from now you can do whatever it is you have to do. Make your report, send teams out looking for me."

"Why don't you tell me your mission? What happens in three days? Who you are working for? If our goals do intersect, I promise I will try to help you."

"No offense, Miss Walsh, but I don't need any help your organization can provide."

She looked to the rifle on his chest and waved an exhausted hand at it. "Again, that's all the help you need?"

"I'm not here to kill people. The last twenty-four hours I have been off mission. Like I said, you would one hundred percent approve of what I'm doing. I just need three days to do it. Your wait will be rewarded."

Walsh did not reply. Court could imagine her giving him three days, just out of curiosity. He could also imagine her running to the front gate of the SI camp and yelling at the UNAMID soldiers to get themselves into their jeeps to chase the white horseman through the night. Ellen Walsh, like all women, was a complete mystery to Court Gentry.

"Three days. Please." He pulled the reins on the horse hard, spun the big animal around, and then galloped off into the dark.

28

Court sat in his tiny hotel room in Al Fashir. Outside the open window above his tattered and soiled mattress on the floor, the morning bustle of the city rattled and whistled and bleated and shouted, as men and animals and vehicles passed by.

He was filthy and wanted a shower, but there was no shower here. Just a hole cut into a closet floor down the hall for a toilet. He'd spent the evening scratching bloody flea bites and had not gotten much sleep but, he asked himself, what did he expect for nothing?

It had taken a day and a half and most of the rest of his Sudanese pounds to get a car and a driver to transport him back to the capital of North Darfur. Court bought a satellite phone with the rest of his cash, using his watch and the two AKs to make up the difference. The man who'd driven him from Dirra had a cousin who owned a filthy boardinghouse in Al Fashir for Darfuris there to work construction on whatever project the NGOs were paying them to build, and the driver and the cousin had spoken and offered Court a room free of charge. The two men even took Court shopping for some local items and paid for them out of their own pockets. Many Sudanese, Court had noticed in his day on the road and in the town, possessed an intense kindness and willingness to give of themselves and their meager property for a complete stranger.

Court had little to offer in return but his gratitude, a few Arabic words of thanks, and an understanding of the body language of the culture. He held his hand to his heart and nodded deeply so many times in the past day he almost felt as if he could pass for a Darfuri, if not for the pigmentation of his skin.

Court had worked in dozens of different places in his career, either as a CIA singleton operator, as a CIA Paramilitary Operations officer, or as a private sector assassin, and many of those places, for want of a better term, sucked. But from time to time he found himself somewhere remote, both geographically and culturally, and completely taken in by the scenery or the people or the way of life in ways that stayed with him after he'd done his job and left the place behind.

He felt this way about Darfur. He wasn't supposed to be here. There *was* much to hate. It was hot as hell and thick with bugs and controlled by a despot and murdering bands of marauders, but Court felt something about this place, the people, the stubbornness and discipline needed to face a miserable day armed with nothing but one's own devices. He could not help but respect the people for scratching out what existences they had, and he appreciated their kindness to him.

He would love to repay the kindness by removing the man from power who was systematically killing them.

He reached across the mattress, picked up his phone, and called a number in Saint Petersburg.

Gregor Ivanovic Sidorenko had not slept. His man had disappeared into the depths of Darfur, the opposite side of the country from where he needed to be, and he had not heard from him in almost seventy-two hours. Furthermore, the international news channels were broadcasting reports from Darfur, reports of an attack on an aid convoy not ninety minutes' driving time from where Gentry was last seen. Details were sketchy, but things did not look good.

Sid sat at his breakfast table in the cold, bit into a hard-boiled egg, and stared at his phone. He'd hardly taken his beady eyes from it in three days.

200

But for once it rang, and it startled him.

The Russian mobster tipped a mimosa in a fluted crystal glass while lurching forward to grab the receiver, fresh-squeezed Florida orange juice, Cuvée du Centenaire Grand Marnier, and Krug Grande Cuvée Champagne drenching his thick, gold-lined fleece robe. He ignored the expensive mess and answered the phone.

"*Slushayu vas.*" I am listening.

"It's Gray. You receiving me okay?"

"Mr. Gray, where are you?"

"I'm back in Al Fashir. I'm safe at the moment, but I can't stay here for long."

"What happened?"

"Nothing to worry about. I got sidetracked."

"Side ...? Mr. Gray, that is not acceptable! You have jeopardized everything! The FSB is very upset."

"It couldn't be helped."

"My people spoke to the pilot. You left the airport to save a woman. A woman!"

"Your pilot shouldn't have left me behind."

"A woman!"

"It's more complicated—"

"This is a very serious damage to our timetable."

"It's no problem."

"How can you say that it is no problem? We do not have another flight to Khartoum scheduled until after Abboud's trip to the Red Sea! How are you going—"

"Can you get a plane back here to Al Fashir?"

"Yes, I have arranged a flight. It will depart today from Belarus. But we can only get you out of the country with that flight. It will not be landing again in the Sudan."

"It doesn't have to land."

"I don't understand."

"Get a pen and paper. I'm going to need the aircraft to bring in some gear I'll require if I'm going to continue on with the operation. Get the FSB to help you put it together. Just relax. This little hiccup along the way will be forgotten."

"If they don't land, how will you—"

"They will need a flight path out of the country that takes them over the Red Sea. They can arrange that. Now, write all this down."

There was a scramble on the other end of the line. "Wait ... okay. I am ready."

Court dictated a list to the Russian mob boss, who scribbled like a frantic secretary. When he was finished, Sidorenko blew out a long breath. "You can do this?"

"Sure."

"The pilot ... he can do it?"

"You will talk to him when we are in the air. *Encourage* him to follow my instructions to the letter."

"*Da*, of course." Gregor Sidorenko was no longer angry. There was a high-pitched tone of excitement in his voice. "This will be ... dangerous for you."

"You are worried about my well-being?"

"Of course. I ... I just want to do what I can to help."

"Anything else?"

"I had a man who was going to take you by car from Khartoum to Suakin. If you proceed as you suggest, you will have to cross territory all alone and on foot. You don't look like a Sudanese tribesman."

"There is a tribe of lighter-skinned Arabs in the area. The Rashaidas. I won't be able to pull it off up close, but with a head wrap and local clothing, someone seeing me driving by in a car or walking across a field is going to peg me for a Rashaida before he pegs me for a white boy."

"You are willing to bet your life on that?"

The assassin answered nonchalantly, "This is what I do."

Sidorenko replied breathlessly, "You are amazing."

There was a long pause on the line. Sid thought the American was going to respond to his comment, but instead he said, "The plan remains in effect. After I'm on the ground, no contact until the job is done."

"*Da*. But the man who was going to take you to Suakin. He is a police officer there in the city of Suakin. He is an occasional informant for the FSB. He may be able to provide you with intelligence that will be helpful. I can arrange a meeting."

Court thought it over. As far as Sid's op was concerned, he didn't really need a police informant. But for Zack's job? Nocturne Sapphire could absolutely stand for one more source of intel about the layout of forces in the area.

"Agreed."

Sid said, "Mr. Gray, please remember. I have women here for you. Many beautiful women. Leave the ones you find in the desert *in* the desert; when you come back, you will never go wanting for women again!"

Court sighed. "Why didn't I think of that?"

Court leaned his head back against the plywood wall of his room. He knew he needed to call Zack; he'd put it off as long as possible. He knew he'd get a tongue-lashing of the highest order. He was right.

After three rings, Zack answered the phone with a marked absence of the customary pleasantries. "What the *fuck*, dude?"

"I got delayed."

"You got delayed? Really? Delayed? Good. I'm glad that's all it was, because for a minute there, I was worried that maybe my watch was running two *motherfucking* days fast!"

"I got caught up with the NSS. And the Janjaweed."

"The NSS *and* the Janjas? You left the airport."

"Yeah."

"This wouldn't happen to have anything to do with some Canadian skank working for the ICC, would it?"

"She spread the word, huh?"

"She didn't spread the word; mushroom clouds over NGO convoys spread the word! You must have charmed the socks off of

203

her; she is saying she doesn't even remember what you look like, but the Darfuris are saying some lily-white fuckwad blew up two of their trucks and killed a shitload of Janjaweed. What the hell were you doing?"

"She needed my help."

"Yeah? Outstanding. But you know what? I need your help, too. I need you to do your goddamned job! Chasin' tail across the desert when you are supposed to be over here getting ready for the most important SAD/SOG operation in the past decade is not going to get the shoot on sight rescinded, Six."

"I wasn't chasing tail. They were going to kill her."

"Cry me a fucking river! As a matter of fact, cry me the fucking *Nile* River, because me and the boys almost had to fucking swim the Nile to get over there to pull your ass out of Darfur."

Court knew the possibility that the CIA would send Whiskey Sierra into Darfur to save Sierra Six had never been on the table. It was a ludicrous assertion. Still, he also knew when it was best to just let Sierra One have his little rant unopposed. Like a forest fire that burns the mountain so thoroughly that no tinder remains to fuel it, Zack's tirade would extinguish itself in a minute if Court didn't fight back.

"Look," said Court, already tired of talking to Zack. "Everything is okay. Sid is sending a plane here to Al Fashir tonight. I'll be in Suakin by tomorrow evening. I'll be back on target in time for the op Sunday morning at six thirty. Everything goes ahead as planned."

"You'd better see that it does, dude. You better get back on target posthaste. There is a hell of a lot riding on this."

"Yeah, understood. Six out."

29

Court kept his eye on the properly functioning GPS computer on his new wristwatch while sitting on the bench in the back of the Antonov. It gave him his position over the land below him, and he had to monitor it constantly to be sure the pilot was doing what he was told.

The plane was an AN-26, a much smaller transport than the one he'd ridden into the Sudan three days earlier. He wondered how many people were on board. He hadn't seen or spoken to anyone in the cockpit since climbing onto the flight nearly two hours earlier. He'd been waiting at the end of the runway at Al Fashir airport, had spent four hours swatting flies and kicking away little scorpions and dinner-plate-sized camel spiders, lying in a hide provided by one of the broken wings of one of the broken planes that lay like slaughtered birds alongside the runway. He'd planned on waiting inside the cabin of the discarded wreckage but found the interior too hot and stuffy to bear, and he had no doubt there'd be snakes to contend with as well. He was down to his last bottle of water when he climbed the fence to get into the airport that afternoon, had drunk the last sip from it an hour before the Russian plane landed, which turned out to be nearly three hours before the plane took off again.

He'd climbed through the hatch that they'd left open on his orders, relayed through Sid, through the FSB, and then on to the Rosoboronexport crew. When he made his way inside the dim cargo cabin, he found all the gear he'd requested cinched to a mesh bench. It was the same pack he'd had with him on his earlier flight, with a few new items, equipment crucial to the change in his operation necessitated by his three-day visit to Darfur. The crew of the Antonov had not bothered to even come out of the cockpit to check and make sure he'd made it in, that he had everything he needed.

These Russians didn't give a shit about him or his job. They were probably annoyed about the unusual flight plan they were ordered to fly, were certainly pissed about the unusual maneuver they'd have to execute, and they would no doubt blame him for the FSB heavies getting in their business and telling them how to do their job.

As far as the man in the back of their plane right now, they made it 100 percent clear with the open hatch left unattended and the lack of a welcoming party when he boarded. They didn't want to know him.

And that worked for a guy like the Gray Man.

He'd spent the first hour of the flight obsessively checking and rechecking all the equipment. He didn't trust these Russians with his life, so he didn't trust them to properly check the devices he'd need to keep himself alive and fulfill his objectives of the next forty-eight hours. Once he was satisfied everything was in working order, he sat back down on the bench and tried to relax.

Court's brain soon drifted off mission. He wanted a pain pill, but he was in no pain. His adrenaline was up, it stayed high when he was about to do this sort of thing, but still, he thought, he worried, he fretted now more than earlier in his career.

He'd once been a well-oiled machine, back with the SAD and before.

Somehow the Canadian woman had gotten inside him. He'd known better than to engage her in conversation, to try to justify himself to her, but there was something about her that got under his skin in ways both positive and negative. He would never admit to respecting her—her line of work and sanctimony he absolutely did not agree with—but he did not meet many real people out

206

here in the black, on the dark side. And even though she was likely some tree-hugging, do-gooding, we-are-the-world-singing, flipper-fucking fool, she was, at least, a fool who went toe to toe with the real dangers of the world.

The aircraft began a steep descent, sending his stomach up into his chest, and Court unlatched the buckle on his seat belt.

Ellen Walsh pushed some of Gentry's buttons during their day together, and even though this woman was likely right now preparing an indictment and opening an investigation and putting all of her energies into tracking him down and seeing that he was thrown in some cage somewhere, Court couldn't say that he did not want to see her again.

He shook his head. *Shit man, snap out of it.*

The Antonov leveled out quickly, causing Court's stomach to lurch in the other direction. With a metallic motorized cranking sound, the rear loading hatch opened behind him. Cold night sky appeared out past the red cabin lighting. The whoosh of air was audible, painfully loud even, but barely felt, as the aerodynamics of the craft kept the wind outside the cabin.

Yes, he'd once been a well-oiled machine.

Court stood, fumbled with all the equipment strapped to his body, and began lumbering towards the night.

He was *still* a machine, he told himself, and he believed it. He *knew* it. He was just a machine that needed a bit more oil than in the old days.

The Gray Man gave a quick test pull to the gear on his chest, between his knees, and on his back, walked slowly down the ramp, and tumbled out into the black sky.

The night air was cool here near the east coast of the Sudan; gentle breezes pulled in from the ocean saw to that. This area of the Red Sea Hills, the topographical anomaly to the west of Port Sudan and to the northwest of Suakin, rose one thousand feet out of the Sahel, a rocky brown disfigurement to the otherwise flat landscape.

At half past midnight, no light shone on the hillside save for a sliver of moon, not a single electrical source for a dozen miles in any direction, but these hills were not uninhabited. The Bejas and the Rashaidas lived out here. They tended goats or small farms on the plateaus, traded at the souks in Port Sudan or Suakin, subsistence-farmed where they could, lived off the hard earth, and did their best to stay out of the way of the Arabs, the tribes that had the power and led the government of Sudan.

There was once gold in these hills. Since pharaonic times gold ore had been sought out and mined and transported overland to Alexandria and Cairo. The mining of precious metals in the area had all but dried up, but gypsum and iron ore and limestone were still scratched out of the rock and sent away to places that actually had a need for the raw materials used in constructing cities and buildings.

It certainly wasn't needed here.

There'd been a war a few years back. Like the war in southern Sudan and the war in Darfur, the eastern minority tribes once tried to throw off the yoke of oppression. They were poorly organized, all but unfunded, and slapped into submission in what had become little more than a footnote after the bigger, badder civil conflicts at the other ends of the large nation.

Now, on a cool, dark, quiet hillside on the eastern edge of a plateau that overlooked the flat coastal plain that ran twenty miles to Port Sudan and then to the waterline itself, there was nothing but rail-thin goats, left unattended during the night by Beja tribesmen. Many of the animals slept standing, a few chewed lazily at tufts of green grass.

A gray Sahelian goat bleated loudly. Another followed, and then another. Soon a chorus of goats called out together, and then the tiny herd parted, ran out from the center, leaving an opening on the grassy hillside.

A large brown backpack crashed into the vacated space, bounced, and rolled down the hill, whipping a twenty-five-foot cord behind it.

And two seconds later a man in dark clothing landed on both boots, seemed to find his balance after a short skid, but the parachute above his head deformed and then re-formed in front of him, sucked in the draft down the hill towards the flatlands, and it pulled him off balance. He lost his footing on the hill, pitched forward, yanking and pulling on the leads to the canopy as he tumbled.

Twenty meters down the hill he came to rest. The canopy deflated and was hauled in, the bleating of the goats subsided, and their community re-formed again as if this odd insult had never occurred.

Gentry sat on his butt, hugged the fluttering canopy to his chest, and looked around in the dark.

"Shit," he said softly to no one, and then he doubled over, leaned on his left elbow, and vomited onto the dry grass.

Once he collected himself, swigged water from a bladder in his pack, spat it out to perfunctorily clean out his sour mouth, he looked off into the distance. He faced east, and to the northeast he could see the lights of Port Sudan, twenty some odd miles distant across the coastal plain. He turned to his right a bit, towards the south. He knew Suakin was out there in the dark, twenty-five or so miles from him now. He needed to get there as soon as possible.

He would have liked to be there already, reconnoitering the area, using the actual terrain instead of a map to fine-tune his plan.

Court stood, found his left butt cheek to be sore and bruised and stiffening, but he ignored it. There were pain meds in his pack. Lots of them. He'd stuffed them deep in a feeble battle with himself, wanted to go as long as possible without taking them.

The battle worked for now; he did not rip open the bag to dig for them. Instead he stood, spent several minutes among the thin goats, hiding his parachute and the other bags he no longer needed in the breeze-swept grasses and thatched bushes on the hillside. He changed his clothes, donned simple dark blue trousers and a dark green short-sleeved shirt, both purchased the day before in Al Fashir. He planned on using two forms of cover.

The Rashaidas, a lighter-skinned Arab common in the area, often eschewed long robes and cloaks for clothing more conventional to Westerners. And if he had to get up close and personal, he knew no one would believe him to be a Rashaida; no native Arabic speaker would buy for a second his piss-poor command of the language, and what Arabic he did know was an altogether different dialect. So his plan was to avoid close contact if possible, but if not possible, he would claim to be a Bosnian Muslim who'd been studying Arabic in Egypt but had decided to complete the hajj, the fifth pillar of Islam, the Muslim's required pilgrimage to Mecca in Saudi Arabia. Suakin was not known for much, but it *was* known, among East African Muslims, anyway, as the port where one could find ferry embarkation across the Red Sea to Jeddah, from where one could make his way on to Mecca. Court had even picked up a simple prayer rug in the souk in Al Fashir to back up this story.

It was, perhaps, the thinnest veil of a cover identity Gentry had ever attempted, for so many reasons Court had stopped counting them. He did not speak a damn word of Serbo-Croatian, the language of a Bosnian. He had concocted no good reason, and not even a bad reason, that a Bosnian studying in Egypt would need to sneak across the Sudanese border to find passage to Saudi Arabia. He would not be able to account for his big backpack, certainly not the sniper rifle and other curiosities inside it, nor the huge amount of money in his wallet and money belt. He would not be able to specify the route he took into the Sudan or even the neighborhood in which he supposedly lived in Cairo.

In any real questioning he'd have to play dumb, which would clearly be the easiest aspect of this cover for him to manage.

No, this particular legend would only work in the most casual of encounters. If he were stopped by police or army or any government official above the rank of the men who scooped camel shit out of the streets, despite his cover story, he would appear to them to be one thing and one thing only: an infidel assassin who dropped into their country from out of the sky.

Just before one o'clock in the morning, the Gray Man hefted his canvas pack onto his back and began walking down the hill.

By eight a.m., Court was sitting Indian style on a pile of straw stacked high on a two-wheeled donkey cart led by two Beja boys. The boys, barely in their teens, wore their hair in wild, messy afros and were dressed identically in baggy beige pants and brown vests, their milk chocolate skin ruddy in the rays of the ceaseless morning sun. Court had given them the Bosnian pilgrim story, they'd bought it, he'd given them a few Sudanese pounds, and they'd taken them. They were heading all the way to Suakin to an uncle's house, delivering the donkey and the hay, and though this means of travel was no faster than Court walking himself, he surely *preferred* this means of travel to walking himself.

He told the boys that he did not want any trouble from local authorities, being a foreigner and all, and they'd helpfully suggested, via common Arabic words and pantomime, that he bury himself and his pack in the straw if cars passed or checkpoints loomed. The boys made a game of it, and he'd bought them lunch and tea at a roadside stand set up for those heading to Suakin to catch the Jeddah ferry. He'd even bought the donkey his own lunch at the stand, identical to what the humans ate, which the kids found hysterical.

In the afternoon, as the Red Sea coastline appeared in the hazy distance, Gentry dug himself deep in the straw and stayed there. He tried not to choke on the dust and avoided thinking too much about the constant creepy-crawly sensations in his pants and his shirt. Traffic on the road had picked up considerably: buses, donkey and horse carts, men on foot, occasionally the odd private car. Twice even military transport trucks passed. Sidorenko had provided Gentry with a good deal of reading on Suakin. Court had ignored the majority of it, other than a map; the folio on the ancient port city had not seemed germane to his mission. But he *had* read a brief article on the city, and he was fascinated by its rich history. As well as being famous for its daily ferry to Jeddah

211

in Saudi Arabia, Suakin was also known as the last active slave port in Africa, only cutting off the traffic in humans in 1946. Suakin was key to the African slave trade, whether Egyptians or Ottomans or British controlled the town. Many of the big, beautiful buildings in the town, virtually all of them in disrepair, were built in the furtherance of this cruel but lucrative industry.

He knew not to expect much as far as infrastructure here, but President Abboud had a farm nearby and enjoyed performing the morning call to prayer in the high gallery of the tower in the mosque that looked out over the Red Sea.

And that's what put it on Court Gentry's travel itinerary.

30

Nightfall found the Gray Man just to the north of Suakin, look-ing out to the water of the lagoon. The Red Sea itself was three miles or so farther to the east. This finger inlet protected the small port and had made the waterway a natural transportation route for centuries, until 1907, when the opening of Port Sudan, forty miles to the north, rendered Suakin irrelevant. Gentry still wore his Sudanese clothing, Western in appearance but not at all out of the ordinary here. With his tan skin and his dark beard and hair, with the dust and grime of a full day of travel, with his white taqiyah prayer cap, he could pass from a distance and in the night as an Arab, perhaps a Rashaida, if no one looked too closely. The Bosnian pilgrim cover story was always there to pull out in a pinch, though it was no more plausible here than it had been twenty miles to the west.

He'd stowed his pack deep in the boulders ten yards from the warm water's edge. He'd found a dark cavelike indention in the rocks, and this he'd made a temporary LUP, or layup position.

The breeze from the ocean was not cool, but it *was* moving air, certainly less hot and stifling than had been Al Fashir or his six hours on the donkey cart. Compared to most of the last ninety-six hours, the steady currents of air off the water here in the dark shade of the boulders felt like the soft touch of a woman, not that Court had much experience with that in the past several years. He lay back, let his mind drift, let his bare feet dangle in a pool of seawater while his head rested on his boots, and he wanted a painkiller to help him relax one last time before the action and danger of tomorrow morning.

But he did not have time to relax now; he had to call Zack, needed to meet with him to pick up some equipment he'd need the next morning. He also needed to meet with Mohammed, the Suakin cop who was on the payroll of Russian intelligence.

He pulled out the Thuraya phone, pushed a couple of buttons, and then waited.

"You here?" Zack was all about the mission now. He was still angry at Court about Darfur, the teasing macho banter of their earlier conversations nowhere in sight.

"Affirm."

"Let's meet at Echo, four-five mikes."

"Roger that. Echo in forty-five."

"One out."

Echo was the code name for the ruined treasury building in Old Suakin, which was an island of shattered coral and stone buildings connected by a causeway to el-Geyf, or the new town of Suakin, which lay on the mainland shore. Court had ignored the causeway; instead he put his shoes and pants and his pistol in a small backpack, slipped it around his neck, and then swam across the lagoon at its narrowest point, not more than five minutes in the crossing. The lagoon channel on the other side of the island was deeper and wider. He could see it in the distance under the light of a large but antiquated-looking prison on the far shore. Several small wooden fishing boats anchored in the water near the causeway; farther on, pleasure yachts moored in the black water, their generators lighting their bows and sails, powering stereos that blasted Western-style music, and no doubt providing electricity to kitchens on board more modern than anything in the darkened city beyond the reach of their mast lights.

On the ruined island of Old Suakin itself he was enveloped by darkness, save for dull illumination from a crescent moon. The wreckage of ancient coral rag buildings, erected in the twelfth century, back when this was a main port in North Africa, had deteriorated down to piles of rubble under majestic walls, stairs to nowhere, regal colonnades and columns alongside overgrown bushes and roads of dirt and broken stone. The only human inhabitants of the island were a few caretakers in wooden huts on the far side. The only other residents were four-legged. Court was nearly surrounded by cats before he'd made it fifty feet inland. He followed a path up a hill, kept low in the dark so as not to be seen, and the cats followed him on all sides. But they were quiet and stealthy like he was; other than an occasional rumbling purr, they did not give away the movement of this odd entourage. After another fifty yards Gentry approached the old treasury warily and heard a noise in the brush too big to be feline paws. He pulled a silenced Glock 19 from his pack, only to find himself staring down his sights at a kneeling camel chewing its cud lazily and staring back at him.

Court holstered his weapon and watched the building from between two large, felled coral pillars, his ears tuned to any noises other than the music from the boats in the distance, the camel behind him, and the cats all around. After a short time a penlight flicked on and off twice from the second story of the building, and Gentry rose and approached across a narrow dirt road.

The building was little more than a two-story facade, a spiral staircase in one corner, and a couple hundred square feet of flooring on the second level. Everything else—roof, side and rear walls, the rest of the second floor—was all in a huge pile of stones and ancient wood piled where the first floor should have been. At the bottom of the staircase Court saw Sierra Two, Zack's second-in-command. The oldest in the Whiskey Sierra clan, Brad wore a salt-and-pepper beard and was dressed in local attire: a white turban on his head, a Kalashnikov cradled in his arms.

Sierra Two nodded, no friendliness whatsoever in the greeting. "Go on up," he said.

The stone steps seemed stable enough, but Court saw proof all around that this structure hadn't been built to last. He walked gingerly up the staircase, found Zack Hightower at the top in the southwest corner of the second floor, the only second-story corner of the building to *have* a floor. Zack sat cross-legged in the shadows, dressed and armed similar to Sierra Two. He'd grown a short beard in the past eight days but otherwise looked the same as he did in Saint Petersburg.

Gentry sat down next to him, and several cats wandered around them both. Zack scooted back farther into darkness, and Court followed him, until they could see one another no longer.

"You aren't wet," Court mentioned.

"We took a Zodiac from the yacht, came in on the dark side of the lagoon. The *Hannah* is anchored fifteen klicks to the northeast," Zack said.

"In Sudanese waters?"

"Yep. We were boarded by a patrol boat and half-ass searched. They think we're Aussies cruising up the coast of Africa, waiting on an engine part to be DHL'd into Port Sudan. We gave them beer and smokes and made friends."

Court picked a black cat up off his leg, sent it on its way with a gentle toss towards the stairs.

"You been in town yet?" Zack asked as he tucked his butt closer to Court on the ruined flooring of the old building so he could talk softer. Their voices carried deceptively far in the night.

"Negative. You?"

Zack nodded. Court could just see the tip of his chin rise and lower. "Major hellhole. And *I* know hellholes. It's got an Old West vibe to it. The only power in town is from generators. There is one paved surface in the city. All the other streets and alleys are hard-packed earth, donkey shit, goat shit, and camel shit everywhere you step. The buildings are made out of cracking limestone and coral, like this shit here. There isn't a structure in the city that I couldn't topple with a brickbat and a half hour. Probably seventy-five percent of the buildings are little huts, made with driftwood and tin and rusted-out fifty-five gallon drums.

"So, no hardened cover when it goes loud," Gentry said, completing Zack's obvious point for him.

"Shit, if it goes loud tomorrow morning, buildings are going to fall down on top of you from the sound waves." Zack shrugged. Court heard the motion in the dark, but he could not see him in the shadows. "Which wouldn't be so bad for the locals. This joint could do for some urban renewal."

"Police presence?"

"Negligible during our recon. A few Chinese AKs on dudes in civilian dress patrolling around. Three or four pickup trucks and a couple of hundred-year-old cannon in front of the police station."

"Cannon?"

"Just for decoration."

Court nodded.

Zack said, "Just so you know, Sudan Station is still shitting bricks about your actions over in North Darfur. Everybody says Sierra Six has gone rogue; he's pulling his own op four hundred miles away from his target. You really fucked up. I don't hear from you for three days, and when I finally do, you don't offer much explanation for all the bang bang in the desert." He looked to Gentry for a reply.

"Yeah," Court admitted with a sigh. "It got weird."

Zack shrugged. "The White House is up Denny Carmichael's butt to know what is going on. I share their concern."

"I told you what happened."

"This woman from the ICC. The Canadian. She can ID you?"

"She doesn't know who I am."

"Is she going to make trouble?"

"Maybe for me, down the road. But not for this op."

"You're sure about that?"

Court thought it over and said, "Yeah. I'm sure. She thinks I'm the epitome of evil ... but she does believe that our interests coincide as far as whatever it is I'm up to here."

Zack sat there in the dark for a long time. He seemed to let it go, albeit slowly. "Tomorrow at oh six thirty Abboud will leave the house where he's staying. It's a ten-mike walk to the mosque. It is five mikes to the square, one mike more to get him right in front of the bank building. The SLA will hit the square from the north at oh six thirty-six exactly."

"They got watches?"

"Sudan Station says they do."

"Whiskey Sierra isn't in direct contact with the rebels?"

"Negative. Sudan Station has a case officer in town; he's running the SLA." He shrugged. Kind of a *What'cha gonna do?* look about the gesture. "I need *you* to be on your mark in the bank when the shit hits the fan."

"Roger that."

"When you snatch Oryx, take him one block south and eight blocks west of the back of the bank. There is a four-door black Skoda Octavia sedan in the parking lot of a brick-making factory. Sudan Station put it there, paid one of the kiln operators to spend the night on the hood to watch over it. Here are the keys."

Court took them. He asked, "Where are you going to be between now and go time?"

"Me, Brad, Milo, and Dan are staying on the *Hannah*. We'll be in place tomorrow morning."

"Where's Sierra Five?"

"Spencer is already in town. He and the case officer from Sudan Station are staying at a hotel called the Suakin Palace. Spencer assures me it's no palace. What it *is*, though, is a decent third-floor overwatch on the square. The case officer is going to leave tonight to get out of the way, but Spencer will stay there, be the eye for us."

"That's good." Court was pleasantly surprised there would be another set of eyes at the target location in the morning, although he was also surprised Zack would want one of his men so close to the action. He didn't press his good fortune by asking about it. Instead he questioned Hightower on the rebels. "The SLA is in place and ready to go?"

Zack shrugged. "Better be. Sudan Station paid four hundred thousand bucks to secure their participation. There are thirty-five rebels who will attack from the north at our command tomorrow morning."

"Thirty-five?"

Zack nodded.

"What happened to one hundred?"

Hightower had promised Court, back when he'd been trying to get him to agree to the op, that a force of rebels one hundred strong would keep Abboud's security and local police tied up. But Zack showed no contrition in explaining the discrepancy. He just waved his hand, like it was a minor matter. "That would have been overkill. A couple of trucks at the square, a couple more at the police station, a couple more on the road into town. We know that if Abboud's personal security detail is close enough to the bank when the raid hits, then they are going to shove him into the bank, no matter how much or how little shooting occurs. We don't want or need a major battle on our hands. Thirty-five rebels is the perfect amount."

"You sound like someone sold that to you, so now you are trying to sell it to me."

Zack smiled a little, the first time he'd been anything but furious with Court since their sat phone conversation when he was flying into Al Fashir, four days earlier. After a second's thought, he raised his hands in surrender. "Yeah. Sudan Station told me one hundred rebels. Then they told me thirty-five. Their explanation was just as I said. It makes sense, especially after looking at the layout of the town, but I sure don't like planning an op under one set of presumptions and then executing it under another set of presumptions."

Court just nodded in the dark. "But you still want to go ahead?"

"Hell yeah," Sierra One said without hesitation. "We're good."

The evening call to prayer came from the minaret in the mosque to the west. If everything went according to plan, Court would be a couple blocks away from that very mosque tomorrow before sunup. He looked at Zack. "You got the stuff for me?"

Zack used his thumb to press a wireless push-to-talk

219

transmission button mounted on the side of the index finger of his glove. He spoke into a small headset angled around his right cheek. "Brad, let's have the ruck."

Sierra Two appeared at the top of the stairs a few seconds later. The rucksack was about the size Court had expected, roughly the same as his other pack, stowed back at the water's edge three hundred yards to the north of this location.

"I need a fucking Sherpa."

"Hey man, you're officially running two ops; for that you need two sets of gear."

Zack next handed over a small plastic box, and Court opened it. It was a C4OPS radio system, the same as the Whiskey Sierra team would be using the next morning. It was new technology, and it had everything but the kitchen sink rolled up into it. A radio, a GPS, wireless PTT buttons to mount on a glove or a weapon, earpieces that also provided noise reduction during gunfire, and a covert microphone headset that was virtually invisible when worn on a face with a beard. Zack had given him a primer on the C4OPS system back in Saint Pete, but before that Court had never heard of it.

"How's the encryption? Any chance the opposition can pick up the transmissions?"

"I'll show you." Zack flipped on the device, pushed the wireless transmit button. He spoke into the microphone in a whisper. "Good evening, all you skinnies and ragheads. My name is Zachary Paul Hightower. My social security number is 413-555-1287. President Abboud sucks camel dicks."

Sierra Two was at the top of the stairs. He turned back to Hightower. "That's *my* social."

Zack smiled. Shrugged. "Is it? My bad, Bradley." He turned back to Court. "You can listen in on our transmissions on this. Just so you know what's going on at our end. But I don't want you clogging the net. Don't transmit. If you need to talk to me, use the Thuraya. I'll have it on at all times, wired into my headset, even if we are in hard contact."

"Why would you be in hard contact? I thought you guys were gonna be out of the way until we rendezvous in the marsh."

"Hey, shit happens, bro. If it breaks bad, who knows what's going to go down? We're all ready to go to shore in support if the situation calls for it. Sudan Station has a van staged for us if we need to move into town in the morning. They also got us local clothes. We brought in secondhand gear. We aren't going in with all US equipment, for deniability's sake. We've got guns from Israel and Germany and Russia, boots from Croatia, packs from China, body armor from Australia."

Court was surprised there had been so much preparation for Whiskey Sierra to be ready to get into the fight, but it had been a long time since he'd been part of a big operation. As a singleton, he normally arranged all the gear and logistics himself.

Zack leaned forward into the soft moonlight. He put a gloved hand out in the dark, and Court shook it.

"Good luck tomorrow. I'll be seeing you, and Oryx, when it's done. We'll party like rock stars on the *Hannah* once we exfil."

"Sounds like a plan. But first how 'bout you guys give me a lift back across the lagoon."

"No prob."

Court searched Hightower's face and body for any signs of deception. He saw worry, anxiety over the op itself, but nothing in his body language gave Court any reason to suspect deception. It comforted him to know that Sierra One did not seem to be working on a different objective in this operation.

31

At ten o'clock that evening Gentry stood on a street corner, just a few blocks west of where he'd been dropped off by Zack's six-man Zodiac inflatable boat. He stood back in the dark, but many local men had passed within feet of him. Some had looked at him with curiosity but not suspicion or fear. In Sid's info on the city he'd learned that the passengers and crew on the Western sailboats and yachts that moored in the harbor were often allowed passes to shop or eat in the town, as long as they paid for the privilege and did not have any Israeli visits stamped into their passports. Court imagined whites were a rare but not uncommon sight, so even if his skin tone raised eyebrows, there was little reason to worry it would raise an alarm.

An old white Mercedes sedan pulled up to the corner. It idled there, its poorly tuned engine coughing into the night air as the driver waited. This would be Mohammed, the local policeman on the payroll of Russian intelligence. Court did not come out of his shadow at first; instead, he searched for any evidence that the vehicle had been followed. Ultimately he decided that unless it had been followed by a donkey cart pulling a fifty-five gallon drum of water, he was clear. There were no other vehicles in sight.

Court climbed into the passenger side, and the vehicle rolled off down dusty, dark streets.

The driver's face was blank, unmoving. Gentry felt that even if there had been light in the car's interior, even if the biggest,

222

brightest bulb from the biggest football stadium in the US was pointed at this man's onyx face, it would reveal no more detail than Court could now discern here in the darkness.

The policeman spoke first, in English. His voice was low and gravelly. "You are Russian?"

This guy had been working for the Russians; there was no reason to confuse him.

"That's right."

"Good. Tell your people I want more money."

"I'm not your agent. Tell them yourself."

Nothing but the man's lips moved. Court had seen vending machines with more lifelike qualities than this informant. "I am in a dangerous position, meeting you, helping the FSB with this. It is now much more dangerous than when I agreed. I want more money before I proceed."

Court wasn't buying it. In Gentry's experience it was the rule not the exception that an informant would ask for more money at the last moment. They often insisted that matters had become more complicated as a means to this end. As far as Court was concerned, this man's main use had been to drive him from Khartoum to Suakin, and since Court had not needed that particular service, he didn't really give a shit whether Sid or the FSB paid the man or not. Still, he'd come tonight to see if the cop could be of any use at all.

It was already looking like this man was not worth the trouble.

"I don't have any money." It was a lie, but Court didn't feel like blowing his stash of cash on this son of a bitch. "If you have information valuable to me, I'll tell my superiors you were helpful."

The stone-faced man pulled over and parked the car. It was pitch-black on all sides of the vehicle, and the headlights shone on the dust cloud created by the car's tires. Mohammed looked into Court's eyes. Court hoped he appeared as dark and threatening as this asshole. "That is not enough."

"Then I guess we're done. I'll tell the FSB you changed your mind. I'm sure you'll be hearing from them soon enough." Court made like he was going to get out, but he knew what was coming.

"Wait."

Court settled back down in his cracked leather seat. His pistol dug into his right hip as he did so.

"There are new developments in Suakin."

Court thought he was about to hear another spiel about danger to justify Mohammed's desire for more money. He sighed, but the informant's next comment got his attention.

"I thought Abboud would only arrive with his regular security detail. Twenty-five men or so. Normally when he comes, that is all. Yes, there are always more up at Port Sudan—they stay with his helicopter—but when he comes to Suakin, usually it is just the twenty-five guards."

"So . . . what's different this time?"

"The NSS arrived this afternoon."

"The secret police are here?"

"Correct."

"How many?" Court looked down to his hands. He picked at his fingernails.

"I saw five men." Then the man in the shadows said, almost as an afterthought, "But there is a lot of military in town, also. You need to watch out for them."

"What's a lot?"

"A company, at least. Infantry."

This made Gentry look up at the driver again. "Any idea why?"

"They say a group of rebels has been tracked to a farm outside of town."

In an instant, Court knew the CIA operation had been compromised.

"Rebels?"

"Yes. SLA. It is strange. They have never operated this far to the east."

"Any idea how many SLA?"

He waved an arm, his first gesticulation. "Not many. Just a dozen men or so."

A dozen. Zack had initially promised one hundred, then cut

224

that to thirty-five. Now Court's most solid intel on the subject was that the real number was twelve. He didn't blame Zack; surely if Sierra One knew his proxy fighters were such an impotent force, he wouldn't have gone this far with the op. No, Court had seen this kind of deteriorating math before. He blamed the local CIA office, Sudan Station, for overpromising and underdelivering. There probably never were going to be a hundred SLA in Suakin; thirty-five was their best guess, and now it was clear that Sudan Station's best guess sucked.

A dozen SLA, already compromised to the local authorities, weren't going to fool anyone. If the attempt to kidnap the president went forward now, the army would roll up the pathetic little force of rebels in a matter of minutes.

Court could still assassinate the president for Greg Sidorenko, but kidnapping him for the CIA was out of the question without the rebel attack. It was obvious to Gentry now that Zack and his mission would be aborted.

"So I want more money to help you tomorrow."

Court needed to talk to Zack before he even knew if there would *be* an op tomorrow. But he realized now he might just need Muhammed's help in getting out of the area. If Nocturne Sapphire was dead in the dirt, then the CIA might want him to do Sid's job and exfil as planned via FSB connections.

"I have two thousand euros."

"I want ten."

Court paused. It wasn't his money, he couldn't care less what this man was paid, but he'd been bargaining for one thing or another in the Third World for most of the past fifteen years, and he knew what he was doing.

He nodded. "Three now, three after." Six grand was probably three times what this creepy bastard made in a year. Assuming the Russians had already agreed to pay him that much or more, this clown was making a serious chunk of change.

Mohammed looked at Gentry a long time. Finally he pulled the car back into the street and began driving. "Agreed."

He and Court discussed arrangements for several minutes as the Mercedes inched around the town. Court tried to reconnoiter while they talked by looking out the grimy windows, but he could not make heads or tails of the confusing streets and dirt alleyways.

Finally Mohammed pulled over again. Court was surprised to find himself right where he'd been picked up a half hour before. The policeman said, "Tomorrow morning I will be at the agreed upon location at the agreed upon time. I will take you to a house in Khartoum where you can wait until it is safe to go to the airport."

Gentry reached into his front pocket and pulled out a band-covered roll of euros. It was Sid's money, of course; the CIA hadn't given him any cash.

Court made it back to his overnight hide at eleven o'clock. He checked to make sure nothing in his packs had been disturbed, and he opened a tepid bottle of water and drank it down. Then he picked up the Hughes Thuraya and made a call.

Zack answered on the third ring. "Just getting some beauty sleep, Six; this better be good." Hightower spoke sleepily.

"You need to abort Nocturne Sapphire. The rebels are compromised."

When Hightower spoke again, he was wide awake. "Says who?"

"Says the FSB informant. He's a local cop. A crew of NSS and a company of GOS infantry is in town because a dozen SLA were tracked here."

"A dozen?"

"Roger that."

"*One* dozen. One-two rebel fighters?"

"His intel seems solid."

There was a long break. "Fucking Sudan Station."

"That's what I'm thinking. Local CIA either exaggerated the shit out of the SLA's ability to get men into the theater, or—"

"Or the SLA lied, fudged the numbers to get a paycheck from Uncle Sam. And then they go and get their bush-league asses compromised!"

"Fuckers."

"Roger that." Sierra One's chuckle came out of Court's phone. "Never thought I'd say this, but thank God for Sidorenko and his local contact."

"Yeah, right? This could have been messy."

"Let me call this in to Denny."

"Tell him you need to abort."

"Let's see what he says."

"Hit me back ASAP, One. I can still do the hit on Oryx; the opposition in the area won't stop me from that."

"Let's see what Denny says," Zack repeated.

Court's overnight hide was, from an operational standpoint at least, a near perfect location to store his gear and lay up for the night. With both large rucks opened and the gear sorted and positioned for his fast access, he found a warm boulder large and flat enough for him to lie on. The gentle tickling of the lagoon's waves against the shoreline rocks was peaceful and would help him rest when the time came.

He'd waited over an hour for the call back from Zack. It came after midnight, just as Gentry's eyes shut and he nodded off to sleep.

He'd wired the satellite phone into his C4OPS system, so when the earpiece chirped in Court's ear, he just pressed a button on the phone to send the call directly into the headset.

Gentry answered quickly. "Yeah?"

"Carmichael says go ahead."

"With Sid's hit on Abboud, right?"

"Negative. We stick with Nocturne Sapphire. Snatch Oryx and exfil over water."

"How the hell can I snatch him with all the opposition in the—"

"Sudan Station doesn't believe it. Thinks either it's bullshit intel your source is feeding you, or bullshit intel you're feeding us. And Carmichael is siding with the local station. We go ahead for now, discount this single source of yours, because local CIA says there are thirty-five SLA here, no reports of major NSS or GOS movements. The SLA say they will hit the square at oh six thirty-six tomorrow morning, no problems."

"I'm not feeding anyone bullshit, Zack."

"I know you're not. Listen, Carmichael says I am cleared to make a game-time decision. I can knock it off at any point if it doesn't look good tomorrow morning. He's given me the go-ahead to be on site."

"You're going to be at the bank with me?"

"No, but we'll be close by. He's green-lighted Whiskey Sierra for direct action if the situation requires it."

Court sucked in the moist air. "Seriously? You guys are going to shoot it out with the bodyguards and GOS troops? What happened to all that deniability bullshit? Why are you even using me in this if you have a green light to—"

"Court, Carmichael has his back to the wall. He's made some promises that he has to keep by any means necessary. He's promised the White House that we can hand Oryx over to the Euros. That means, basically, that we *have* to hand Oryx over to the Euros. The future of the Special Operations Group rests on this op."

"The future of my *ass* rests on this op. You promised this would come down to a few of Abboud's bodyguards against one hundred rebel forces. Now it's the bodyguards, a company of GOS troops, and an NSS contingent of unknown size, all against a couple of pickups full of untrained dipshits who've already been compromised!"

"I told you, Sudan Station doesn't think they've been compromised. And even if they have, Whiskey Sierra will be the force multiplier. We'll get it done."

"This plan needs an enema, Zack."

"Kid, back in the day, how many of all the Goon Squad's ops went to plan?"

Court thought. Shrugged. "Can't think of a one, but—"

"Exactly. This plan is the best we got, and if it all goes south on us, we'll come up with something else on the fly. Just like always."

"I don't like it."

"I will make note of your dissent, and I will place it in the 'who the fuck cares what Court thinks' file." Zack laughed at himself. "What did I tell you back in the day, Six? You don't have to like it—"

"You just have to do it," Court finished the thought. He was pissed, but he was a beaten man on this. He'd do his job, and Hightower knew it.

"You want to get back in the fold? You stick with your part of Nocturne Sapphire. You will make Carmichael a very happy and very appreciative man. Don't worry, dude. Whiskey Sierra will be around to help you through."

After a long pause Gentry muttered, "Six out."

32

Court awoke and looked down at his watch. Tiny bits of tritium gas-filled tubes illuminated the hands, told him it was time to get up.

It was four thirty in the morning; the air was cool with the ocean's breeze. He rolled into a sitting position and filled his lungs.

He'd slept fitfully for a couple of hours at most. The operation ahead had kept him tossing and turning, his mind spinning with details and contingencies and with a multitude of if/then statements that he could not seem to reconcile. No matter how he looked at it, he couldn't imagine this day being anything other than a massive cluster fuck. He felt like a train wreck was coming, he was on the train, and it was too late to jump off.

From the pack Zack had handed off to him the night before he retrieved a peanut butter Soldier Fuel bar, a vitamin and protein-fortified energy bar created by nutritionists in the US Army. He opened the package and ate it quickly and efficiently, his game face hardening by the minute as the day's operation approached. He washed it down with water from his CamelBak bladder.

Gentry crab-walked down the boulders to the water's edge. As he relieved himself into the lagoon, he considered changing clothes into something more tactical, but decided against it. He'd love to have pants with more pockets—pockets were important to an operator—but his grungy, grimy, local attire—clothes that he'd hiked in, swam in, slept in, even ridden on a donkey cart in—just looked too authentic to eschew for something clean and alien to the environment.

He crawled over to his Russian backpack, the one provided to him by Sid. He hefted it over a shoulder and stepped into the cool black water of the lagoon. The heavy bag was watertight and built with an air chamber that would allow it to float, and Gentry hung on to it as he swam across.

Twenty minutes later, his head appeared at the top of the minaret on Old Suakin Island. He climbed into the gallery of the structure, the open room just under the crown at the top of the tower. Back when the island was alive and the mosque open, two hundred years ago at the most recent, from here the muezzin sang the adhan, the five times daily call to prayer. Now it was dormant and home to birds; Court's arrival stirred pigeons from their sleep. They flitted off, but the noise and movement was no worry to Gentry. The cats around here certainly harassed the feathered creatures often enough to where a small group of them taking flight in the night would not raise the alarm. Court crawled carefully across the minaret, smearing fresh pigeon droppings with his knees and gloves, pulling his pack behind him. He was less concerned with being spotted and more concerned with the structure giving way, falling apart and falling down, taking him along with it. But it held, and Gentry unzipped his pack and pulled out the pieces of the Blaser sniper rifle and began assembling the weapon.

All of this was merely misdirection. He was not going to use the rifle, not going to snipe anyone today. This was all aimed at encouraging Sidorenko to believe the story that his top assassin had been compromised somehow and captured or killed outright by CIA assassins. When Abboud turned up alive, his shackled form on television from The Hague, Sid would wonder what happened to the hit man he'd sent to kill him. Carmichael had promised that Langley would let it be known that a SAD Paramilitary Operation's team had finally caught up with their most wanted man, killed him dead on the coast of the Red Sea, just moments before he killed again.

Court had no way of knowing for sure if this ruse would work. Sid was no fool. But, Gentry decided, the more evidence he could plant on site that would indicate that he was, in fact, in place for the Abboud hit, the more likely Sidorenko and his people would get word that the leaked story matched with the physical traces of Gray's last known location.

So the American took his time, laid out the scene exactly as he would if the sniping, in fact, were about to take place. The rifle was placed in position on its bipod, the scope cap was unsnapped, and the optics were ranged properly for a 400-meter shot in negligible winds. The gun was loaded, and extra cartridges were lined up neatly on his right-hand side.

Finally, when he was satisfied with his ruse, Court took one last look at his sniper's hide. How easy it would have been for him to assassinate President Abboud, make his way to a speedboat at the far edge of the island, shoot hard and fast over the gentle Red Sea waters to an awaiting larger craft, and then churn away into international waters. Sure, the Sudanese had gunboats—he might get unlucky and run into one during his escape—but the odds of avoiding the Sudanese navy were likely a hell of a lot better than they were for the success of Nocturne Sapphire. Court shook his head slowly. A shitload of things beyond Court's control needed to go very very right in the next few hours.

Gentry backed down the stairs. Out again on the predawn dirt roads of Old Suakin Island, he backed his way the three blocks to the water's edge, ensuring that no tracks of one man coming and going were anywhere to be found. He hefted his much lighter pack and stepped back into the warm water. It was as placid as a swimming pool, though the brackish smell left little doubt that it was not chemically cleansed.

When he was neck deep, holding on to his floating pack with both hands, he looked back at the island. When his planted evidence was found, whether in hours or in days, he would be linked to the scene. It would appear to everyone that the assassin had made it to his sniper's nest, set it up as per his requirements, and then lain in wait for his prey.

And then it would appear to everyone as if the sniper just simply vanished into thin air.

The Gray Man smiled darkly as he turned, gently kicked his feet, and began floating towards the shoreline one hundred meters away.

There wasn't a soul on the dirt streets of New Suakin at five in the morning. First light was not for another hour, Oryx would not pass by for ninety minutes, but Court was already in position, tucked deep into shadows at the long, tin-roofed fish market that composed the southeastern corner of the square. With him was his CIA backpack, nearly fifty pounds of gear stowed inside. His satellite phone was attached to the left side of his belt under his loose-fitting shirt, wired into the C4OPS radio hooked alongside it. The wireless earpieces were tucked in both ears, and the thin rubber-and-wire tube lay flat on his cheek as it snaked down to his mouth, allowing the covert headset to be nearly invisible in the hair on his head and of his beard.

Under his shirt on his belt he carried his suppressed Glock 19 and two extra magazines. Forty-six rounds of 9 mm ammunition in total. Not a lot for a battle, but this morning's action was supposed to go on *around* him and not *on top* of him.

Still, he sure as hell would have liked some more firepower.

Court took his time to tune himself in to his environment. Loose camels roamed the streets; donkeys were in corrals or tied to wooden hitching posts. The town around him looked, quite literally, like something from biblical times, with the one big exception being the old, crumbling mosque in front of him. There were no mosques here in the time of Christ, but surely this particular view that he had, sitting at the open-air fishmonger's stall, must not have changed one iota since the twelfth century. He imagined himself back in those days and wondered if some spy or assassin had crouched at this very place at this very time of morning, with nefarious designs on a target in that mosque or in that ancient-looking building across the square.

Only then did he notice the few anachronisms in the scene. Several donkey carts were in view, but all had thick rubber tires instead of ancient wooden cartwheels. Much of the metal roofing and siding of the shacks in view were rusted oil drums or even large tin coffee cans. A broken blue plastic bucket hung from a rope outside a second-story window.

Without warning a voice spoke, close. It startled him, and he grabbed for his pistol and rose, bumping his head on a loose wooden shelf above him in the shack before recognizing that the voice was Zack and that it had come through his headset. He knelt back down, mad at himself.

"Good morning, Six, wherever you are. Me and the boys are just finishing our second cup of coffee, then we'll get geared up and head to shore." The sound of a long stretch and a sigh. Obvious dramatic effect. "Damn. Sure as shit is nice working for the man, not running rogue, sitting scared by yourself in the dark somewhere, hoping like hell that rat running up your leg doesn't bite you in the balls because you can't afford to move and give away your position."

Court looked down. There was no rat on his leg. He chastised himself for looking.

"Pretty soon, bro, you'll be back workin' with us. Of course you'll still be the outsider, but I promise I'll let you join us for a cup of joe from time to time."

Gentry nodded. It would be good to be part of a team again, even if there were a few caveats to the relationship.

"First things first, though. Let's get through this morning. One out."

"Roger that," whispered Court to himself; he did not transmit to Hightower. He rose slowly, avoided the shelf above, and crossed the tiny alleyway towards the side entrance to the bank. He picked the lock in under thirty seconds; it was a simple tumbler job that needed just two narrow tools and a few jiggles of the torque wrench to defeat.

Inside it was pitch-black; stale dust wafted in the moonlight shining through circular and arched windows. Court pulled his penlight from his pocket and turned it on, put it in his mouth, and crossed down a small colonnade that ran along the eastern side of the large, open building. This place had been around for hundreds of years, Gentry could tell, but apparently banking was no longer such a big deal in Suakin. Most of the space was open and empty, with a few desks and telephones, wooden filing cabinets, and steps that went down to a basement. Court continued on to the main entrance and found it exactly as drawn up in the diagrams Zack had provided him. There were stairs to the left and the right of the front double doors. The steps went up to a narrow atrium over the doors, where large windows looked out over the square. Gentry took a few minutes to stage his gear, hustling a half dozen times up and down the spiral stone staircases to position equipment where he would need it when Oryx and his security detail came storming through the door, thinking they were saving themselves from an attack in the square.

Court looked out the open windows of the atrium, getting a good look at the square for the first time. It did not look like a square, in the sense that Court knew the word from his travels in Europe, Asia, and Latin America. It was the size of two football fields, completely unpaved, not a blade of grass, just a big, flat expanse of hard earth. On the opposite side of the bank were some rickety looking two-story buildings, whitewashed colonial-style architecture but dingy, their filth obvious even in the moonlight shine. To the northeast, the right side of the square, it was nothing but shacks—handmade driftwood, plywood, tin, and junk hammered together or tied together or, Court imagined with slight exaggeration, simply leaned together with a prayer to Allah and a hope for the best. The shacks stretched down a hill several blocks to the water's edge and the causeway to the island of Old Suakin.

To the left of Court's vantage point, the western side of the square, he saw the finest buildings Suakin had to offer. The hotel was there, the Suakin Palace. Court looked at the third floor and wondered if Sierra Five was watching. Gentry stood in pitch-blackness inside the bank, but he figured Spencer would have night vision gear of some sort. He raised his hand tentatively.

"Sierra Five to Sierra One," the transmission came over the net a second later.

"Go for One," Zack's tinny voice responded.

"Sierra Six is in position."

"Never a doubt in my mind," said Hightower. Court lowered his hand. It felt odd to be watched, especially at a time like this. He continued scanning the rest of the buildings of the square. They were whitewashed limestone and coral, looking as old as Methuselah, Gentry thought, then he wondered if Methuselah was from around here.

He eyed the street from where the SLA trucks should come, assuming they'd come at all. If they did not, then Court assumed he'd leave all his gear here and just scoot on out the side door of the bank. The Sudanese would find a curious array of gadgets lying around the building where their president was set to come if there was a ruckus, but the CIA would not be positively implicated in any sort of attack or potential ambush. All of this gear was available outside of the USA, and all of this gear had been procured outside of the USA.

But the CIA local field office, Sudan Station, had assured everyone involved, in no uncertain terms, that their rebels would come through. Everyone involved had believed them, to the extent that Court's source was discounted as unreliable for providing intel that said otherwise.

Fuck, thought Court. This is not how he operated his solo hits. Everything was so much simpler as a private contract killer.

33

The Gray Man had finished his work inside the bank by ten after six. He'd just returned to his perch on the second floor when a transmission from Zack came though. "Whiskey Sierra in position. Three is on a rooftop on the northwest corner of the square; Five is in the third-floor window of the Suakin Palace on the southwest corner. The remainder of us are together and mobile, three blocks northeast of the square. We are in a beige ... break .... What the hell is this piece of shit? A beige Ford Econoline van. The SLA will hit from the west. They should be getting into position right about now. First one that sees or hears any sign of them, call it in." A staccato pair of "Roger thats" from his men at the square followed the transmission.

Dawn began in the east ten minutes later. The town sloped from the square down to the water, so from his second-floor vantage point Court could see the distant sea glowing with morning light where it met the sky. Oryx would appear on the other side of the square in minutes, yet still no one had seen any sign of the SLA. They should at least have been somewhere staging to move, and the two Whiskey Sierra operators west of the square should have either heard or seen them by now.

But there was nothing.

Gentry saw what Zack meant when he said the town had an Old West feel. Looking out of the window at the dirt, the simple buildings, the hitching posts and water troughs, the donkey carts and wooden awnings, guns at the ready for a shoot-out, Court realized he could be in another world and another time.

Gentry sipped water in his high perch. He checked the layout of items in the pack on his back for the fourth time.

Tension built quickly in his stomach.

"One for Five," Zack said in his mike.

"Go for Five, One," replied Spencer, the muscular black team member who had been an Army Special Forces sergeant before moving into CIA black ops.

"Still nothing in your sector?"

"Don't see anything over here by the hotel."

"Three?"

"Not a peep to the northwest, boss."

Hesitation from Hightower. Court wondered if he was about to abort the mission. "All right. Looks like we're gonna have to go ahead with Bravo."

In the dark atrium of the bank, Court Gentry's eyebrows furrowed almost to the point of touching. What the hell was "Bravo"? If there *was* a plan B, then Court sure as shit hadn't been read in on it.

"Roger that, boss," said Three. "I've got the RPG ready."

The RPG? Cold sweat formed on the Gray Man's temples.

Court began to reach down to push a button on his sat phone to call Zack to find out what the hell was going on.

But he didn't have to.

"Okay, Six. Let me fill you in before you blow a blood vessel." Zack's disembodied voice sounded somewhat contrite. "Denny and I were worried that the SLA might not be able to come through for us. Sudan Station kept promising . . . but you saw how their numbers were diminishing before our eyes. Your source, the cop, and his intel that the SLA had been compromised, pretty much sealed the deal.

"Brother, even without the SLA, we are still going to go ahead. You don't need a battle, you just need a diversion, a little attack to get Oryx moving to his security team's rally point. Well, Six, we're gonna give you that little attack, aren't we, Three?"

"Roger that, One."

"Three and Five are going to lay down some direct fire, just enough to get Oryx and his close-in bodyguards through the door of the bank. Then we're going to hit the remainder of the guys in the square from the northeast, just to keep their heads down for a minute or two. After that you'll be clear, break." There was a long pause. "This is Denny's plan, by the way. I didn't want to tell you before now because ... well, shit, I hoped the SLA would show. Hope you're not too pissed."

Court wasn't pissed; he was white-hot fucking livid. One hundred rebels had turned to zero, and Zack had neglected to mention the company of infantry that was supposed to be in the area. Court had thought that he would have plenty of time to get Oryx to the car and out of town while the bodyguards were fighting it out with rebels. But now he only had the support of five men in the square, and they would break contact almost immediately, giving Court virtually no time to get Oryx out of the bank, move him ten blocks to the car, and then get him on the road and out of town.

Court had been ordered not to transmit on the C4OPS radio, but he did not care. He pressed the talk button on his belt. "You son of a bitch! I can't get him out in time—"

"Off the net, Six!" Zack ordered. As team leader, his radio had been set to override the transmissions of all others. "Oryx and his detail are in sight. They are entering the square, northeast corner. Get ready to hit the rear of the party, Three."

"Three has targets in sight," said Dan, his voice low.

Court looked out the window at the dawn. He could just make out movement, the mass of dark-suited men in the distance, appearing in the square. He looked down at the staircase, thought about running, although he didn't really know where he would go. It was too late to continue on with Sid's operation now; there was no way he could get back to the Blaser rifle and shoot Abboud, and if he did not complete that objective, then Sidorenko would not help him get out of the country.

Conversely, if he did not go through with Nocturne Sapphire, Zack and the CIA would not help him get out of the country, either.

He was stuck, past the point of no return, and this was the reason Hightower hadn't told him of the change in the mission to direct action.

He'd have to continue on with Nocturne Sapphire now.

"Two hundred yards to the bank," said Five. "I'll hit them when they are passing by the door."

"Roger that."

Gentry took one last look at his gear around him on the atrium; it was all in place. He calmed himself. This was different from most of his other operations, but they'd snagged some terrorists back in the Goon Squad days, so Court was no stranger to this sort of action. Still, this was big. This was the biggest, most complicated, most time-sensitive mission he'd ever been on. It was a mission that stank of desperation on the part of the CIA.

Court's mentor, Maurice, had always told him, "Any mission you can't afford to walk away from is a mission you should *run* away from."

"One hundred fifty yards," came the call from Sierra Five.

Maurice had another saying that popped into Court's mind right then. "A plan is just a big list of shit that's not going to happen." Court had found this to be the one constant in his missions, in his life. Plans were good. Plans were necessary, but ultimately, most plans were bullshit.

"Sierra Three to One."

"Go for One."

"Boss, I got a truck passing below my position."

"SLA?" Court could hear the hopefulness in High-tower's voice.

"Wait one, break." A short pause. Then, "Negative. It's GOS troops."

"Five for One ... I got troops over here, too. Two blocks west of me heading towards the square."

"Goddammit," said Zack as way of reply.

Shit, thought Court. The GOS was nearby, but the SLA was not. Who were the GOS looking for?

Court squinted across the square. To his right the sun began to rise over the water like a fresh red blister. Dawn's light gave an eerie glow to the whitewashed buildings to his left. Abboud's entourage, some twenty or more men, closed on his position.

"One, this is Three. What we doin', boss?" Court's earpiece was alive with Whiskey Sierra's traffic, though he was under orders to not transmit himself.

Court whispered to himself in the cool, dark atrium, willing with every ounce of imagined magic projection he could muster. "Abort. Abort." He stayed at the window, but he was ready to run down the stairs and out the back door of the building. He could get away, not to the car left for him, but to the water. There were little boats tied up all around the harbor; he could grab one and go.

Hightower's voice came over the net. Court knew each inflection of the man, to where he could hear the stress concealed between the words. "Say number of tangos, over."

"One, Three. Could be about thirty. Three-oh, break. One long flatbed. Small arms and RPGs sighted, break. Might be some PKMs in there too, boss, over." PKMs were big Russian belt-fed machine guns.

"Roger that," said Zack flatly.

"Five to One. I've got about the same number over here. They are patrolling in columns, doesn't look like they're too jacked up for trouble."

When Zack said nothing else for a few seconds, the net crackled to life again. "One, this is Three. I can engage right now. Once they disperse it's going to be hard—"

"Understood, Three. Wait one," said Zack.

"Abort," whispered Gentry again. And then, again under his breath, he said over and over and over a line that he'd used many times in the past when life and death was all up to Sierra One, and Court was on the tip of the spear awaiting the decision. "Be cool, Zack. Be cool, Zack. Be cool, Zack."

Court knew everything, literally his very life, likely depended on Sierra One's next transmission; a safe, quiet exfiltration, and then an investigation into how Nocturne Sapphire fell apart so completely.

Or the alternative.

World War *fucking* Three.

"Be cool, Zack."

Then it came. "Sierra One to all elements."

Be cool Zack.

A long hesitation. "Let's knock it off. Everybody stand down. Hold positions until Oryx's entourage gets in the mosque; then I want a quiet egress back out of the area—"

Court let out one of the longest sighs of relief of his life.

Each member of Whiskey Sierra came on the net, in turn, and confirmed that they understood the order to stand down. These men were consummate professionals; they betrayed no emotion, neither relief nor disappointment, that the mission had been scrubbed at the very last second.

Gentry took one last look at President Abboud, walking briskly through the square with his entourage towards his position. Disappointing to be so close and yet so far, but Gentry was a pro as well. He'd been here before, a second or two before the point of no return but unable or unwilling to proceed. Court wasted no time turning away from the window and moving back towards the stairs from the atrium to the front door entrance to the bank. He walked down the dark colonnaded hall. He'd almost reached the back door when his headset came alive once again with Whiskey Sierra's radio traffic.

Zack Hightower rested his rifle between his knees and leaned his head back against the headrest of the passenger seat in frustration as Brad/Sierra Two put the dirty beige cargo van in gear. Behind them, in the very back of the van, was Milo, Sierra Four. He sat facing the closed back door of the vehicle, with a big HK21 between his legs. The shoulder-wielded machine gun carried the same powerful cartridge as many hunting and sniper rifles, but it fired them faster and from a 100-round box magazine. Milo was the designated "trunk monkey," the man ready to shoot out the back doors to keep opposition off of their tail. He was low-profile now, with the doors closed and no targets to fire at, but if the operation had gone ahead, it was likely Sierra Four would have been the man sending the most hate downrange.

The van had been waiting in the deep shadows of an alley a few blocks from the square, far from where the government of Sudan infantry had been reported. Other than chickens and goats in the road, they'd seen no movement at all, so they pulled out of their hide and began moving south. This was in the direction of the square, so Brad made his first turn to the left, which would take him closer to the port and allow him to avoid Abboud's guard force.

But the alleyway turned into a dead end at a camel corral. It was a large circular structure crafted out of driftwood and scrap metal, with a few hulking animals kneeling in the dirt, and there was no way around it.

Brad began backing up the truck. Both he and Sierra One looked into their rearview mirrors.

Zack saw them first and shouted to the van and over his radio to the team.

"Troops!"

Sierra Two slammed on the brakes. Twenty meters behind them, at the mouth of the alleyway they had just entered, stood half a dozen green-clad soldiers, their Chinese-made Type 81 rifles raised in front of them and pointing at the van. One of the soldiers shouted a command.

"What do we do, boss?" asked Brad from the driver's seat.

The delay from Zack was brief. When he spoke, he transmitted to the entire team.

"All elements. Belay my last command. We are a *go* for Nocturne Sapphire. I say again, execute! Light 'em up!"

In the back of the van, Milo kicked open the rear doors with his boots. They locked open wide. He lifted his machine gun and fired spurting bursts at the six soldiers at the mouth of the alleyway.

Three soldiers died where they stood. The rest dove to the ground and returned fire.

Behind Milo, Zack unbuckled himself and spun between the seats, lifting his Israeli Tavor TAR-21 assault rifle and firing over Sierra Four's left shoulder. Brad shoved the gearshift knob forward, from reverse to drive, stomped on the gas, and the big Ford van crashed through the fencing of the corral, sending massive brown camels clambering out of the way.

The Gray Man's shoulders dropped in resignation.

His fingertips were a foot from the latch to the back door of the bank. On the other side of the door would be a dark alleyway. Beyond that a few quiet twists and turns, and he'd be at the port, in the water of the lagoon or on a small boat. He'd be out of danger in minutes.

But Zack's transmission and the gunfire to the north changed everything.

Now Three was on the net. "Three's going loud." and then the explosion of an RPG, close to Gentry's position.

And now Spencer was joining the action. "Five's on the trigger." Submachine gun fire emanated from the Suakin Palace.

It was on. Abboud would be storming through the doorway behind Court in seconds.

The Gray Man turned, reached for the suppressed Glock 19 holstered on his hip.

Just outside, the square cracked to life with return pistol fire from Abboud's men. Court sucked in the musty air of the old bank building, brought his shoulders back, and clenched his jaw before saying, "Here we go."

He ran up the stairs and got into position.

Seconds later the double doors in the lobby below him burst open.

Welcome to World War *fucking* Three.

34

The men below Gentry shouted and screamed, but not in panic.
No, these were trained bodyguards. Their commands were to their
principal, the president of the Republic of Sudan. Court knew the
drill. They would hustle into the room in a tight cordon, with
Oryx in the center. Once inside they would secure the door and
then lead him towards the most secure portion of the building,
likely the basement vault. Gentry didn't know how many protec-
tors had come in with Abboud; that would depend on how they
were positioned when the gunfire started, if any had been hit by
Sierra Five or Three, and any number of other factors. But ultimately it did not matter whether there were two men or twenty
downstairs; Court Gentry had a surprise for them.

Court pressed a button on a handheld remote device he'd left
on the windowsill. By doing so he activated electromagnets on two
bolt locks he'd attached to each side of the double doors below,
firing the three-inch long iron bolts across the space between
the two doors and holding them fast. This ensured no one else
came through.

Next he lifted a twelve-pound device off the cheap linoleum
flooring of the atrium by its carry handle, jammed his thumb
under a switch cap, and then pressed the button. One second later
he hefted it over the side railing. It fell towards the lobby, but it
was attached with a six-foot cord to the railing itself, so when the
acousto-optical nonpyrotechnic less-lethal stun device reached the

eye level of all the men in the lobby, its two-second countdown clock beeping and flickering, thus ensuring all eyes would be upon it, it would create maximum effect. Court threw himself to the atrium's floor, tucked into the fetal position with his eyes shut tight and his hands covering his C4OPS earpieces.

The device was a prototype built by the CIA's Directorate of Science & Technology, and Zack just referred to it as the Big Bang. It was designed to cause both physiological and psychophysical disorientation, with incredible lights and sound. The eggheads at Langley had been careful to only use off-the-shelf equipment in the device, mostly from Japan and France and Germany, to avoid having a virtual "Made in the USA" label affixed to the contraption.

Even with his eyes closed, its bright burst of light reflected off the walls around him and burned into his eyes, and even with his noise-reducing C4OPS headset in his ears and his hands covering them, the high-pitched one-second siren's wail was deafening. Its advertised optical effect was akin to staring into the sun for 110 milliseconds, and acoustically it battered the eardrums and even concussed those within twenty feet of it when activated in an enclosed space. Court felt the teeth in his jaw rattle, and coral rag and other material from the ceiling above him rained down on his body, but he ignored pain and the falling debris, and jumped to his feet instantly.

He had no time to wait.

As he ran down the stairs, he raised his weapon in front of him, not 100 percent certain of what he would find. Gentry entered the lobby quickly. He found them all incapacitated to one degree or another, six men in total, one of whom would surely be Oryx. One of the guards was up on his knees, both hands feeling around on the carpet for his weapon. Court shot him in the back of the head, and the man fell forward, his face slamming against the pistol on the floor that he sought. He then stepped over two unconscious guards' lifeless forms to reach an older man, who was lying faceup. Yes, this was his target. Oryx was out cold, and next to him, two younger guards were conscious but completely disoriented. They lay on their backs and writhed in their own vomit. Immediately Gentry ripped open the thick president's white dress shirt and pulled his tie loose. Stepping in front of him, he knelt down, reached under his underarms, and hefted him until their chests were leaning against one another. Court ducked down, let the dead weight settle on his right shoulder, then he used his legs to rise up again into a standing position, heaving Oryx up with him into the fireman's carry. The American walked the big Sudanese man over the legs of another bodyguard and out of the room. At the dead-bolted back door he laid him back down gently and drew his pistol again.

Court hurried back towards the lobby. Though his ears rang from the siren he'd just set off, he could hear incredible amounts of gunfire outside. He was thankful all the heavy fighting was to the north and west, which would not interfere with his escape route.

Inside the lobby Gentry raised his pistol and fired one suppressed round into an ankle of each of the four living bodyguards. He looked around the room hopefully for a dropped rifle or submachine gun but saw nothing but a few Lado pistols, which he ignored.

Outside, men beat on the front doors, yelling to be let in. Gentry left the lobby and the injured men behind. They'd recover soon, some perhaps in under a minute, and their heads would kill them for hours or days. Their ankles would incapacitate them for longer, but more important, they would require immediate care, care that would take more guards, police, soldiers, and other first responders to organize and carry out, leaving fewer available to hunt for the kidnapper.

Gentry returned to the back door while reloading his pistol, and here he rolled Oryx onto a two-wheeled hand truck that he'd been given by Zack. It was a small, collapsible, lightweight device, made principally of telescoping PVC pipes with a hard honeycomb plastic floor plate and fat rubber tires. He positioned the heavy body on the two-wheeler, took a moment to tuck the arms inside the attached bungee cord, and then paused a moment to catch his breath.

The gunfire outside continued in short bursts. It sounded confused, spread out.

It sounded like trouble, but still he heard nothing around his side of the building.

Court unhooked the dead bolt at the back door and opened it, looking first to the left, the direction of the square. It was clear.

Then he looked to the right. Two civilian men stood in the dirt road. They looked like Beja fishermen, and their arms were empty of weapons. Court pointed his pistol at them, and they raised their hands immediately. He told them to go in Arabic, and they just stood there. But when he waved the pistol with its long silencer attached, in a motion to mimic their getting out of the street, they seemed to understand, and they disappeared in seconds.

A minute later, Gentry jogged in the shadows, pushing the hand truck with the president on it in front of him. He'd made it two blocks to the south and had only seen the two confused civilians, who had done nothing to impede his progress. Court then ran past a long, low wall and turned inside an open gate to a private residence. In the small dirt courtyard he lowered the two-wheeler to the ground and knelt beside it. He was a hundred yards away from the front door of the bank now. He'd made one right turn and then a left down narrow passages and was semi-confident he had neither been spotted nor left any sort of a trail with his feet or his wheels.

The crackle of gunfire from the square continued.

As if on cue, Oryx's head began to roll to the left and the right. Court unstrapped the president and sat him up, slapped him a few times across the face. He pulled flexi-cuffs out of his backpack and fastened the Sudanese president's arms in front of his body. He reached for a bottle of water staged for quick access in a side pocket of his pack, opened it, and splashed it liberally across the big black man's face and poured a quick shot over his bald head.

Oryx came to fully. He was still disoriented, and his pupils were dilated. Gentry made him take a few swigs of the water, then he slapped him again.

Oryx spat the water up immediately, most of it hitting Court in the face. Abboud then tried to reach out and swat away the phantom bright lights in front of his eyes.

Gentry shouted over the inevitable ringing in Abboud's ears. "Wake up! Hey. Open your eyes! Look at me! Look at me."

He had the man's full attention now. His eyes were wide but clearly whited out in the center from the blinding light of the Big Bang. He took in the scene and the man in front of him by looking at him in a sideways glance. He was clearly shocked but recovering from what must have appeared little more than a dream a few seconds earlier.

Oryx shook his head, attempting still to clear out confusion, the bright dancing lights, the ceaseless ringing in his ears.

Court had been flash-banged many times in training, but the gizmo he'd used on Oryx and his guards was new, and it was nasty. Gentry was glad he'd never been on the business end of an acousto-optical stun device of this magnitude.

In Arabic Oryx shouted, "Who are you? Where ... what is happening to—"

Gentry responded in English. "Listen up. I was sent to kill you. That was my job. But someone else wanted me to kidnap you instead. Do you understand?"

The president nodded slowly, as if he were still not certain this was not all some sort of a cruel hoax. Court stared him down several seconds, and then a wave of panic flashed in Oryx's eyes.

"I'm going to *try* to kidnap you, but here's the deal. If that gets too complicated, I'm going back to plan A. Plan A pays a lot more than plan B, anyway. Things get too rough, you make too much trouble when we try to get out of here, and it's plan A all the way. Plan A is a bullet between your beady eyes, and I leave you in the street, go home, and count my cash.

"You understand?"

249

Oryx nodded again. The panic was there, but there was an acquiescence in his expression. He understood now.

"So your job is to make sure plan A isn't the easy choice for me. Got it? We need to be on the same team here, so this all goes smooth, okay?"

"American? You are American?"

"Absofuckinglutely." Court was proud to say it. It had been a while since he'd operated in the interests of the United States.

"Good. What is your rank?"

"No rank."

"No rank? You are an officer, yes?"

Court laughed as he pushed the two-wheeler up against the wall to shield it from view of anyone walking down the street outside. "Just a grunt, dude. It was this or peeling potatoes, and I drew the short straw."

Oryx did not understand the joke. He shook his head again to clear the lights and declared, "I wish to surrender to your senior commander."

Gentry chuckled. "Sorry, I'm all you get for now."

"Very well." He said it in a disappointed tone. "My head—"

Gentry pulled two pills from his front pocket. "Take these for now."

Oryx took the pills in his hand, looked them over, but did not put them in his mouth.

"They're just mild painkillers. I promise you will thank me in a few minutes."

Abboud popped the pills in his mouth slowly, swallowed another swig of water and choked on it, but did manage to keep the pills down.

"Can you run?"

"Run? I can barely see!"

"Can you move fast, then? Say no, and plan A is my best bet, because we're going to have to haul ass to get you out of here."

Oryx nodded helpfully. "I can run."

"Good man. Now, I'll help you stand."

250

Oryx looked around. He seemed to just now notice all the gunfire. "Who is shooting? What is all this shooting?" Court realized his prisoner really wasn't quite caught up to what was going on yet. It was no surprise.

"Friends of mine. They are keeping your friends busy. We are going to head through the back of this house here, go south a few blocks, and get in a boat. You ready?"

Oryx nodded again. He was helpfully conspiratorial in his own kidnapping. Even though he was clearly still disoriented, he recognized the alternative and had no doubt in his mind, looking at the serious American man in front of him, that it would be no problem for him to carry it out.

"Let's move," said Court. And he pushed Oryx around, shoved him hard to propel him towards the little stone house.

Sierra One, Two, and Four bounced around the inside of the cargo van as it bottomed out, lurched back into the air, and began climbing a little hill. The back doors were wide-open, but Four had strapped himself in with a belt tied to the bolted-in center seats and affixed to him with a quick-release buckle. No one knew where they were exactly, even though they had all spent weeks studying maps of the town. Brad even had a satellite photo of Suakin taped to the steering wheel in front of him. But all the streets looked the same, all the alleyways looked the same, the endless sea of dilapidated burlap and driftwood shacks looked the same, and apparently all the road signs had long ago been used for roofing material or firewood.

The three men had spent the past three minutes stumbling into and then out of little engagements with government of Sudan soldiers from the Sudanese People's Armed Forces. The GOS units in town seemed disorganized as hell. As often as not, Brad had turned their van onto a road only to find themselves *behind* a column of men. Twice they'd come face-to-face with army trucks, and both times not a shot had been fired as both vehicles backed up to get out of danger.

This was a confused ambush, if that's even what it was, but what the government troops lacked in organization, they made up for in sheer numbers. As the Whiskey Sierra van blasted through the little streets lining a seemingly endless vista of hovels on the north side of town, more and more Sudanese troops seemed to be coming out of the woodwork. Sierra Four had emptied an entire magazine from his weapon at enemy threats during and since breaking through the corral, and now Milo reloaded quickly, certain there'd be more fighting to come.

Sierra Five's voice came over the net between bursts of automatic fire a quarter mile from the van.

"Yo, One. I could use some help over here. GOS has backed up out of my line of sight, and I've repositioned to a second-floor window, but it won't be long before they come back and blow the shit out of this hotel."

"Roger that, Spence," said Zack. "We're coming to pick you up ASAP; we're just a little turned around over here."

"Just follow the sound of the shooting. I've got a dozen or so of Oryx's guards taking potshots at me from the square. You ought to be able to orient yourself on that."

"We're trying," Zack replied, as Sierra Two made two quick turns to his left, pulled right behind an army jeep with an unmanned Russian machine gun mounted on its rear bed.

Brad made an immediate right.

"Sierra One to Sierra Three, gimme a sitrep on your position."

Dan did not stop firing to communicate. "They're hitting me from two alleyways." Two cracks of his rifle distorted the transmission in Zack's headset. "Not coordinated fire, and I've got the high ground on the roof here, but there sure as hell are a lot of them. They get in below me, and I'm toast. How copy?" Several more cracks delayed Hightower's response.

"Good copy. We're on the way."

"Contact rear!" Milo shouted from behind Zack. In the small metal space of the van, his machine gun sounded like a jackhammer amplified by a heavy metal band's amp stacks. Zack spun around to engage with his Tavor, but Brad made another quick turn that took them out of the line of fire.

"One, this is Three. I've got eyes on a chopper approaching from the north."

"A chopper? Civ or military?"

"Uhhh, wait one, break. He's military. Big, fat fucker. Looks like he's about seven or eight klicks out, low and fast, headin' this way like he's got someplace to be ... Looks like an Mi-17."

"The Mi-17 is a Hip. The Sudanese don't have Hips." Hip was the NATO designation for the Russian-built Mi-17.

"Pretty sure it's a Hip, boss."

"Roger that, goddammit," Zack growled. Not much he could do about an assault from the air right now.

"Five for One!"

"Go Five."

"I've got small arms fire to my west. Not on my position. Sierra Six isn't a klick to the west of the square, is he?"

"He shouldn't be. Six, if you are able to transmit, let me know if that's you."

"Six, to One." Court came over the net. His voice was sure and succinct. "Negative. I have Oryx, and we are southeast of the square. We're making a try for the harbor."

Zack thought it over as the van made another hard turn, this time to the left. "Must be the SLA rebels. Better late than never, I guess. I'll take whatever I can get at the moment. Sound like much, Five?"

"I'm not impressed. Doesn't sound like half of what I've got going on right on top of me!"

"Wait a sec," interrupted Sierra Two from behind the wheel of the van. "This is that alley that runs into the northeast corner of the square."

"You're sure?" asked Zack. He had no idea. It looked the same as the last dozen alleys they'd driven through.

"Yeah. We stay on this, we're in the square in thirty seconds. We want to do that?"

Zack thought it over for a second, then said, "What the hell. We don't want to get lost again, and Spence and Dan are going to run dry if we can't pick them up."

"There are gonna be troops in the square. And Abboud's guard force," Sierra Two noted as he drove on.

Hightower just nodded. He began transmitting, "Three and Five, we'll hit the square in twenty seconds, blast through it shooting, whip around behind the bank, and pick both of you up outside your positions in the alley one block west of the square. Keep your heads down!"

A pair of "Roger thats."

"Four, it's gonna get crazy," Zack shouted back to Milo.

"Bring it on!" came the shout from the trunk monkey behind him.

Gentry was less than five blocks from the square when the Whiskey Sierra van drove through it. He heard squealing tires, then questioning and answering rifle and pistol fire that continued unabated.

He also heard a smattering of fire farther to the west, probably outside of Suakin, AKs both inbound and outbound, and this he took for the lopsided battle between a portion of the GOS force and the SLA guys the CIA had managed to browbeat into showing up. They were getting their asses handed to them, from the sound of it. It would probably be a while before Sudan Station convinced the SLA to do any more fighting at its behest.

With all the action in the early morning town, as near as Court could tell, his sector was clear. He and Oryx were on their knees under the shaded lean-to that covered an old brick oven and served as a tiny open-air bakery. They were only fifty yards from the boats. He could see the little wooden craft on the still water of the bay, red hulls rocking back and forth invitingly. Just fifty yards, yes, but fifty yards of open ground. Gentry worried about GOS men to the north along the beach or the causeway to Old Suakin Island, but more than this, he worried about the reports of a helicopter above. Even if he and Oryx could snake down to the boat, traveling over the water would leave them totally exposed to that chopper.

He thought it over for a few more seconds. "Forget the boat," he said aloud, then turned to Oryx. "I have a car, eight blocks southwest of the square. *That's* where we're going. Now!" Court pushed Oryx into the alley, and they both began running.

They'd made it just one block up an alleyway when Oryx broke off quickly to the left, dodging down an even smaller alley that ran up a gentle hill. Court chased after him, reached out to grab the big man by the neck and get him back on track, but a squad of five GOS soldiers on foot came out the back door of a small coral building, not fifteen feet from their president. They raised their weapons in confusion, took a moment to size up the situation they had just stumbled upon. Court took advantage of the delay. He put himself between the soldiers and Oyrx and shoved the president out of the way roughly, raising his weapon at the same time. He fired two rounds from his pistol into the chest of the first man in the squad, got his free hand around Oryx's tie, and yanked his prisoner back out of the tiny alleyway as he dropped another soldier with a round to his forehead.

The remaining soldiers scrambled for cover in the building they'd just exited, and Court let go of Oryx, darted towards the rifle lying next to one of the dead trooper's bodies. But a long burst from an unseen shooter's rifle stitched bullets down the alley just feet in front of Gentry, so he turned and retreated back around the corner, grabbed his prisoner again, and ran away as fast as he could with one hand on his weapon and the other on the neck the president of the Sudan.

35

Suakin is a town filled with Rashaidas and Bejas, mostly, but as it was a market and a port town, and somewhat of a port city still, there were transplants from all over the country. Dinka, Fur, Nuba, Masalit, Nuer, most all of the tribes came here to trade and to live. There were also some Nubians, dark black non-Arabs who congregated principally around the Nile River to the west.

One such Nubian family lived in a burlap, driftwood, and tin shack to the southwest of the square. The shack was also their business, as the man of the house made goat-hide sandals with tire-tread soles and sold them in the dirt alleyway in front of their hovel.

The man's son was dead, so the sandal maker helped raise his four grandchildren: three girls and one boy.

The man of the house huddled over the girls, called to his twelve-year-old grandson Adnan to come over to his side of the shack and lie in the dark with the rest of the family, but Adnan refused to cower. Instead, Adnan opened an old chest next to the sleeping mat, and from this he took the prized possession of his dead father, a longbow. As his grandfather yelled at him, young Adnan scooped up three arrows before running out of the house and towards the sound of gunfire.

His shack was on a hill, and from the front door he could see smoke and flashes of light towards the square. There was more shooting behind him to the west, but it was farther away. Adnan ran to a flight of rickety stairs that led down his hill. He leapt down the stairs, took them three and four at a time, his young, sinewy, coal-black legs comfortable with the exertion. With the gunfire around, he instinctively tucked his head tight into his neck as he ran.

He passed an old man on wooden crutches standing in front of his shack. The cripple shouted to the child, demanded he go back to his home, but Adnan wasn't listening.

Adnan was going to save his family and his town from whoever threatened it.

The Nubians were fearless and ferocious warriors since the times of the pharaohs, and their weapon of choice had always been the bow. Nubia itself means "land of the bow." Nubian archers served as highly coveted mercenaries in ancient wars as far away as distant Persia.

Adnan's family had descended from a dozen generations of bow makers, but bows made them no money, as AK-47s and the Chinese AK knock-off, the Type 81, hung from the shoulders of everyone around here with cause to wield a weapon. An AK is more powerful than a bow, an AK is easier to master than a bow, and, it could be argued, an AK is only slightly more technologically complicated. For this reason Adnan's grandfather switched to making sandals, but Adnan had learned as a child how to use the large bamboo bow with leather at the handgrip, with bone and horn inlaid at the tips and just above the leather wrapping.

Adnan barreled through a small driftwood and baling wire gate, into another dusty alley. The gunfire from the square reverberated on the walls and carried down to him. He tucked his neck in tighter as he turned to race towards it, his father's weapon in his right hand and the arrows in his left.

Other townspeople were out now, running away mostly. Adnan passed them at a sprint as he moved towards the action.

He rounded a narrow passageway and stumbled to a halt. Thirty meters ahead, at the entrance to this alley, a black man in a black suit skittered around the corner, as if shoved from behind. His hands were bound in front of him, and he slipped and stumbled forward on the shiniest shoes Adnan had ever seen in his life. The young Sudanese boy ducked quickly into an unused doorway to the back of a derelict butcher shop, hid himself in a morning shadow, his back to the wall, and then lowered to a squat. He ducked his head around the corner and saw the black man being pushed towards him by a bearded white man.

An infidel.

The white man held a long pistol in his right hand, and he shouted as the two men ran up the alley towards Adnan's hide. "Move! Move! Move!" The foreign word meant nothing to young Adnan, but the tone told him he was forcing the black man forward.

Adnan had never seen the president of his country and had no idea of the identity of the big man with the bound hands.

Here was Adnan's moment. In seconds they would pass, and he had no doubt he could put a steel-tipped arrow through the back of the infidel. He only had to wait a few seconds and take him down from behind.

As the footsteps and the angry foreign shouting closed on his position, Adnan changed his focus to the other side of the doorway, one meter from the tips of his bare feet. A dead rooster lay in the shadow, his feather-covered carcass maggot-infested and putrefying. The Sudanese boy's eyes narrowed with purpose. He chose an arrow and laid the remaining two on the dusty stoop next to him. He pointed the razor-sharp barb of the arrow in his hand at the most rotten morsel of the dead bird and stabbed it deeply, turning the point around to the left and the right like a key in a lock.

Covering the tip of the missile in bacteria, a determined smile covered the young boy's face.

The suited black man passed the doorway, again nearly falling forward. Behind him no more than a few steps was the shouting infidel, his long black handgun a blur as he ran.

Adnan rose and stepped into the alleyway behind his target. He threaded his arrow into the bow, pulled back the bowstring tightly as he raised the tip to eye level, and centered it on the sprinting white man, who was nearing the turn to the back of the building.

The man wore a backpack, so Adnan adjusted his aim so that his arrow would strike high in his target's neck.

"*Allahu Akbar.*" Like two thousand years of proud Nubian archers before him, Adnan let the missile fly.

"Left turn! Left turn!" Court shouted at President Abboud. The older man stumbled; no doubt his balance was affected by his bindings, but also no doubt, decided Court, the man was crafty enough to willfully hamper their escape. Gentry was having none of it, though, and he lifted his right arm high to strike the man in the back of the head, to convince him of the urgency of the situation.

Just as the butt of his gun connected with the president's sweaty head, Court felt an excruciating pain in his left shoulder blade above the top of his backpack, just three inches from his spine. The impact knocked him forward and spun him slightly, not to the ground but nearly, and he stumbled past the president but then caught himself as he followed the man around the corner.

"Ugh!" He grunted with the impact; the blistering sting did not dissipate as he slowed and looked back over his shoulder.

A long brown arrow protruded from his shoulder blade.

Court's run slowed as he stared at it. His brain had difficulty processing what was right before his eyes for a long moment. He looked down to his chest to make sure it had not gone all the way through his body. It had not. He then tried to reach back for it and failed. Finally, he began jogging forward again, still looking back at the arrow. Softly, he muttered, "No fucking way."

The beige van slammed on its brakes at the side entrance to the three-story hotel, a colonial-style building that must have been an architectural gem a hundred years earlier. With wooden balconies, gabled hoods above the windows, white shutters, and ornate latticework columns, the hotel looked more New Orleans than Arab African. Zack looked through the windshield, scanning for targets, but he could not help but notice the dilapidated state of this building and those on either side of the road. Spencer ducked into the side door of the vehicle, and it lurched forward again. Milo fired a pair of bursts down the street to keep the infantry's heads down, but it appeared that the SLA attack to the west had drawn many of the troops away from the southwest corner of the square.

Spencer had been roaming Suakin in cover for two days, therefore he was dressed in local attire and carried only a small Uzi submachine gun. Quickly he grabbed a chest rig with body armor that had been waiting for him inside the van. He struggled to put it on in the back as the Econoline bounced on the bad road.

Whiskey Sierra's vehicle turned north and accelerated quickly up a wider unpaved road. Civilians' heads could be seen in windows and doorways and peering through the gates of walled buildings. The locals were staying off the roads themselves, which was good for them and good for Zack. He had no doubt the Sudanese Army would not think twice about collateral damage, though he and his men were doing their best to avoid it.

Less than thirty seconds after collecting Sierra Five at his hotel, the van again slammed on its brakes, this time at the doorway to a two-story building. Spencer opened the door.

They were parked less than a second before Zack transmitted. "Three, we're not gonna sit here all damn day for—"

A crash on the roof of the van shook it to its chassis, the impact like a dull thud to the battered eardrums of the occupants. It was Dan, jumping from the roof of the building. He slid off the side of the vehicle and ducked into its open door. Sierra Three slammed the door shut behind him, and Sierra Two once again stomped on the gas pedal.

Zack called into his headset for Court, "Sierra One for Sierra Six, break. I've got my guys, and I'm getting the fuck outta here. You are on your own for now. Good luck, and watch out for that damn chopper. One out!"

They'd made it no more than fifty yards up the paved street when three policemen in dark uniforms stepped to the edge of the roof of a small blacksmith's shop. Each man heaved two large concrete blocks off the roof. The heavy cement arced into the air in front of the van, forcing Brad to jack the wheel to the right, nearly scraping the paint from the right side as he passed an old parked Chevrolet sedan. He pulled back to the left and just missed a pair of unoccupied rickshaws by the side of the road.

Another group of locals was up ahead on the roof of another building with cement blocks and large tires, ready to throw them at the van. Hightower knew it would be dangerous to try to drive under them.

Zack shouted from the front passenger seat, "Left up here, Brad, hard left!" The van turned hard into an alley even narrower than the road they'd just left.

Before he could even finish his turn, Brad shouted to the passengers of the van, "Contact front!"

The windshield of the van popped and cracked. It did not shatter entirely, but a stitch of white-rimmed bullet holes drew across it from right to left, from low to high.

Zack felt a vicious tug to his forearm and stings to his face and neck. He lifted his rifle over the dashboard and fired back through the glass fully automatic, emptying his thirty-round magazine at targets in the road in front of him and pulverizing the windshield into bits of white sand.

The van veered hard to its left. Zack knew there was no room for error at this speed in such a narrow alleyway. He braced for impact, and the impact came, a hard jolt to the left, then the vehicle bounced back hard right, and this time Hightower knew the impending impact would be vicious and directly on his side. He pulled his legs up just as the big van slammed into a white building on the right, slowed, and came to a stop four feet from the broken wall of concrete blocks.

Steam from the radiator shot into the air in front of the broken window. The van was dead.

Zack shouted without hesitation, "Bail! Bail! Bail!"

After ordering his team to de-bus, Hightower rolled out the front passenger-side door, fell to the hard ground, landed on his shoulder and hip, and found himself facing away from the direction from which the gunfire had come. He looked back over his shoulder. One of his men had already tossed a white smoke grenade to obscure the view of the gunners ahead of them in the road. A decaying but occupied coral stone building was just a few feet away from his head, a window waist-high just above him, and Zack wasted no time scrambling to his feet, launching himself from the street and into the air, tucking into a ball, crashing through the plate glass, and slamming again hard now onto the ground floor of the building. It was a dark office of some sort. There was a government feel to the setup, but no one was inside this early, and the generators for the lights were not running. Zack rolled quickly to his knees and began reloading his rifle. He could not help but take note of the blood; it was on his arms and his gloves and the shattered glass and the floor where he landed, and it was smeared all over his tan-colored gun. But he went about his work, did not pause an instant to check the severity of his injuries.

Gunfire outside in the street continued ceaselessly. Just as he racked a fresh round into the chamber and began to stand, Sierra Two came flying through the same window. Their bodies hit, a glancing blow, and Brad slammed to the ground, his unslung FAMAS F1 rifle skittering free of him and sliding several yards across the floor.

"Four is hit!" came the call through Zack's headset; it was Dan's voice, and Dan was still outside in the street full of flying lead.

Zack shouted into his mouthpiece. "I'm suppressing to the north; Two will open the door by the van. Get Milo in here!" Hightower leaned his rifle out the window and fired short bursts up the alley. Without looking he knew that Brad would already be rushing to the building's back door to help the others inside.

Zack did what he could to conserve ammo, but his weapon soon ran dry. He called for cover, but the other men on his team were still fully involved with the rescue of their injured colleague. Hightower dropped his empty rifle and pulled his Sig pistol from his drop-leg holster, fired out the window and up the street with his right hand, had to lean his head out and expose his upper torso to do so, while his left felt for a fragmentation grenade in a pouch on his chest.

As his pistol's slide locked open with the firing of the last round, Sierra Five shouldered up on his left and opened up with his small Uzi. Zack threw the grenade as far up the street as he could. "Frag out!" He then stepped back inside the room to reload and assess the situation.

Four sat on the floor. With his HK machine gun in his hands he covered the door through which he and two others had entered the building. His lower right leg was bloody, and Three checked it quickly. Two had already crossed the big room, pushing desks and chairs out of the way as he did so, and was looking out a window on the south side, trying to find a fast exit to get the team moving again. Hightower noticed that Sierra Two was limping as he moved.

Zack reloaded; he had six rifle magazines left. His 150 remaining rounds did not seem like a lot of ammo, considering he'd already blown through ninety in a sporadic fight that was less than five minutes old.

As he moved across the room to link up with Brad, he took a look at his own wounds. There was a clean, almost perfectly round bullet hole in his right forearm. Blood ran from it, soaked his brown shirt and his gear, but his hand and arm seemed to be working just fine. He then found an exit wound just above his elbow. Both arms and hands were covered in blood, but he could find no more injuries other than some abrasions from the broken glass on his cheeks, just under his goggles.

"Three, can he walk?" Zack asked into his mouthpiece as he arrived at Two's side.

"Affirmative. I think his fibula's cracked, and he's losing blood. He'll need treatment ASAP, but he can walk for a few minutes, anyway."

"Good enough. Everybody on me, we're busting out of here now. We are *not* gonna let these knuckleheads surround us."

36

Court heard Zack's transmission to him while he was still running with Oryx, then, a half minute later, he heard the crash in the distance. The continued transmissions on his radio told him Whiskey Sierra had made it out of the street, but it was clear they were knee-deep in shit.

But Court had his own problems. He and Oryx had ducked into a hovel full of locals to hide from a platoon of troops running towards the square. It was a dark and filthy open room, the only light coming from holes in the walls where the corrugated tin did not match flush with the driftwood. Gentry held his Glock to the president's temple. The Gray Man panted from the exertion of his run and the adrenaline pumping through him, wincing in pain with each breath as the muscles around the arrow tightened and spasmed. As he did all this, he stared at a family of nine who just sat on the floor and stared back at him. There were children in the room, small and black with big, wide eyes that made it clear to Gentry that he was the strangest sight any of them had ever laid eyes on.

The adults' eyes showed some fear and some surprise, as well, but more than that, there was a prideful anger, that this white man with his gun and his prisoner should just bash his way into their simple home and threaten them with his presence. These people's lives were borne of hardship, austerity, disease, work, hunger, an absence of liberty and free will. One more danger, one more insult to their existence, was met more with derision and fury than terror.

Though the adults *had* noticed that this white man had not pointed a gun at anyone except the man in the suit.

These people had no idea they were in the presence of the leader of their country. He meant nothing to their lives.

Court had ignored the arrow in his back as well as anyone could ignore such a thing. From the pain he could tell it was deep in the bone of his shoulder blade, but he could move his arm and shoulder. He recognized that he was lucky it had not hit him harder. Three inches deeper, and the bolt would have pierced the top of his heart and he'd be dead already, lying facedown in the alleyway where he took the hit. He guessed the bowman must have shot him from a great distance, or else it was a woman or a young boy; otherwise, the sharp projectile would have surely penetrated all the way through him.

It stung like hell, but it wasn't killing him, though he was certain it would not be long before he accidentally slammed the protrusion against a wall and really ruined his morning. Again he tried to reach back and grab the arrow, but again he could not quite get his hand to it. He thought briefly about having one of the locals help pull it out of his back, but right now he just wanted to get the fuck out of town, and he absolutely did not want to pause for what would surely be a slow and delicate procedure executed by a person he would not trust to do it correctly.

Soon the soldiers in the road were gone. Court nodded to the patriarch of the family, an ineffectual show of gratitude for not making trouble and a show of contrition at the inconvenience, and then he was out in the road again with Oryx. They made it to the car; it was parked where Zack said it would be parked, and Court got Abboud in with no trouble, then ran around to the driver's side. It was difficult for him to crawl into the seat with the arrow in his back and his backpack still in place; he had to lean forward and let the backrest down and turn slightly to the left. Finally he turned the key, and the engine started.

He felt his shirt, wet with blood, sticking to his back.

As he shifted the little two-door into gear, the helicopter flew right over their heads at no more than one hundred feet. The noise was so loud, the *whump-whump* of the rotors so malevolent, that Court ducked low in his seat.

The chopper moved on, directly towards the gunfire from Whiskey Sierra's battle a half mile to the north.

He released his boot from the clutch, pressed on the gas, and they lurched forward. The motion caused him to bump the arrow hard into the seat behind him.

"Fuck!" he shouted, the pain a jolt of blue flame in his back and up his arm and into his neck. Screaming, he made eye contact with the terrified president. Court shouted at him, the adrenaline and anger of the moment getting the best of him. "What the fuck, dude? What kind of a backwards-assed, piece of shit country are you running here? A fucking *arrow*? Seriously?" Court's right hand left the steering wheel, formed into a fist, and punched Abboud in the face. In doing this, he brushed the arrow again against the seat, and again he screamed.

Whiskey Sierra had broken out of the office building and into the alleyway to the east. They then leapfrogged as a team through a neighborhood of tents and shanties, burlap and canvas or corrugated metal and rusty car parts turned into the barest of housing. By zigzagging towards the northeast at each opportunity, Zack and his men were both changing their direction to throw off their pursuers, as well as slowly making their way towards the water. The helicopter was overhead, but Whiskey Sierra ducked under overhangs and stayed tight against the walls of the structures and kept running. If it was a Hip—Zack hadn't seen it to be sure—then it might have air-to-ground munitions mounted to its hard points. Even if it did *not* have ATG ordnance, it could still carry two dozen combat-outfitted troops, more than enough to make trouble for Whiskey Sierra.

Their run through the slum was slowed significantly by Milo.

His right leg was bloody, and his foot wasn't cooperating. He was down to a hobble, weakening by the minute, and it was just one more thing Sierra One could not do a damn thing about.

Zack was losing blood himself, but his arm wound didn't even rank in his top ten list of priorities at the moment.

Still, it was remarkable how easily they had managed to break contact with the GOS forces. The warrenlike layout of the shanty town, with many passages no more than five feet across, made it a great place to not only hide but to move through without being seen from any distance.

Zack and his team would have been even farther away from their last contact point with the enemy if it wasn't for all the traffic in the alleyways and passages. Civilians were everywhere now. Dark-skinned men, women, and children ran all over the place, rickshaws nearly as wide as the paths they rode on bottlenecked locals who could not get out of the way of bloody, screaming, gun-wielding *kawagas* even if they tried. Twice Hightower literally bashed the butt of his Tavor into the side of a little hut to push the structure's corner, walls and roof included, just enough so he and his men could press through. They waved their rifles at anything that moved in their path, but these civilians did not want any part of this fight, so Sierra One and his men had not had to shoot any locals just yet.

Whiskey Sierra came to the end of the neighborhood of shacks and tents and found themselves on a ledge. In front of them a steeply graded hill, completely devoid of vegetation, ran down fifty yards to a road, on the other side of which lay the marketplace. There were tented stalls and wooden stalls and completely open-air stalls where the produce or other goods were simply laid out on fabric on the dirt, but there was also a cement building that ran three city blocks and housed permanent shops and small storage and warehouse facilities.

In the team's study of the town, this structure had been dubbed Mall Alpha.

On the other side of these buildings was another row of

permanent structures, dubbed Mall Bravo, and just east of this was the waterline.

As One considered ordering his men down the hill, Sierra Five shouted at the back of the tiny five-man team.

"Contact rear!" He fired a burst from his Uzi. "Here they come!" The GOS had found them.

Zack knew in an instant they'd have to expose themselves on the hill. They needed to get to the heavier buildings to have any chance of holding back the troops on their tail.

The helicopter was a quarter mile to the west and low, but beginning a shallow bank that would bring it back around on Zack's position in twenty seconds. "Let's go. Three, help Four!"

The injured Milo ripped out of Dan's grasp, spun back to the approaching enemy up the alleyway, and dropped to his knees.

"You guys go! I'll stay back and hold them off!"

Zack Hightower just grabbed the younger man by his gear, yanked him back up. "Yo, hero! Shut the fuck up and do as you're told! This isn't Hollywood, goddammit."

"Sir!"

Zack shoved him roughly to Dan, who grabbed him around the waist, and they all started down the hill.

Within seconds Hightower lost his footing on the decline. It was earth hard as stone, covered with a thick powder of dry dust. His boots had no chance for traction, so as he ran, he fell forward and rolled and slid down the hill. He'd just made it to the bottom, climbed back up to his feet, and turned when Brad and Spencer slid down right next to him. Spencer jumped right up to his boots and turned back to cover, but Brad had gotten his rifle's sling caught up in his gear, and it took him longer to stand.

Dan and Milo were still scooting down the hill on their haunches, their weapons held high out in front of them for balance as well as to keep the barrels from getting fouled in the dirt, when Zack saw Sudanese troops appear on the ridge. He and Spencer each dropped a soldier with a burst to the chest at fifty yards, and this sent the rest of the GOS riflemen diving for cover at the top of the hill.

Hightower screamed over another long burst of covering fire from Spencer, ordered Brad to help Dan get Milo in the first door in the first shop of Mall Alpha. The wounded twenty-nine-year-old Paramilitary Operations officer was all but out of the fight for now; he could not get up to his feet without the other two men pulling on his massive amount of armor and gear. They moved out, and Spencer's rifle clicked empty.

"Cover!" called Sierra Five.

"Covering!" answered Zack, dropping to his knees and firing a single round at a head that appeared at the top of the hill. His round went low, digging into the hard dirt and creating a tiny avalanche of dust and rocks.

Spencer got his gun reloaded and back into the fight just as the helicopter flew over the hill directly in front of him and Hightower. Zack could confirm now that it was, in fact, an Mi-17 Hip, a Russian-made chopper that the government of Sudan was not known to possess. He did not dwell too long on this revelation, as the Mi-17 opened fire with a heavy machine gun hanging from one of its outboard pylons.

"Move!" Sierra One screamed to Sierra Five, and both men turned to run for their lives.

37

Court pulled the little Skoda Octavia into the open gate of the private home ten kilometers northwest of Suakin. The brown wall stood eight feet high all around, and from the looks of the security gate, Gentry expected to see a large dwelling inside, but once in the gate he found just a tiny, single-story building with glassless windows and several loose goats chewing on hay all around the dirt yard.

And Mohammed's filthy white Mercedes was there, parked in a back corner of the courtyard.

Court could no longer hear gunfire in the distance, and his radio attached to his headset was out of range of any transmissions, so he had no idea what was going on with Zack and his team back in Suakin. He couldn't see the helicopter in his rearview mirror, but that meant nothing, as the chopper had been flying so low that it would not be visible from this distance anyway.

Oryx was behaving himself. Twenty milligrams of OxyContin saw to that. He remained conscious—alert, more or less—but he didn't really seem like he gave a damn about what was going on. He sat quietly in the passenger seat, buckled in with his hands secured together in his lap, and he just looked out the window at the scenery on the drive like he was a first-time visitor to the country he ruled. They'd passed many donkey carts full of people getting the hell out of town, desperate to avoid whatever craziness was going on in their normally quiet streets on a normally quiet

Sunday morning. There was the regular morning commercial traffic of the day, as well, and even this far from the city, trucks and buses and camels and donkey carts were heavy on the road, even in front of this house. And Oryx just took it all in. He wasn't smiling, he wasn't freaking out, he was just watching everyone go by.

He was just the way Gentry wanted him.

Court, on the other hand, was miserable. The sharp pain in his back got sharper with each bump of the tiny car, and there were a hell of a lot of bumps on the road from Suakin. Sweat drained into his eyes, and some bug that looked like a horsefly and flapped around like a small bird had harassed him the entire drive, causing him to swat and duck and inevitably to jab the motherfucking arrow deeper into his motherfucking shoulder.

Court parked the car and took a look at Oryx. *No, he's not going anywhere.* He climbed out of the vehicle and stood up straight for the first time in fifteen minutes. He drew his Glock and held it down to his side. Mohammed was nowhere to be seen. Court assumed he was sitting in his car waiting, but he couldn't see into the tinted windows and had no idea if the police official was in the car or in the house.

As he approached, Mohammed climbed out of the Mercedes. His hands were empty, so Court holstered his gun. The tall Beja man looked agitated, which did not surprise Court in the least.

Mohammed walked towards Court, who stopped not far from his own car. Clearly the policeman had not noticed the black man in the front seat, nor had he noticed, apparently, the arrow in Court's back. Some policeman, thought Court, but the man's mind was focused on other confusions at the moment. "What has happened? On the radio they say there is shooting. A *lot* of shooting!"

"Yeah, it's nuts down there."

"They were shooting at you? The army was shooting at you?"

"Some of them."

"Did you do it?" Mohammed asked.

Court shrugged. "I did what I came to do, yeah."

"But if you are here ... who are they shooting at *now*?"

Court looked back over his shoulder, past the arrow in his back, and at his car. Mohammed followed the white man's eyes.

"Who is that?"

"Some guy I picked up along the way," said Court.

Warily, but not warily enough, Mohammed passed by the white man and knelt down to look through the open passenger window. His body stiffened in shock. Quickly he rose back up. "It's His Excellency. I don't understand. I thought you were supposed to—"

Mohammed spun around, the irises of his wide eyes narrowed on the silencer three inches from his forehead.

He did not hear the gunshot that killed him.

"Who is this man?" Abboud asked as Court helped him out of the car. Already the American had lifted the man's car keys out of the dirt, had wrapped the bloody head in a blanket. He turned away from the president and began dragging Mohammed by his arms to the back of his own vehicle.

"Local policeman. He was working for the people who hired me to assassinate you."

"What?" And then, "Traitor!"

The American opened the trunk of the Mercedes. With the arrow piercing muscles in his upper torso it was torture to scoop the dead weight off the ground and then lift it, then roll it into the back. But he got the job done. He then looked up at Abboud. "How's your heart?" He unzipped his pack and retrieved a clear plastic bottle of water.

"My heart?" Abboud asked, unsure if he understood the question. "My head feels a little strange. But my heart is good. Why?"

"Your health okay? Blood pressure? Any respiratory issues?"

Abboud walked closer, stood behind the car next to the white man with the arrow in his upper back and the odd questions. The man dropped the water bottle in the trunk with the body. What sort of insanity was this white devil a part of?

"I am very healthy. What are these inquiries about my condition? And why do you give a dead man a bottle of water?"

Court pulled the president's tie from around his neck, then he unbuttoned the remaining buttons of his starched white shirt. He pulled it free of his black slacks and let it hang loose, exposing a white V-neck undershirt. "It's not for him. Hop in."

"Hop?"

"Get in the trunk. Now!"

"With—"

The white man pulled Abboud by the back of the head, shepherded him more than pushed him into the back of the car, then used a folding knife to cut out the internal trunk release cord. The thick Sudanese man pushed the dead body out of the way to comply with his instructions. He did not want to cross this man.

He did not *want* to assist the man attempting to kidnap him. He did not *want* to climb into the dark sedan with this bloody carcass of a traitor to his country.

But more than anything, he did not want the American's operation to switch to plan A.

Ten kilometers southeast of Gentry's position, Zack Hightower had managed to get all of his men into the first of two long, symmetrical, uniform, two-story buildings. The shopping center had a nongovernmental-agency cold and efficient construction look to it, and handmade wooden stalls with low-hanging eaves were built haphazardly around it. It was more like a low-rent urban flea market than an American mall. The floor inside the building was full of dirt, like runoff from the hillside washed through the ground floors during the rainy season. Also, along with the goods for sale inside shuttered and gated kiosks, trash was everywhere in the open center, as if squatters were common. This was no great surprise, considering these buildings were a hell of a lot more secure than the actual homes of the majority of those living in and around Suakin. Hightower assumed there must be some security here, but the security had apparently cleared out when five wild-eyed and bloody white men, dressed like soldiers and firing machine guns at helicopters and government troops, came rolling and sliding down the hill outside.

The row of buildings was ruggedly built but certainly not impenetrable. There were waist-high windows without glass, doorways without doors, and behind this shopping center was another, identical two-story block of shops, literally dozens of windows and a long rooftop from which someone could get line of sight into an open window on Whiskey Sierra's position.

And the motherfucking helicopter was circling right over them now.

Four's leg was a mess, bleeding from multiple points. Zack guessed he'd lost well over a liter of blood already. Most men would not have been on their feet, much less still in the fight, but Milo was a former Navy SEAL; he'd been pushed physically further than 99.99 percent of the rest of the American population, so he could shrug off this battle wound for a few minutes more.

But, Zack knew, once he'd lost two liters, he'd be down, unconscious or close to it. He was desperate to find his men some cover, to tend to Four's wounds, to consolidate ammo, to catch their fucking breath.

They were three blocks from the sea now. Two had used a hatchet to knock a hole through the wall of a small basket shop into the back of a post office. It was only just after seven a.m., so the office was still closed, but there were voices coming from the other side of the shuttered front door and windows. The team moved into the room, low and behind the counter. Five went to the front door, cracked it open, and then quickly closed it. He turned back to Sierra One, who had positioned himself to cover the hole in the wall they'd just crawled through.

"No dice, Zack. GOS out the wazoo. They're hanging back, thinking it over, but they'll see us if we break cover."

"Roger that," said Hightower. He knew this force against him must at least be entertaining the possibility that the president of their nation was a captive of the men they were shooting at. It should have made them think twice before engaging, giving an advantage to Whiskey Sierra. But this was a chaotic and confused situation, and Zack knew he could not trust the training and reasoning of his enemy to check their fire.

He nodded to a metal circular staircase that rose into a dark hole above them. It looked more like a small storage space than a second floor. "Three, punch out and try and get access to the roof, but watch for that chopper. We want to keep moving southeast, towards the port."

Dan, the dark-bearded Paramilitary Operations officer, complied. He moved quickly with his French-made FAMAS F1 assault rifle high towards the darkness. When he was gone, Zack looked to Two, then nodded to Four. "We've got to stop his bleeding, or they'll be able to track us."

Two began limping over to Four before Zack finished the thought. Four guarded the hole in the wall with his machine gun while Two dropped to his kneepads next to him and began pulling medical supplies from his small pouch on his chest rig.

A minute later the helicopter flew by low and slow, trying to get a look inside the windows of the second story.

"Dan." Zack used his radio to call Three on the roof.

"Yeah, boss?"

"I need you to do something about that Mi-17."

A pause, and then the reply, "I'd love to, chief, but I left my Stinger missile in my other pants."

Brad and Milo laughed. Spencer was down a hallway that led to an open room, doing his best to cover a half dozen points of entry by himself. Zack barked, "Three, that chopper has *got* to go. I don't give a fuck how you do it, but *you* don't come down till that Mi-17 goes down, how copy?"

A hesitation, but the answer was firm. "Good copy, Zack."

"We're gonna pass Four's HK up to you. That's better than your FAMAS." Zack looked to Four, who, though prone with his back propped up against the wall and covered in blood from his right knee down, did not seem happy about relinquishing his weapon. He handed it over to Brad who, in turn, passed his F1 to the wounded man. Brad ran up the staircase with the big gun. A few seconds later, he came down with Dan's weapon around his neck and went back to work on the bloody leg.

Hightower spoke into his headset. "There is no way we can get out of this city with that bird overhead. Once we're on the open road, there will be nowhere to hide from the air. We defend this building until that chopper is dealt with. If Dan can get the Mi-17 out of the way, we are going to head east, to the waterline. We're going to swim out of here. Everybody copy that?"

"Four can't swim, boss," said Two.

Zack looked at Four, who's face was whitening with the loss of blood.

Four said, "Fuck that shit. I'll swim if you tell me to swim."

Zack looked back to Two. Brad shook his head emphatically. Milo started to protest, but Hightower raised his hand. "You cut that macho man bullshit right now. Nobody is impressed." Then he transmitted to the team. "Okay, we head to the water anyhow, make 'em chase us, then we disappear. We'll double back over ground we've already covered. If we're lucky, then they'll think we went for a swim. We're going to need to use a little subterfuge."

To a man they nodded as one. They understood the stakes. They knew no one would be coming for them. They knew they were on their own. They had only themselves to rely on.

And the Gray Man.

Zack reached to the satellite phone on his chest rig and punched the number six on the keypad. He noticed his bloody arm again, wondered how much longer he'd be operational if he could not stop the bleeding. He pushed the concern from his mind as Gentry answered.

Sierra One asked, "Yo, brother, things as fucked-up on your end as they are over here?"

"Oryx and I are clear. It sounded like you guys were engaged pretty heavily."

"Still are."

"You got a plan, Charlie?" Gentry's sarcasm was directed at plan Bravo, which hadn't turned out so well.

"You know it."

"I doubt it."

A pause from the other side. "I'm workin' on it. Where are you?"

"We're fifteen klicks northwest. I've switched out the wheels I left town with. Nobody followed us."

"Well, shit, kid, sounds like you're sitting pretty compared to us. We're hemmed in, two casualties, ammo short. The army has backed off, hoping this Hip flying overhead can frag us so they don't have to expose themselves again. I guess they either don't think we have their president, or else they don't care."

"A Hip? I didn't know the GOS flew Mi-17s."

"It's definitely a Hip."

"Who are the casualties?" Court asked.

"Milo took a round in his leg. We've controlled the blood loss, but he ain't walkin' out of here on his own power."

"And the other?"

"Yours truly."

"You operational?"

"Hell yeah, I'm fraggin' skinnies like there's no tomorrow. Just caught a little ding to the forearm of my non-shooting hand, although on a day like today, all hands are shooting."

"Shit. One casualty here, too."

"Who?"

"Who the fuck do you think, Zack? You sent me in alone, remember?"

"I know that, dickhead. I didn't know if you were talking about Oryx."

"Oryx is fine."

"You get a boo-boo?"

"Something like that."

"Where are you hit?"

"Upper back, with an arrow."

"Uhhh, repeat last?"

"I got shot with a damn arrow. Haven't taken it out yet. I'm working up to it."

"So there's an arrow sticking out of your back? For real?"

"Affirm."

"What the hell? Ain't nobody shooting arrows around here."

"Well, I didn't fucking back into it, Zack! I never saw the shooter. Beats taking a 7.62 from one of those PKMs the army's blasting back there."

"An arrow. I'll be damned."

"Look, Zack. I can get to you guys. I'm pulling into my hide right now. I can zip-tie Oryx to a support beam and haul ass back to you. I've got my Glock and a mag left, maybe I can—"

"Negative. You stay put and protect the package for now. I don't need you charging in like Custer and losing the president in the process. We'll keep trying to wiggle out of this shit on our own."

"Understood."

"How you gonna get that arrow out?"

"I'm going to ask the president to help me."

Zack whistled. "He may be disinclined to cooperate."

"Yeah. I'll have to persuade him."

"Well, good luck with that. But while you're over there playing cowboys and Indians, the grown-ups are shooting real guns in my neck of the woods. So get your principal secure and your shit straightened out and check back with me."

"Roger that."

Zack disconnected the call. Just as he looked back up, gunfire from a heavy machine gun hit the north side of the building, scattering plaster and concrete through the dusty air of the room like thick smoke. All three men dropped to their chests and returned fire into the wall. Zack shouted into his mike, "Come on, Dan! Clear my fuckin' sky already!" But his words were drowned out by the incredible noise.

38

By eight a.m., Whiskey Sierra was completely pinned down from the west and from above. Spencer had scooted back into the room with the other men. He'd taken a three-round burst from an AK-47 into his big chest plate and was bleeding from several shrapnel injuries to his neck and face.

Dan was still up on the roof. He'd found some concealment from the chopper and was trying to get an opportunity to bring it down, but he would need to expose himself to do so, and the Hip was circling too damn close to try it. The other four team members were flat on the ground of the first floor. The machine gun on the back of the jeep Brad had almost rear-ended earlier had found a crew, and it had been pulverizing the portion of the mall where Whiskey Sierra was hiding. Zack and his team could not even get their heads up to return fire, so withering was the enemy's attack.

"Dan, can you make it to the side of the roof to get a shot on this machine gun?"

"No fucking way, boss. The Hip is hovering right in front of my position. I stick my head out, and I'm going to lose it. I can't even engage it till it moves away." The noise of the helicopter came through the headsets with Sierra Three's transmission.

"Roger that."

Brad shouted over the noise from the incoming fire, "They are going to flank us here in a second!"

279

"Yeah," agreed Zack. It was his job, as the team leader, to think of a way out of this seemingly impossible predicament.

He looked at the hallway. Other than the windows and front door, it was the only exit to the room. "Spence, think the GOS has taken that next room yet?"

"I wouldn't doubt it. Lots of access from the street."

Hightower nodded. "Okay. All elements, here's what we're going to do, break. This ain't pretty, but it's all I got. Brad, on my command, you are going to throw all your smoke as far as you can out the window towards the west, try to get it on the road between us and the machine gun. Dan, stay down, but throw your smoke from the roof in the same direction, as far as you fucking can."

"Roger, boss."

"Spencer, throw your smoke out the window to the east, into the market between the malls. How copy?"

"Good copy."

"I'll pop smoke along with Spence. Then, on my command, Spencer goes out the window to the east, fires at the Hip, and hauls ass. You're going to try to get the chopper to go after you. As soon as he does—"

Dan finished the transmission. "I'll dump eighty rounds from the HK up its ass."

"Good man. Then Spencer continues on to Mall Bravo. Tries to make the GOS think we've relocated over there, while the rest of us keep heading south in this complex via the second floor."

"Roger that," said Spencer. Going out into the open like that was all but a death sentence, but the man did not show a moment's hesitation or an ounce of fear.

"We'll link up as soon as possible," said Zack.

"Sounds good," Sierra Five said. Still no indication that he knew he was likely about to die.

"Brad, Milo is your responsibility."

"I got him, but we're going to have to shit-can his gear so he can keep moving."

"Do it." A pause for Brad to get the assault vest and backpack and utility belt off his injured patient. And then, "All right, guys, let's make this happen. Go!"

Smoke grenades arced out of the windows and off the roof. Men under direct fire scrambled to their knees. Milo, though injured and weak, rolled to his knees and fired his borrowed weapon, threw a fragmentation grenade to the west.

"Frag out!"

Within seconds opaque red and white smoke had spurted from canisters in the streets on two sides of the building.

Spencer had unhooked much of the gear from his back and hips, and with only his UZI, a pistol, and a few magazines, he leapt out of the window of the shop, began sprinting across forty meters of market stalls and open ground to try and make it to the other strip mall. He was somewhat obscured by thick white and red smoke, but above and behind him the Hip turned on its axis and plunged through the air after him.

The big black operator slowed and turned to fire at it, raised his impotent weapon for a long burst, but the Hip fired first. The chain guns ripped up the wooden stalls to the left and right of him, and Spencer turned and began running again.

The Hip moved closer, creating distance between itself and the roof of the building behind it. Dan, Sierra Three, stepped out of his low concealment and brought the machine gun to his shoulder.

He lined the big rifle's red dot sight on the tail rotor assembly at the back of the big bird. He opened fire with quick controlled bursts to combat the recoil, and he did not stop, firing eighty rounds and turning the barrel white-hot.

A small puff of black smoke appeared in seconds. The aircraft shuddered and angled to the right, breaking off his chase of the man in the market. He banked harder and harder. Dan thought he was trying to fly back around and engage him, but an explosion at the rotor assembly, much larger than the original puff of smoke, sent the Mi-17 spinning on the vertical midline of its main rotor.

It was eighty feet in the air, completely out of control, and

Dan ducked back into the stairwell with a warning to Sierra Five, "Spence! He's goin' down hard! Get clear of the market!"

The tail of the Mi-17 slammed into the second story of the mall Zack and the majority of Sierra Five occupied. It dipped forward and hit the ground nose first. It was only a drop of thirty feet or so, but the big machine was moving at speed, and the resulting explosion and fireball ensured there would be no survivors.

Hightower knew exactly what happened to the Hip, though he had not seen it take the hits from Dan's rifle nor had he watched it auger into the dirt between the two shopping centers. But he heard all the noises and the transmissions from his man on the roof, and when the chopper burst into flames, he and the two men with him were just coming out of the second-floor stairwell and passing a window, and the light and heat off his left shoulder left no doubt as to the fate of the Mi-17 and those aboard.

The three men continued down a short hallway, where they met Dan just as he came down a ladder from the roof. Brad and Dan each took hold of Milo, and Zack led the way as they tried to put some distance between themselves and the last point of contact with the enemy.

"One for Five," Zack called into his headset as he warily moved through a long sundry store that apparently took quite a bit of heavy machine gun fire. All around papers, woven baskets, ceramic pottery, everything in the room, was shattered or shredded.

"One for Five. How copy, Five?" Nothing. "One for Five. Spence?"

The team's headsets were silent.

Court entered the thatch-roofed dwelling, cleared it with his Glock in under five seconds. The walls were primarily burlap, and a fifty-five gallon drum had been pounded flat to use as a door. Treads from tires had been worked in with driftwood, plywood, and other refuse material to augment the burlap on the walls.

The inside was dark and sweltering, the air still and thick, an absence of the smells of food and smoke from cooking fires that made the American assume the owners had been gone awhile and were not coming back soon. He wiped away some cobwebs, kicked at some trash in the corner to make sure no one was hiding there and nothing dangerous came slithering out, and then used his knife to cut holes in the fabric walls to provide light and draft.

He had lucked into finding this hide. After High-tower's last transmission, the Gray Man had decided to not go all the way up to the marshland as he'd originally planned. Instead, he wanted to be closer to Suakin in case he needed to get back there to help extract Whiskey Sierra. So he pulled off the main road, wandered aimlessly down a lonely dirt track, passed a few donkey carts and one small village, looking for any place to park the car and find a few minutes' peace. The abandoned dwelling was surrounded by high grasses and was barely visible from the road, and immediately he knew it would do, although the grasses looked like they would certainly be full of all sorts of poisonous snakes and angry insects.

Gentry holstered his weapon and carefully retraced his steps back to the Skoda to get his human luggage out of the back.

Oryx was awake and alert. His eyes were wide and filled with alternating signs of relief, disdain, and a bit of drug-induced contentment. He'd downed the entire bottle of water and somehow even managed to get his undershirt ripped off of his body. His white shirt was literally clinging to him, soaked with sweat. His large bald head dripped.

The trunk had already begun to smell like death.

"You are not with the American government," Oryx proclaimed as he was led towards the dwelling. "The way you executed that man. The way you hit me, threw me in the trunk. The talk of money and assassination. These are not the actions of an American serviceman."

"Nope."

The president stopped and turned. "You are a soldier of fortune."

Gentry pushed him forward. "After expenses, I'm really more like a soldier of the middle class."

"I know who sent you to kill me."

"Do you?"

"Of course. It's obvious. Who has both the resources to pay you and to plan this, and hates me enough to set this in motion? Those American actors who are so against me and have so much money. I have seen them on television for years, speaking to your congress, making movies of lies that they call documentaries. I knew some day these infidels would make an attempt on my life."

Court wasn't in the mood for chit-chat. The barb in his back was causing all his muscles to seize and cramp in pain; even walking was difficult now. As they approached the open doorway, he said, "That's right. I'm gonna be a primo player in Hollywood when this is done. Fucking star on that sidewalk and all that shit."

"And I also know who sent you to kidnap me." His voice trailed off at the end, as he stopped at the entrance to the tiny structure. "Where are we? What is this place?"

"Keep going."

"What are you going to—"

Court struck him soundly on the side of the head with the butt of the gun. The big man staggered, turned to the shack, and began walking forward with no more questions. Once inside, he continued to the center of the dimly lit room, and then he turned around. Gentry could see his confusion.

"You are working with Bedouins?"

"Shut up."

Abboud shook off his confusion and began a sales pitch. Court had expected nothing less. "I can arrange to pay you more, more than you are getting to do this, I assure you."

"Shut up."

"Not money from Sudanese banks, no. I have accounts all over the world. Friends in the West and in Asia. This could be a larger monetary event for you than you now realize. You can just double what you are being paid and I will see—"

"Shut up and listen!" Court holstered his pistol again, the agony showing in his face as he reached across his body and gingerly removed his backpack by unbuckling the shoulder straps. Then he began working on his brown shirt, tearing at it with grunts and winces. After several tugs it tore free, and he stood bare-chested in the dim shack. "I need you to help me get this out."

"The arrow?"

"No, the coffee stain on my crotch. Yes! The arrow!"

The president's thick eyebrows rose. "What if I do not agree to help you?"

"I will kill you."

Court could see the gears turning in Abboud's brain. The crafty man knew his kidnapper needed something from him. He was now trying to find a way to play it to his advantage.

"What will you do for me if I do help?"

"I won't kill you. Yet."

That slowed the gears down a bit.

"What do I have to do?"

"I am going to lie on the ground, facedown. I need you to put your foot in the center of my back, grab the arrow just behind the head, and pull it out of the bone."

There was a flicker of fresh light in the president's eyes, and Court Gentry knew exactly what he was thinking. "You will want to drive the arrow into my back or neck when you pull it out. If you do this, you better find the place on my neck that will kill me instantly, because I am going to roll over and shoot you sixteen times if you don't."

"Why sixteen?"

"Because my gun only has sixteen bullets. Remember, I gave you a lot of dope back there in Suakin. You are slower than you think, you are weaker than you think, and right now, you are not half as smart as you think you are. You need to consider your actions very carefully before trying anything stupid, because I swear I will blow off your fucking nuts and watch you flip around till you bleed out if you don't succeed."

Silence hung in the air like the cloying heat. Oryx's face showed the unpleasant mental image dancing in his head.

Finally, Court asked, "Are you ready to try this?"

President Abboud paused a long time. Finally he said, "This will be extremely painful for you."

"And that's a problem for you, why?"

"You may think I am trying to kill you when I am only trying to help."

"I will expect pain in my back, where the arrow is. If I feel pain anywhere else, then the president of Sudan will lose his balls. That means no more little baby despots for you. You understand?"

Abboud nodded. Court drew his pistol and worked his way slowly to his knees, then onto his stomach. The arrow was into his scapula. It would not come out easily, and when it did, Court knew he would bleed considerably. He had a small trauma kit with him but no real way to dress a wound he could neither see nor reach, and having the president of Sudan bandage him just seemed too damn weird to bear.

And while Oryx's drug-induced lethargy and diminished capacity worked to Court's advantage as a kidnapper, it certainly did not benefit him as a patient. For all he knew, big Bakri Abboud was going to fall on top of the arrow instead of pull it out, and thereby pin Court to the floor of this shit hole shack like a butterfly in a bug collection.

Any way he looked at it, the Gray Man knew this was going to suck. He wanted to pop some pills, but he was smack-dab in the middle of a massive operation. That the thought of narcotics even entered his brain at this moment was disappointing to him.

Court fingered the Glock in his right hand. For a while he heard or felt nothing. He wondered if Oryx was trying to sneak out the door. Finally the booming African's voice called out from above. "Can you release my hands? It will make it easier for me to—"

"Hell no. Just grab it and pull."

He felt the pressure of the large sole of a big shoe between his shoulder blades, the painful adjusting of the arrow in his muscle and bone as it was grabbed hold of, and then an excruciating yank that caused Gentry's eyes to fill with tears and his throat to emit a cracking scream. The burning and tearing did not stop. Instinctively, Court flipped onto his back, raised his Glock at the attacker above him, and ran his finger tip from the trigger guard down to the trigger.

He sighted on his target, just a couple of feet from the tip of the gun's barrel.

Oryx stood above him, his hands bound together and shielding his eyes. The bloody arrow fell from his fingers onto Gentry's chest.

He'd done it. Oryx had not tried anything and, Court realized, he'd come incredibly close to shooting him between the eyes nonetheless.

The pain in his shoulder did not subside, but still he rose to his feet, found himself more mobile if only because he no longer had to move carefully to avoid bumping the long projectile.

"Good."

"What is your name?"

"Call me Six."

"Mr. Six. Fine. And you may call me President—"

"I'll call you whatever the fuck I want. Now, shithead, I need to make a phone call, so I need you to sit in the corner and be a good boy. Can you do that?"

39

Zack and three of his men had made it out of the last kill zone. After the chopper went down, the GOS seemed to back off both in fear and in an attempt to regroup. Hightower and company followed the second-floor hallway of Mall Alpha through laundries and rug shops and bakeries and storage rooms. They'd engaged two GOS men who were surprised to see them and certainly sorry they did in those last few seconds before they were silently killed with daggers. Brad and Dan scavenged the Type 81 rifles from the men's bodies, since both of their own weapons were down to the last magazine. Brad passed his FAMAS to Milo to use as a makeshift crutch, and it had increased the mobility of Whiskey Sierra significantly. At the end of the mall they'd gone back downstairs, where they saw the GOS infantry on the street pulling back a couple of blocks, so Zack gave the order for the men to break cover and head through the souk, one block closer to the water, to the other concrete row of buildings he'd dubbed Mall Bravo.

The crash of the big helicopter had started a fire in the souk, and the black smoke from fuel and fabric and rubber and wood had helped obscure the depleted team as they crossed the open ground. They received no return fire from the retreating GOS, and it seemed likely their repositioning had gone undetected. It was almost too much to hope for, but so far, he'd seen no evidence that the opposition knew where they were.

Hightower had seen enough combat in his life to recognize that the main thing they'd had going for them was the confusion on the part of their enemy. He was certain the Sudanese Army had no idea they were only up against five men, and these five men were not holding their president hostage as a human shield. If they *did* know the only threat was right here in these buildings by the souk near the water, they would simply concentrate all their forces here, blast the hell out of the malls, and kill everything that moved inside.

Five men, no matter how good their training, could do nothing against that sort of assault.

And it was starting to look like five men had become four. Spencer had not transmitted since disappearing out the window to divert the attention of the helicopter ten minutes earlier. It was possible he'd lost his radio or the signal between the buildings was broken, but Sierra One thought it likely that Sierra Five had made it across the souk, only to stumble into a superior force of GOS infantry on the other side.

Still, Zack and his men were heading carefully through mall Bravo now in an attempt to find their comrade.

Hightower's sat phone vibrated. He pressed the answer button, which put the call through to his tactical headset.

"Hey, Six. You chillaxing on the beach with a mai tai?"

Gentry's voice came through the line. "We're secure. You?"

"Knee-deep in it. About fifty yards from the water, three blocks north of the causeway. Still in sporadic contact. Haven't been able to shake the GOS long enough to slip away. How's your back? Run into any more Comanches out on the trail?"

"I'll live. You need me there?"

"Sure you can put Oryx on ice?"

"Affirmative. I'll tie him up and drug him. He's not going anywhere."

"Alright, then get on your horse and get over here ASAP. We need you to bring us some wheels, get us some kind of sitrep as to the concentration of OPFOR in the streets. I was thinking you might be able to come in low-pro from the west, score us a ride, and then move close enough to lead our exfil back to it."

"Shit, Zack, want me to pick you up a fucking Happy Meal while I'm at it?"

Zack chuckled as he knelt in a shop that made and sold tin pots and pans. Brad was ahead, clearing a doorway with his scavenged Type 81 rifle. Dan was behind with Milo. "Man, where did you learn to be such a smart-ass?" It was a rhetorical question; Zack knew the answer. "The only burger meat around here is going to be Whiskey Sierra unless you come and pull our asses off the grill."

Zack heard the sigh, but he also knew his former operator would comply with nothing more than a little bitching and moaning. "Roger that, I'm on the way. I'll use the radio when I get in range."

"Good boy. On your way over here, I want you to call the *Hannah* and let them know where you stashed the president. Just in case none of us make it out, they can come in and pick him up."

"Roger that. Six out."

It took a half hour for Gentry to get Oryx secure, change his shirt to something less torn and bloodstained, cover his head with a turban, siphon fuel from a parked cargo truck to gas up the Mercedes, and get back into Suakin's city limits. He almost took the truck and left the Mercedes behind, but the old, heavy, diesel sedan was serving him well at the moment, it had not been compromised by the enemy, and the truck looked like shit, even by the lousy standards of what passed for motor vehicles around here. Heading back into the target zone, he passed army trucks and police cars moving in all directions, and bewildered civvies doing the same.

Overhead a pair of old American F5 fighter jets, flown by the Sudanese Air Force, etched figure-eight-shaped contrails in the bright blue sky.

There did not seem to be much cohesion to the movements of the military forces, which Gentry took as a good sign. From the look of it, the Sudanese had no idea how big an opposition force they were up against. With Gentry's movements to the southeast of the square, the two operators in buildings in the square, the van shooting its way around the entire town, and the brief engagement with the SLA to the west, it must have painted an incredibly confused tactical picture for the GOS military commanders. With the massive volume of gunfire and the shouted radio traffic reporting enemy contacts on all points of the compass, they may well have thought the president had been kidnapped by a local force one hundred men strong.

As Court downshifted his Mercedes to negotiate the narrow passageways between two rows of shanties, an army jeep shot up an alley from his right and passed directly in front of him as it continued to the north. At the paved road a two-ton truck full of troops pulled out into traffic next to him, and it was nearly T-boned in the process by an identical truck heading east.

There was no shooting in town, and the helicopter was gone. Sirens whined, and a thin pillar of dark smoke drifted over the harbor and lagoon to the east.

It looked like a battle had been fought here, and it looked like the battle was over.

Gentry parked the car on an open dirt soccer pitch four blocks west of the square. Immediately he was approached by men trying to sell turnips, even with the local equivalent of the Battle of the Bulge just a few blocks away less than an hour earlier. He wondered who the fuck would be thinking about buying a turnip for that evening's soup at a time like this, and he brushed them away with a wave of his hand, trying to keep his beard and his shades and his turban covering as much of his face and head as possible while he moved. He purchased a long white thobe robe from a vendor in a shallow stall a block from the soccer pitch, and stepped into an alley to don his new garment.

There were cops everywhere now. Gentry figured most of them must have come down from Port Sudan, forty miles to the north. If so, then they would have just arrived, run face-first into the chaos and confusion of the scene, they would be trying to glean intel, and would be unsure about jurisdiction and jostling for real estate with the local cops and the military and the NSS. Now would be the last possible time to accomplish anything in Suakin for the rest of the day, and Court knew he needed to hustle. Up ahead he spied a disorganized police checkpoint next to a long wood and corrugated tin lean-to structure that covered hundreds of wooden cages, each cage housing an individual chicken or rooster. Dozens of locals were milling about. Only a few were going about their business; most were standing around and talking, trying to pick up gossip about what was going on. A few of them were getting hassled by the cops at the checkpoint, so Court looked for a different route.

The dust kicked up by the vehicles on the streets all but obscured the road, like a miniature haboob. Gentry could barely see fifty feet, and he hoped the cops and the other curious eyes in the streets were having the same problem so he could move closer to his objective with a bit more confidence.

To avoid the checkpoint, he made a left down an alley. In seconds he was lost. There were so few main roads in this town, it was easy to feel like you were caught in a maze of arbitrary passageways between shacks that went on for miles. But the town was set on a gentle slope towards the harbor, and Gentry's objective lay at the harbor, so Court just kept moving downhill and away from people, and soon enough this led him into the square.

In daylight the square seemed smaller, even more dirty and congested. It was full of men and beasts and machines. Camels and goats and donkeys mixed in with military vehicles and government sedans and "technicals," Toyota pickups with machine guns mounted in the back and filled with men. Two transport helicopters sat idle in the square, their troops already out hunting for the kidnappers of their president. Ambulance sirens blared from all ends of the open area, and men shouted and screamed at one another. A half dozen dead soldiers had been dumped in a pile by their fellow brothers-in-arms, and the wounded were everywhere. Court saw a makeshift clinic for injured civilians. Even from a distance some of the wounds looked serious, and he quickly turned away from them, worried there would be hurt children, and he could not bear to witness their suffering.

"We had to destroy the village to save it," he muttered under his breath and inside his hot turban.

His Thuraya buzzed on his hip under his clothing, and the call came through his covert headset. He answered with an explanation. "Almost to you, One. Need about five more minutes."

"That's good. We've been waiting on your ass so long the landlord is hitting us up for first and last month's rent. How's the town?"

"It's getting stuffy, a lot of jurisdictional issues all these organizations have to iron out. Plus the dead and wounded everywhere adding to the confusion. We need to take advantage of this disorder. The time to move is right now."

"Negative, we can't exfil just yet."

Court stopped in his tracks. "Why not?"

"Sierra Five is MIA. I need to know what happened to him."

"Copy that. I'll find us some wheels and get set. Six out."

Zack had his three men ready to move seconds after Court hung up. They had spent the last half hour on the roof at the northern tip of Mall Bravo, not forty meters east of where the Hip crashed in the souk between the two malls. Their rooftop position did not give them any view, however. They'd found a ripped and rotting green tarpaulin held up by driftwood and wire, under which someone had stored firewood and empty water tanks, and Whiskey Sierra had ducked into the deepest recesses of the structure for maximum concealment. There they sat and waited, bled and perspired, thumped scorpions off of each other with gloved fingertips.

The four men had patched themselves up as well as possible. Zack had bandaged his forearm and effectively stopped the bleeding, consumed water and salts from his rations to replace that lost in his profuse sweating, and consolidated all his partial magazines of ammunition into one thirty-round mag in his gun, plus a partially loaded mag in his canvas chest rig. Brad now wielded a fully loaded Type 81. He'd hurt his back and knee while crashing the van. He thought he might have cracked a rib or two on his right side but had not reported himself as a casualty to Sierra One. Dan carried a scavenged Type 81 as well. Dan was the sole uninjured member of the team.

Milo was stabilized for the time being. Dan had used massive amounts of duct tape to secure Brad's F1 to his leg like a stiff-legged splint, and he'd rebandaged the young Croatian American's shattered leg. But Sierra Four was without a rifle; he only carried a 9 mm H&K pistol, and all of his armor and gear had been left behind or passed around the team so that he could continue to move. He vigorously protested everything done for him, insisted he was good to go, but his bluster just annoyed the shit out of the older, more experienced operators. They understood his condition better than he did, and they treated him professionally, even if they continually berated him for trying to tell them he was fine.

The four men left the roof in a tactical train, descended two floors in a tiny and darkened metal stairwell, and ended up in an east–west alley. Milo stumbled twice on the stairs. Zack then ordered him to keep his pistol in his right hand and Dan's shoulder in his left. This helped his balance.

The alleyway ran towards the harbor, and the team took it slowly. Men's voices were heard on the other side of a wooden door, and Whiskey Sierra formed around it, but the voices faded. Sirens in the distance mixed with the guttural roars and cries of camels. The team did their best to shut out all the noises that were not tactically significant. Soon they made it to the mouth of the alleyway, and here they warily stepped into sight of the harbor.

Dan was first out of the alley, into the open street in front of the water. The others moved close behind him.

Dan stopped dead in his tracks. "Contact front!"

40

Fifty yards in front of the mouth of the alley, atop the crystal green water in front of the island of Old Suakin, sat a Sudanese Navy coastal patrol boat. It was one hundred feet in length; men stood on the deck behind a 12.7-mm machine gun. Quickly they turned the barrel of the big weapon towards the white men appearing in front of them.

Zack ground to a halt next to Dan. "Disperse!" shouted Zack, and his men broke left and right. High-tower himself grabbed the injured Sierra Four and pushed him back to the right, fell with him into a shop that wove and sold fishing nets.

The time for well-coordinated movements was gone. No more covering fields of fire, leapfrogging from one piece of concealment to the next. The four men began running, crawling, and leaping over obstacles as fast as possible.

The braying of the ship's machine gun was ungodly. Its rounds sawed through the building above Zack's head. He grasped Milo by the drag handle on his Australian body armor, found the shop had a back room, and the back room had a bent metal door that Hightower kicked open by spinning on his back on the dirt floor and shoving both boot heels up hard towards the locks. Through the door was another shop, and then a hallway that headed south. Zack crawled on his hands and knees, pulling Milo along with him.

The patrol boat brayed again, shredding wood and metal and

stone and fabric above their heads. A jug of black lubricant split in two on a shelf above them, spilling warm grease over their gear and clothing.

A third burst came from the guns, and then it was quiet for a moment. "Whiskey team, report," whispered Zack into his mic.

"Sierra Three, I'm good to go. I'm with Two. His headset came off, but he's cool."

Zack breathed a quick sigh of relief. "One and Four are okay. That's going to bring the army down on us quick. We've got to get the fuck out of here, break. Sierra Six, are you receiving on this channel?"

Court replied, "Affirmative, One."

"Good. When you *do* come for us, do *not* go east of Mall Bravo. That ain't the Love Boat out there."

"Roger that. Any sign of Sierra Five?"

"Negative. Doesn't look like he made it to the waterline, though. We'd have heard that belt-fed bitch light him up. We'll move north a couple of blocks to see what we can see. And all elements: keep your heads down while we link back up."

Court spent the next fifteen minutes finishing work on a project he'd just begun when the patrol boat's loud machine guns opened up a quarter mile to the east. He'd come across a four-man squad of young GOS infantry guarding a dirt track to the northwest of the square. The track ended at the one paved road that led out of Suakin to the west, where it linked up with the north–south highway that continued up to Port Sudan and down to the rest of the country. A gas station lay at the intersection. The station was surprisingly modern, considering the rustic nature of the town. Court attributed this to the fact that it was on the highway, and Sudan did possess a relatively robust system of bus travel between major cities.

The soldiers' jeep was parked in the unpaved lot of the gas station, and a Russian PKM light machine gun sat mounted in the back under a black plastic cover. Many locals stood around the station, finding refuge there after having fled the center of Suakin, and the soldiers had their hands full with the crowd of people milling about.

Court had walked up to the jeep, careful to keep his turban covering virtually his entire face, and he took a look inside. The keys were not with the vehicle, which meant he needed to figure out which of the soldiers was the driver.

He had a plan boiling in his head, but for now he just needed to wait for Zack.

The two malls and the shacks and shops erected all around them were a flutter of activity now. Everywhere soldiers moved with weapons up, screaming at civilians to get out of the way, and the civilians screamed back. Beasts of burden clogged the alleyways, and a bucket brigade of rail-thin men dumped water on the last of the fire in the souk that surrounded the blackened helicopter and the charred remains inside. The soldiers pushed these men away, as well, but the locals re-formed their line and went back to work, so desperate was their need to keep their subsistence-level incomes alive by preventing their shops and their wares from going up in black smoke with the chopper.

But Zack, Brad, Dan, and Milo were not moving, were not running away or blasting themselves clear to safety. Instead, they lay prone, fifty yards north of the two malls, on the second floor of a two-story mud-brick building ringed by a low wall. The men all looked out the open arched passageway to the balcony, across the balcony, over the wall, over the road, and across a sandy runoff depression that led east to the harbor. On the other side of the depression, some two hundred meters away, was the bus station. And outside the bus station, sitting in the dirt, propped against a wall and surrounded by over two dozen soldiers, was a muscular black man, obviously wounded but obviously alive.

Sierra Five.

Through the four-power scope of Hightower's TAR-21, the only weapon with optics left on the team, he could see that Spencer's shirt had been removed, and he bled from the face and neck and shoulders, and blood stained his brown pants. His torso was covered in the gleam of perspiration along with the crimson shine of his blood. He'd been handcuffed behind his back, he was conscious, and a civilian man knelt in front of him, talking to him. Every now and then, he turned the American's face towards him to ask him a question, then slapped him or punched him. Zack knew Spencer wasn't going to say a word in response to a little rough stuff, but he also knew the harsh treatment he was now being subjected to would deteriorate in seconds into real torture.

And there was nothing he could do to save him.

"Sierra One for Sierra Six."

"Go ahead for Six."

"You ready to try an exfiltration?"

"Affirmative. I just need to know where you are. As soon as you find Five, let's do it. Every second we wait is another second where I risk compromise."

Zack relayed his exact coordinates and then said, "They've got Five. We have eyes on. He's alive but unreachable."

No transmissions came through the headsets for several seconds. Finally Court responded. "Okay. Understand you have line of sight?"

Zack nodded in the darkened room. A dingy white curtain blew in the hot breeze in front of him, momentarily obscuring his view of his man. Zack knew what Court was asking. Court was a pro among pros. Of course he understood what must be done.

Hightower flipped the safety on his Tavor, rendering his weapon hot. "Affirmative, Six. I have line of sight. He's at the bus station just north of us."

Gentry's next transmission broke a short still. "*I'll* do it. I'll head down the hill and get eyes on. You just sit tight, and I'll take care of it."

The other three men in the room with Zack said nothing. Hightower knew that they all understood what was going to happen, but only Gentry offered to do it.

Court Gentry was one hell of a guy.

"Negative, kid. I appreciate it, but this is my job. It's what they pay me for, I guess."

"You sure?"

"Affirm. Just tell me you're ready to pick us up."

"I've got a diversion set up here. I'll need about thirty seconds to be under way, and another two mikes to be right on top of you guys."

"Roger that. Make ready. We go on my mark."

Dan was closest to Zack, just two feet off his left shoulder. He reached out and patted his boss on the arm, gave him a sympathetic squeeze.

Hightower shrugged off the hand.

Everyone on the team knew what was about to happen. They played by a set of rules that included this eventuality.

"Goddammit," said Zack softly. The men beating the shit out of Spencer now were blocking his shot; the aiming reticle on his Tavor was lined up on the tailbone of a secret policeman. Hightower wanted to squeeze the trigger, but killing one NSS officer was not worth exposing their position.

At this point, there was only one thing worth exposing their position: preventing Sierra Five from revealing his identity or mission to the Sudanese. He wouldn't do it willingly, but he would do it, and there was only one way to stop it.

Just then Hightower squinted into his scope. There was a ruckus of some sort on the other side of the secret policeman. Soldiers ran forward, one fell back in the dirt, another spun away down to his knees. The NSS officer blocking Sierra One's view was pushed aside, and then Sierra Five appeared, bloody and shirtless still, his hands shackled behind him.

"Six, execute in five seconds," said Zack.

"Go in five, roger," came the terse reply.

Spencer ran free of the scrum of men, showing incredible balance and fitness to do so. He head-butted another soldier and made it ten yards closer to Hightower's position, near the edge of the sandy depression.

"He's trying to get away," said Milo, watching without benefit of a rifle scope.

"No, he's not," said Zack softly. He blinked. "He's trying to help me get a better shot."

To the west, they heard handgun rounds and the boom of an explosion, Court's diversion, and in his scope Zack saw Spencer drop to his knees, saw his bloodied mouth move in a shout, and an instant later the distant sound made it to Hightower's position.

"Send it!"

"Sending." Sierra One pressed the trigger on the Tavor, sent a 5.56-mm round down the barrel, through the arched passageway, across the depression, and into the forehead of his man. Spencer's head snapped back, and he dropped still in the dirt, his body coming to rest on top of his restrained arms.

Within seconds, close gunfire began pocking the walls in the room, the white curtain whipped and tore and shredded, and dust from impacts between steel and clay bricks turned the air around the remaining members of Whiskey Sierra a smoky brown.

41

"Sierra Six is Oscar Mike! ETA four-five seconds!"

Zack acknowledged Court's transmission. "Six is on the move, roger."

Court drove out of the gas station in the open-topped jeep. Behind him flames rocked seventy feet into the air from a burning fuel line that spun and bounced across the concrete, swinging wildly in all directions from the gas pump.

Two of the soldiers were dead by Court's gunfire, and two more had been stabbed in the liver and lay facedown and injured in the street. Civilians ran for their lives, sprinting away from the flamethrower igniting everything in sight with a wild mind of its own. Minivans and buses slammed into one another in attempts to get clear of the station. Locals in the street, safe from the flames, now found themselves forced to dive out of the way of the military jeep that lurched in a wide arc to turn around, heading down the hill now and driven by the maniacal turbaned *kawaga* who had started this catastrophe.

Court headed east as fast as the jeep would go. The cover had popped free of the machine gun on the fixed base behind him; in his rearview he could see the weapon bouncing with the undulations of the uneven dirt track.

A pack of hobbled camels crossed in front of him, and he yanked the wheel to the right, crashed through a wooden stall selling fruit, sending a dozen bunches of bananas hanging from ropes flying into the air. He kept crashing through to the other side of the stall and found himself a block south of the road that would have led him to Whiskey Sierra's hide site. Just then, two military jeeps pulled up to the intersection in front of him.

Fuck!

Court whizzed past them, and they turned in behind and began giving chase.

"Tangos on my ass, Zack!"

"Copy that."

"Can you go one block south, or do I need to come to you guys?"

"We'll meet you in the alleyway, a left turn behind the hotel. When you pick us up, scoot over. Brad will drive." And then, "You never could drive for shit."

"Roger that." Court did not deny Hightower's charge.

The passages and alleyways were a thick congestion of man, animal, machine, and other impediments to an operator trying to make haste in a motor vehicle. Gentry leaned on the horn as he drove. A rickshaw and a donkey cart with a fifty-five-gallon water drum blocked the way just ahead of Court on his new route, so he jacked the wheel, went right one more block, and then took another hard left. Here he was forced to slam on the brakes to avoid a small crowd of children and sheep in the street, and he knew the two army jeeps pursuing him were right behind. Quickly he pulled the emergency brake, leapt up in the driver's seat and vaulted into the back, his shoulder injury protesting even through the painkilling effects of the massive amounts of adrenaline coursing through him. The two jeeps made the turn, and they, too, skidded and stopped, a huge lingering dust cloud formed by the act. Court spun the PKM machine gun back around at the vehicles, and pulled back the charging handle to rack a round. He was close enough to see the eyes of the driver of the closest jeep widen in surprise, and the black soldier ground his transmission, frantically yanking his gearshift into reverse. Court pointed right at the hood of the jeep and pulled the trigger of the big Russian weapon.

Click.

The weapon was unloaded.

Goddammit!

Court drew his Glock 19 and fired an entire magazine at the two jeeps as they backed around the corner, their green bodies slamming into one another more than once in a desperate attempt to flee the withering handgun fire. It was no belt-fed machine gun, but at the moment the nine-millimeter handgun was a hell of a lot more valuable.

As soon as they disappeared from view, he leapt back into the front seat, released the brake, and lurched forward.

He'd popped the clutch, stalling the jeep.

The windshield next to his head exploded in a spiderweb of cracks as a rifle round struck it.

"Shit!" He refired the engine and launched forward again.

Thirty seconds later, he finally made it to the rally point, and he found the surviving four members of Whiskey Sierra engaged in a fierce firefight, their weapons cracking and snapping as they sent rounds towards a row of buildings at the end of the alleyway to the east. Enemy grenades exploded just short of their targets, and return fire whistled by. Court put the jeep in park and leapt into the back—again his left shoulder hated him for doing so—and he went to work immediately loading a can of ammunition to the machine gun. Sierra Two climbed into the driver's seat. Brad carried only a pistol now, which he fired over the front windshield.

Seconds later Hightower leapt into the passenger seat, took up a forward firing position, and Two dropped down behind the wheel to reload his sidearm and put the jeep in gear. Sierra Three next came out from behind a row of barrels next to a big generator; on his back was Sierra Four, and in his right hand was a Sudanese Marra pistol that, Court assumed, he'd gleaned from a fallen enemy. Dan dumped his wounded colleague in the jeep's bed next to Court and then dove in on top of him.

Brad hit the gas, turned the jeep to the left, sending Court reeling in the back; only his handhold on the machine gun kept him upright. Court reracked the slide on the now-loaded weapon and opened up with a burst on the barrels on the corner as they drove off. Immediately the fuel inside ignited, and a massive explosion erupted across the alley, black smoke obscuring the Americans' retreat.

In under a minute they were on the paved road that led out of town. Twice they'd passed infantry while negotiating the maze of alleys in the shanties, but the speed and the confusion of the quick encounters had kept both meetings bloodless. Sierra Three remained at Gentry's feet, his handgun and his eyes trained on the six o'clock to nine o'clock sector around the vehicle. His pistol could not do what Six's machine gun could, but if he saw threats, he knew he could direct the Gray Man to engage them with the jeep's heavy weapon. He also knew the Gray Man would cover from three to six o'clock, and Brad and Zack would cover the two quarter-slices of the pie in front of them.

Sierra Four was in the back, as well, but he was unconscious now from blood loss.

Court leaned nearer to Zack's head and shouted over the noise of the speeding vehicle, "Hey! You make a left up here, and I can get us a new ride!"

Zack thought it over for less than a second. "Let's do it!" He instructed Brad to follow Court's instructions. They made the turn to the south at the top of a hill and ran directly into a military checkpoint. Easily a dozen GOS infantry were in the middle of a road lined on both sides by clay walls of private homes. Court aimed the PKM and blasted a parked technical, exploding the pickup truck and blowing men down to the dirt at twenty yards. Other troops fired at the Americans as they shot up the road at fifty miles an hour. Brad sped through the smoke and came out on the other side. To the left of the jeep a wounded infantryman lying on his back in the street rolled quickly to his knees, raised his weapon, and raked the open-topped vehicle with automatic rifle fire from fifteen feet. Court had been shooting in the opposite direction and therefore saw the threat late, but he spun the PKM towards the gunfire, blasted the soldier back against a brown wall in a splatter of blood, and then looked down at his exposed body, fully expecting to see he'd been shot.

Miraculously, he had not.

"Hang on!" shouted Brad, and Court knelt in the jeep with his hands on the machine gun just as the vehicle went airborne at the top of a crest in the road, sending it crashing down on its axle before it bottomed out and cleared the area.

A few seconds later, Brad reached for his chest rig, hugging himself with his right arm while he drove with his left. "Dammit."

"What is it?" asked Zack, still scanning his sector.

"Think I fucking popped a rib when we hit back there."

"You good?" asked Hightower.

"Yeah, I'm good, I just—"

The break in the response turned Sierra One's head to his driver. Brad continued to hold the wheel with his left hand, his foot almost to the floor, but his right hand was up in front of his face.

His fingers were coated in thick, rich, blood.

"Son of a . . .

Sierra Two's hand slowly dropped in his lap, his head bobbed to the side and then fell forward towards the steering wheel.

"Three, drive!" Zack pulled Brad out of the driver's seat and across his own body. The entire left side of Two's torso was drenched in blood. An enemy round had pierced his side between his underarm and his armor.

Dan crawled over the backseat and slid behind the wheel as the jeep began veering to the left. He pushed down on the accelerator and turned just in time to avoid a crash with a high gravel mound by the side of the road.

Gentry knelt over Dan seconds later and yelled to be heard. "Hey, man. I think you're hit. There's fresh blood all over the place back here, and I can't find a leak in me!"

As he drove, Dan felt over his own body. After several seconds Gentry leaned back over again.

"GSW, left shoulder!"

Dan looked, found that he'd taken a gunshot wound high in the front of his left shoulder, less than two inches from the jugular vein in his neck. He bled like a stuck pig but kept driving on.

Soon they arrived at the home where Court met Mohammed earlier in the day. The small Skoda sedan was still in the courtyard. It took Gentry a couple of minutes to find the keys where he had tossed them in the dust. During that time, the wounded Dan took the one rifle left with the team and guarded the front gate, and Zack gave CPR to Brad on the ground next to the jeep.

"Come on, Bradley! Don't fucking chicken shit out on me! Walk it off!" he shouted at a man who, Court could tell even from across the yard, was clearly dead. But Zack didn't want to see it himself. Court wondered if Sierra One was trying to revive both Sierra Two and Sierra Five with the futile treatment.

Zack did not give up for nearly five minutes. By then Gentry had the injured Sierra Four in the back of the Skoda, with Dan bandaged perfunctorily and sitting next to him. He helped Zack put Sierra Two's body in the trunk. Court then led Hightower to the passenger seat. Court took the wheel, and the vehicle left the gate of the home and headed north, its four white men of war hidden behind tinted windows.

42

Twenty minutes later the Skoda drove under a flight of four Sudanese Army helicopters that were following the highway from Port Sudan down to all the activity in Suakin. The choppers continued on and disappeared in Gentry's rearview mirror.

Hightower had not spoken at all. He seemed utterly spent, dejected, nearly unconscious. The injured Four was passed out in the backseat, and Three looked like his moderate blood loss from the shoulder wound, plus the other wears and tears of the morning, had left him completely worn out.

After a while, Zack pushed himself up from his seat with difficulty. He had Court lean forward over the steering wheel as he drove, and Sierra One pulled the robe off his shoulder to check his wound.

"Your back smells nasty."

"Yeah," Court replied distractedly, scanning the skies ahead for another chopper. This tiny team of wounded and virtually unarmed men was in no condition to fight anyone. Gentry was desperate to keep them away from any threat more potent than a head cold.

"I know this place is filthy, but how does a wound get that kind of putrefied stink in four hours?"

"Dunno. You got any antibiotics?"

"Negative. We just brought basic trauma shit. Used most all of it, didn't we, Danny?"

307

"Yeah, boss." But Sierra Three took some of the clean bandaging from his shoulder wound, tore it free, and handed it up to Zack.

Hightower took some tape from his med pouch and positioned Three's gauze over the hole in Gentry's back to stanch any more bleeding. It was a perfunctory job, just marginally better than nothing. "You'll make it. When we get to the *Hannah*, we'll get you fixed up."

"Cool," said Court. He wasn't that worried about it, though it hurt like hell.

Hightower's satellite phone buzzed in its chest pouch. The device was blackened with dirt and soot and oil and blood, but at least it was still functional. Sierra One had pulled off his headset while attempting to revive Sierra Two, so he just pressed the speakerphone button.

"Go for Sierra One."

It was Denny Carmichael. There was no "Hello." No "How are you?"

"I just got a call from the White House. They say the US ambassador to Sudan is asking if there is some sort of Agency involvement in what he is describing as, and I quote, 'a Black Hawk Down incident up in Port Sudan.' How am I supposed to respond to that?"

Zack smiled, his head back on the headrest and his eyes closed. His face was black from filth and red from the blood that had smeared to nearly every square inch of his body, except for where his eye protection had kept the mess away.

"Well, sir, if I were you, I'd say that it looks like State's intel sucks as bad as CIA Sudan Station's intel. We're forty miles *south* of Port Sudan."

"That's not the point, is it? Do we have, or *did* we have, a Black Hawk Down incident?"

"Absolutely not. You didn't outfit us with any Black Hawks to go down."

"Don't get snippy with me, One. Did you secure Oryx?"

"He's secure."

"Have you extracted him to the *Hannah*?"

"Negative. But that's the next item on my to-do list."

"Sierra Six has him?"

"Uh, negative. Six is with us, what's left of us. I lost a couple of operators to enemy fire. Thanks for asking about my guys, by the way." Court turned to look at Hightower. It was shocking, even after all that had happened in the past several hours, that Zack would snap at his superior like that.

Denny's response showed his focus was on Nocturne Sapphire, not on the health of the team members of Whiskey Sierra. "Who is with Oryx right now?"

Court Gentry answered while driving. "Oryx is secure. He's not going anywhere."

"Why are you and he not in the same damn place?"

"Whiskey Sierra was compromised. I came back to help. I did *not* put Nocturne Sapphire in jeopardy."

"And if you had been killed?"

"I transmitted the location of Oryx to the *Hannah* before I set off."

Denny's anger and frustration were evident in his voice. "It is not the job of the men on the *Hannah* to extract Oryx from the Sudan. The *Hannah* does not have operators of your supposed caliber, Six, although I can't possibly express to you how disappointed I am with your decision-making abilities in the past week! You should have gotten Oryx out of the country before going back for the others."

Court began to respond, but Zack grabbed the phone and pulled it up close to his mouth. "I've got one hundred percent casualties! Two KIA! We just spent almost four hours battling an infantry force several hundred troops strong, with supporting air assets. Infantry and air that was *not* supposed to be there. And our local support, support that *was* supposed to be there, didn't fucking show!"

"My information from Sudan Station is that they did show, albeit a few minutes late."

309

"Sudan Station may have paid four hundred grand for a donkey cart full of rejects to each fire a magazine up an alley and then run away, but other than that, we didn't get a goddamned bit of assistance."

There was a significant pause. Court expected a little contrition, but none was forthcoming. "Nevertheless, you should not have allowed yourselves to be compromised. And Six should not have gone off mission to extract you from your own mess. You knew the risks." There was an annoyed sigh audible over the satellite transmission. "Now ... pull yourselves up by your bootstraps and continue on with Nocturne Sapphire. I will do what I can to negotiate the political fallout over here. That is all." The line went dead.

Zack dropped the phone into his lap. It rolled down his legs to the floor. He was too tired to pick it up and resecure it to his chest rig.

Court said, "Damn, Zack. Your boss is an asshole."

"Tell me about it."

An hour later, Court Gentry parked the Skoda at the shack hidden in the marsh grasses, climbed out, and entered with his pistol raised in front of him. The dark hooch was just as he'd left it, though even hotter and stuffier.

Oryx was just as Court left him, as well. Gentry had injected the Sudanese president with a syringe preloaded with a sedative that would knock him out for roughly two hours, and then he'd flexicuffed his hands behind his back and around the sturdy central support beam of the shack. Upon return he was cross-legged, and his head hung down as if sleeping. Between his knees Gentry had left an open bottle of water. He didn't really know how Abboud would have drunk from it, bound as he was. But as it turned out, it appeared that the president had slept the entire time.

Thirty minutes earlier Court had dropped the surviving members of Whiskey Sierra, and one of their two dead operators, at the ocean-side pickup point fourteen miles north of Suakin. The men immediately concealed themselves and their fallen colleague in a thick mangrove swamp. Zack handed Court a small receiver that picked up a transmitter on board the *Hannah* so he could know where the boat was at all times, even if coms went down for some reason.

The original plan had been for the Zodiac dinghy from the *Hannah* to come to shore and pick up the team, but there was no way they would attempt that in daylight now. Instead, one of the crew on the CIA ship would pilot the two-man mini sub into the swamp and pick up each man, one at a time. It would take the rest of the day to effect this retrieval but it was felt by all that this was far preferable to having four injured men sitting chest-deep in brackish water for eight hours while waiting for a night pickup by the Zodiac.

Court had been instructed to return to his hide and get Oryx ready to move at a moment's notice. It would be late evening before someone could return for the final two trips to bring out the president of Sudan and the Gray Man, but if the pickup site became somehow compromised, Gentry would need to be ready to scout out a new location on his own.

Court unhooked Oryx from the support beam of the shack, laid him on his back, then placed next to him his bottle of water and a bag of raisins that had been in his backpack.

"Eat," he instructed.

Oryx did not move.

"You aren't unconscious, asshole. That hypnotic I gave you has worn off."

The president continued to lie still.

"Dude, I'm really not in the mood to play right now."

The man did not move.

Court knelt down above him and lifted his meaty left arm into the air by his wrist. Gentry acted like he was taking his pulse, but he held the arm over the prostrate man's face and let it go. If he were unconscious, the hand would have hit the president in the nose, but instead it lowered slowly and then flopped dramatically to the side.

"Sit up," Court said angrily. The man still did not react.

Court pulled a multi-tool from his pack, opened the wire cutters, and placed the president's pinky finger between the cold metal pincers.

Immediately President Abboud opened his eyes. He smiled sheepishly, his white teeth a stark contrast to his coal black face. "That is a clever trick, holding the patient's arm over his face like that and letting it go."

"Glad you liked it. Get your ass up, or I clip off this finger. Turning you over to the ICC with nine fingers instead of ten is just as good as far as I'm concerned."

Oryx sat up in the dirt. He took the water and drank half of it before placing the bottle back down.

"I feel sick."

"Just the meds. It will clear out soon enough. And you probably have a mild concussion from the Big Bang this morning."

Oryx nodded. He asked, "How is your back?"

"It feels like some asshat shot me with an arrow. How do you think it feels?"

"Did you rescue *your* men from *my* men?"

Court looked into the man's eyes. "Some of them."

Oryx nodded slowly. "I regret the loss of life on both sides of the battle today."

"That's incredibly comforting, douche bag."

A genuinely offended expression covered Abboud's face. It remained as he asked, "What happens now?"

"We wait."

"How long?"

"I don't know."

"You don't know?"

"Nobody tells me nothing," Court said as he pulled items out of his bag. "For now, eat your lunch and stop asking me questions."

Oryx shrugged and opened the package of raisins. He seemed more relaxed than Gentry would have expected. As he picked at the tiny pieces of fruit, he said, "Mr. Six, you must admit I am

312

not giving you any trouble. I do not know why you show so much anger towards me."

Court began taking off his shirt. The burning sting deep into the bone of his scapula made the action miserable. "Remember, I *was* coming in to blow your head off, so I honestly don't think you're being treated so bad."

"I was talking about your words to me. Your striking of me back in Suakin. You are not the image of the honorable American soldier that your country tries to sell to the world."

"I am *not* an honorable American soldier."

"Then what are you?"

"I'm the guy they send in when some asshole does not deserve to be treated honorably."

As Oryx chewed raisins slowly, he looked across the darkness at his captor. "But, sir, this is your profession. You are here because of what the West considers to be war crimes in the Darfur region. That does not involve you personally, nor, I will venture to say, does it involve members of your family. There is no reason for you to treat this as a personal vendetta. Can we not keep our relationship at a professional level while we are together?"

Court did not respond. Instead, he opened a tiny bottle of disinfectant he'd retrieved from his bag. He leaned forward, reached back, and did his best to pour it where it would run down his shoulder and into his wound. Oryx continued, "Back in the car. You hit me in your moment of rage because you cannot control yourself. Your anger is more base, more degenerate, than the calm reason that I apply to the war in Darfur for which I have been indicted by this kangaroo court of yours."

Gentry winced as the medicine penetrated the swollen hole in his back. But he looked at Abboud across the three feet of dim space. "You think I hit you because I was out of control?"

"Of course you did. I saw it in your eyes. You were scared and angry, and your emotions controlled you. You lashed out—"

"Look in my eyes now. Am I in control?"

"Yes. In this moment you are, but—"

Court punched Abboud in the face again. The man's beefy head snapped back and then forward, his lip fat and red immediately.

"What is wrong with you?" Oryx covered his face as he shouted.

Gentry tossed the empty container of antiseptic back in the bag. "All sorts of things."

"Maniac."

"Yeah. You might want to remember that."

43

Gentry spent the next ninety minutes telling president Abboud to shut up while writhing in agony from the pain in his back. The extraordinary heat and humidity simply piled on to the misery of the afternoon. Twice Court fished through his backpack for hydrocodone pills, but both times he refrained from taking them. His pain was real, as was his body's desperate need for a moment's respite from the agony, but Court knew he should hold out and wait to hear from Zack.

Zack finally called around four p.m. He and Milo were back on the *Hannah*; Dan would be arriving in the mini sub within the hour. Court was told it was likely they would use the same exfiltration point in the mangrove swamp, as they had not been compromised. The pickup time would be midnight, meaning Gentry would just have to sit tight for the next seven hours or so before getting Oryx to the water.

Court hung up the call with Zack and looked at Oryx. The president stared back at him. His black bald head was covered in sweat beads that hung like ornamentation, glistening whenever a warm breeze fluttered one of the torn burlap walls enough for the sunlight to filter in to illuminate them. His hands were unbound.

Court next looked to his backpack. Seven hours, with nothing to do but sit here and suffer ... he thought about the pain and the cramping in the muscles around the pain site and the fact that he would need to have his body and his muscles as limber as possible for any eventuality as soon as he was on the move again. The only means to that end, he told himself, would be to get some relief for the pain now.

He did not need much convincing.

Sixty seconds later, Oryx had his right wrist zip-tied to the center beam of the shack. His left arm was free to drink water or eat food or to take out his manhood and piss in the dirt if he were so inclined. Gentry made sure there was nothing within reach he could use as a weapon or a tool. Court told himself that Oryx was secure, and Oryx could take care of himself for a while.

Next the American opened his backpack, went right past the hydrocodone pills, and pulled out the most potent injection of morphine the CIA had given him. He tore the preloaded injector from its sterilized package and popped off the plastic tip to expose the needle.

Oryx backed away, afraid.

"Don't worry," said Gentry. "This one's for me."

He injected twenty milligrams of the heavy opiate into his left arm. Immediately he sat down and leaned back against the wall of the shack, out of reach of his captive.

Within a minute and a half his eyelids began to flutter, his pupils became smaller, and the pain began to subside.

Oryx could clearly see the effect the injection was having on his captor. "Madness. What kind of a soldier or spy takes drugs during a mission?"

"Shut up," Gentry said. The room around him softened into a gentle blur. He then said, a tad too defensively, "The pain will slow me down later if I don't take the edge off now."

"And your heroin will not slow you down?"

"It's not heroin, asshole," Court snapped back, but he knew the drug was similar in effect to heroin, though it did not produce its high for as long a duration.

"You are a drug addict," Abboud said flatly.

"And you are a genocidal despot. Get off my back."

Any self-flagellation Gentry may have felt for taking the heavy narcotic while operational went away in seconds, as the rush of the drug's initial effect gave way to an exaggerated sense of well-being. Within ten minutes of injecting himself, he was deep in conversation with Abboud, a 180-degree turnaround from his earlier behavior.

But Court was not entirely incapacitated. During the course of their polite conversation over the next half hour, Oryx asked him for his real name and his home address, asked to borrow his phone, and asked if he could get a closer look at his very fine pistol. The Gray Man was under the influence of a mood-altering opiate, but he was not insane. Each time he just smiled genuinely. When the gun was requested, he even laughed and replied that Abboud had made a nice try.

By a quarter till five, Court was at peace in the dark shack. It was a chemically induced peace, and a peace at a decidedly inopportune time for a warrior like Gentry. As he chatted with Oryx or talked to himself, he found himself incredibly proud to be on this mission, proud to be sent along with the brave men of Whiskey Sierra, God rest the souls of two of them, and proud to be trusted by the legendary Denny Carmichael.

With his eyes closed in blissful tranquillity, he began to fall asleep, the heavy sedation edging out the loss of inhibition that had him deep in conversation with his captive. Just as his head lolled to the side, his phone beeped.

Court stared at it, his eyes as wide as saucers. He looked up at Oryx and smiled. "Oh shit. I'm in trouble."

He answered it. "Hello?"

Hightower said, "Okay, Six, we're gonna have to push up the timetable."

"Oh boy. Um . . . I don't know. How is everything out there on the boat?"

"Fine, but I'm going to need you to recon another site for the pickup. I think the north side of the mangrove is going to be better at low tide. Get over there and see if it's clear of civvies. There are some Bedouins that have built structures up and down—"

"You mean ... right now?"

"No, dude. At your fucking leisure. Of *course* I mean now."

"Oh, okay. I mean, no. Don't be mad ... but I need to hang out here a little bit longer."

"To do what?"

Court looked up at the ceiling. He noticed the intricate weave of the thatch; even in the dark it was as if each strand of the thick straw had its own personality, its own purpose, its own path through the others as it tucked into and out of the—

"To do *what*, Six?"

"C'mon, Zack. Don't be pissed off. I just need to ... " Court's voice trailed off.

"What the hell is wrong with you?"

"Nothing. I wish you could see the ceiling in this hooch though, it's fucking beautiful. They dry the reeds and then tie them into little bundles, and then they tie those together to make bigger bundles that—"

"Jesus, Court! Are you high?"

Court laughed into the phone.

"Where's Oryx?"

"He's sitting right here. You wanna talk to him?"

"Fuck no, I don't want to talk—"

"Here he is."

Court got up, carried the phone over to Abboud, who reached out slowly and took it with his untethered hand.

"You are speaking to President Bakri Ali Abboud. Who is this?"

Hightower did not answer at first. When he spoke it was slow, tentative. "What's happened to my man?"

"Your man has injected himself with some sort of tranquilizer."

"Accidentally, you mean?"

Oryx looked at Gentry. He'd gone back to the wall and leaned against it. His eyes were open, fixed on the ceiling of the shack, his head back against the burlap and driftwood wall.

"Deliberately. Very deliberately, in fact."

It was clear Zack Hightower did not know how to respond to

this. "Okay. Well ... you listen. I've got many more assets in the area. You try to take advantage of this situation and—"

"Don't worry, Mr. CIA. Before your man decided to enjoy himself, he made sure I was restrained. Your operation is delayed, but I am unable to escape."

"Give the phone back to him."

Oryx looked down at the Thuraya and smiled. He pushed a red button to end the call. Six's eyes were still on the ceiling. They were unfixed, the eyelids sagging low. Desperately the Sudanese president tried to think of the phone number to his office, to his security detail ... to anyone. Yes, a secretary at his Khartoum presidential palace; the number just popped into his head. He did not know where he was, exactly, but he could move an entire army into the area north of Suakin, south of Port Sudan, west of the coastline and east of the Red Sea Hills with a single order. He still thought it likely that Six, if he could, would kill him if he felt his kidnapping operation was no longer feasible. But if Six stayed incapacitated for a while, there might just be enough time for a rescue!

He began thumbing the numbers on the phone.

He looked back up to his kidnapper as he brought the phone to his ear.

The small black pistol with the long silencer was centered between his eyes. "I'm going to need that back."

"Yes."

"Nice try, though," said the American.

Gentry slept for two hours and awoke at dusk. He was still heavily under the influence of the morphine, still felt relatively free of the pain in his back, though the euphoria had dissipated enough for him to dread his next conversation with Hightower. Oryx himself had nodded off in the heat, and Court took the quiet moment to sip bottled water and eat a Soldier Fuel bar. As he chewed, he idly picked up the phone and saw that Sierra One had called six times in the past two hours.

Court set the phone back down in the dirt and finished his

dinner. Then he built a tiny fire, using grass and twigs and bits of larger pieces of driftwood lying around. He hardly needed the warmth, but the light was helpful now that darkness had fallen on the eastern coast of the Sudan.

"How are you feeling?" Oryx asked from the center of the room. Gentry looked up to see him standing, facing away and relieving himself with the aid of his free hand.

"The back feels better. The rest of me feels great." Court smiled at his own humor.

"Your phone keeps ringing."

"Yeah," said Court. "I'll need to call them back in a bit. In a couple of hours I'll be hauling your ass to the coast. In a day or two, you'll be locked up." Court smiled at him, "I guess you figured killing four hundred thousand of your countrymen wouldn't have a downside, huh?"

"You have killed more people today than I have, friend."

"We're not friends."

Oryx sat back down and wiped his face, smearing the sheen of sweat across his forehead. The soft firelight danced over his ebony features in the reflection of the dampness. "I think we are more than friends. We are almost brothers."

"You need to take a look in a mirror."

"I mean, our sensibilities are similar. As is our chosen course of action. We both kill, and we both have decided that it does not bother us to do so."

"You've all but eradicated a people. You and I are not—"

"So then it's not the act of killing that bothers you. It's merely the scale of the killing. But I could counterargue that what I do, I do through political policy, not with my own hands. I think it takes more cruelty to kill a man, face-to-face, than a people via laws and declarations of war. *You* are the more dangerous man here. Just think how many people you would kill if you ran a nation, an intelligence service. You would slaughter everyone you were against."

Bakri Ali Abboud, president of Sudan, leaned very close now, his head just above the burning wood, the sheen of sweat glowing across his face. "Just like me ... brother." He smiled. "You and I, Mr. Six, are the same thing. Eradicators of the debris of humanity." Oryx let the phrase hang in darkness a moment. "Only I am better at it than you, so I am deemed more evil than you. Interesting how one's perspective commands one's concept of right and wrong."

Gentry stoked the fire with a long stick. He recognized that it was the opiate in him causing him to continue the conversation. "You *were* better than me, but the party is over. You'll be locked up for the rest of your life."

Oryx smiled again.

Court eyed him in the firelight. "You don't seem so worried about spending the rest of your days behind bars."

"Oh, if that were truly going to be my fate, I would be extremely disturbed, I can assure you. But I will *not* spend the rest of my days behind bars."

"Not if I change my mind and shoot your ass right here."

President Abboud laughed, low and rhythmic. "I don't know if you can operate your weapon in your present condition.

"Try me."

"No, no," Oryx waved his hand. "I am happy to have you for an escort to Europe."

"To prison," Court said.

"Oh, for a few months, I'm sure you're right. But offers have been extended to me, offers that I have refused until now, that will allow me to seek exile in any one of many third-party nations. The Ivory Coast is close to home, but at the moment I am leaning towards a certain Caribbean island that has been suggested. I enjoy the occasional cigar, though I pray you do not tell my wives."

Court sat up straight, still Indian-style, against the wall of the shack. "Bullshit."

"Diplomacy," answered Bakri Ali Abboud with a smile.

"The Europeans are going to let you walk?"

The president shook his head slowly. He exposed his teeth in a smile. "Not just the Europeans. The Americans, too."

Gentry was gobsmacked. He knew he was way too fucked-up to evaluate the micro-expressions set off by the president's limbic system, to check for clues of deception. But the bastard unquestionably *seemed* sure of himself.

Abboud's smile remained, but through it he said, in an exaggerated American accent, "As you said before. Nobody tells you nothing, eh, Mr. Six?"

"Why?" Gentry's voice cracked.

"For the good of the world," Abboud chuckled again. "What do you think would happen if I were assassinated in my hometown by SLA rebels? A civil war ten times larger than what we have now, except this would be worse. China wants their oil, so they will back my successor just as they did me. But Russia will support a military coup of the civilian successorship, and they will aid our neighbors to the west. Chad will invade, take north Darfur, and hand the bulk of the oil there to the Russians as payment. The IDP camps will be threatened, and UNAMID will be forced out, since the original agreement was with me and not with the government of Chad. China will push my successor towards a total war with Chad to retake Tract 12A, and my successor is, fundamentally, a weak man. He will submit to their will in ways that I would never agree with. China can own him with weapons and power and money.

"One year after I am gone, East Africa will be the center of a superpower conflict, tens of thousands will be dead, another million uprooted."

"But won't kidnapping you have the same effect?"

"There will be short-term chaos, but I will agree to terms that have been offered to me in secret for three years now. If I reveal details of Russia's illegalities here in the Sudan, if I tell my followers, directly and forcefully, that the Russians are prepared to fan the flames of war against us, then there will be no Russian influence on the citizenry, and consequently, no civil war. If there is no civil war, then it is doubtful that Chad would invade. I can even let it be known that China was involved in my kidnapping. This will hurt Chinese interests in the region and return the minerals of the Sudan to the Sudanese."

"China had nothing to do with this kidnapping."

Abboud shrugged. "My followers will believe me. There is evidence to back me up, as well. Chinese Special Forces have been secretly training my troops in Port Sudan, to provide security to Tract 12A along the Chad border. China has known good and well that Russia covets their oil, and they knew that Russia wanted me dead. I can convince the Sudanese people that China and I had a disagreement, so they decided to get me out of the picture by trading me away."

"That's brilliant." Court said. It sickened him to say so.

"Thank your coworkers. This was all part of a CIA plot, a plot to get me to voluntarily turn myself in to the ICC. As I said, I turned their offer of exile down." He shrugged his shoulders good-naturedly. "So here you are to enforce the offer."

"So you are more beneficial alive than dead."

Abboud shrugged. "Apparently so. You get me out of here alive, and I will play my part. As you said early this morning in Suakin, you and I are on the same team. Only you did not know the truth of that statement."

The Thuraya phone rang.

44

"Hey, Zack."

"You back with us, or are you still high as giraffe nuts?"

"I'm good to go; sorry about before. I was hurting pretty bad and accidentally pulled the wrong dosage of—"

"Forget it. We've got a problem. This whole op just went tits up."

"What happened?"

"Langley says we greased some Chinks."

"Say again?"

"We killed some Chinese guys."

Court thought back to what Oryx had just told him. "Combatants."

"No doubt, but apparently that's still a no-no."

Court knew who they were. "Special Forces, here training the Sudanese up in Port Sudan."

"Yeah, that's what Denny thinks. Probably from their Flying Dragon unit. Sudan Station didn't even know they were in country."

"Shit, Zack. How bad is it?"

"It's not good, from the sound of it. Langley is dealing with the White House right now. The White House didn't sign on for a dustup with a superpower."

Court rubbed sweat from his eyes. The wound in his back was better from the meds, though it still stung. "How many Chinese did you guys kill?"

"Close to thirty, apparently. We're guessing that Mi-17 Dan shot down was full of troops and a flight crew. That would account for that number of KIA. But seriously, BFD. Aren't there like two billion Chinks? It's not like they'll miss them."

"Dan didn't, apparently."

"Ha. Yeah, no shit."

"What's the fallout going to be on this?"

"Your guess is as good as mine. I am to reestablish coms with Denny in thirty mikes. Worst case, we bug out."

"With Abboud, you mean?"

"Let's just wait till we hear back."

"Roger that, Six out."

Zack called back just after nine in the evening. Court had spent the last forty-five minutes talking to Oryx about the offer he'd received from the West. He seemed willing to do whatever he had to do to stay out of prison and to make his way to Cuba as a free man.

It was sickening, but Court understood that it was unquestionably the best of a long list of shitty outcomes.

Zack said, "Six, I need you to get far enough away from Oryx to where he can't hear your side of this conversation."

"Copy that, wait one." Court looked at Oryx, still shackled to the center beam of the shack, turned, and left the tiny hooch. Outside in the cooling evening, he lowered onto his haunches and sat down at the rear bumper of the Skoda. "Okay, I'm alone."

"I've got a big-time change to your op orders, Six. You ready for this?"

"Affirmative, go ahead."

Zack paused. Then, "The Chinese are saying that this morning's engagement in Suakin killed twenty-six noncombatant civilian advisors."

"Bullshit. They weren't civilians."

"Of course not. They're lying through their noodle-slurpin' teeth, but they can do that, and everyone will believe them."

"Go on."

"The White House has officially shit their britches. They want nothing more to do with this operation. Seems they have been working secretly on some big-ass trade deal with the Chinks, were going to announce it next month in Beijing."

"So?"

"So the White House has ordered the director of National Intelligence to order Denny to order us to exfiltrate immediately, just drop all our shit and go. They do not want CIA fingerprints anywhere near the Sudan operation, for fear it would jeopardize the deal."

"What about me?"

"I'm going to pick you up in the sub. I can be at the mangrove swamp at midnight. Can you make it by then, or do you need to go on another bender with your party drugs?"

"I can be there, but what's all this going to do to Nocturne Sapphire?"

"There *is* no Nocturne Sapphire, and we all need to forget that there ever was. The rug's been pulled out from under us. We just need to get out of Sudanese waters, get down to Eritrea, and not get compromised. Sudan Station will dump all the blame for this on the SLA."

Court looked out at the grasses blowing in the evening breeze. "But ... what the hell am I supposed to do with Abboud?"

"Give the fucker a dirt nap," Zack said flatly.

Court hesitated. "But ... he's the one that can convince his people what the Russians are up to."

"We're not supposed to be here. There is no way we can hand Abboud over to the ICC now. Think about it! If we hand Abboud to the Euros, the Chinese Communists will get wind of it, and the Chicoms will pull out of the deal."

"But Abboud is more important alive than dead. Isn't that what the White House has been thinking all along?"

"Yeah, but the knockdown of the Chinese chopper was a game changer."

Court shook his head in disbelief. "It's a trade agreement. What is one trade deal in the scheme of things?"

"It makes the politicians look good."

"So would ending an African genocide!"

"Not by risking a superpower war! The average Joe in the USA does not want to hear about us shooting it out with the Chinese over some dumb savages living in mud huts."

"The Chinese aren't going to go to war over this."

"What are you, a fucking poli-sci PhD now? You are an operator, not a diplomat. The dips have their job and you have yours. Abboud needs to die! Kill the fuck! That's an order!"

But Gentry would not let it go. "The *only* way to stop what is going to happen is with Abboud alive, in front of a camera, laying out to his people the involvement of the Russians and Chinese in his country's internal affairs. That was the original motivation behind Nocturne Sapphire, because that is the only thing that will work. It *can't* be done any other way."

"Well, that's not going to happen. You're going to cap him and get your ass to the northern tip of the mangrove swamp for the exfil. What the hell is wrong with you? I thought you'd be happy to dump some hollow points into that bastard's snot box."

"C'mon, Zack! We extract Abboud from here, get him to The Hague, and we can stop a war!"

"It's not our job to stop a war! It's our job to do *our job*, and our job is to waste Abboud, dump his corpse by the side of the road, and then get our happy asses out of here!"

Court's jaw tightened, and he leaned his head back on the rear bumper of the Skoda sedan. "I need to think it over."

"Think it over? Who the fuck do you think you are? You do what—"

"I'll call you back. Six out." Court ended the call. He dropped the phone to the grass and dropped his head into his hands.

Dammit. Court knew he could stand up right now, walk back into the shack, and put a nine-millimeter bullet into the head of the president of the Republic of Sudan without a single shred of remorse for the act. The man was a monster, certifiable and dangerous.

Go kill him. Just get up and go kill him.

But he understood the logic that Oryx's power could now be turned back against the atrocities and used for good. Yeah, it was complete and utter bullshit that down the road he'd get the last laugh. He'd be banging hookers in Havana after a lifetime of murder and corruption.

But hell, Court thought, that's a problem for another day. Gentry himself could go to Cuba on his own dime and settle that score. He'd kill Abboud for his crimes, but not until the impending chaos of a post-Abboud Sudan was minimized.

And that could only happen with Abboud alive.

Court had been played by the Russians, lied to and manipulated to where he almost helped start a war, and now, he realized, killing Oryx would mean he'd been played by Langley into the same thing.

No. He would *not* kill Abboud. *Could* not. He would bring him to the International Criminal Court to stop one war and prevent another.

It would, no doubt, get the shoot-on-sight sanction reinstated, but it was the only hope for thousands of innocent Sudanese. Court put his head between his knees and covered it with his hands. He realized he wanted to storm back into the shack not to shoot Abboud but instead to shoot himself up with more of the morphine.

Its effects were wearing off quickly, with the struggle to concentrate obviated by the events of the past ten minutes.

Court picked up the Thuraya and called Zack back.

Hightower answered immediately. Court knew he must have been furious, but he masked it well. "You back with the program, bro?"

A long pause. "No can do, Zack."

Court felt the tension on the other end of the line. He'd never defied Zack Hightower a single time in their five years together

328

on the Goon Squad until, of course, that day when it all went to hell. Finally Zack spoke. His voice was light, but the menace was more than implied. "Look, kid, I've already lost a couple of really good guys today. I don't want to lose you, too. Let's make lemonade from lemons, here. Shoot that asshole, get yourself to where I can come and pick you up, and you and me will sail off into the sunset. Langley will drop the SOS, we'll get debriefed, we'll shit, shave, and shower, and inside of seventy-two hours we'll be tossing back two-for-one Budweisers at a lobby bar in Bethesda. One for us and one for our homies. Cool?"

"As awesome as that sounds, Zack, it's not going to happen. I'll go it alone if I have to, but I'm getting Abboud to the ICC alive."

Anger welled in Zack Hightower's voice, as if every word served as a demonstration as to how his frustration grew exponentially. "How the hell you going to do that? You got a boat, a plane, an army?"

A pregnant pause, a quiet "Negative."

"No, you don't, do you? I'll tell you what you *do* have. You have a hole in your back that stinks so bad it could knock a buzzard off a shit wagon. *That's* what you have! You need a doctor a lot more than you need some fucked-up one-man crusade to save the most hated man on God's green earth. I know you think of yourself as the fucking Lone Ranger, but you're on a fool's errand if there ever was one. From where I'm sitting, you need four things to accomplish your objective. You need guys, guns, gear, and guts. Court, you got the guts, I'll give you that. But you are sorely lacking in every one of the other categories. No singleton operator is going to get that fucker out of the Sudan! You've got the Sudanese Army, the NSS, and Abdul Q. Public on your tail.

"Everyone is looking for their president and trying to smoke the guy who snatched him ... You really want to cross *me* on top of that?"

"You're going to come after me?"

Without hesitation Hightower said, "Yes, I am. I swear to God if you don't cap Oryx right this second, I'm going to report it to

Denny, and you and I both know he'll send me after you. Neither of us wants that to happen, Court."

Another long pause. "See you, Zack."

A pause again, this time on Hightower's end of the conversation. Then, "No, Gentry. I'll see *you*, right through the scope of my Remington 700. Just before your head turns to pink mist. We wanted to make you part of the team again, but you know what? You've been solo for too long; you never *were* going to fit in, dude. Guess it's inevitable that it had to end like this."

Zack ended the call.

Court rose from his position of the past hour, against the bumper of the car. Slowly he stepped back into the shack. Oryx was there, of course. Standing in the middle of the dark room. It was clear he had not overheard the specifics of the phone conversation, but certainly he'd picked up some of the tone.

"What is going on?"

"Nothing. We need to move." Court had given the location of the shack to the CIA operators on the *Hannah*. He knew he needed to get out of here before Zack or someone else came calling.

"Tell me, Six. What was all the arguing?"

Court cut the president's zip tie from the center beam with a small folding knife. He said nothing to the man as he closed the blade and slipped it back into his pocket.

"What is happening?" Abboud was extremely agitated. Court imagined he himself would be even more stressed-out right now but for the remnants of the drugs in his system. He wondered how much it affected him. Would he be able to drive? Would he be able to find a new hide without stumbling into all the people who were searching for him and his captor right now?

Oryx began to ask once more about the phone calls. Court stood in front of him and pulled two new zip ties out of his backpack to restrain the man's hands in front of his body. Before he had done so, Court shrugged. Whatever. "I've been ordered to kill you."

"By the American actors." The big black man made it as a

statement, but it was clear he was asking. He pulled his hands back and away.

"Negative. The CIA wants you dead, too. It's pretty much a unanimous consensus, at this point. Give me your hands."

Oryx's face contorted in shock, like he'd been doused with cold water from an ice bucket. "No! We had an agreement. They need me alive. The European—"

"Shut up! We need to get out of here so I can think without worrying about them—"

"I can help them with their—"

"Calm down! Give me your hands!"

"They cannot just change the arrangement like—"

Court pulled his Glock. The drugs slowed him, and his stiff gun arm wavered. He pressed it against Abboud's throat.

"I said, calm the fuck down!"

Oryx's hands went up in surrender, and then they went for the pistol.

45

President Abboud was a big man, taller and broader and thicker than Gentry by a wide margin, but he was sixty-six years old and did not possess even a modicum of the training in the brain and muscles and soul of the American warrior. It should have been no match.

But for the morphine. Abboud knocked the Glock pistol away with his first strike, wrapped a meaty hand around each of the American's wrists, and pulled their bodies together. Six moved slowly and sluggishly, did not even realize he was being attacked for the first few seconds of the action. He thought Oryx was just freaking out about the possibility of having the CIA's backing pulled out from under him and was just slapping at Court like a frustrated child.

But when Gentry hit the ground, slamming into his wounded back under the weight of the huge Sudanese president, the danger of the situation became apparent to him through the dulled reality of his doped-up senses. The drugs were not enough to block the flash fire of excruciating agony as it registered in his shoulder and then transferred to his brain. He screamed out, and a series of punches rained down on him from above. Court covered his face, focused on the pain in his back to wake his adrenaline, to jump-start his muscle memory and to get this big bastard off of him.

From the light of the tiny fire, Court's narrow eyes located the next punch, a right hook already on its way from on high. Gentry short-circuited the attack with an attack of his own: he hit Abboud hard in the nose. The president's hook landed a quarter second later, but it was weak and poorly targeted, the fist turned quickly into a hand that reached up to his face as he fell on his back, holding his broken nose and wiping free-flowing blood from the swollen nostrils.

Gentry kicked Oryx off of him the rest of the way, rolled over, and began crawling around looking for the pistol. He found it against the wall, retrieved it as he stood, then retrieved Oryx by his shirt collar and pulled him into a standing position. Within seconds he had the moaning man's hands zip-tied behind his back, and a minute later the Skoda tore through the high grasses on its way back to the main road.

Gentry thought over his options, and this did not take long, as there were so few. He had no idea where he was going, other than to just find some new hide so he could work out a plan. Oryx rubbed his face against the upholstery in the backseat of the car because he could not use his hands to wipe the blood away, and he moaned and cussed softly in Sudanese Arabic.

The phone rang. Gentry had no interest in listening to one more petition from Zack to do what he was told, but he answered the phone anyway. The rage and adrenaline from the fight in the shack still had his emotions in high gear.

Court said, "The time for talking is over, asshole. If you're going to come after me, come on, because the quicker I kill you once and for all, the quicker I can break cover and get my job done!"

But it was not Zack on the other end of the line. It was Denny Carmichael. He said, "Young man, Sierra One explained the problem at hand. I am calling to see what I can do to rectify it."

Carmichael was scared, nervous about having one of his men on a rogue mission. Court could hear it in his voice.

"I'm sorry, sir. Killing Oryx at this point will create a disaster I am not prepared to be a part of."

"I understand how you feel. I was one of the architects of

Nocturne Sapphire. All along, we knew that if we could take him alive, he could be very useful to us and to his country. But unfortunately we cannot leave any trace that the CIA or any US operator was in Suakin yesterday. If evidence comes out, then we will have a massive international superpower crisis, which is, frankly, a hell of a lot more important than civil war in a third-world nation."

"So you agree there will be war. A civil war with the backing of the Chinese and Russians?"

"Civil war, yes, in the short term it is likely. But we do not see the superpowers playing an active role."

"Maybe you don't have the assets in place to see it happening."

"I can assure you, we have close contact with officials very high in the Sudanese government."

"How close is your contact?"

"Extremely close."

"How high are the officials?"

"Extremely high."

"Well, I have the fucking president sitting in the backseat of my car, so when you can get a source higher and closer than that, *maybe* you'll impress me."

There was a long pause. "There is an important trade deal in the works."

Gentry couldn't care less. "Yeah, so maybe we take it on the chin from the Chinese. That sucks. But we'll get over it."

"That's not for you to decide."

"Actually, it is. I've got the president. I intend to get him to the ICC alive. I am going to do the right thing here. There are a lot of people in this country who are depending on it. You guys had the right idea; Nocturne Sapphire was the right op. Yeah, it was hopelessly fucked-up because Sudan Station doesn't know its ass from a hole in the ground, but we were damn close to pulling it off. I'm going to finish this. You guys at Langley need to realize that what I am doing here is the right thing, and you need to rethink your—"

Denny's calm but annoyed countenance of all their earlier conversations morphed in an instant to screaming, shouting vitriol. "I don't have time to listen to a sermon from a pissant like you! Let me explain something. The past four years have been a cakewalk for you. There are people up here who have a soft spot for Court Gentry. You did good work for a long time for precious little thanks, and that earned you a great deal of respect in the SAD. When the shoot--on--sight went out on you, there were some in the bureaucracy here who were borderline insubordinate in their conviction to the cause, and the operation to eliminate you suffered for it.

"But *now*, Mr. Gentry, *now* there is not a man left in the agency who's on your side. Not only will I reinstate the SOS, but I will bump it up to the top of the priority list. It won't be some half-assed Echelon tracking, intradepartmental memoranda and Interpol watch request. It will be coordinated teams of tier-one hunter-killers, SAD/SOG Paramilitary Operations officers, Combat Applications Group, proxy teams of bounty hunters. I will personally arrange that every available SAD asset will be brought to bear against you.

"There won't be a rock big enough for you to crawl under, a handler foolish enough to sponsor you, a country brazen enough to allow you inside its borders.

"Zack is going to hunt you down. He will stop you, and he *will* kill you. You may still have a pulse for a bit, Mr. Gentry, but as of this very moment . . . your life is ended!"

Carmichael did not say anything else. Neither did Court. He liked getting the last word . . . but at this moment it seemed as if the last words on the subject had been spoken. No clever quip could blunt the impact of Carmichael's rant. This man was not threatening anything that he did not have the power to put into motion.

After an extremely long pause, the man from Langley spoke quietly. It sounded to Court as if he were hanging up the phone as he did so.

"That is all."

46

Tuesday was Ellen Walsh's first day back in her tiny office in The Hague since leaving for the Sudan five weeks earlier. Her supervisors in the Office of the Prosecutor for the International Criminal Court had offered a week for her to tend to herself upon her return from Africa, but the thirty-five-year-old Canadian had only taken a day to go to a local dermatologist to look at her sunburned face, and a GP to give her a prescription for migraines she'd been having since the truck explosion on the road to Dirra.

When she appeared through the elevator doors to her office, her coworkers were shocked to see her. Snippets of her adventure had made it out. The international media had covered the attack of the Speranza Internazionale convoy and the murder by the Janjaweed militia of world-famous Mario Bianchi and two of his local staff. There was no mention in the reports that other Westerners had been in the convoy, but Ellen herself had spoken to the administrative heads in the Office of the Prosecutor, and the story had filtered its way downstairs like water poured through cracks in the flooring. From there, administrative assistants of the top brass told friends and friends of friends who worked throughout the building. Her brutal sunburn and a sad and distant look in her eyes lent credence to the rumors, and Ellen knew it would not be long before she would be forced to send out an email thanking everyone for their concern, and simultaneously asking everyone to please respect her privacy and understand that she just wasn't quite yet up to talking about what she had witnessed in Darfur.

On her computer in front of her were two reports, neither finished. One was an incident report upon which she was to put in writing as much as she could remember about her discovery of the Russian Rosoboronexport aircraft in Darfur and the men on board, along with any names, corroborating witnesses, et cetera, et cetera. She had only opened the template and put in information regarding her initial plan to enter Darfur with false credentials. Even this part of the document was difficult for her to write. So much had happened since her time in Khartoum, skulking around other NGO offices looking for her way into Darfur, that it seemed to be relegated to the portion of her brain reserved for distant memory.

The other was her report about the murder of two wounded and defenseless gunmen by an American John Doe who had flown into Al Fashir with the Russian aircraft. She'd all but finished this report. She could not get it out of her mind, but she was not sure if she was writing it in an attempt to purge her thoughts of the atrocity, or if she would, indeed, file the report and open an investigation into this man. She was torn by her official obligation and her feelings towards this stranger. He had helped her and convinced her he was not evil, but she was concerned that he was an individual teetering on the edge, a man who needed to be stopped before more atrocities were committed.

And what to make of the news that the president of the Sudan had been kidnapped during a massive battle with rebels on the east coast of the country? Could Six have had some involvement with that? The timing was right, but Six did not seem like a man who could control a force of Sudanese rebels.

He could barely control himself.

Her desk phone rang. "Ellen, there is someone calling himself 'Six' on the phone for you."

"I'll take it." And then, "Hello?"

"Three days are up. I thought you would have caught me by now."

"Where are you?"

Instead of an answer to her question, he said, "We need to talk."

"This ... situation, going on in Sudan right now. There is not much information ... I know there has been a battle. The president is missing. It happened right when you said something would happen, so at first I assumed that you somehow had something to do—"

"I have Abboud. I have him right here with me."

Her voice was soft but intense. "Oh my God."

"Crazy, huh?"

Ellen breathed nervously into the phone. She looked out of her office door, then stood up quickly and shut it, nearly pulling the phone off her desk while doing so. "What ... Who are you ... What are you going ... Why are you calling me?"

There was no response at first. She could hear the pounding of her own heart.

"Do you want him?"

"What?"

"Abboud. He's yours if you want him."

"Me?"

"Yes. And just so you know, I didn't kill any Chinese. That's on the news these days, I hear."

"Yes, it is."

"That wasn't me. I kidnapped Abboud, but now I don't really know what to do with him."

Ellen's voice was still barely a whisper. "Didn't you ... think about that beforehand?"

"Yeah ... plans change. Deals fall through. You know how it is."

"Right." She had no idea what he was talking about.

"Look. He has information about Russia and China. He says the two are going to start a proxy war over Sudan unless he does something to stop it."

"Yes, there have been rumors."

"What do you think?"

"Well ... I'm not an expert in that; I am more involved in the armaments—"

"I'm pretty sure you are the most expert person I can get on the phone for a chat at the moment. I'm asking you what you think."

"I think President Abboud is absolutely correct."

Court filled her in on what he'd learned. She admitted to knowing part of the story, but she was fascinated that Six's information came directly from the president of the Sudan himself.

"He says a deal was in the works for him to turn himself in to the ICC."

She cleared her throat and spoke in a normal register. "Above my pay grade, Six."

"Well, how 'bout this? How 'bout you go tell the big shots at your organization that if they can find a way to pick me and Abboud up from the Red Sea coast, then they can have him. That ought to bump up your pay grade a bit."

Ellen bristled. "I'm not here for the money."

"Okay, donate it to charity; I don't give a shit. I just want to stop the situation here from getting any worse."

"That's your only motivation?"

"Yes."

"How can I believe that?"

"I've been ordered to kill the fucker. I would *love* to kill the fucker. I think you, of all people, can believe that. But I'm not going to, because I think he can actually save lives."

Gentry imagined Ellen still more or less in shock over what happened in Darfur. He knew she probably didn't trust him, and this phone conversation was surely another surreal event that her brain was having trouble processing, so he was not surprised that she hesitated for a long time. Finally she cleared her throat. "I'll go upstairs right now, talk to the prosecutor himself. We'll find a way to come and get Abboud."

"Excellent."

"Will you be coming to The Hague with him?"

Court sniffed. "And deprive the International Criminal Court of another fruitless manhunt?"

She chuckled. She had a nice laugh, throaty and unguarded. Court was pretty sure he'd never heard it before. She answered finally, "I have not begun the process of preparing an indictment against you."

"'Yet,' you mean?"

Another pause. Gentry could tell by the breaks between her words that she had been wrestling with this very issue. "There's a good man in you, Six. I can see him through the cracks in your hard shell."

"You're a shrink now?"

"Bad news. It doesn't take a shrink to see the cracks in you."

"You don't know me."

She changed gears. "I know you are not CIA. I made some calls. My sources say they don't have anyone in Darfur."

"Like I told you."

"But if you are not CIA, then who *are* you?"

"It doesn't matter."

"It absolutely does, Six. The ICC will not help you if they don't know who they are dealing with."

"I am privately contracted."

"A private party has hired you to kidnap the president and hand him over to the ICC?"

"Yeah."

"Then they told you to kill him."

"Right again."

She paused a long time, disbelieving, perhaps. Finally, "Who is this private party?"

"Can't tell you."

"You *have* to."

Court knew it would come to this. He tried to sell it with a straight face, though he was speaking on his satellite phone. "Okay. I've been contracted by private US citizens. People in the arts and entertainment industry, mainly." Oryx himself had given him this idea.

340

"In the arts and . . . So . . . are you saying *movie stars* are paying you to do this?"

"Well. Yeah. I guess I am."

"*That* is your story?"

He smiled. She was a smart woman. Too smart to believe him, but also too smart to not turn away the president handed over to her organization on a silver platter. She'd play along. "And I'm sticking to it," he replied.

"Okay." It was said with a worried tone, like she wasn't sure she'd be able to sell this fantasy to her superiors any better than Six had to her. "I'll call you back. Are you safe for now?"

Court exhaled. "Oh yeah, snug as a bug, Ellen."

"I'll hurry."

47

Dawn rose over the still waters of the Red Sea as Court drove the Skoda north on the coastal highway that led from Port Sudan to the Egyptian border. Out the driver-side window he could just see the Red Sea Hills, and out the passenger side, past Oryx's bruised and impassive face, he looked out over the water as the blackness of dark warmed into the softness of the predawn.

An hour earlier he'd skirted to the west of Port Sudan under cover of darkness, and now the Skoda had the flat road to itself. Court had worried about military checkpoints, but there were none. He'd seen several police cars hours earlier, but in his dark car he never once felt exposed.

The coastal road turned inland for a few miles, towards the hills but not that far to the east, and then it cranked back to the north. At seven a.m. he turned off the highway and followed a sand and dirt and coral path that headed back towards the water. He passed small towns on both sides of the road. They were higher than the road on rocky plateaus that continued on to the sea.

It had taken a full day for the ICC to put a plan together to take possession of Oryx, and Court was not privy to many of the details. All he knew was that he was to drive himself and his captive to a Dutch-run seaside scuba diving resort just twenty miles from the Egyptian border and wait for a pickup by a team of ICC investigators who were on their way from Greece. Ellen

Walsh would not be with them, and Court found this unfortunate, though he did not want her exposed to danger.

Gentry himself had no intention of leaving with the ICC team. No, he would put Oryx in the speedboat, or the helicopter, or the SUV, or however the president was to be extracted, and then Court would go in the other direction. He figured he could get a small dive boat from the resort and head north towards Egypt. He'd run out of gas before the border, but then maybe he could land and hitchhike farther north, make the border crossing in the desert in the night with some friendly Bedouins.

He'd have to do this all with a raging infection in his back and no antibiotics or pain meds. He'd poured the last of his antiseptic on his wound before he and Oryx set out from their second hide the evening before, and he'd dumped the narcotics in a ditch fifteen minutes later, so great was his desire to consume them. He'd have to do without a respite from the agony, and he told himself that this would make him tougher, sharper, more ready for what was to come around the next corner.

But mostly it just made him even more miserable.

He still had the receiver that broadcast the GPS coordinates of the *Hannah*. He'd taken the time to disassemble the device with his multi-tool to ensure there was no tracking transmitter hidden inside that would have sent his own position back to Hightower and the *Hannah*. The receiver told him the CIA boat was still to the southeast, in international waters. Hightower had not called him in a day and a half, and Court was worried by the long silence. Zack could be anywhere, either on the *Hannah*, back in the States, or standing in the road just up ahead with an anti-tank launcher.

Zack was scarier than the GOS, the NSS, certainly scarier than the ICC.

The unpaved road turned to the north and continued on, but a driveway led towards the ocean and the resort. In the quickly growing sunlight Gentry could see a medium-sized main building, and on either side of it little individual bungalows on the beach, backlit by the orange sun one-third exposed on the horizon's line of the Red Sea. But a heavy chain sagged three feet off the drive, locked to upright posts in cement on either side. The chain did not look particularly formidable, but there was no way the little black Skoda was going to successfully ram through it and then keep going.

Two hundred meters, low sand dunes on either side, brown sea grasses blowing gently in the warm breeze. They'd have to walk the rest of the way.

Court pulled the car to the side of the road.

"Out," he ordered Abboud.

"I've never been here before," said the president. "But I know what this place is. There is decadence here. Alcohol was found once, five years ago. We could not punish the owners, a European couple, with more than fines. I think maybe they were shut down for a summer." He sniffed through his injured nose. "Infidels."

"Out," Court instructed once again. He climbed out of the driver's side and moved quickly around the front, opened the passenger-side door, took the president by the shirt, and lifted him to his feet.

"When will the transport arrive?"

"I don't know."

"How will they get past the coastal patrol boats?"

Court pushed him forward towards the bungalows. "I don't know."

"Where will the ship go when it leaves here? All the way to port in the west or will we—"

"I don't know."

"Mr. Six. You have no real plan, do you? Let me get in touch with some of my contacts in the West. I can make arrangements that would be satisfactory to everyone."

"No."

"We, my friend, are on exactly the same team here. You understand that now, don't you? I will contact some people with whom I have done business for many years. They are very loyal to me—"

"That's what I'm afraid of," said Court distractedly. He pushed the president forward again up the sand-strewn driveway, past a low sign in Arabic, but his eyes were off to the right, into the distance, into the deep morning shadows. Some six hundred meters away, a half kilometer back from the coastline to the south, the terrain rose sharply at the rocky plateau. There, in the morning shadows, the sun reflected off of the windows and tin roofs of squat, square buildings. Court could see no movement, no sign of life at all, but he felt exposed nonetheless.

He'd made it just over halfway to the bungalows with no more protest from Abboud. Then the president spun around abruptly. Court's eyes had drifted back to the south, but he quickly turned his attention back to his captive.

"I want you to make a promise to me. If we are still here tomorrow, it will be very dangerous for both of us. For you especially, because, unlike you, I *do* still have *some* friends out there, looking for me, wanting to help me. If we remain here for twenty-four hours, you can be sure that someone, one of the staff, one of the owners, someone who saw the car along the road to the beach, someone will report us. Then they will come, and by 'they,' I mean everyone. Friend and foe will descend upon us. I was a general long before I was president, and you have chosen for us absolutely indefensible ground. Our back to the ocean, our front to tens of thousands of square meters of sand dunes. This is a deplorable place for us to fight—"

"Shut up."

"—and you don't even know when help will arrive, or in what form the help will come? I should think you could have chosen a better—"

"Shut up!" Court said again, shoving Abboud forward, angrier than ever at the man, principally because the man was absolutely correct in everything he said. This was a mess, this one-man extraction attempt in denied territory by an unknown force.

Court shoved the president again. It made him feel a bit better to deflect some of the focus of his wrath on someone other than himself.

His phone rang.

Seventy meters to go.

He answered it. He hoped it was Ellen with details that would cause his mood to improve. "Yeah?"

"S'up, Court? How's life treating you?"

Fuck. It was Zack, and a conversation with Zack right now would do nothing good for Gentry's disposition.

Still, Court thought, maybe he could glean some intel from Sierra One. If Zack was calling, that meant Zack was not sneaking up behind him at that very moment. "Things just could not possibly be any better, High-tower. Thanks for asking."

Sixty meters.

"Yeah? You come to your senses and draw a knife across your boyfriend's throat yet?"

"Sure did."

"How come I don't believe you?"

"'Cause there just isn't enough trust in the world."

"Yeah. That *is* a shame, isn't it? Look, bro, I just wanted to give you a bit of good news because, despite your bullshit, I think you could probably use it."

Abboud turned around as he walked, tried to ask Court who was on the phone, but Gentry just stiff-armed him forward again.

"Good news? Well, okay, I guess I'll take it."

"Figured as much. Here it is. Today, buddy, is your lucky day."

Fifty meters.

"Okay. I'll bite. Why is today my lucky day, Zack?"

There was a long pause. Court thought he could hear Zack's face rubbing his mouthpiece, his stubbled beard scratching the microphone. Finally, Sierra One answered. "Today is your lucky day, because *you* are my secondary target, and I am pretty sure I'm only going to have time to get one shot off."

Forty met—Huh?

Court stopped in his tracks. Jacked his head to the south. To the buildings some seven hundred meters distant. A flicker of light in a deep morning shadow flashed from the roof of the highest building on the plateau.

In less than one half second, Gentry turned his head back to president Abboud, propelled his body forward towards the walking man, reached out both arms, and dropped the sat phone. At the same moment he also screamed a single word.

"Down!"

President Bakri Ali Abboud's shoulders raised in surprise of the scream from behind. Then the right side of his neck seemed to quiver, as if slapped hard. The left side of his neck blew apart, blood and tissue flung towards the sand dunes to the north side of the road, leaving Oryx instantly decapitated save for some skin and muscle that remained. His head spun around on its axis and flopped backwards as his torso went limp and dropped straight to the sandy driveway.

Court landed on top of him as blood gushed about, recognized the man was dead in another instant, and then rolled off of Abboud to flatten himself on the driveway.

"No!" He shouted out to the air, just as the report from a sniper rifle rolled across the dunes. His collision with the president's body and his impact with the ground created excruciating agony in his shoulder blade. Still, the anguish he felt at the loss of the president, the loss of his mission objective, the loss of his opportunity to stop the civil war and the impending invasion, was paramount in his mind.

Flat on the ground now, he looked up towards the buildings. The roof where the sniper's bullet came from was behind the tip of a peaked dune just off the side of the road, but Court knew Zack would reposition after that shot, and if he managed to get any higher on the hill, he could get line of sight on Gentry's position on the drive. So Court clambered to his knees and shot forward, scooped up the Thuraya on his way to the dunes. He dove into a tiny gully off the drive, rolled to his right, to the east, back towards the car, and flattened out again.

He punched a blood-drenched fist again and again and again into the sand in utter frustration, the morning heat cloying against his clothes and sticky sand and dust coating his skin where Abboud's blood had smeared.

"Sweet!" It was Zack's voice over the phone in Court's hand. Quickly Gentry brought it to his ear. "Six hundred ninety meters, low light in a half-value eight--mile--per--hour crosswind. That was a Sierra Six quality shot, you gotta admit it!"

Court pressed his forehead in the dirt and sand. All his exhaustion, his infection, everything just sucked the life out of him right now. He began to sob and shake.

Hightower's booming voice continued to pour forth from the little speaker. "You are one quick son of a bitch. If you weren't so sick with that festering back, I bet you could have gotten in the way of my .308 boat tail and caught that round instead of your lover boy. How cool is this, Court? Last Christmastime you capped the ex-president of Nigeria, and I just bagged me the sitting president of the Sudan. Give us time, and you and me just might clean up this shit-assed continent, whaddya say? Wait a sec. Scratch that. You aren't going to live long enough to whack anybody else. Either the infection is going to get you, the thousands of GOS chuckleheads on your tail are going to get you, or *I'm* going to get you."

Court continued to lie there and shake, as if from extreme cold, a near complete physical and mental breakdown. His body and clothing were caked with matted bloodred sand. He gulped air for a long moment before saying, "You had ... *one* chance to stop me from killing you. I was in your sights, and you made your choice. You chose badly, Zack."

There was a pause on the line. Court sensed concern on the other end. "Whatever, dude. You just need to stay in that hole and die. I'll be out of the country before you can pick Abboud's brain matter out of your teeth. And if you *do* make it out of the Sudan, Denny has already told me I'll be leading the task force set up to hunt you down."

"I'll save you some time. Come on down here right now. I'll be waiting."

"Love to, brother, but I think I'll get out of here before Johnny Law shows up to see about that dead president smeared all over your shirt like pizza sauce. But I won't be far. Milo and Dan and the rest of the guys on the *Hannah* have already hitched a ride out of the theater. It's just me and you now." He chuckled. "Oh yeah, plus the five hundred thousand members of the Sudanese Armed Forces."

"And I will burn through each and every one of them to get to you, Zack. Six out."

Hightower spoke up as Gentry made to end the call. "Court, Sierra Six was one of us, and you are no longer one of us. Your code name is no longer Sierra Six, it has reverted to Violator. You're the enemy again. Just in case you're keeping score. One out." Zack hung up the phone.

Court was sick as a dog, half-dead in a ditch, outmanned, outgunned, and outplayed. He had failed. He lay in the sand as the full sphere of the sun appeared between the bungalows on the water. Slowly he made it to his knees and began crawling towards the resort, head low in case Zack was still peering through a rifle scope up on the plateau.

48

The moon had gone for the month; the Red Sea caught and amplified the light of a million stars, but it was not enough illumination for Gentry to see the *Hannah* in the distance. He squinted to the southeast, following the direction indicator of the GPS beacon locator in his hand. He was less than a mile out, so he cut the engine of the four-man rigid inflatable boat.

His GPS also told him he was four miles offshore now, but he could not see the land in the dark. With the engine off there was all-encompassing nothingness, dark in all directions but up, and up was untouchable infinity.

The ocean was not still. It rose and lowered silently, no breakers or whitecaps out here, just gentle surges that lifted the Gray Man and his boat a few stories into the air and then let him back down again. It was more felt than seen in the darkness, but an occasional reflection off the water's surface showed him hills and valleys all around, hills and valleys of black water that undulated with the undercurrents of the Red Sea.

It had been a long day. After making his way to the dive resort, he'd found it empty except for the husband and wife owners of the establishment. The few Western guests had all been rounded up and trucked to Port Sudan for lengthy interviews, a fishing expedition by the NSS for the kidnappers of the president. Court did the greatest favor he could imagine for the Dutch couple. He leveled his Glock at their heads and tied them up in the dining room of the establishment. He knew the Sudanese would find the president's body close by, and he knew these two senior citizens would be questioned. If Court had, in any way, made them accessories after the fact, then they might have tripped over their stories or provided some sort of evidence that would incriminate them. It was also very likely that the NSS had installed listening devices throughout the Western resort as a matter of course.

So Gentry played the role of the bloodstained maniac to the hilt, shouted and ordered the frightened Europeans. He took from them food and water and medical supplies and a pickup truck and a small RIB with an outboard motor and dive gear without so much as a nod of thanks. He drove the truck ten miles to the south, waited in a mangrove swamp until dark, and then set off for the *Hannah*, following the coordinates on the GPS tracker.

He knew the two surviving members of Whiskey Sierra other than Zack had already been evacuated from the area, along with the rest of the crew. It was Gentry's hope that Hightower was still on the mainland searching for him, but he knew it was possible that Zack had come back to the *Hannah*. He had the mini submarine, after all, so he could easily come and go as he pleased. Court wanted to get to the *Hannah* to use it to flee the Sudan. His earlier idea about crossing the border was fantasy now. When the body of the president was found, that part of the nation would be 100 percent impassable.

So Gentry hunted the black ocean for the yacht with the idea of stealing it and steaming away to safety, though he knew next to nothing about yachting.

Court's boat moved with the gently rolling surface of the sea. The GPS tracker indicated the boat was not far ahead, so Gentry waited to catch a surge that brought him higher than the other waves so he could see the yacht in the distance.

There, a quarter-mile off, a blacker silhouette on a sea of dark, dark gray. Not a single light visible aboard.

Nobody home?

Court strapped a mesh bag to his waist. Inside were his Glock

19, down to the last seven rounds of ammunition, a folding knife, and his satellite phone in a plastic, waterproof bag.

Next he slipped a buoyancy control device over his shoulders, upon which a scuba tank had already been attached. Then he put on his mask, snorkel, and fins. He took a few test breaths into his regulator, and slipped silently into the warm water.

As he swam, he focused on his mission to keep his mind off the excruciating pain in his left shoulder, a pain that was always there, but a pain that snapped to the forefront of his consciousness every time he reached forward in his breaststroke.

Soon his mind slipped off-mission, and onto one of many of the hundreds of tidbits he'd gleaned about this theater of operations, whether by reading Sid's material or Zack's material. This particular tidbit didn't seem that important at the time, but at present it was all-encompassingly crucial.

Nurse, white-tip, gray reef, hammerhead: the four species of shark common to the Red Sea.

Court kept swimming, pissed that he could not get the thought of being eaten by a hungry fish out of his mind.

He remained just below the surface and checked the compass on his wristwatch from time to time to make certain he was headed in the right direction. After ten minutes he surfaced silently, waited for a moment to catch a lift to get a better vantage point. It came soon enough, and the yacht was right there, some seventy yards ahead.

As he began dropping with the wave once again, the bow of the yacht caught his eye. The name of the boat was written on the black hull at the bow, written in either white or yellow lettering.

Arabic lettering.

What the hell?

He had never seen the *Hannah*, but he was pretty sure it wasn't disguised as an Arab boat. No, he was more than sure. Zack had told him they'd passed themselves off to the Sudanese as Aussies. This would have been difficult to do with a yacht with an Arabic name.

Gentry dog-paddled closer, squinting in the dark to try to read the bow. At forty yards he could make out the characters, but his written Arabic was even poorer than his spoken Arabic.

He said the letters aloud. "F-a-ti-ma." The *Fatima*.

Not the *Hannah*.

But the homing beacon was emanating from the yacht, which meant, clearly, that someone had taken the transmitter from the *Hannah* and placed it on this vessel.

Someone? No, not someone.

Zack Hightower.

It also indicated one other thing to Court.

Goddammit, he said to himself.

This was a motherfucking setup.

Court looked back in the dark. There was zero chance he'd be able to find the skiff he'd left behind him ten minutes earlier on the open water.

He'd have to press on.

He lowered his mask back over his eyes and began to submerge again but stopped himself. He thought he'd heard a noise. He shook water from his ears and cocked his head.

A man shouting.

Boom! A gunshot, immediate and unmistakable across the quiet night sea, Court dove under the water's surface in fear he'd been spotted.

But no. Underwater it continued. More gunfire. One gun responding to another, and then another. There was a shotgun in the mix, Court's practiced ear could discern, but a handgun was firing as well. Quick and controlled.

Another scream. Court surfaced again to try to make sense of what he was hearing.

He felt his body lift in the warm water, he surged upwards towards the stars, and Gentry saw the flashes of light in the sky above the yacht before the vessel even came into his line of sight.

And then there it was. Court saw the yacht, but no one was visible on deck.

There was another volley of gunfire and the flashes in the

portholes. The fight appeared to Gentry to be down in the lower decks of the eighty-foot-long vessel.

All was quiet for a moment, but this still was broken by the sound of a small outboard motor coming to life. Seconds later a wooden skiff appeared from behind the stern of the *Fatima*, one man on board controlling the motor, and he pushed the little engine's throttle to the limit as he streaked off into the darkness.

What the hell was all that? Court wondered if Zack was on board the boat and had been surprised by a group of soldiers.

He swam above water the rest of the way, keeping a wary eye on the deck and upper levels of the yacht. He strained to hear any noise at all other than the gentle lapping of waves from the departed skiff against the side of the big fiberglass hull, but there was nothing.

Until he arrived at the boarding ladder at the stern of the yacht. Just then, a single small-caliber pistol shot cracked from below-decks. It was answered almost immediately by a larger handgun.

Silence again, save for the lapping waves.

Court pulled off his fins, unfastened his scuba gear, and let it drift away. He grabbed hold of the ladder and climbed up as slowly and as carefully and as quietly as he could. He rolled over the guardrail and onto the teak deck in his bare feet, winced along with the fresh burst of pain in his shoulder, and held his waterlogged but dependable Glock out in front of him. Carefully he moved to the companionway to descend to the lower decks of the darkened yacht.

The first two bodies were at the top of the stairs. Two black men in combat uniforms, bullet wounds in the chest. The men didn't look like they were Sudanese Navy, but that was no surprise. The Sudanese Navy was so small, and the mission of the day, checking and rechecking every floating object off its coast, so large, that it was very possible the GOS Army just co-opted boats and boaters to ferry soldiers out to all the yachts and freighters and fishing boats to board and search.

Next to their bodies were wire-stocked Kalashnikovs. Court wanted to pick one up but was worried about making noise while doing so.

Blood smeared the mahogany of the companionway steps. Court followed it down, his pistol at the ready.

He entered the lower saloon and saw the carnage in the soft green light of a fish tank's glow against the wall. Two more black men, dead, and one white man, flat on his back in the middle of the floor, with his feet towards Gentry and the staircase.

He was unarmed; his chest was bloody.

But he was not dead.

Court flipped on the overhead light of the lower saloon, keeping his weapon trained on the wounded man. He called out to him from across the room. "Zack?"

"Know why they call it a sucking chest wound?" Hightower asked without looking towards Gentry's direction. His voice was weak.

Court nodded slowly and answered, "?'Cause it sucks."

Zack nodded sleepily. His right arm was heavily bandaged both above and below the elbow from where he'd been shot two days earlier.

"What happened?" asked Gentry.

"Fucking backup gun. You'd think I'd have learned my lesson after you popped me with that Derringer back in '06."

Court looked again at the two men at the foot of the stairs. Both had shotguns by their bodies, but a small automatic handgun also lay next to one of the men's hands.

The man appeared clearly dead now, but Court shot him in the back of the neck anyway, and then slipped his Glock back into his hip bag. "Whose boat is this?"

"Dunno. The GOS has boarded everything they can up and down the coast, pulled a lot of people into Port Sudan, trying to find someone with knowledge of the president's kidnapping. I figured if I got on board one of the empty yachts, the GOS goons wouldn't come back and check them again. There was no reason for these dudes to be here. I figure they came back to loot it, and we just all got unlucky to bump into each other."

"What about the mini sub?"

Hightower looked Gentry over through thin eye slits for several seconds. "I scuttled it. Denny's orders. I was going to use this boat to get down to Eritrea."

Court regarded his former team leader for several seconds. He said, "I can stop the bleeding. Stabilize you. Get us out of here."

"No, thanks."

"Suit yourself. You're going to die if you don't get some help."

"There will be a GOS naval gunboat on top of us in a few minutes. The pilot of the skiff that brought these guys is probably on the horn to the navy already."

"Then I'd better get busy. I'll patch you up, but before I do anything, I want some answers from you."

"Give it a rest, Court."

"Why was I burned? Who put out the shoot on sight? What the hell did I do wrong?"

"When the gunboat gets here, they aren't going to board us, they are going to blow the living hell out of this prissy yacht. All that sexy Court Gentry, Gray Man, faggot ninja shit isn't gonna help you when their deck gun opens up."

"I thought you wanted me dead."

"Hey, it's not what I want; it's my job. If you put a pistol in my hand right now, I'll shoot you, but I don't guess that's gonna happen, so maybe you'll take a little professional advice and go for a swim. This yacht might be able to do twenty-five knots; a Sudanese coastal patrol boat can run thirty-five, chase us down in no time."

Court wasn't listening. He wanted answers. "Who burned me? Was it Matt Hanley?"

Zack's eyes were glassy, but they rolled in frustration nonetheless. "I don't know."

"Was it Lloyd?"

Zack's brows furrowed now. He looked up. "Who the fuck is Lloyd?"

Court's shoulders slumped. Then shrugged. "That's what *I* said."

49

"Zack! Listen. You aren't too far gone. I can treat you. You can walk away from this. Just tell me who put the hit out on me and why."

"Fuck it, Six. I ain't walking, and I ain't talking."

"What the hell is wrong with you?"

"I'm a good soldier, Court. My orders are to make you dead. Not to make you dead, unless you can save me, at which point my mission is no longer valid. Look, man, you are a good guy. I'm rooting for you here, I really am. But I'm not lifting a finger to help you out. Can't do it. It would go against my op orders."

"You are fucking crazy."

Zack smiled. Gentry could see the pain on his face. "I just do my job. More sons of bitches should do their jobs. No offense, Violator."

"Dammit, Zack!" Court shouted it in frustration. He stood there over his former boss, thought for a long moment, and then he left the saloon and ran up two levels to the cockpit of the ship. Here he found a first aid kit. In seconds he was back, and he knelt down next to Sierra Six.

Zack turned his head slowly to face him. "What the hell are you doing?"

"You know what I'm doing. You are an asshole, but I can't just stand here and just let you die." Gentry ripped open Zack's shirt, exposed the wound. It was small, two inches below his right nipple, Court knew the bullet would have gone through the lung. He reached under Zack to feel for an exit wound.

"You patch me up, and I'll kill you!"

"No, you won't."

Hightower looked up at the ceiling with his half-mast eyes and shook his head slowly in disbelief. "You are a terrible judge of character, Court."

"Tell me about it."

Five minutes later, Gentry had Hightower stabilized, at least for the time being. There was no exit wound, which meant there was a bullet or fragments of a bullet somewhere in his damaged chest cavity. Court used a folded cover from a magazine from the bookcase and duct tape from the aid kit to create a valve over the chest wound that would allow air to escape from Hightower's lungs when he breathed out, but not allow air into the chest cavity when he breathed in.

It was all he could do at the moment.

Then Court left Zack and returned up two flights to the helm of the ship. Within minutes he'd turned all the systems on, ignored most everything except the engines and the compass and the wheel and the autopilot. He ran down to the deck and checked to make sure the anchor had not been lowered. He was sure there was some way to check from the helm, but he figured eyeballing it would be faster than trying to figure out which computer monitor displayed that nugget of information. He refrained from turning on any lights; he wanted to move as stealthily towards international waters as an eighty-foot luxury yacht possibly could. He knew he would not hit a shipping lane for some time, but he hoped that any civilian sea traffic out there in the dark had radar on board, because Court did not know how to operate that particular function of the big multifunction display at the center of the mahogany and brass helm, and he did not want a collision with some other boat.

Court pushed the throttle gently, and the big boat surged forward. When the craft reached twenty knots, he set the autopilot to hold the present course and then he ran back downstairs.

Court entered the lower saloon to find Hightower crawling on his side, halfway under a table that folded out from the wall. Court followed the wounded man's eyes to a titanium snub-nose revolver on the floor against the wall, just within Hightower's grasp. It was the same gun Zack had pressed to Gentry's forehead in Saint Petersburg. Slowly, Hightower's left arm crept out on the floor, reaching for the gun.

Court did not have to hurry; he just stepped across the floor and kicked the pistol away.

Gentry said, "I don't think your heart was in that attempt."

Zack nodded; his eyes closed again. "My heart has other pressing matters to attend to at the moment." He winced with pain. "Pulmonary pneumothorax. Air pressure in the chest cavity is stopping my heart."

"If you promise to stop trying to kill me for a minute, I can help you."

"No promises," Zack said, but he rolled back onto his back and cried out in pain as he did so. His breath was shallow and labored. Court quickly flipped open his knife, found a spot between the second and third ribs on the right side of Sierra One's chest, and then punched a shallow hole through the skin and muscle. Zack cried out. Immediately air escaped from the hole with a slight whistling sound. Court went to the fish tank in the corner, pulled some rubber tubing and a filter out of the water, and returned to his patient. He slid the tube in the fresher of the two chest wounds, stuck the filter in the open end and laid it on the ground next to Zack's arm. "When we get out of this, you and I are going to need most of the antibiotics in the Western world."

Zack coughed. A little blood appeared on his lips. "Seriously, dude. The gunboat will be here any minute. Just where do you think we are going?"

Court sat down next to Zack, exhausted and sore and sick from the infection in his back. He pulled the satellite phone out of his bag. "Time to kiss a little Russian ass."

*

Court got through to Sidorenko on the third try. "Hey, Sid. It's Gray. It's done."

"Yes, it is all over the news. President Abboud is dead. Everyone in Moscow is very pleased."

"The body has been found?"

"Yes. Near a resort sixty miles north of Suakin. Very curious."

Court breathed a hesitant sigh of relief. "Yeah. I'll explain everything when I see you. We need to move up the extraction, though. I've got to get out of here immediately."

"Do you?"

"Yes. Too much heat to lay low as we originally planned."

"Is that so?" Sid's voice held none of his earlier excitement. Gentry sensed trouble.

"Yeah. I'm wounded."

"Wounded?"

"Hey! Sid! Stop with the questions. Yes, I'm wounded. I need some help."

"I'm afraid your benefits package does not include health insurance, Mr. Gray."

Court said nothing. The muscles in his jaw twitched.

The Russian mobster continued. "Abboud is dead, this I know. But I also know that you did not kill him. He was killed by a sniper while you were trying to protect him, to get him out of the country to deliver him to the International Criminal Court. You used my operation to gain access to the president, in order to take him alive for some other actor."

Shit. "Where did you hear that bullshit?"

Sid's reply was delivered with a sudden scream, his Saint Petersburg accent more pronounced and the words less intelligible. "You take me for a fool! Well, Courtland Gentry, Gray Man, I am no fool. You can stay there and die for your treachery!"

"I'm going to kill you, Sid!"

"You just told me you could not survive without me, and now you make threats about what you will do to me? Ha. You were a dangerous man, Gentry, this is why I liked you. But you're not so dangerous, now that you are alone, injured, scared. Not so interesting, either. I had a man with a problem. Soon there will be no man and no problem!" Sid laughed as he hung up the phone.

"Dammit," said Court. He dropped the phone on the floor by his side and lay back against the wall of the saloon. The infection was sapping the last of his energy reserves.

He thought Hightower was unconscious, but his patient turned his head slowly. With his eyes still closed, he asked, "What did Sid say?"

"He said, in so many words, 'Fuck you.'"

Zack's dry, cracked lips tightened into a slight smile. His voice was soft. "Damn, dude. *Your* boss is an asshole."

"Yeah. Who knew?"

"Face it, nobody's coming for us. I'm disavowed, and you're the enemy. We are pretty much the definition of fucked. You can back-stroke back to the beach; that's pretty much your only option."

Court reached above him to a small bar and grabbed a water bottle. His back screamed in pain while doing so. He unscrewed the cap and took a few swigs. He poured a few splashes over his head. Distractedly he drummed his fingers on the water bottle, his legs splayed out on the rising and falling deck.

Nothing was said between the two men for a minute. Court felt each second tick. He thought he sensed the boat pulling to the right slightly, but he pushed it out of his mind. The autopilot had been set, so the course should be true.

"I'm open to suggestions, One," Gentry said idly. But there was no reply. Sierra One was unconscious, though breathing better than before with the introduction of the tube to release the air buildup. He'd still likely bleed to death if he didn't get to a hospital soon.

Court reached for the first aid pack to see what pain medicine was kept there. He wondered if the Arabs who owned this fancy yacht were the type who abstained from such peccadilloes.

Court's eyebrows rose. A sudden thought struck him.

Why the hell not?

He reached for the phone again and leaned his head back

against the teak walls of the cabin. He dialed a number with his thumb and held the phone to his ear.

One ring, two rings, five rings. Court looked at his watch.

The phone crackled as it was answered. The battery meter showed the device was quickly running out of juice.

"Cheltenham Security Services," said a woman's voice.

"Don Fitzroy."

"May I ask who's ringing?"

"Court."

"Certainly, sir. One moment."

The pause was brief. The phone was almost dead. It was possible Zack had his own Thuraya around here somewhere, but Court was too tired to hunt for it.

Don Fitzroy, Sir Donald Fitzroy, had been Court Gentry's handler before Gregor Sidorenko. The previous December the two men had a falling-out, and Court vowed to stay away from the English spymaster as long as he lived, even if he became desperate.

But desperate events, Court now saw, warranted desperate measures.

Fitzroy's low, gruff voice came over the line. "Well, hullo, lad. How are you?"

"Been better, to tell you the truth."

"I'm sorry to hear that. What's wrong?"

"You've been watching the news?"

A nervous chuckle. "The only news of interest to a man like me is taking place on the western seashore of the Red Sea. I *truly* hope you're not involved in all that ruckus?"

Court sighed, "I guess I'm just about the nucleus of that ruckus."

Another pause. Then, "Good Lord. Whispers about say it is the CIA at work. So you are back with the agency?"

"Unofficially."

"*How* unofficial?"

"Well ... actually, they're trying to kill me."

"Sounds like a bloody unofficial relationship, then. In fact, isn't that the *opposite* of being 'with' them?"

"It's a bit fucked-up, yes."

Instantly the Englishman said, "How can I be of service?"

"Just like that? I'm in the shit, Don. You can squeeze me dry if you want. My leverage is nonexistent."

"We'll work it out later. You are a man of your word. Let's just try to get you out of there."

Court hesitated, then said, "Do you have any assets at all in the area?"

"I'll need to make some calls. Nothing of my network, but I have colleagues in Eritrea, in Egypt. Maybe by tomorrow afternoon—"

"Negative. I can't wait. I have to have something faster."

Don seemed momentarily flummoxed. Court's slightly buoyed spirits sank anew with the delay. He closed his eyes and leaned his head back again. Then he opened them.

"I *do* have a boat. I'm making twenty knots towards international waters."

"A boat? Well, that's something."

"But the GOS Navy is on the way. I can't outrun them." Court gave his general coordinates to Fitzroy, who wrote them down hurriedly.

"You must try to dodge the Sudanese."

"If I had something to shoot for, a ship or a boat or even a damn buoy to hang on to, I'd feel a lot better."

Don said, "There should be a handheld FM beacon on board. Find it straightaway. I'll call a friend who's a maritime underwriter at Lloyds of London, get a list of every boat, ship, or yacht within three hours of you. If I don't know the owner or operator of one of those ships, I will bloody well find someone who does. You go due east from your location, get out into the sea as fast as you can, as far as you can. When you're in international waters and clear of the Sudanese, sound your distress beacon."

"Understood. Thanks, Don."

"Thank me later. You have a navy to outrun." Court hung up the phone and ran back to the cockpit to speed up the engines.

50

Court found the handheld FM distress radio in the cockpit, slid it into his hip bag, and then made his way back to the helm. Here he pushed the throttles all the way forward. There was less than an hour left until daylight, and Gentry had his bow pointed right where the burnt orange sun would appear. He only hoped he'd be around to see it shine.

Suddenly the cockpit was awash in bright light. Court ducked instinctively, turned in all directions looking for the source of the blinding beam. He found it astern on the starboard side, a spotlight no more than one hundred yards away.

The twin 12.7-mm machine gun of the coastal patrol boat opened up one second later, tearing into the cockpit and ripping through mahogany and bronze and glass.

Gentry dove to the deck next to the helm, used the deeply waxed teak flooring to slide like a snake towards the stairs to the lower decks. He slid down the stairs face-first, his shoulder killing him but his fear of supersonic metal taking precedence in his priorities.

On the main deck Court waited for a short respite from the near constant fire and grabbed both rifles dropped by the dead men on the companionway. The weapons were old and poorly maintained. Court knew firing on the gunboat would be extraordinarily reckless, but not firing on it would allow it to come as close as it wanted, shine its spot on the hapless yacht, and rake its machine

364

guns back and forth to its heart's content until the engines stopped and the yacht sank in the black water.

Court wasn't going to make it *that* easy for them.

He crawled to the bow, staying out of sight. The braying 12.7-mm guns seemed to be concentrating on the helm, the waterline, and the stern of the ship, most likely to destroy the controls and the propellers and stop the boat's retreat to international waters, as well as to kill anyone hiding out belowdecks. But the bow was still mostly shrouded in the dark shadows of the upper saloon and cockpit, and Gentry used this to mask his movement. He flipped the selector switch on the weapon to fully automatic, lined the 81's iron sights up on the spotlight beam, and slipped his finger into the trigger guard. In the brief pause he took to concentrate his senses before he fired, he noticed the deck below him was not moving forward in a straight line. No, he felt a very noticeable and very strong pull to the right of the eighty-foot craft.

He had no idea why, guessed only that the machine guns had already damaged the rudder.

He pushed this out of his mind and pressed the trigger. The light exploded in a flash of sparks. Suddenly the *Fatima* was enshrouded in darkness, and the gunboat across the water was the bright spot, as its windows and electric lighting exposed all the men on the deck.

Court fired the remainder of the first AK's magazine in full automatic mode at the men, killing two and sending the rest diving to the deck of the hundred-foot craft. When his weapon ran dry, Court dropped it and ran to the port side of the yacht. He knew the bright flash of the gun would have attracted attention, and he needed to get as far away from the bow as possible. He made it back to the stairs to the lower decks just as the machine guns on the yacht again began belching hot steel. On the stairs he saw his boat was sinking now, leaning to the port side, although its forward propulsion still pulled to starboard.

Court returned to the lower saloon and dropped to his hands and knees. It was below the waterline and therefore mostly safe from direct gunfire. He found Zack lying in the same place. His bare chest was covered in the ersatz bandages and a thick sheen of sweat. His eyes were open and blinking.

"Fucking navy," Zack said as Court crawled up next to him. A passing sweep from the machine gun sent splinters and glass and seawater throughout the saloon just above their heads. Seconds later the engines stopped, and the *Fatima* began to drift.

But the gunfire continued. Court had to scream to be heard. "We're going up on deck!"

"Don't forget the sunscreen."

"We're sinking. We're going to have to go over the port side. Maybe we can wait a while, transmit the distress on the VHF when they leave."

"Not gonna work. We're nowhere near international waters. The Sudanese will hear the distress, come back, and finish the job."

"I'm not going to sink that navy boat. I don't have any other alternative."

Zack laid his head back flat. "Do what you gotta do, bro. I'm staying right here."

The machine gun fire stopped abruptly. Court looked around. He noticed the water bottle he'd left on the floor earlier had rolled to the port side. Within seconds other items in the room began to slide on the mirrorlike finish of the deck.

"We're dead in the water," Court said. "The engine room must be filling up. But why aren't they shooting?"

Zack said nothing.

"I'll be right back." Court climbed the stairs on his hands and knees. The yacht was sinking incredibly quickly. Already it leaned to port at a ten-degree angle. On the deck he laid flat, so he was concealed to the starboard side by the list to port. He crawled to the railing and peered over carefully, looking for the gunboat. The navy vessel was moving out of the area, away from the yacht, and Court could not imagine why. Quickly he looked into the sky, worried about a fighter plane with a bomb or some other attack that would necessitate the patrol craft hauling ass. But the starry skies were clear.

He was about to turn to slide back to the companionway when he noticed it, above the waterline, just below his position at the railing. In the darkness it glistened and hung there like a big, wet tumor on the hull of the *Fatima*.

It was attached to the hull with cables and suction cups, and had been below the waterline before the yacht began listing hard to the opposite side.

Cigar-shaped, black as onyx, and twenty feet long, an enclosed prop and rudder at the rear, and a clear plastic canopy on the top.

A mini submarine.

Court shook his head in disbelief and mumbled with a little smile, "Zack, you rat bastard."

Court realized now why the boat had pulled so hard to starboard at speed.

Hightower had neglected to mention it because his primary mission was to kill the Gray Man. His secondary mission would be to save his own life.

Court had an incredible respect for Sierra One's mission focus, even if it did piss him off.

Court looked back to the Sudanese patrol boat and realized they must have seen it, too. But apparently they had taken it for a large torpedo and decided to back off lest one of their machine gun rounds set it off.

The Gray Man turned away, slid down the sharply angled deck to the companionway, and returned to the saloon. Zack was still on his back.

"Would it have killed you to tell me about the sub?"

"I was hoping it would kill you if I didn't."

"You going to tell me how to drive it?"

"You've never piloted a mini sub?"

"Who the fuck *has* piloted a mini sub?"

Zack smiled and said nothing.

"Don't suppose there is an instruction manual lying around anywhere."

No response.

"I feel like ripping that tube out right now, Zack."

No response.

"God, when I'm done saving you, I swear I'm going to kill you." Court knelt and lifted Zack onto his wounded shoulder. He screamed in pain.

Zack screamed as well from the agony of being hefted by his bandaged right arm, but Gentry did nothing to make his patient feel better.

51

Court pulled the small canopy shut. From the difficult action of the closing mechanism, and the absence of a good handhold on the inside of the Plexiglas, he got the impression there was some sort of a button or knob that would cause an automatic shut and seal, but Court couldn't even see the dials and gauges in front of him in the dark, so yanking it tight with his fingertips would just have to do.

He'd managed to get Hightower inside without one iota of assistance from him. By the time they'd made it back on deck, it was listing at twenty-five degrees. Every bit of strength in Court's good arm was put to use sliding Zack up to the railing and over the side. Skittering together down the wet hull to the sub, the satellite phone popped out of Gentry's pocket and bounced off into the ocean. Court found a latch on the outside of the canopy and popped it open. He struggled to get Hightower's dead weight slid into the rear recumbent position. Court buckled him in like a child in a car seat and scooted down into the front.

Exhausted, once enclosed in the small cockpit, he took a few seconds to recover. Then he called back to his unwilling passenger, "Come on, buddy! Give me a hint! What do I do?"

"I'd love to help, bro. But my orders are to terminate you. This is kind of a roundabout way to achieve my objective, but . . . " His voice had grown much weaker after the strain of movement, even if his attitude remained in full effect.

"Fuck your orders. Let's go for a ride!"

Zack did not reply.

Court went back to feeling around at the controls.

A sudden, loud screech filled the air, and a shell landed in the water twenty-five yards short of the sub. The small craft shuddered, and foamy water splashed on the Plexiglas like a mini-hurricane was passing overhead.

"I guess their smoke break is over," muttered High-tower from the backseat.

"Shit!" Court began fingering all the dials in front of him, found nothing that felt right to flip or twist or punch. He wanted to activate everything; it might still come to that, but he was scared to do so. He really had no idea what he was getting himself into, only that the alternative was to sit on a sinking ship and dodge high-explosive shells from the patrol boat's deck gun.

He ran his fingers faster on the controls, feeling for some sort of power button, which he imagined to be larger and more pronounced than what his fingertips had so far come across in the darkness. His hands next moved to either side of him, to the outside of the vinyl armrests, along the walls. On the left side his hand wrapped around a simple lever with a ball extending three inches horizontal from the wall. It was in the "up" position. With nothing else feeling right, he pulled the lever.

Immediately the front of the sub disengaged from the cable attached to the suction cup on the hull of the yacht. The nose dropped towards the water, and Gentry slammed forward into the cockpit controls.

He had neglected to fasten himself in the seat harness as he had Hightower behind him.

He screamed in pain. With all his might he leaned back, felt above him for a lever aft of the one he pulled, and he found it and yanked it down.

The rear cable disengaged, and the midget sub slid off the angled side of the *Fatima* and plunged five feet down to the black water, nose-first.

Upon hitting the sea, the craft righted itself for a moment, and

Court used the time to fumble back into his cockpit chair. It was difficult to do, but he managed, had only just snapped the clasp when he felt the weight of gravity on his right side. The water around the Plexiglas's bubble was an opaque dark green, so Gentry waited for the sub to come back up to the surface so he could get his bearings.

For five seconds he waited to resurface, and all the while he felt the pull harder and harder to the right, as if the sub was somehow beginning to roll.

At ten seconds he realized it was rolling, but the pull to the right seemed to stop. The sub was still submerged.

He pulled the small folding knife from his pocket, held it in his lap, and let it go.

The knife flew upwards, just missing his chin and nose, before bouncing on the plastic canopy and sliding forward.

Court realized then that they were inverted, and they were sinking.

"Zack! Zack!" Gentry's ears popped, and he fought a wave of panic. He had no situational awareness whatsoever now, completely entombed as he was in a dead craft in dark water.

Hightower did not reply.

Above him he heard a shell hit the yacht, a two-stage explosion, the first being the warhead and the second, undoubtedly, the fuel tanks. A shock wave buffeted the bottom of the sub.

Gentry could wait no more. His hands reached out in front of him, his right index finger found a button, an arbitrary button, as there were dozens, and he could not even see what color they were much less any writing on them.

Fuck it. He pressed down.

Nothing.

His ears popped again, and a sustained pressure entered his head. He had no idea how deep the water was here, but he neither wanted to keep dropping nor hit the bottom, especially canopy first.

He reached for the next button. Pushed it. Then a third. Then a fourth. He wondered if he was releasing fuel or opening a cargo door or triggering a self-destruction sequence.

Court did not know the first goddamned thing about submarines.

He pressed a fifth button, and immediately warm infrared lighting illuminated the cabin.

His head was killing him, and nausea ripped through his body from his intestines to the back of his neck.

With the new light he quickly scanned dozens of choices, looking for anything to turn on. His finger stopped at a button labeled HUD, and he pressed it without hesitation. The laser head-up display came online, projecting all sorts of data on the windscreen in front of him. Speed and Current Depth increased by the second, an artificial horizon turned slowly clockwise, and a compass heading revolved steadily around the dial.

He wanted situational awareness, and he got it. Now, after the onboard computer told him that he was corkscrewing down to his death, he realized that he really didn't want that info after all.

The pain in his head worsened. He vomited water and bile; some of it spewed through his nose and followed gravity's path, running into his eyes. He smeared away the burn with his sweaty arm, put his hand on the joystick on his right, and tried to right the craft, but it had no effect whatsoever. He pushed the lever that he took for a throttle with his left hand. Again, nothing doing. He stomped his bare left and right feet down, kicking out for rudder pedals that were not there.

The submarine passed sixty feet.

Court fought another wave of nausea and a further increase in panic.

Then he stopped playing with the controls, brought his hands into his lap.

"Zack. You awake?" Court's voice was calm now, no sign of panic or threat to the other man in the doomed submarine.

"Yeah. Just enjoying the ride, bro." Zack's voice was incredibly weak. He'd likely be dead soon, Court realized, no matter what

372

happened to Court. Still, Gentry knew Zack well. He was not as calm as he pretended to be.

Zack Hightower didn't want to die, either.

"I can't make this thing work." Gentry pulled his Glock-19 and held it up in the red light for his rear passenger to see. "But I *can* make *this* thing work."

"Really? You're threatening to shoot me? That's all you got, dude? Pretty fucking lame."

Court ignored him. He said, "I've trained without oxygen at depths of one hundred thirty feet. If I blow this hatch in the next minute, flood the sub, and make it to the surface, I figure I can find some floating debris from the yacht to grab on to. With a little luck I should make it back to shore by nightfall."

"And *then* what?"

"I make it out of the Sudan."

"Right. *That's* gonna happen."

Court paused. Then said, "I'm the goddamned Gray Man, remember? I'll get it done."

All quiet in the rear seat now.

"But that's one ride I can't take you along on. You understand, don't you, *bro*?" He mimicked Sierra One.

Again, Zack did not respond. Court took that as a good sign. Hightower was never at a loss for words.

"So I'll live, and you'll die. Which means you fucked up. If you would have helped me with the sub, we both could have made it, meaning you could have lived to kill me another day. Ultimate mission success by temporary delay of mission resolution. Even Denny Carmichael would agree that that is a valid strategy for a good soldier like you to take. You just aren't smart enough to know a good deal when you see it."

Still nothing from behind.

"I'm sure there's a better way to pop this hatch, but the only control I know how to work in this goddamned tub is the trigger of this gun. Wish I could leave the Glock behind for you to shoot yourself before you drown, but it may come in handy onshore."

Zack remained silent. Court hoped he was thinking and hadn't just fallen asleep.

Gentry's head was killing him. His sinuses felt like they would burst open any second with the pressure and the acidic puke in his nose.

"Passing one hundred ten feet." Court began filling his lungs with air. A rapid deep breathing to increase lung capacity. In between breaths he said, "It was a pleasure serving under you most of the time, Zack. I'll send a letter to Langley and tell them you went down with the ship." A few more deep breaths.

Court pushed the barrel of the gun to the Plexiglas's canopy, ducked down away from it.

Zack coughed weakly.

Fuck, thought Court. *He's not going for it.*

"See ya," Gentry said, stalling an instant more, and then he moved his finger to the trigger and sucked in a full, deep breath of the cabin air.

Here we go.

"Down by your right knee. Dial that says BAL. Turn it all the way to the left to neutralize the ballast. Next to that is a square button that says PROCON. That's propulsion control. Push it now." Zack's voice was weak, but the words sure as hell came out fast.

Gentry lowered the gun, found the dial, and turned it, then found the button and pushed it. Immediately a loud metallic noise filled his aching head. A 2-D computer rendering of the submarine appeared on the HUD. It started as a cigar-shaped image, but when the metal noise stopped, the image had wings and tail fins and looked like a single-engine fighter plane.

"Give it some thrust. Just a touch."

Court tipped the throttle, and he felt a slight engine rumble and sensed gentle forward movement. A HUD reading that had been zero slowly climbed from 5 percent to 10 percent to 20 percent as he pushed the throttle a bit more.

"Now, use the joystick to level her out. It's fly-by-wire. Pitch,

374

yaw, roll, all controlled by the joystick. Kind of like an airplane."
Zack coughed. "You crashed a plane once, didn't you?"

"Crash-*landed*," Court clarified. He'd gone from near post-panicked resignation of his imminent death to near jubilant euphoria at his high prospects for survival, all in the last thirty seconds.

"That was in Kiev, wasn't it?"

"Tanzania, Zack. You were there."

"But again, in Kiev? You crashed there, too, didn't you?"

"No comment."

Quickly he had the descent under control, and then the machine leveled out. A few seconds more, and he had the compass heading pointing due east.

"Headlights," instructed Zack from behind.

"Where?"

"Have you ever been in a car, dumb-ass? Same place."

Court reached to the left in front of him and, yes, the light switch felt just like it did in most wheeled vehicles he'd driven.

He flipped it on.

And shouted in shock. "Oh shit!"

The sub moved quickly along the sandy ocean floor, which was not more than ten feet below.

Court began hyperventilating slightly. He pulled back on the joystick and pushed the throttle forward to 40 percent.

"Okay. Now, a four-position dial on your left, about eleven o'clock."

With the dim red lights it was hard to find, but Court got his fingers around it.

"Turn it all the way. Oxygen scrubbers. We're breathing each other's carbon dioxide at the moment. This will clean the air."

"Roger that."

After Zack's tired voice instructed Court through turning on the O2 system and activating the sub's laser collision avoidance feelers, Court piloted the sub to the east for another minute, getting the feel of the craft. Once confident he had the hang of it, he called back to Hightower again, "How am I doing?"

"You suck. You can't drive cars for shit; you can't fly planes for shit. You'll probably steer this thing up a whale's ass in a minute."

Court could hear the relief secreted in the injured man's admonitions.

Two hours later, Court felt certain they were well out in international waters. He could hear soft moaning and an occasional wheeze from the man behind him. Zack babbled incoherently at one point. Gentry knew High-tower could still die from his wound or from an infection, even if he made it to top-flight medical care in the next hours. Sir Donald would have to come through big time to rescue them.

The irony was not lost on the Gray Man. He'd saved Sir Donald a few months earlier, told himself he'd never trust him again, and now the portly knight was Court's very last hope.

The sub finally surfaced at eight fifteen in the morning. The sun was well up now, straight off the bow of the little vessel. Gentry used it to orient himself as the HUD was difficult to read with the bright daylight penetrating the cockpit. Court activated the FM beacon and waited.

They bobbed up and down on the open sea.

A little after ten he saw the ship. It was a huge tanker, and as it loomed above the submarine, loomed above Gentry's head right at the waterline, it seemed as high as a skyscraper and menacing with its jet-black hull. The ship took nearly a half hour from first sight to the point at which a ladder was lowered to the sub and Court popped his canopy. He called out for help, and two men came down on separate ladders, secured Hightower in a harness, and had him lifted three stories up to the railing.

Court climbed up the ladder under his own power, though his shoulder burned with the strain, and he vomited in the heat as the huge ship rose and fell with him hanging on alongside. He'd nearly made it to the top when he passed the big letters on the port side bow. He had to lean back to read the name of the craft that rescued him.

"LaurentGroup Cherbourg."

"Perfect," he said. Court had had dealings with LaurentGroup, the huge multinational corporation that had tried to kill him the previous year. He never thought he'd willingly climb aboard one of their vessels but, again, desperate times called for desperate measures.

Court continued up the ladder to the railing and was pulled over the side by a crew of Indonesians.

Zack was laid out on a stretcher and rushed hurriedly away. Court himself fell to the deck, was lifted by his arms and legs, and then more dragged than carried into a cool hallway in the superstructure of the ship. Within minutes he asked for morphine, a syringe appeared, and shortly thereafter, he was out.

When he awoke, he'd already been transferred to another boat, a tall sailing ship owned by a Welsh media tycoon and, as it turned out, a friend of a friend of Sir Donald. Court asked about the condition of the man brought aboard the tanker with him, but the crew of his new vessel had no information.

Four days later, they made port in Alexandria, and Court Gentry slipped ashore and away. The crew of the sailing ship never saw him leave.

They just awoke one morning and found him gone.

EPILOGUE

Of all the eighty nations around the globe to which Rosoboronexport sold arms, Il-76 senior pilot Gennady Orloff most enjoyed his layovers in Venezuela. It was not because of Caracas's nightlife, which had taken a hit with the austere Communist demagoguery that President Hugo Chávez had advanced in the past few years. And it was not because of the natural, rugged beauty of the country, as Gennady rarely had more than one day until his turnaround flight back to Russia and therefore insufficient time to leave Caracas proper, the smoggy urban jungle of five million.

No, Gennady enjoyed Venezuela because of a woman. *One* woman, which was hardly the norm for a bon vivant such as Gennady Orloff. On his flights to Bolivia, in contrast, there were three women from whom he was forced to choose. In Cuba, there were seven, although a couple were getting a bit long in the tooth for Orloff's taste. In Vietnam there were nearly a dozen ladies whose company he enjoyed for a single night, though half accepted dong or credit cards for the service, and none of them would have been able to keep his wandering eyes or other body parts from straying had he any forty-eight-hour layovers in Ho Chi Minh City.

But Miss Venezuela was different. She was the only woman in the country that he had eyes for. He'd met her on the Internet, which was de rigueur for the forty-four-year-old Russian husband

and father. For the past eighteen months he'd made at least one flight a month to Caracas, ferrying missiles or warship parts or seemingly every major item from the Russian military catalog with the exception of the Kalashnikov rifle, as the Russian government had licensed a plant in Maracay, Venezuela, to produce AK-103s domestically. And virtually every time he came to Caracas, twenty-nine-year-old Tanya del Cid was waiting for him in a junior suite at the Gran Meliá Caracas, arguably the most opulent five-star hotel in all of Venezuela. Tanya was a cashier at a Lexus dealership, and she had a girlfriend who worked as a concierge at the Gran Meliá, and both women traded secret overnight loans of the goods and services of their employers. While Tanya enjoyed her dashing Russian pilot in a junior suite, Maria cruised Avenida Principal de las Mercedes in an SC10 convertible "borrowed" off the lot.

Two weeks to the day after his flight to Al Fashir, Gennady Orloff and his crew said good-bye at Ground Transportation of Simón Bolívar Airport, with plans to see one another the next afternoon for the return flight. The four other Russians ran through a late afternoon downpour to jump into a shuttle bus to ferry them to a nearby airport inn, while Gennady climbed in a cab with instructions to rush him to the Gran Meliá.

Thirty-five minutes later, the rain-soaked shoes of Gennady Orloff squished down a beautiful hall on the seventh floor of the hotel, his weathered canvas flight case and nylon overnight bag rolling behind them. Gennady's tension, both nervous and sexual, made him feel like he was back in school. He arrived at room 709 and found the door cracked. Curious but not worried, he pushed the door open slightly.

Rose petals lay in a wide path through the sitting area, disappearing down the candlelit hallway to the bedroom. Soft Latin music, a somber serenade by María Teresa Chacín, played on the stereo.

Gennady smiled. Ah, this again.

Inside he left his cases at the door as he shut and locked it. He kicked off his wet shoes and yanked off his soaked socks, quickly pulled a long-stemmed white rose from an arrangement on the coffee table, and walked down the hallway. He paused at the door to savor the moment, the smell of lavender wax from the candles, the feel of the moist petals between his toes, the perfume of Tanya, which wafted gently in the air.

Gennady opened the door, his eyes following the petals all the way to the bed.

Tanya sat on the bed, fully clothed. Her arms were tied behind her back at the elbows, she'd been gagged with panty hose, and her eyes were wide from fright and red and puffy and dripping tears.

Gennady heard the hammer of a pistol cocking behind his head. He dropped the rose.

English words: "Hands high. Walk backwards down the hall. Slowly."

Gennady Orloff did as he was told. His frightened eyes locked with Tanya's. She tried to say something, but only a series of high notes and a quarter cup of spit came out of her mouth through the panty hose.

Once back in the living room, the music was turned down. He waited several seconds for instructions, but when none came, he put as much masculinity into his voice as he could muster and said, "I am turning around slowly."

A man in a suit sat in a leather chair, his back to the far wall, a raincoat folded beside him. Both hands were empty now; they rested on his knees. To the man's left the thunderstorm raged in the window, the light on his face coming from outside and, through the water streaming down the glass, made it seem as if his face was melting before Orloff's eyes.

The face. Gennady knew that face.

It was the American assassin he'd flown into Sudan, the one who'd caused him so much trouble. The Russian tried to not let his nervousness show. *"Chto Novava?"* What's new?

"Nichivo." Nothing much.

"Shto ty hochesh?" What do you want?

"For starters, I want to speak English. Sit down."

Gennady sat on the sofa across from the American. He moved slowly, warily, but the bearded man in the leather chair gave no indication of threat. He seemed thinner somehow than in the Sudan. His face appeared drawn and gaunt, though again, his face *was* somewhat obscured by the rain-diffused lighting.

The Russian pilot switched to English. "All right. What do you want?"

"I want to have a conversation with you."

"You caused me a lot of problems after Al Fashir."

The American shrugged. "Apparently everything is okay now. You are still flying weapons for Rosoboronexport."

"*A kak je?* Why wouldn't I be? I did nothing wrong."

"Other than violating sanctions, you mean."

Gennady relaxed a little. He waved his arm like shooing a fly from his face. "Politics. I don't have anything to do with those decisions. I am just a pilot."

The American shrugged. "We all have our expertise."

Gennady swallowed, stopped himself from asking about the American's expertise. He knew he was a killer, and did not want to bring that up.

"Did you . . . do anything to Tanya?"

"Depends on your definition of 'anything.' I put a gun in her face. I tied her up. I scared the piss out of her, quite literally, as a matter of fact. Yeah, I did 'something' to her." The man seemed distant for a moment. But his eyes retrained on Gennady in a second. "She's a spook, by the way." He said it nonchalantly.

"What?"

"Yeah. She's GIO."

Gennady just stared back. He did not understand.

"General Intelligence Office."

Still no comprehension of what he was being told.

The American sighed, frustrated. "A Venezuelan spy. I pulled a wire from her." He dangled a tiny listening device with an antenna no wider than a strand of wet spaghetti out in front of him, then swung it across the coffee table to Orloff.

Gennady caught it and looked it over. He laid it down on the table. "You lie."

"No . . . I kill. I do not lie."

Orloff believed. For several seconds he all but forgot about the American in front of him. He wanted to stand and return to the bedroom to beat the shit out of the little lying Latin whore, make good use out of those restraints holding her arms back.

But the American? What was his angle?

"You work for Gregor Sidorenko. The FSB told me this when they questioned me about your disappearance. Are you here to protect me from Venezuelan intelligence?"

"No."

"Then what?"

"Does your wife know about the affair?"

Gennady's eyes narrowed. "Not this one, no. But she would understand. She knows I am a man who is loved by many women."

"Especially those paid to sleep with you."

The Russian sighed. Shrugged. "I love my wife."

"Do I look like I give a flying fuck about your marriage?"

"Then what is this about?"

"I don't know what the Venezuelans plan to do with the intelligence they've gotten from you, but you have to ask yourself if you have ever said one thing in bed with the beautiful Tanya del Cid that you don't want the FSB to know about. Nothing negative about home? About your work? Nothing significant that could hurt you if Russian state security heard it?"

Gennady shrugged. "I am just a pilot. And a proud Russian. I have said nothing that worries me."

"You are certain?"

The Russian nodded slowly, perhaps not so sure but unwilling to reveal anything to this American.

The American seemed unfazed. "I need you to do something for me. I am prepared to pay you a lot of money."

"What do you want me to do?"

"Something that you already do well. Talk."

"Talk about?"

"Talk about flying into Darfur. Talk about ferrying in an assassin from the Russian mafia to do a job for Russian state security. Talk about the types and quantities of weapons you brought into the country, weapons that won't show up on any invoices. Show the West Russia's crimes, and show the Sudanese that the Russians killed their leader."

"What will that prove?"

"What many people already assume. But it will put pressure on Russia, get them kicked out of the country. Damage their influence. It just might prevent a war."

"Why the hell would I do something so crazy as this? The FSB would kill me if I did."

"Not if they could not get to you."

Gennady shook his head. This discussion was madness, completely out of the question. "I have a family. They could get to them. My wife and three children—"

"Five children, actually." The American said, his voice menacing. "Must be hard to keep up, isn't it? Three with your wife, Marina, in central Moscow, plus a six-year-old girl with Mina, a Thai factory worker, and a twelve-year-old boy with Elmeera, a Tunisian flight attendant."

"Yes," said Gennady slowly, frightened now that the dangerous man knew so much about him. "But my family in Moscow, even if the FSB couldn't get me. If I talk about Sudan, Sidorenko or the FSB will kill them."

"A team from the International Criminal Court is in Moscow now. You call your wife and tell her, and I will call the team, and your family will be taken from Russia, to safety, within the hour."

Gennady shook his head without reservation. "No way. Just leave now, American, and I will not report this. But do not—"

"Your family will be safe if you say yes to my offer. And you will be a wealthy man. Relocated in the West with a new life. A good life. But if you say no . . . " The American leaned forward. His face moved away from the rainwater's reflection but darkened to black as it lost the light from outside. "You will have no life at all."

"You are threatening to kill me?"

The American shook his head. "I wish it were that easy. But we need you. You are important. You know important things. We need you to stop the war."

"Then, what are you—"

"You talk to the ICC, or I will take from you what you hold most precious."

Gennady Orloff's face went slack. He felt a weakening in his gut that threatened to cause him to lose control of his bowels. The man in front of him was a cold-blooded, heartless killer. "My children?"

No words were exchanged for a half minute in the living room. Finally the American sat back up, lightened a bit, and said, "But I don't see it coming to that."

"I will kill you!"

The assassin shook his head slowly. "No, you won't."

Gennady's fury was absolute. But his fear of the man in front of him was equally powerful. He did not dare attack him. He was a pilot, not a killer. Instead, he thought of his children, about his predicament, and he slowly broke down. He cried softly for a long time on the sofa of the dark room. Only his sobs and the rain outside broke the stillness. The American assassin sat quietly in the chair.

Twenty minutes later Court stood in a phone booth on the avenida el Recero, a block away from the hotel Gran Meliá. The rain fell in torrents, and his raincoat was soaked, fogging up the glass inside the tight space. Outside passersby with umbrellas jammed the sidewalk, heading to cafés and concerts and hotels and bars. They moved like the water rushing along the gutter in front of Gentry.

His eyes focused on the water and followed bits of trash floating by the phone booth, traveling downstream. He knew he should be scanning the crowd around him for threats—he was operational, after all—but the narcotics in his bloodstream sent his brain off on little errands that served no purpose. He tracked a crushed can of juice that shot by and watched it swirl down a metal grate in a deluge. He looked for another bit to follow on its path to—

"This is Ellen Walsh."

Court forgot momentarily that he was holding the phone to his ear. Quickly he refocused and said, "He agreed. I moved him to my room: 422. I didn't want to leave him there with the girl."

"I'll have his family picked up immediately. We will debrief him here at the hotel tonight."

"You are here? In Caracas?"

"I just arrived an hour ago."

Court watched the tiny river of runoff flow down the street while he carefully chose his next words. "Are you here for Gennady Orloff, or are you here for me?"

There was a long pause. "I am here for Orloff. I have decided to leave the events on the road to Dirra, back on the road to Dirra. You will not be indicted for what happened."

"Thanks."

"Six, I am worried about you. I don't know what you said to Orloff to get him to agree to provide evidence to the ICC, but I assume it was not something I would approve of."

"It was not something *I* approve of. But the ends justify the means."

"For your sake, I hope you believe that. I told you I was worried that you might become that which you most hate."

"I'm okay," he said, but his tone convinced neither Ellen nor himself.

"Listen. Why don't we meet right now? In the lobby. Orloff can sit and stew by himself with my team. We'll have a quick drink, you'll see that I'm not here to put you in shackles, and I'll take a look at you, just to make sure those cracks I was worried about haven't gotten any bigger."

Court smiled a little. He was not happy, but it was a moment of contentment.

385

"Please?" she pressed.

"Ten minutes. I need to make a call first."

"Great. You probably won't recognize me with a shower and clean clothes."

Court smiled again. "I look pretty much the same, I'm afraid."

She giggled. "See you in ten," and she hung up. Court knew how to read voices. Ellen was happy, excited.

One drink wouldn't hurt a thing.

He put more money in the phone and dialed a number written on a small scrap of paper taken from his pocket. When the line was answered, he put the scrap in his mouth and swallowed.

"Hey, Don. It's done."

Sir Donald Fitzroy said, "Did he believe the story about the woman being an intelligence agent?"

"He did."

"That was a brilliant idea, lad. Put the fear of the FSB in him, did it?"

"No. He didn't bat an eyelash. Nothing to hide, I guess."

A pause. "I see. Then you used some other means to secure his help."

"I did."

Fitzroy's voice was strong, more serious than usual. "You don't sound happy."

"I don't *feel* happy. I told him I'd go after his kids."

Another long pause. Gentry felt like the man on the other end of the line was judging him. But then, "You helped prevent a shooting war, Court."

Gentry said nothing.

"No one wants to see the sausage made, but everyone loves the sausage. It is a dirty business, threatening one's family. I should know. But it is damn effective. And it needed to be done."

"Yeah," Court said, again unconvincingly.

He leaned his forehead on the glass of the phone booth and watched the water some more, flowing faster by the minute as the rain picked up.

He just wanted to hang up the phone and go see Ellen. He was already thinking about two drinks now. Maybe they could even get in a cab, get away from the hotel, find a small place for dinner, some quiet local cantina without work for her or worry for him. He'd like that. He *needed* that.

"I need a vacation," he said into the phone but mostly to himself.

"You need more than a vacation, lad. Listen carefully to what I'm about to tell you. All over the world, they are after you."

"Who?" Court lifted his head from the glass.

"*Everyone.* The Russian government, the American government, Sid Sidorenko's Nazis. It's not like before; this is full-time. The CIA is putting out feelers all over the earth. They'll work with anyone, pay any price to find you. *Please* take my advice. Wherever you are right now, whatever you are doing . . . run. Get up and go and go and keep going. Don't tell me where, for God's sake. They will get to me to get to you. Don't tell a soul. They are close, and they *will* find you if you do not run straightaway."

"What about the ICC?"

"The ICC? I haven't seen anything about the ICC hunting you. I would bloody well know it, too. International organizations are an intelligence sieve. No, that particular organization may be the only group *not* pursuing you at the moment."

Court looked up at the lights of the Gran Meliá up the street through the rain on the Plexiglas. He said, "I understand."

Fitzroy continued talking, fast and nervous. He sounded as if *he* were the prey instead of Gentry. "And forget every stash you have; don't access your bank accounts; ignore all the cash you've made that's not in your pocket right now. They are putting their foot down on the Swiss, desperate for information on your finances. The Swiss will balk for a time, because that is what they do, but the Swiss will fold up soon enough, because that is *also* what they do. Do what you must for money, but stay off the grid. Run, keep going. Absolute paranoia is your *only* chance for survival."

"Yeah." The Gray Man's head moved on a swivel now, up and

down the street. The drugs in his brain seemed to evaporate with the infusion of adrenaline.

"Six months, nine months, whenever you have to, you don't call me, but you contact someone who knows me, find some way to get in touch, and I'll get back with you. If you want work, I will give you work. If you just need money, I'll find a way to get something to you to help out."

"Thanks, Don."

"I've done nothing, Court. My debt to you is not paid by this. Run now, go, and don't look back."

"I'm serious, I really appreciate—"

"Run, boy! Hang up the phone and *go!*"

"I'm gone," Court said, and he hung up the phone. He stepped out of the booth and looked up to the bright lights of the hotel for a moment, but only a moment, then he looked away.

Towards the darkness.

He melted into the foot traffic and disappeared in the evening crowd flow, like warm rainwater down the drain.

HAVE YOU READ THEM ALL?

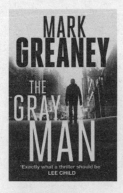
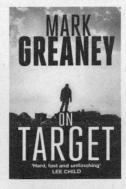
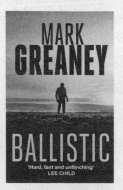
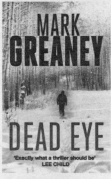
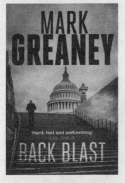
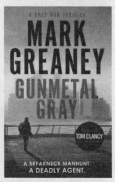
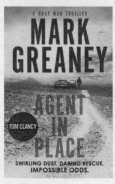
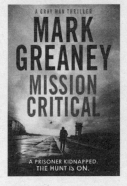
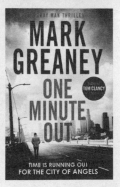